DETERMINANT

Book 3 of The Guardians of Vesturon

A.M. Hargrove

Determinant

For more information about A. M. Hargrove and her
upcoming book releases,
please visit her at:

www.amhargrove.com
www.twitter.com/amhargrove1
http://www.facebook.com/AMHargroveAuthor
www.goodreads.com/amhargrove1

ACKNOWLEDGMENTS

Many thanks to my family (Henry, T.A.C and McIntyre) and friends for all their support and contributions to this latest addition to The Guardians of Vesturon. I'd also like to thank all the Determinant Beta Readers—Terri Thomas, Midu Hadi, Lissa Smith, and Rebecca S. Hammer for their awesome contributions in this whole process. I couldn't have done it without you!
I'd also like to thank my son T.A.C for his ingenious idea for the character of Tak. This requires a bit of explaining. Tak was originally named Tak Herdekian. My son wanted to be named for a villain so I decided to grant him his wish. He and I sat down one night and he came up with the name "Herdekian." When the story began evolving and the character Tak Herdekian developed, I discovered he could not be put to rest with this one book, for he had his own complicated story to tell. In fact, I decided that his species, The Praestani, deserved a book of their own (or perhaps even a series). I also realized that this spin-off would have to be written in the adult genre, since Tak, whom I have since renamed as Jurek Herdekian, is the ultimate bad boy and will play by no one's rules (but perhaps his own)!
And finally, I'd like to thank my editor, Jennifer Nunez for her patience, skills and all the hours she spent with me on the phone!
I hope you enjoy *DETERMINANT*...

Prologue

T he six men moved through the city streets in a triangular formation. Not a single soul paid them a bit of attention. Dressed unusually, even for a large metropolis such as Atlanta, they were donned in snug black leather pants, black vests and wore unusual criss-crossing bands on their bare chests. They looked like a scene from a fantasy movie. Their bare arms were heavily tattooed and their hands were covered in black gloves. However, the few that glanced their way didn't notice any of that. Utilizing an advanced form of technology, unknown to humans, the men had altered their appearance and speech. To anyone watching, they appeared as six jean-clad men in their late teens—college students perhaps, out for a night of fun.

Conversation between them was minimal. The language they spoke, while it sounded like English to any human within hearing distance, was most definitely not. It was a guttural mix of sound that didn't exist on Earth.

The men were tall and self-assured. Their eyes were an unusual color—a blend of lavender and indigo with flecks of silver. No one stopped to look at them long enough to notice, and if they had, all they would have seen would have been six pairs of brown eyes. The men weren't exactly handsome, but they were nonetheless impressive, with their rugged features. Power, strength, and fearlessness emanated from them.

Never hesitant in their steps, they moved along in an unhurried, but purposeful manner toward their destination, as if they had been there dozens of times before. The leader directed them not with speech, but by the movement of his head. They carried no weapons that one could see, but they were most definitely armed. A single glance from one of them could annihilate an entire city. Not only were they their own deadly weapons, they also possessed strength, unknown to humans, and powers that would be considered impossible by any human standard.

The group separated as they neared their destination. To avoid suspicion, they would access the building using two different entrances. Once inside, they would reconvene near their goal.

Minutes later, the façade of the Centers for Disease Control and Prevention came into view. Three of the men entered through the main doors and the other three went in through a side entrance. It was late evening when the premises would be mostly vacated, except for essential personnel, so it would be unlikely anyone would interfere. That wasn't much of a concern for the men. Interfering humans were quickly indisposed by a few simple tricks. Locked doors and high security areas didn't pose a problem either. It would be a simple task to retrieve what they came for and they would be gone in a moment, leaving no trace of their break-in.

They moved as a group of six again and traveled through the maze of corridors as if they had done this daily. It was a surprise to them when the figure of a young woman came into view, for most employees should have vacated the premises by now. What surprised the leader even more was her proficiency at mind communication, which was an impossibility for humans. He knew with certainty she was otherworldly, but from where, he could not discern. Her pale eyes intrigued him and he experienced the briefest feeling of regret for what he was about to do. He forced himself to shove that thought out of his mind, as the choice was not his to make. His family would die if he weren't successful in this mission.

His fleeting encounter with her ended as quickly as it had begun and he was on his way to completing his task at hand. He moved through the secure area and headed for the cryogenic containment section where the variola major specimens were located. He gathered the most deadly of them with efficiency and replaced them with the influenza specimens given to him by the lab director he had so eloquently threatened. Moments later, his group was back on the streets of Atlanta, putting into motion stage two of their mission.

This phase would be completed rapidly. Entering various locations, they would spread the virus. He was glad his species was immune to this deadly disease. Humans had eradicated this illness in the 1970's and had ceased vaccinating against it. Since he had stolen most of the viable strains, the feasibility of recreating a vaccine was nonexistent. The disease would spread rapidly and a pandemic would ensue. Once again, he felt the brief pangs of his actions, but pushed the thoughts out of his head. His family was more important to him than a group of unknown humans, no matter the number of casualties.

The virus needed to be spread quickly. Infected aerosols would be the most rapid mode of transmission, so the mercenaries released some of the virus into the ventilation system in the building before he exited. His group then proceeded to enter a few of the dorms on the Emory University campus to repeat their actions. The summer session was ending and the students exposed would shortly be traveling home before the fall semester would begin. This would give the disease a wide and various possibility of dissemination. His goal was to have an epidemic in place before he left Earth.

The men visited the most populated buildings in the city and lastly they arrived at Hartsfield International Airport. This was the ultimate place for disease transmission. With travelers moving around from plane to plane, and country to country, it wouldn't take long for this illness to manifest itself worldwide.

BOOK ONE

January St. Davis

Present Day

T he fever consumed me. I gripped the steering wheel until my knuckles were white and close to bursting through my skin. I was wracked with chills, which I thought odd. How could I be freezing and burning up at the same time? I had never been sick a day in my life, not a cold, strep throat, nothing. Payback was hell and I was living through it now, literally burning in it. What a way to make up for eighteen years of health.

I must have contracted the flu. I had worked with the influenza virus all summer at my internship with the Centers for Disease Control and Prevention in Atlanta. My eight-week program had ended and I was on my way back to Cullowhee, North Carolina to resume my fall semester at Western Carolina University where I would start my junior year.

The fever had begun last night. I felt flushed and went to bed thinking it would be gone in the morning. I forced myself to pack up my scant belongings and dragged my achy body to the car for the drive home. It was just past noon when I left. I had anticipated arriving by four as it was about a three and a half hour drive.

I hadn't been in the car for thirty minutes when everything went south. What in the world is wrong with me? The chills hit first. Then I was alternately burning up and shivering violently. It was hard to keep my car in the lane with my uncontrollable shaking.

The headache turned into a crushing vise. My head was piercing with pain. It started inching its way down my neck and into my back.

My stomach rolled with nausea. I finally pulled off the road into a rest area. I fumbled around in my purse, hoping to land on some Tylenol but came up empty handed. Leaning my head against the steering wheel, I dozed.

I opened my eyes to the darkness of the night. Geez, how long did I sleep? My eyes tried to focus on my watch but my vision was blurred. Did I sleep or pass out? My goal was Cullowhee, so I pulled the car back on the road, heading in that direction. God, please let me make it home.

My vision was deteriorating. I could barely discern the trees as I passed them. Even though it was dark, I shouldn't have trouble seeing the trees. I knew I was very ill and my heart skipped a beat as I wondered what was wrong with me. I began to worry in earnest about whether I could make it back to Cullowhee. Oh God, what am I going to do? I don't know if I can keep driving! I didn't have a choice. I was in the middle of nowhere, Timbuktu if you will. There wasn't a hospital or motel anywhere near me. I pushed on, praying I would make it back safely.

The chills and fever continued. I was using my air conditioner and heater back to back. I realized I was becoming disoriented and dizzy. I knew I should stop but I forced myself to continue driving. I was trembling, whether it was from fear or the chills from fever, I didn't know. The road began to move, like a wave. I made several turns and the fisting of my stomach made me aware I was hopelessly lost. Where am I? None of this looks familiar! I stopped my car.

Looking for a place to sit, I wandered. My little brother and sister, Tommy and Sarah, were up by a tree, so I stumbled toward them. Oh, thank God! They can help me. Right as I was about to reach them, the ground came up to meet my face…

Chapter One

Three Years Ago

T he incessant chirping of those pesky birds awakened me. They loved to perch on the huge tree right outside of my bedroom window. Sometimes I wished I had a BB gun to silence them. I loved animals, I honestly did. However, at 5:30 a.m., the only thing I wanted to do was sleep. Those tiny peeping creatures with ten thousand decibel chirps were doing their dead level best to prevent that. It was blissful to imagine a chirp-free morning though…where I could wake up to my alarm instead. I flung my pillow at the window hoping to scare them. It didn't work.

I rubbed my eyes as I sat up in bed and realization dawned on me. Today was the day. It was graduation day at last and I would be giving my valedictory speech! My dreams had come true and all of my hard work paid off. I was graduating first in my class! My heart started banging in my chest. Oh no! I could feel my palms getting sweaty. I rubbed my hands across my quilt and took a deep breath to calm myself. My nerves roared at me as the thought of public speaking made me quake.

Focus on the positives, January. That's it…at least pretend you're excited. Maybe you can redirect that anxiety into something good.

Well, I was looking forward to one thing. Perhaps he would finally notice me. No matter what I did, how hard I worked or what I accomplished, I never received any acknowledgement from my father. Nothing…nada. Maybe today would be different. This is what I had so diligently focused on over the years. A single nod or maybe a brief congratulatory comment…anything at all would make me ecstatic. I know it's a stretch, but maybe, just maybe he would tell me how proud of me he was.

I threw back the covers and clambered out of bed, slamming into the wall in the process. After a few minutes of hopping around while nursing my wound, the pain in my baby toe subsided so I hobbled down to the bathroom.

My bedroom was in the attic…a place I had been relegated to when I was four years old. I would never forget the first night I spent up there. My terror had paralyzed me and my parents wouldn't allow me to come back downstairs. I sat awake, jerking at even the tiniest of creaks, shivering and praying the monsters under my bed wouldn't snatch me up and carry me away.

When morning finally arrived, I bolted down the stairs and begged my mom not to make me ever go back up there. No such luck. That night I was back up there again, trembling and scared to death. Sleep eluded me for a long time. I got into tons of trouble at school that week because I kept falling asleep at my desk, on the playground, or anywhere I could. I was so sleepy my eyelids weighed a ton. I was only in preschool, but napping was not allowed except during the rest periods.

Every day I was sent home with a note explaining to my parents that I had a complete disregard for the rules. As a result, I was punished again and sent to up my monster-filled torture chamber without dinner. I often wondered why they hated me so. What did I do to deserve such horrible treatment? It would be something I would continually ponder through the years.

I took a quick shower and when I say quick, I mean light-speed. My showers were restricted to two minutes and if they lasted longer than that, my next one had to be taken in ice-cold water. I'm not quite sure why my parents insisted on this, but they did. It only took me once to get the two-minute shower thing down pat. Turn the water on, hop in, lather up then rinse. I was, if anything, very efficient in that regard.

Next, I quickly brushed my teeth. For some odd reason I felt different today. When I glanced into the mirror, the reflection looking back was still the same old me…stick straight white hair and weird looking pale ice-blue eyes. Admittedly, I was a bit freakish. I knew in my heart my father thought so. I could tell by the distasteful looks he threw at me, not to mention the thoughts I could hear as they shouted to me from his mind. That was an anomaly I never discussed with anyone. Besides, I never felt like I fit in with the rest of the kids.

Quit feeling sorry for yourself. This is your big day so stick a smile on your face and enjoy it.

I darted back up the stairs to my own tiny world and picked out my clothing for the day. I decided on my blue dress since it was the best one I had. It was a plain shift that ended above my knees. It had capped sleeves that made my arms looked scrawnier than they truly were. Thankfully, my gown would hide them. I grabbed my strappy black sandals and threw them into the bag that contained all my graduation paraphernalia—cap, tassel, sashes, etc. I lifted my eyes to the ceiling and was bathed in memories of the years gone by. I would be leaving this room when summer neared its end. I had grown to love this little haven of mine. I often mused that I was the complete opposite of Harry Potter. Instead of "the boy beneath the stairs," I was the girl up in the rafters.

My attic bedroom was miniscule. It had those stairs that folded up and closed, acting as the door as well. On one wall it had one teeny round window that was up at the peak so I really couldn't look out of it. My parents had never finished it off so it was bare-bones—rafters and insulation only. I had a small chest of drawers, a twin bed, a clothing rack and a mirror. My bed doubled as my desk. I used a piece of plywood for it that I stored beneath the bed. I never invited any friends to spend the night because I was embarrassed about my room…no pretty wall colors, no flowery comforter, or anything to give it that homey appearance. Be honest with yourself January, Mom wouldn't have let you invite anyone over anyway!

It was puzzling to me why they had put me in the attic in the first place. I was the only child until I was eight. Then my mom had my little brother Tommy and two years after that, Sarah was born. We had three bedrooms so initially two of them were empty. Then one went to Tommy and the other went to Sarah. I told my mom over and over that I wouldn't mind sharing the room with Sarah, but she always ignored me.

I quickly finished getting dressed…everything I did was accomplished in record speed with good reason. It was the best way for me to avoid the criticism my parents like to dole out. I gathered everything I would need for the day because I would not get a chance to come home before the actual ceremony. I was on the set-up and decorating committee and was needed before and after rehearsal since I was the valedictorian. That meant I had to take my dress, cap, gown, sashes, adornments and shoes with me this morning.

With my arms full, I carefully navigated the narrow stairs, and dumped everything into my car. Then I went back inside and put the coffee on. I ate a bowl of Frosted Flakes, filled up my go-cup with coffee and headed out the door.

When I got to my car I looked at my watch and started laughing. It was only 6:30 am and I didn't need to be at the auditorium for another hour. I glanced at the passenger seat and the tickets for graduation caught my eye. Oops! I nearly forgot to leave them at home. I went back inside and wrote a quick note to my parents.

Good Morning Everyone!

Well, today is the day. I am so excited I can hardly stand it. Sorry I had to take off before you all woke up but since I am on all those committees, I needed to get there early. I also need to practice my speech. Wish me luck on that!

Here are the tickets…you must have them or they won't let you in. Make sure you arrive early if you want a seat. I'll look for you in the parking lot afterward…that's where everyone will congregate for pictures.

Can't wait to see you!

Love,

January

I jumped in my car and headed down the street. Watching the sunrise at the neighborhood park beckoned to me. If I didn't hurry, I would miss it. Early morning was always my favorite time of day. It must have stemmed from when I was little and scared of the dark. The sky quickly lightened from grey to light blue and the huge orange sphere inched up in the sky at last, casting everything in its warm glow. Morning had broken, so I headed over to the auditorium.

The day flew by since there was so much to do but seven o'clock in the evening arrived entirely too fast. We all lined up for the processional into the auditorium. I looked around trying to spot my family, but didn't have any luck. I wonder where they're sitting?

When I heard the MC say, "I'd like to present our valedictorian for this year, Ms. January St. Davis," I found myself making my way to the podium. With sweaty palms and trembling hands, I held the pages of my speech. I had practiced it over and over and knew it by heart, but I was nervous nonetheless. This was the first time I would be speaking to a group this large and it was a bit daunting, given the fact that I was only sixteen years old—I had skipped two grades and was graduating earlier than usual. Relax January. Pretend you are all alone. Take a deep breath.

And so I began. Initially, my voice shook and all the saliva in my mouth seemed to have evaporated. Water! I need water! My mouth felt like I had swallowed a huge gulp of sawdust. Just when I thought I was a hopeless failure, a miracle happened. Everything fell into place and my speech went off as smoothly as I hoped. It must have struck a chord because as I looked across the room, everyone was standing and applauding and I noticed several people were wiping their eyes. I was shocked because I never imagined I'd receive a standing ovation! I felt a huge grin spread across my face. Where are Mom and Dad?

We marched across the stage to individually receive our diplomas, and then we were all filing outside and throwing our caps into the air. When we finished, everyone tore off in different directions to find their families.

I scanned the crowd but soon realized my family was nowhere to be found. I puzzled over this because I knew I had left the tickets on the kitchen counter. I bet they left early to avoid the crowds.

I snuck away from everyone and drove home as fast as I could without speeding. When I pulled in the driveway, I noticed my mom's car was missing. I ran in the house anyway, yelling out in excitement, "Did you hear it? Did you hear my speech?"

No one was in the kitchen so I tore into the den to find only my father there, sitting on his recliner watching TV.

"Well?" I asked my voice laced with excitement. "Did you hear my speech? Can you believe I got a standing ovation?"

"I wouldn't know…I wasn't there," he responded in an emotionless tone.

"W-w-what?" I stammered. "Where's Mom? Did she see it?"

"She's not here and no she didn't."

"What do you mean? Is she okay? Are Tommy and Sarah okay?"

My stomach gave a sick twist as I thought that something happened.

"Everyone's okay. Your mother took them to Charlotte to Carowinds and they are spending the night."

"Wait. You mean she didn't come to my graduation?"

I felt like someone had just nailed me in the gut with a full fisted punch. Every bit of oxygen had been sucked out of the room.

"No, she didn't go," he mumbled, sounding as if he didn't have the time or energy to speak to me.

He never took his eyes off the TV. I turned away and started making my way to the crummy staircase that would take me up to my crummy little room when his voice stopped me. I was having difficulty processing this news.

"There's no need to go up there."

"Well, I need to change out of this," I murmured, motioning to my gown.

"Your stuff isn't up there anymore. I took the liberty of moving it into the garage."

"The garage? But why?" I was puzzled by his comment. I was also feeling the first stirrings of alarm.

"Because as of this moment, you no longer live here."

"I'm sorry, what did you say?"

"You heard me...you don't live here anymore," he said with a satisfied smugness.

"I'm not sure what you mean."

"Come on January! I thought you were a smart girl! After all, you graduated first in your class. What about, 'You don't live here anymore,' do you not understand?" He asked me in such a nasty manner I was speechless.

My mouth had turned into a big O and I couldn't respond for a moment. "But what am I supposed to do? Where am I supposed to go?" I stammered.

"That's not my problem."

I opened and closed my mouth several times, but no words would come forth. I didn't even realize I was crying until a tear fell on my hand.

"All of your belongings are in the garage. You can load up your car...I'm sure everything will fit since there isn't much. Your cell phone has been paid until August. When you move to North Carolina for college, you will have to get one on your own." His eyes bore into mine but I felt like I was in the middle of a bad dream.

"But why? Why are you doing this? What have I done to make you hate me so much?" I croaked. It was a question that I had wanted to ask for a long time.

"January, I'm not the only one that hates you. Your mother abhors your very existence." He smiled then, enjoying my anguish.

"Why?" I choked out.

"You mean you haven't figured that out yet? I thought a smart girl like you would be a bit more perceptive. Haven't you ever wondered why you were named January? Shall I tell you? It's your mother's least favorite month of the year. Cold, gray, usually nasty."

Memories from my childhood suddenly flooded my mind. My father would egg me on to do things that I now realized he knew would result in injuries. A slip down some stairs, a misstep on a tree limb; he would often dare me to do things that landed me in the emergency room with a broken something-or-other. Then I heard the words…horrible words that I knew he was thinking. How much he hated me…how he was glad I had finally graduated because now his obligation to me was over…how he couldn't wait to see me out of there…how happy he was when I was moved to the attic. He totally loved the fact that I was scared to death. Who is this man? All these years I wondered about the treatment I received from him but now I was questioning his integrity.

"Come on January. How did you not figure all this out? You're so perceptive. You have to know I am not your biological father. Lucky for you, your mother decided to give birth to you instead of having an abortion. You see, your very existence is the result of a rape." Again, he gave me that smug smile.

His words, uttered with sheer joy, sucked the air from my lungs. I dropped to my knees in shock. This can't be true. The fact that my mother was raped and I was the product of that nasty deed wasn't the worst thing I was experiencing. It was the fact that the man before me, the man, who for sixteen years I thought was my father, was enjoying delivering this horrific news to me. His sadistic enjoyment of my pain was the very thing that was crushing my heart. How can he act this way?

His thoughts assaulted my mind. I had always been able to pick up bits and pieces of things others were thinking, but now it was as if an information highway had been opened between us and I could hear everything in his head. It scared me because his thoughts were so vile and filled with absolute hatred. What have I done to him to make him hate me so? But wait…how could I be hearing his thoughts so clearly? I shook with fear. I had experienced this from time to time, but never like this. It was so…explicit!

I fell back on my bottom and dropped my head into my hands. I have to get out of here! It was imperative that I put some distance between this man and me. His thoughts were so nasty and vicious they were making me tremble.

I slowly stood, still dizzy from his words and stumbled to the garage. My paltry belongings were strewn across the floor, making it obvious to me he hadn't cared if he had broken anything in the process. One by one, I placed everything into my car. It was pitiful that everything I owned fit into the trunk and back seat of a Toyota Corolla.

The car cranked on and I backed out of the driveway and away from the only home I had ever known. I made it as far as the parking space of a nearby church. My tears were blurring my vision, making it impossible for me to drive.

I dropped my head to the steering wheel and cried. Where can I go? What will I do? I had to work in the morning. Could I stay here and sleep in my car? What would I do for a shower? I didn't have many close friends. My parents always discouraged any of my friendships and the few times I had spent the night out, I was never asked back. I'm positive now it was because I never reciprocated. I was never allowed to.

This sheer helplessness was overwhelming. As I sat there, I began to think about my ability to hear my father's thoughts. It was frightening because I had literally been reading his mind. Was it because he hated me so? Was it a temporary thing? Or would it plague me forever? What is wrong with me? I was a freak…I had always felt I was different but now I knew for sure. Maybe that's why they hated me so much. Maybe they had known about this aberration all along…maybe that's why they had deposited me in the attic, segregating me from little Tommy and Sarah. They didn't want me to infect them with whatever it was that possessed me. Maybe I was possessed…maybe the devil had invaded me. I didn't feel evil. It was all so confusing. My head was throbbing.

I must have slipped into a light sleep because I awakened to someone tapping on my window. Whoever it was had one of those LED flashlights and he was shining it in my eyes, blinding me. My spirits briefly rose when I thought that perhaps it was my dad, coming to take me home.

I shifted my head so the beam from the light would not be directly in my eyes and realized there was a police officer standing next to my car.

"Miss, roll your window down please," he ordered.

I immediately complied. "Yes, officer."

The police always made me nervous and on top of my earlier episode, I found myself trembling. My heart was hammering in my chest, threatening to explode. I dragged my fisted hands across my eyes and face in a futile attempt to wipe away the mascara that I was sure had streaked down my cheeks.

"Miss, what are you doing here?"

"Um, nothing sir. I was just sitting."

"May I see your driver's license and registration?"

I fumbled around a bit before my hands landed on the required items.

"According to this, you live right around the corner from here. Is there any reason in particular why you're parked here?"

"No officer."

"I'm going to have to ask you to step out of the car."

I did as he asked.

"Miss, have you been drinking?"

"No sir. I don't drink." I dropped my head and stared at my twisting fingers.

"Hmm." He cocked his head to the side, inspecting me. I was assaulted by his thoughts and I immediately responded by taking a step back.

"She doesn't seem to be intoxicated but it is graduation night and there's been a lot of drinking going on. Why else would she be parked two blocks from her house? She must be afraid to go home."

Without thinking, I responded, "Sir, I swear to you I've not been drinking. I don't drink... I promise. I'm a good girl. I really am." The stress of the entire evening, along with his presence overwhelmed me and I suddenly found myself sobbing.

"I think it's best if you allow me to drive you home."

"No...no, please. Officer, I promise I'll go straight home. Please don't drive me there." I couldn't bear the thought of the humiliation of having to tell him the truth.

"Miss, you've just turned sixteen. That's much too young to be sitting out here alone at this hour. It isn't safe for you to be out here like this. Now tell me the truth. Why are you here?"

After I could control myself enough to speak I decided to tell him the whole ugly story. There was no reason to belabor this any longer, as he was not going to leave me sitting there. I had nowhere to go. I felt like he had left me with no other choice.

"I can't go home because my father—well he isn't my father but I didn't find that out until tonight—he's kicked me out of the house."

"Why? What did you do?"

I bristled with anger as I wiped the tears from my face. "I didn't do anything except be the unfortunate offspring of my mother's rape." The more I thought about this, the more it angered me.

"Excuse me?"

"Yep, you heard correctly. My so-called father informed me tonight that my mother was raped and I happened to be the result of that. And then he kicked me out of the house. He said his obligation to me was over now that I had graduated from high school. Honestly, I believe he enjoyed saying those things to me."

"Miss, are you sure you're not making this up?" His cynical tone indicated his disbelief.

I sighed as I dropped my head and stared at the pavement. How embarrassing to have to tell some stranger that your family doesn't want you to live with them anymore. To make matters worse, that stranger now thought I was making it all up. I drew in a quivering breath.

"No, I swear officer. I wish I were though. I came home from my graduation tonight. I'd searched for my family after the commencement but couldn't find them." I paused because I flashed back to earlier in the day. Initially, I didn't even realize I had started speaking aloud. "When I woke up this morning, I thought this would be the greatest day of my life. My whole life..." I had to pause and swallow the gigantic lump that had lodged in my throat. "My whole life was spent trying to get my father to notice me…to get him to say one word of encouragement…have him tell me he was proud of me…anything. I never heard him utter anything positive to me. So today when I woke up I thought that this would be it. I was graduating today and giving the valedictory speech. They never even showed up. My mom didn't even come. She took my little brother and sister to Carowinds to spend the night there. I'm only sixteen, I graduated two years early and I was the valedictorian. And they didn't even come to my graduation."

I was silent for a few moments, trying to regain my composure as my lower lip quivered. Then I lifted my eyes and asked, "Why in the world would anyone do that to her child?" It was a rhetorical question, but he answered me anyway.

"Miss, I don't have an answer for you." Then he did the oddest thing. He opened his arms to me but I backed away. Never in my entire life had anyone done that. My mother never held me…not to comfort me when I was scared or sick or even to show love. My father certainly never did. I was so unused to affection that I didn't quite know how to respond.

"I'm sorry Miss; I didn't mean to offend you." He sort of shuffled his feet. I realized my reaction had made him uncomfortable.

"It's okay…I've never…I mean, well never mind and you didn't offend me," I sniffled. I looked at him for the first time—I mean really looked at him. He had sandy brown hair and a kind face with soft hazel eyes. He was tall, maybe six feet or so and a bit on the heavy side. My guess would be that he was in his mid-thirties.

"Where will you go tonight?"

"I was planning on staying here in the parking lot until you blew my plans." I made a poor attempt at giving him a lopsided grin. For some reason I felt really sad that I had made him feel awkward when he was only trying to comfort me.

"Look, let me make a quick phone call." Before I could respond he was on his cell phone and seconds later he was speaking with someone. When he ended the conversation, he turned to me and said, "Follow me in your car. You're going to stay with my wife and me tonight. I know it sounds weird and all, but I wouldn't feel right leaving you out here by yourself."

"Oh, I don't think…oh no sir, I can't do that. I don't even know you or your wife. Please sir, can you just pretend you never came here…that you never saw me here? Please?" I was most uncomfortable with this. I prayed he would just leave me be.

"Look Ms. St. Davis…"

I interrupted him, "It's January…please call me January."

"Okay then, January. Look, if I leave you out here I'm going to feel miserable. But, that's nothing compared to what I'll feel when I go home and you're not with me. My wife would kill me and you don't know what it's like being around her when she's mad at me." He gave me a wink then and I couldn't help but give him a watery smile.

"That's awfully kind of you sir, but I don't even know your name. I'm not comfortable with any of this."

"Well, I'm Seth and my wife is Lynn…Campbell. And if you don't follow me, I'll just have to handcuff you and drive you over in my cruiser here," he said with another playful wink.

He made it impossible for me to refuse so I followed him for a couple of miles until we pulled into a driveway in a neighborhood that I wasn't familiar with. The light over the porch was on and the door opened to a slightly heavy woman in a bathrobe. She had long brown hair and huge brown eyes. Her friendly smile eased my trepidation about staying with these strangers.

"Hi," I said sheepishly.

"Come in, come in," she said. We made our introductions and Seth left to go back out on patrol. He wouldn't be finished until 2 am. Lynn and I sat at their kitchen table for another two hours while she held my hand (a first for me) and I poured out my heart to her. Then she led me to a small bedroom and I crawled into bed and promptly fell asleep.

Chapter Two

When I awakened I was disoriented. Where in the world am I? At first I didn't recognize anything until it all came crashing down on me. I couldn't breathe and my heart started hammering in my chest. My throat felt like it was closing up on me. I struggled for air but the room seemed devoid of any. I stumbled out of bed, banging into things and somehow made it to the hallway before Seth intercepted me.

"What is it January?"

"Can't breathe..." I strained to get the words out.

He took a long look at me and said, "You're having an anxiety attack. Come."

He grabbed my arm and tugged me into the kitchen. He quickly opened a drawer and pulled out a paper bag. In the meantime, I felt my vision darkening and pins and needles were piercing my skin everywhere. He pushed me into a chair and held the bag over my mouth. I looked up at him and he said, "Slowly take some deep breaths. You're hyperventilating and this will calm you down."

I began to breathe in slowly and at first it didn't work. I started to panic again as I felt myself suffocating.

"January, I promise you're going to be fine. Just keep taking long slow breaths."

Seth continued to encourage and coach me and eventually, I began to feel the panic subside. My breathing eased and I was finally feeling some relief. I continued to hold the paper bag and lifted my eyes to his. He nodded and took the bag away.

"Better?" he asked.

I nodded, afraid to even speak yet. I sat there and then I took another deep breath and asked, "What was that?" I started to shake and I could feel my cheeks burn with embarrassment.

"You just had an acute anxiety attack. Don't be alarmed though, you're totally fine."

"I'm so sorry. I didn't know what was happening," I said.

"There's nothing to be sorry about. I'm surprised this didn't happen sooner, with what you've been through and all."

"I'm so embarrassed. I feel terrible for putting you and Lynn out like I have. I think I need to be going." I struggled to stand but felt the room start to sway.

The next thing I knew, I was laying on the couch with a cold cloth on my head.

"Are you back with us?" Lynn asked.

I nodded.

"January, when was the last time you ate anything?"

I couldn't remember.

"Did you eat anything yesterday?"

I thought for a moment and realized I hadn't. I had been so busy during the day and I was expecting to eat after the graduation ceremony. A pained expression must have come over me because Lynn quickly said, "Honey don't you worry about it. I'm just going to whip us up a big Saturday morning breakfast."

What seemed like moments later, I found myself devouring a stack of pancakes with warm maple syrup, some scrambled eggs and bacon with a glass of milk and a cup of coffee. Wow, I must have been hungry because I normally didn't eat that much.

I lifted my eyes to see both Seth and Lynn grinning at me.

"What?" I asked.

"Oh, it's nothing. We just like to see someone with a hearty appetite enjoy their food!" Lynn said.

"Er, yeah, I normally don't eat like this. But it was so delicious, I couldn't help myself."

"That's just Lynn's cooking. Why do you think I have such an awesome six-pack?" Seth laughed as he grabbed his belly.

"Honey, you know it's not a six-pack. You have a pony keg!" Lynn said as we all chuckled.

An awkward silence descended on us and I stared at my fidgeting hands. I suddenly remembered that I needed to shower and get ready for work.

"Oh my gosh, I have to go to work today. What time is it?" I screeched as I leaped out of my chair.

"It's 9:15," Seth replied.

"Shower…may I take a shower?"

"Why yes," Lynn said as she lead the way to the bathroom. She showed me where everything was. I dashed to my car and grabbed the bag my clothes were in, frantically searching for my work uniform. I worked at George's Meat and Produce, a local market, and I was supposed to be to work at 9:30. I was in a panic trying to get ready.

I took my usual two-minute shower, stuck my hair in a ponytail, threw on my uniform and made it to work by 9:40, apologizing profusely for being late.

Mr. George was fine with it. I was never late so I guess he knew I must have a good reason for running behind. We were so busy that 7 p.m. arrived in a flash.

I went to my car and then it hit me. Where should I go? I knew I needed to go back to Seth and Lynn's, if only to thank them for letting me crash with them. I refused to ask them to let me stay another night. I was still reeling with humiliation over everything that had happened. I was agonizing over my dilemma when I heard the tap at my window. I looked up to see Seth's face.

"January, Lynn and I want you to stay with us…"

"I can't do that Seth." I said as I chewed on my lower lip.

"Please hear me out. We want you to stay with us until you can find somewhere to go. You leave for school soon, right?"

At my nod, he continued, "You can stay in our spare room until then or until you find somewhere else to stay. Okay? And if you decide to stay with us, there will be rules to follow, like there would be in any family situation. So, what do you think?"

I couldn't help feel suspicious. My head was swimming with all sorts of unpleasantries. Not about them; they had been nothing but kind to me. I just never experienced kindness such as that and it made me extremely suspicious and confused.

"I'm not sure," I answered him.

I noticed his expression fall as his eyes drooped a bit.

"Look, I know you're probably overwhelmed with everything that's happened, but you'll be safe with us and you'll have a roof over your head. We really don't want you out and about on your own. It's simply not safe January."

I nodded. He did have a point. I was honestly scared out of my wits. The idea of being thrown into the world unexpectedly was still a shock to me. And it did feel wonderful to sleep in a soft comfy bed and eat that tasty breakfast. I was definitely warming to the idea.

I looked at Seth and nodded. "Okay, but only if you let me help with the cooking and chores and allow me to pay room and board," I added with a smile.

Chapter Three

I t was decided that I would stay with the Campbell's for the summer before I headed to college. Initially, the whole prospect of moving in with them was a bit daunting. I wasn't sure if it would work out. My timid personality had me constantly damp with sweat. I worried about saying or doing the wrong thing and I felt so out of place...like that proverbial third wheel.

The Campbell's didn't have children and their house was large enough for three, but somehow I felt like a spoon in the fork drawer. Out of place and awkward, the summer couldn't pass by quickly enough for me.

Several times over the next weeks, I drove by my old house hoping to catch a glimpse of Tommy and Sarah. I was finally rewarded for my efforts one day and I swung in the driveway as I saw them playing in the front yard. As soon as they saw me, they barreled through the grass and reached my car by the time I could pull it to a stop and throw it in park. I jumped out and—oh my gosh—it was so great to see them. I pulled them both into my arms and nearly squeezed them to death. I didn't want them to see my tears but I didn't have a choice as they squirmed out of my arms.

Tommy was pogo sticking up and down in excitement and Sarah was grabbing my hand and swinging my arm back and forth.

"January, Mommy said you moved to college," Tommy accused.

"Not quite sport. I'll be going in August." How interesting that they lied to the little ones about me.

Tommy asked me in his own sweet way, "But where're you staying?"

"Well, honey, I moved a few blocks away from here. So what have you and my favorite little squirt been up to?" I asked as I grabbed little Sarah, picked her up and swung her in the air. She giggled and Tommy launched into a play-by-play description of what they had been doing all summer. I was thankful I was able to change the subject and get their attention off of me.

When he finally finished his chronicles of their days spent at the neighborhood pool, I gathered them both in my arms.

"Listen you two, you know how much I love you, right?" When they nodded, I continued, "I'm going to be moving to North Carolina soon but I wanted you to know that I think about you every single day. I'm going to miss you so much I can hardly stand it. Now Tommy, you're the big guy here and while I'm away, I want you to take care and watch out for Sarah, okay?"

He looked at me with his big brown eyes and dirt-smeared cheek and nodded his head vigorously up and down.

"It's a very important job to look out for your little sister."

"I'm not widdle! I'm a big gewrl!" Sarah insisted.

"Right you are Miss and you have an important job too! You need to look out for your big brother!" She nodded her head but Tommy interrupted.

"I'm all grown up and I don't need her to look out for me," he said petulantly.

"Oh Tommy, I only wish that were true. Everyone, including me, needs someone to look out for them. It's important that you do that for each other. You got it?"

"But January, who'll look out for you?" Tommy asked.

Oh crap...I cannot cry now. No way!

I swallowed the ginormous lump in my throat and tried for a few seconds to speak as I fought to stop my lower lip from trembling. I was finally able to push back the surge of tears and I squeaked, "Well, I'm hoping my new roommates will. And I'll look out for them in return."

My beautiful, precious siblings looked at me with their guileless eyes and it nearly split my heart in two. The thought of leaving them forever was the knife that was shredding my heart into pieces. I took a deep shuddering breath to calm myself. I just couldn't let myself break down in their presence but I was having great difficulty keeping it at bay.

"So, I want you two to behave and mind Mom and Dad. But most importantly, look out for each other. I love you two and I promise to write you as often as I can."

I heard a creak and looked up to see my mother storming out of the front door with daggers in her eyes. Her thoughts assaulted me in rapid succession…Freaky thing…what is she doing here…I wish she would just disappear. They went on and on to the point I had to close my mind to them. They were making me ill.

"What are you doing here?" her voice dripping with hatred.

"I stopped by to say hello to Tommy and Sarah," I mumbled. I was numb from her vile thoughts and the iciness of her tone. I couldn't believe she was treating me like this in front of the kids.

"Tommy, Sarah, in the house…now!"

"That won't be necessary. I was just leaving."

I darted a look at the kids and they were so confused I reached out my arms to hug them one last time and tell them everything was fine.

"Don't you dare touch them! Just…get out of here and don't ever come back."

I staggered backwards from the vehemence of her hatred. She had always been a passive woman, not saying much of anything. I was told she abhorred me, but I hadn't let myself believe it. I knew it was the truth now. Her tone and actions conveyed it all to me. She despised me…bottom line.

"I love you two…more than I can ever tell you." I blew them a kiss and smiled.

"Tommy, Sarah, in the house I said. Now!" she yelled at them.

They scurried to the porch and disappeared inside.

"That wasn't really necessary, was it?" I whispered.

"Yes. It was. You are an abomination and I want you gone from here. Now!"

"Why didn't you abort me when you were pregnant?" The words tumbled out before I could stop them.

She cocked her head and was silent for a second. Her eyes seared me as she said, "That was the biggest mistake of my life and every day I regret my decision to not end that pregnancy." She spun and went inside, leaving me standing in the driveway, mouth agape. The brutality of her words made everything I had previously felt pale in comparison.

My body felt as though it had been physically abused. I dragged my battered and beaten self into my car and drove until my tears blinded me, forcing me to pull over. I stopped at a wooded park and sat in the parking lot for I'm not quite sure how long. I lost track of time.

When the bone-crushing pain of her words began to recede, I drove back to the Campbell's. They immediately knew something was wrong.

"I'd rather not talk about it. Please excuse me. I think I'll go to bed now," I mumbled, my face etched with pain.

I stumbled into bed and cried myself to sleep, telling myself things would be better the next day. I was wrong. Eventually the stark pain of my mother's words began to dissipate, and I ultimately came to terms with the fact that I had been raised by two people that hated me. It was a horrific feeling, but at least I knew the truth.

Chapter Four

At nine o'clock on a sultry August morning, after hugging and thanking Seth and Lynn, I backed my Toyota out of the Campbell's driveway and began my journey to Cullowhee, North Carolina. I was moving to Western North Carolina University to begin stage two of my life. Stage one hadn't been so hot so I was tentative in my hopes for this one.

Seth and Lynn offered to accompany me, and although they had been nothing but kind to me and I don't know how I would have made it without them, I wanted to escape everything that was Spartanburg, South Carolina. One of my roommates was also from here, but she wasn't heading up until the week after next. I was going early to search for employment. I'd been granted an excellent academic scholarship, but since I had no financial means, I'd have to work and earn as much money as possible. Medical school was my ultimate goal, and the debt accompanying that would be mountainous.

I don't think excited could aptly describe my frame of mind. Anxious was more like it. I was ready to start phase two and was looking forward to meeting new people who were disconnected from my past. I wanted to give the former part of my life a speedy burial and be reincarnated into a new January. Now was that time.

My forever sweaty palms latched onto the steering wheel and navigated my Toyota up the mountains to college town. I normally enjoyed this drive as I was surrounded by the beauty and mystery of the mountains. However, since graduation night, I had existed in a perennial state of anxiety and my thoughts were clouded with worry that day. My jumbled and twisted nerves made it impossible for me to eat much as my stomach was on a continuous carnival ride of loop-t-loops, and as a result, I had lost weight. My clothing resembled sacks more than anything but unfortunately, they would have to do since buying new ones wasn't in my budget. I was hoping that my nonexistent appetite would reappear and claim my body once again.

It only took about two and a half hours to get to my destination. I'd rented a room for two weeks in one of those efficiency-type motels, as I couldn't move into my dorm yet. It was reasonably priced and Seth had checked it out through his police network to ensure I'd be safe. It was bare bones but it was clean and conveniently located. I missed my room at the Campbell's and all their warm chatter, but it wouldn't do for me to dwell on it.

I carted in my clothes and toiletries and then the job hunt began. Luckily, I landed two jobs by the second day. One was a waitress position at the Purple Onion, a restaurant in Waynesville, which was about a 35-minute drive from Cullowhee. My second job was at the university bookstore. This was a real coup, as I'd be getting a twenty percent discount on all my textbooks. So far so good!

I loaded up on my work hours to get as much in beforehand as possible. I knew when classes started I'd be forced to cut back. Besides, I didn't know anyone so I didn't have anything else to do. The ever present clenching of my stomach eased a bit, due to the jobs and the fact that I would be earning some money.

The restaurant owner was awesome. His name was Lou and he was so accommodating with my schedule. He was a large, balding, grey haired man in his early fifties and he sort of treated me like a daughter...or at least what I thought a daughter would be treated like. I got along famously with all my coworkers and the chef kept telling me he was going to fatten me up. The food was scrumptious. The menu was higher end with a variety of seafood, chicken, beef and vegetarian dishes.

My favorite was the seared tuna. It was mouth-watering sashimi grade tuna seared with sesame seeds on the outside. I balked at trying it at first. I'd never eaten tuna other than from a can. Everyone laughed at me when I said that. It was true, however. I didn't know tuna fish actually came fresh like that. The first time I placed that tiny morsel in my mouth, I felt it melt and I couldn't seem to get enough after that!

My job at the bookstore, on the other hand, wasn't so great. It was exhausting work hoisting and unpacking the heavy boxes and stocking the shelves. The manager, Karl, was okay I guess, but he wasn't Lou. I suffered through it though because I was jonesing for that textbook discount along with the extra cash.

"January, you're going to have to hustle a bit more. Tomorrow things are going to pick up and everyday will get busier and busier," Karl said.

"I'm working as hard as I can Karl. I can't lift the heavy boxes as easy as the guys can," I retorted. He expected me to have super strength. I was half the size as some of the others. "Maybe I could do a different job."

"No, I need you here, doing this. Textbooks are heavy. You knew this when you accepted the job."

"Yes, sir. I'll do my best," I mumbled.

"See that you do."

Between the two jobs, I barely had time for anything but sleep. For two weeks, every night I crawled between the sheets and crashed. My sleep was anything but refreshing. I awakened each morning feeling every bit as weary as I did when I went to sleep. I attributed it to my mounting uncertainty on whether I could pull off going to school full time and working two jobs.

The day arrived when I could move into my dorm. I packed up my meager belongings and drove to my next residence. I felt like a vagabond due to four moves in the space of three months. It was a good thing I didn't own much. That was my way of keeping the glass half full.

I was the first of my suite mates to tackle this event. I'd be rooming with Carlson Kittredge from the Raleigh, North Carolina area. My other two suite mates were Madeline (or Maddie as she preferred to be called) Pearce, whom I knew from high school, and Catherine (Cat) Newman from Asheville. I rapidly moved my few belongings in, made up my bed with the set of sheets and comforter the Campbell's had given me as a going away gift, and headed to the bookstore for my shift. Things were heating up there as more and more students arrived for the semester.

I was starving and exhausted by the end of my shift, but I made my way to the Purple Onion to work. My mouth watered as I thought about what I would soon be eating. My shift didn't end until midnight and by the time I returned to my dorm, everyone was asleep.

The next day, Sunday, was pretty weird. Everyone was gearing up to start class on Monday but I was so busy with work, I didn't even think about checking out where my classes were. I was carrying a tough load: Biology, Chemistry, Physics, Calculus and English. Everyone else was excited about parties and meeting boys, but I was worried about whether I could manage it all. My anxiety was obvious by my ragged nails and chewed up lower lip.

"Did you check out where your classes are January?" Cat asked me that evening. "Maddie and I did but I am still so nervous about getting lost and being late. I know I won't sleep a wink tonight."

"Same here," Maddie agreed. "I wish I had at least my first class with one of you."

Carlson piped in, "What are y'all so worried about? Just ask a cute boy where you should go if you get lost. That always works for me!" Sweet as she seemed to be, evidently Carlson didn't have a clue. Maddie must have been thinking along the same lines because I glanced her way and caught her eyes rolling. I chuckled.

I shook my head saying, "I didn't have a chance today. By the time I got off work, it was dark."

"You work too much girl," Carlson said.

"I have to. It's my only means of support," I confessed as I dropped my eyes to the floor. I started wringing my hands as this was headed to an area in which I had no desire to venture.

Even though I tried my best to ignore my ability to hear thoughts most of the time, I knew it would be asked and I just knew the question would come from Carlson. "What about your parents? Isn't that what parents are for anyway?"

Bless Maddie! She darted her eyes my way, but then answered Carlson before I even had a chance.

"Carlson, not everyone is lucky to have parents with unlimited amounts of cash to dole out to their kids. Everyone has their own situation. Please think about that before you throw out comments like you just made."

I felt the corners of my mouth turn up.

"Gracious me, I didn't mean to offend anyone. I'm so sorry!" Carlson exclaimed.

Like I said, she really didn't have a clue.

"Well, I'm just saying," Maddie concluded.

I looked at Maddie, smiled and mouthed a "Thank you" at her. She nodded.

"I'm sorry January. I meant no harm," Carlson added.

"No problem Carlson. Don't worry about it. Some of us are luckier than others so do me a favor and thank your parents. You're one of the lucky ones," I replied.

That night I fell asleep thinking about Tommy and Sarah, wondering if they were missing me as much as I missed them. My stomach clenched every time I thought of how their sweet faces looked when last I saw them. I reminded myself to write them a letter the next day.

The first semester sped by and Thanksgiving was the following week. Seth and Lynn begged me to join them in Spartanburg, but I declined their kind invitation. Even though we spoke frequently, and I missed seeing them, I had no desire to return there. My memories of it did nothing but bring me down, making it a depressing thought altogether.

I loaded up my work hours again. Lou couldn't have been happier because the Purple Onion was open on Thanksgiving and everyone was vying for the day off. I said I would work as long as he needed me so some of the others could spend time with their families. All my roommates would be gone so I didn't mind doing it. Besides, those extra greenbacks would come in handy.

Maddie was going to Cat's for the holiday and Carlson was heading home to Raleigh. I had applied for permission to remain at school so I was the only one in our suite. While it was a bit disconcerting, it didn't bother me much. On a whim, I decided to try to call my parents (as I still thought of them) hoping, but not expecting, to speak with Tommy and Sarah.

I punched in the numbers on my cell phone before I lost the nerve. Please let Tommy answer the phone. Please, please, please...

"Hello."

Oh no, it was my mom!

"Hi! It's me, January. Happy Thanksgiving." My voice shook.

"What do you want?" Her tone indicated this wouldn't go far.

"I was hoping to speak with Tommy and Sarah. Please Mom, let me speak with them. I won't say anything bad, I promise. I just want to hear…"

"I TOLD you not to EVER come around here again. I meant it. And that goes for phone calls too. Don't EVER bother us again!" The phone slammed in my ear.

Her mean spirited words left me shaken and rattled, not to mention how they had thoroughly spoiled my Thanksgiving. What I wouldn't give to hear Tommy and Sarah's voices. The gnawing ache in my belly reared its angry head again.

I had avoided thinking this way, but I finally had to admit to myself that phase two wasn't working out quite the way I'd envisioned. I never had time for anything fun because I was working, going to class or studying. In frustration, I threw my cell phone across the room.

Maddie and Cat were great. They both tried to get me to open up, but honestly, I simply didn't feel like discussing it with them, or anyone else for that matter. It humiliated and embarrassed me to even admit to myself the horrid circumstances of my birth. I was sort of close to both of them, but definitely not that close. I wanted this secret buried and buried deep so it would never resurface.

"January, I'm worried about you and your schedule. You're burning the candle at both ends and I'm afraid you're going to burn out soon," Maddie commented one day. Her concern was genuinely written all over her face.

"I'll be fine Maddie. I appreciate your concern but honestly…"

She placed her arm on mine and halted my words, "Do you want to talk about it? I know something's wrong and I may not be able to help, but I'm a good listener."

I felt guilty not giving her what she wanted, but I couldn't bear to open up that topic. I just couldn't do it. I hung my head because I dared not look into her eyes. Tears were close to escaping and if that dam broke, no telling when the flood would end.

I cleared my throat and finally eked out, "Thanks Maddie. Your concern's touching, and I do appreciate you…I really do. But I'll be fine." I had reined in my emotions so I was able to look her in the eye.

Her pity was palpable. I had to get away from her…and fast or I would lose it. I turned and quickly walked away.

Maddie had dealt with issues of her own, losing both of her parents by the time she was eighteen. Cat, on the other hand, grew up in a houseful of rambunctious kids—four to be exact, with Cat being the second oldest. Her home life might have been warm and loving, but her family's financial situation wasn't the best. I didn't know the specifics, but I knew it was bad enough that she might have to move home to Asheville. I know either of them would have been great sounding boards for me, and perhaps it may have eased my anxiety a bit, but I simply couldn't bring myself to speak of my situation with them.

The one thing I did talk to them about was how fiercely I missed my little brother and sister. I craved their company…yearned to hear their sweet voices and hold their warm little bodies in my arms. Not being able to at least talk with them made my belly fist up in knots every time I thought of it. I often wrote them sweet little notes, but I was positive my mother didn't pass them along. I swore to myself that someday, I would find a way to talk with them and they would learn the truth from me.

Chapter Five

Christmas was fast approaching and finals were consuming my every spare moment. I wasn't sleeping much and couldn't wait to get my exams behind me. It seemed that's how I spent the entire semester…hoping time would fly and move me to the next stage.

My grades were finally posted online and I was not pleased with my results. I made a 3.2, which was okay, but not nearly high enough for my standards. I should have expected as much with the hours I was working. I was averaging three to four hours of sleep per night. At this rate, I wouldn't make it to forty. College wasn't turning out to be the great experience I had prayed it would be. Way to go January!

Everyone left and I found myself back in the little efficiency motel for the holidays. The university closed the dorms for the three-week period.

Maddie called me the day after I received my grades.

"How did you make out with your grades January?"

"I ended up with a 3.2," I said sullenly.

"That's awesome!" Maddie exclaimed.

"Not really. If I want to get into med school, I need at least a 3.8 or better."

"January, you're so smart, you'll get those grades up. I know you will. I can't believe you did that well, with all the hours you work. I don't know how you did it."

"Thanks Maddie. It wasn't easy. I will say that," I said earnestly.

"That's an understatement. Well, I'm getting my stuff ready for my backpacking trip. I'm up on the trail for Christmas and then I'm going to drive down to the Keys for some fun in the sun!" her voice radiated excitement.

"I'm so jealous. Soak in some rays for me, will you?"

"You bet!"

"Hey, be careful up there. Don't forget to take that bear pepper spray stuff you talk about!"

Maddie started chuckling. "Don't worry, I won't! I'll see you in January, January!"

"Ha ha! Very funny!"

As I drove to work one day, I marveled at the view. Initially, I had dreaded this drive, thinking I would hate the time in the car every day. I couldn't have been more mistaken. The drive between Cullowhee and Waynesville was magnificent. The constant changing hues of the sky, coupled with the glorious peaks of the Smoky Mountains were a sight to behold. Cat and Maddie bragged about it all the time, saying how unmatched the splendor of the mountains was. They frequently hiked and backpacked in the national park, and examining the views as I drove, gave me a better understanding of why they loved it so much.

I was getting extra hours again at the Purple Onion and I was having a grand time. Since I didn't have classes or exams to worry about, I was truly enjoying my burden-free vacation and the gorgeous drive to work made it feel special.

"January, what are you doing for Christmas?" Lou asked me a few days before the Holidays.

"I was planning on working," I replied as I carried a load of plates into the kitchen.

"No, that's not what I meant. I meant for Christmas dinner. We close at five that day and I was wondering what you were doing afterward."

"Oh." I hadn't bothered to give it much thought. Truthfully, I had avoided thinking about it altogether. What I wanted more than anything was to see the joy on Tommy and Sarah's faces when they came downstairs to see what Santa left for them.

"Um, nothing I guess," I mumbled. I had a feeling where this was heading.

"Well, the wife and I want you to come to our place. It won't be fancy or anything, and it's just the two of us, but you know the food will be good."

"Oh, Lou, that's awfully kind of you but…"

"No buts January. You already said you weren't doing anything and we'll have more than enough food. You know Diane…she'll have enough for an army," he insisted.

"Thank you, but…"

"I told you January, no buts. You're not going to make excuses to get out of this one. It's settled. You're coming home with me right after we close here. And if you want, you can spend the night. We have plenty of room and that way you won't have to drive home." He was not going to take no for an answer.

"Are you sure?" I asked hesitantly. I didn't want to burden them.

"I wouldn't have asked you in the first place if I didn't want you to come. Now quit jabbering and get back to work," he said with a wink.

I wish Lou and Diane were my parents. They fussed over me that night and I'd never felt anything like it before, except maybe for my short stay with Seth and Lynn. That gnawing ache in my belly had lifted and I ate more than I had in a long time. Maddie always mentioned the "warm fuzzies" and I think I finally got what she meant by that.

The week after New Year's would bring that feeling of comfort to a screeching halt. Maddie had gone backpacking over Christmas and was supposed to go to Cat's for New Year's. She never called or showed up. She simply fell off the face of the Earth.

The search parties checked everywhere for weeks and the only things they found were her backpack and a bloody sleeping bag. They brought in search and rescue dogs but were unable to find anything. Her scent disappeared off the trail and the dogs could never pick it back up. She had simply vanished into thin air.

I never had been afforded the chance to sleep much before, but now my nights were filled with scary dreams. The churning tension in my belly threatened to erupt every day. I could hardly bear the thought of her in the hands of a kidnapper. Or what if she had been lying somewhere injured, with no one to help her? How could this have happened? I couldn't get those awful thoughts out of my head.

"Wake up January!"

What? Who's that?

"January! Wake up! Come on, you're scaring me. Wake UP!"

Someone was shaking me…and hard. I struggled to open my eyes. My lids felt like they were glued together. I hoisted myself on to my elbows and opened my eyes to see Carlson's face right in front of me.

"What's going on?" I asked.

"You were screaming in your sleep. You scared the daylights out of me!" She was clearly agitated.

"Sorry," I mumbled, rubbing my eyes. I was, in fact, relieved she had woken me up. I had been dreaming about my parents and that was something I wanted to keep buried.

"I guess it's all the strain of Maddie's disappearance."

"I guess so. Don't do that again, okay?"

"I'll try Carlson," I said drily. As if there was any way I could control it.

If I thought my dreams were bad, they were nothing compared to what Cat was experiencing. To put it bluntly, she was going crazy. She and Maddie had become inseparable, almost like sisters. They were the best of friends and Cat was struggling with all of this.

"Any word?" Cat asked as she barged through the door.

"Nope," I answered, kicking my toe against the doorjamb. We would repeat this sequence daily. Somehow, Cat and I were steadfast in our refusal to give up hope.

One day though, I came home and Cat was grinning from ear to ear.

"You are not going to believe this!"

"What…don't keep me hanging!" I yelled.

"She's back! They found her! You won't believe this but she showed up last night at the hospital down in Spartanburg. Random, I know. It's pretty weird too because the hospital doesn't know how she got there. The staff said that one minute she wasn't there, and the next minute she was!"

"I'm not following you," I said.

"Well get this. Maddie doesn't remember a thing either. Nothing at all. She doesn't know where she's been or what happened to her. The doctors say she had some bones that were broken but have pretty much healed. The bad news is that her spine was injured so she's lost the use of her legs."

"Oh no!" I couldn't imagine that. What must Maddie be feeling?

"But she's okay otherwise. This whole thing has been so bizarre!" I could tell Cat was on cloud nine with joy.

"Yeah, definitely bizarre. This is hard to process." I was dazed.

"I know. I'm heading down there tomorrow to see her. You want to come?"

"Yeah! Oh darn. I can't. I have hours at the bookstore and Karl won't let me switch. I'm sorry. Please tell her how happy I am she's back!"

While we were ecstatic she was alive and as well as could be expected, we were heartsick over what she had endured along with the fact that she had decided not to return to Western. We all attempted to change her mind, but she was adamant about staying in Spartanburg. Cat was devastated by this but she understood that Maddie was much more comfortable in her home and we realized it was the best decision for her.

We visited her several times and she was making awesome progress. She even had learned to drive. We'd joke about how she was hell on wheels. She wasn't the greatest of drivers before, but now…well, get the women and kids off the road. Maddie was clumsy at best, but behind the wheel of a car without the use of her legs…it was a scary thought indeed! I finally felt the burning pain in my stomach ease and at last I was able to eat. It was short-lived though.

A couple of months later we were reliving the nightmare. I can still remember the look on Cat's face when she answered her phone that fateful day.

"Hiya!" Cat said. She liked to answer the phone like that. She loved how goofy it sounded.

"What? No! When? Call me as soon as you know something!"

The look on Cat's face was frightening.

"She's gone again," she whispered.

Maddie left Cat's cell phone number as next of kin with her home health care nurses. One day, when they went to her house, Maddie was gone. She had vanished again and this time it was seemed she wasn't coming back.

Several scenarios went through our minds…suicide for one. Except nothing added up. She had seemed happy. Her nurses even said she was spunky and in great spirits. The police couldn't find any evidence of foul play. It was baffling.

During our last visit, Cat and I both noticed that Maddie had been a bit agitated. She had complained of headaches but the doctors said that was part of her recovery and they would diminish as time went on. I knew something was fishy, but again, the police couldn't find a trace of anything to indicate what might have happened.

Nothing from her home was missing, not even any clothing. Everything was intact and the only fingerprints the police located were the nurses' and Maddie's. Everyone was downright perplexed by the situation.

I had even begged Seth to see if he could help since he was connected to the police force.

"January, this isn't something you want to hear, but I talked to the detective in charge of Maddie's case and there isn't a shred of evidence. They've dug into as much as they can, but nothing is missing. I hate to ask you this but are you sure she didn't…you know, maybe take her own life?" Seth asked one afternoon over the phone.

"Seth, I know Maddie and she wouldn't do something like that. And, if on the off chance she did, I know she would've left a note or something. She wasn't depressed like that either. People just don't disappear into thin air Seth!"

"Calm down January. Getting all riled up like this won't help."

"Well, someone has to," I shouted into the phone. "Something's happened to her and we need to find out. She may need our help. Someone has kidnapped her or something. She didn't go anywhere. How could she? Her car is still at her house and she can't walk for cryin' out loud!"

"Okay. Look, I'll keep checking with the detective, but calm down January. You're being upset won't help us find her any faster," he admonished.

"I suppose you're right but Cat and I feel like you all are just not doing enough to find her."

"Well, I wasn't going to mention this, but they've ruled out kidnapping. Kidnappers always demand a ransom, and there haven't been any demands at all," he informed me.

"What if someone abducted her and they don't want a ransom. What if they want her dead or something?" My voice had risen again.

"January, get a hold of yourself. Let me worry about that on this end. I'll let you know just as soon as something turns up, okay?"

"You promise?"

"Have I ever steered you wrong?"

"No," I said sullenly. "And Seth...thanks. You know I appreciate you doing this."

I hit "end" and kicked the wall.

"There's nothing Cat."

"How can that be January? What can we do?" Cat asked.

I shook my head, not knowing what else to say or do. I could hear her thoughts and how upset she was. She wanted to help find Maddie, but didn't know how.

Weeks turned into months and Cat's state of mind deteriorated. I was worried to death about her because she would barely speak to anyone. Cat, why won't you talk to me? Her wooden responses to my questions were scaring me. The end of the semester was upon us and she hadn't attended classes for weeks. She had sequestered herself in her room and only did the bare necessities to get by.

Her parents came to move her home and they both shuddered at her appearance. She was wan and haggard and had lost a great deal of weight. They were as emotionless as the rest of us as they robotically crammed her things into bins and boxes.

Her dad walked her to the car and stuffed her into the passenger's seat. I followed them out but I wasn't sure of what to say. It was awkward for everyone. I reached through the window and squished Cat in a hug as I felt tears tracking down my cheeks. She never even lifted her arms to hug me back.

"I'll call you Cat. Take care of yourself," I sobbed. I looked at her dad as he stepped into her car to drive off, but he gave no indication he even saw me. I stood in the parking lot for a long time staring at the empty parking space before I went back inside.

Chapter Six

Two Years Later

I had just turned nineteen and my second and third years of college were behind me. My grades were horrible. Try as I might, I couldn't seem to bring them up. I had lost my academic scholarship and my student loans were probably more than I could ever repay. My freshman year had destroyed me, and the last two years I had struggled to recover, but my mind didn't want to cooperate. I kept thinking things would turn around, but I had this ball and chain called bad luck I couldn't break free from.

After all this time, Cat still suffered from deep depression. She had been hospitalized for a time, and for weeks she wasn't allowed any phone calls. She was eventually released but still lived at home. She took classes at the local college, and had made tiny improvements, but she never quite recovered from Maddie's disappearance. For some reason, she blamed herself, even though none of it was her fault. I still called her daily but our conversations, if you could even call them that, were repetitious.

I punched in her cell number. *Please answer and be the Cat I used to know.*

"Hey January," the dull, lifeless voice drifted over the phone.

"Cat. Um, how're you doing today?" I prayed for the right answer.

"Same, I guess." Gone was the vivacious young woman I had once known. In her place was a wooden doll, barely able to converse with me.

"Cat, I want you to get better."

"I know. I'm trying January. How are you? Still working crazy hours?" The questions were asked out of courtesy and not because of her desire to know.

"Always. Work and school. I miss you and…" my voice trailed away. I almost said Maddie but stopped before I totally screwed things up. I didn't want to add to her burden…she had enough on her plate right now. "I miss the way things used to be."

"Yeah, I miss that too. Things sure ended up different, didn't they?"

My finger traced the outline of my phone as I spoke. "Yeah, different. An understatement. If you want I can come visit," I suggested, my voice hesitant, knowing what her answer would be. It was the same every time.

"Thanks, but I'm not up to that yet. Okay? Reminds me of the bad stuff."

"Okay. I understand. Just let me know when you are. Take care, Cat. I mean, well, just take care. I'll call you tomorrow." I hit the end button and absently massaged the gnawing ache in my belly that was my constant companion.

What a couple of years! Could it get any worse? *Gawd, I hope not. I can't take much more.* I hadn't talked to Tommy or Sarah in over two years, Maddie's disappearance had never been solved and Cat was in Asheville still recovering from her breakdown. My grades stunk, I lost my scholarship and I had been fired from my job at the bookstore for my bad attitude. What chaos my life was.

I stared at myself in the mirror and the pathetic image looking back at me shocked me. *Is this really me?* I was a bad awful mess. My weight had dropped to nothing. I was skin and bones and my stomach had never recovered from its carnival ride. I knew I had major issues, but there wasn't anything I could do about it. My palms stayed sweaty, along with the rest of me, and my nails were chewed to the quick. My white stringy hair had never been attractive, but it was downright ugly now. The dark purple circles beneath my eyes emphasized the hollows of my cheeks, making them much more pronounced. They could probably qualify as caves. Even the great food at the Purple Onion hadn't helped. Mainly because I could barely choke it down whenever I attempted to eat it. Nerves…anxiety…worry…call it what you will but I was riddled with it.

My dreams of medical school had been ripped totally away. I couldn't work full time, go to school full time, keep my grades up with these courses and continue to live through this nightmare of a life. My attitude wasn't pleasant either. I had no friends and who could blame anyone? I snapped at everyone and was downright surly.

One shining star was that I had been offered a summer internship at the Centers for Disease Control and Prevention in Atlanta, working in the microbiology department. It was a surprise to me at how I landed it, but it would be a full time paid internship in which I would earn six credit hours. It was the first time I felt excited about anything in a long time! I adored microbiology and had changed my major to it since I had all but given up on medical school. At least I would be able to find employment with that degree.

I would be moving to Emory University the next day to start at the CDC. I had booked up my work hours so I could have some extra cash and tonight was my last shift at the Purple Onion until I returned in August.

The evening went well. The summer tourists were beginning to arrive and I was surprised when Lou told me we would be closing early. Usually he had extended hours this time of year. At ten o'clock, I escorted the last patrons out of the restaurant and locked the doors behind them.

I went back in the kitchen to see what I could pilfer to eat, but all the lights had been turned off. My heart leapt in my chest because a few minutes ago, the room had been filled with employees. As I fumbled in the dark, suddenly the room was blazing in light and everyone was yelling, "Surprise!"

They had decided to give me a surprise going away party! Chef made some of my favorite yummy food (seared tuna for one) along with a huge cake and at the end, Lou presented me with a going-away check for $500. I was speechless. No one had ever shown me such kindness.

I kept blinking, trying unsuccessfully to keep the tears at bay.

"January, you've been a faithful employee since you started here and you've worked harder than anyone, including myself. I wanted to make sure you had a little extra money because things can be mighty expensive in Atlanta," Lou announced as he patted my back. He had learned long ago I didn't know how to handle a hug.

"Lou, I don't know what to say," I sniffled. I felt miserable for the way I had treated these people lately and they were the only ones who had stuck by me.

"Just say you'll be back in August!" he replied.

I nodded as I swiped my palms across my cheeks to rid myself of my tears. I was going to miss him so much!

Everyone hung around for a long time and I finally became conscious of how bone achingly tired I was. I told everyone goodbye and plopped into my car to go home. I felt the weariness of the day hit me during my drive and several times I felt my head bobbing. In the next moment, I discovered myself sitting in the parking lot of my dorm, not remembering how I got there. It scared me because I had been exhausted before but I never had gotten to the point where I couldn't remember what had happened.

I lumbered up to my room and barely made it to bed before I was fast asleep.

Chapter Seven

W orking at the CDC was amazing! I had never been this happy that I could recall. Food began to taste good again and, surprisingly enough, I had even put on a few pounds. My co-workers were incredible. They all went out of their way to teach and explain things to me. The lab itself was something I couldn't have dreamt up. It was state of the art with top of the line everything.

On my first day, I was given a tour of the entire facility, down to the super duper secure lab where they kept all the deadly specimens of things like the *ebola* virus, anthrax, and *variola* or smallpox virus. The deadliest of viruses were kept in a cryogenic state and the layers of security were unreal. The lab director escorted me around, as you needed special clearance to be allowed there. Security consisted of fingerprint and retinal scans and that would only gain one's entry to the exterior room. More layers of security existed for one to gain access to the storage freezer. It was all controlled through a central computer with many checks and balances to ensure the specimens were not tampered with. They had those metal tubes you see in the movies for the frozen specimens. A robotic arm would grasp the tube, lift and open it and either close it or deposit another sample within it.

My job was to run tests on the influenza virus. The CDC was responsible for predicting which strain of flu would be prevalent each year. This was done based on the past year's strains and they constantly checked the viruses to see how they mutated. My job was to inspect all the strains and watch for mutations or evidence of the possibility of upcoming mutations.

I was in the fourth week of an eight-week internship when things began to turn sour. My supervisor, Angie Mitchell, started to heap piles of extra work on me, making it difficult at best to complete my normal tasks. I was scolded for running behind and she threatened to remove me from my post. Her personality seemed to have undergone a complete overhaul. I noticed her thoughts had taken on a nasty edge. I was still hearing other's thoughts, but I had learned to slightly tune them out. Sometimes, if they were especially spiteful, it was tricky to avoid them, much like I was presently experiencing.

Something was up with her and I wanted to know what it was.

"Angie, is there something wrong?"

"Of course there's something wrong. Your performance has been less than adequate lately and I have deadlines to meet. Honestly January, I don't understand why you can't complete a task," she said in frustration.

What? How can she think that? I've been working my butt off!

"But Angie, I am working twelve hours every day, trying to get everything accomplished. In the last week alone you've tripled my workload. Have I done something to upset you?" I asked as I pushed the hair out of my face.

"That would be an understatement," she said bitterly.

I was lost in the weeds. This was a person that had initially taken me under her wing and spoon-fed me information about everything necessary for me to be successful here. She had flooded me with praise for several weeks and her reviews on my performance had literally glowed. She had gone from thinking I was the greatest employee ever, to an incompetent and inept one. I mentally examined my activity to see if I had changed anything, but I knew I hadn't.

"Angie, I thought you were pleased with my work here. Can we try to work together to get back on track?" I asked. I did not want to lose this position and something had gone wrong.

"January, I've given you proper direction and it seems you disregard everything I tell you."

Disregard everything? What is she saying?

My mouth formed a huge O. I had taken meticulous notes and kept a journal of everything she had instructed me to do. I was implementing all the proper steps and yet she was finding fault with all of my actions. I was at a loss.

As I looked at her, I inspected her appearance. She was disheveled and her clothes were not very clean. She wore a lab coat so I hadn't paid much attention to these details before. Now I was noticing little things about her appearance that had changed. Something was going on. Angie was married with children, in her forties and very attractive, in a smart-woman sort of way. She had long dark hair that she normally wore twisted up in a bun. She wore glasses and was usually quick to smile at things. I couldn't recall that last time I saw her smile.

"Angie, please talk to me. Is there something wrong? Are you okay?"

"I told you I'm fine! Now leave me alone and get back to work," she screamed at me as she stormed out of the lab.

Things continued down this deteriorating path for another week. I did my best to keep out of her way and I was very good at it. I had become an avoidance expert as a young girl in order to evade constant criticism. It bothered me though that she had such an abrupt change in her demeanor that I made the decision to unleash my internal information highway. I was going to make a point to get into her thoughts to see what was eating her. On the Friday before my final week at the CDC, Angie stormed into the lab. Her thoughts were screaming out at me, making my decision to read her thoughts unnecessary.

"He said he would kill my kids if I didn't do this. What am I supposed to do? I can't hide this stuff anymore. My boss is going to notice and when January leaves next week, it'll all become evident that I've been falsifying those records. He said to blame it on January, but I just can't do that. What am I going to do?" Her distress went on and on.

This was awful and I didn't know exactly how to handle this. Someone was threatening her. She needed to tell the police, but I couldn't stand there and not offer her help.

"Angie," I began softly but I startled her out of her thoughts and her eyes were filled with panic and horror.

"It's okay, it's just me Angie. I didn't mean to frighten you."

She released a deep sigh and I became aware of the tears on her face.

"Hey, it's okay. Please, let me help you. I know you're in some kind of trouble, but maybe I can help."

Her face suddenly hardened and her eyes became chips of ice. "You have no idea what you're saying. I don't need your help and I've told you to leave me alone. Just butt out where you're not wanted," she gritted out.

I couldn't let it drop. I should have walked away, but I just couldn't. "But Angie, I know you're upset about something," I pressed on.

I should have trusted my gut instinct but didn't. She swung her hand at me and I heard rather than felt the crack as her palm came into contact with my face. My head snapped around and then I felt my cheek begin to sting.

I reached my hand to my cheek and was paralyzed with shock. I never expected this. She turned away from me and I was still standing stock still as I heard the slamming of the lab door.

I was stymied. I wanted to help but couldn't. I could hardly go to the police and explain how I discovered this. I could see it now, I thought as I massaged my still stinging cheek.

"Why yes officer, I read her mind. I know someone's threatening her."

That would gain me a ton of credibility, I thought sarcastically. I wracked my brain trying to figure out what to do but I kept drawing a blank. Predicaments ruled my life but this was one for which I had no solution. I hated this freakish ability of mine and I fervently wished it would go away! I wrung my hands in frustration.

It was Friday and my pile of work kept me busy until nine that night. I had dwindled it down to nothing when I glanced at the clock. Realizing the lateness of the hour, I looked around and noticed how empty the lab was. I was lost in the events of the day and the amount of work I had and I was still nursing my wounded ego as I headed out of the lab. As I made my way down the corridor, I noticed six men advancing toward me.

It wasn't their actions I noticed so much or even the way they walked. And though it was an oddity for them to even be here at all, it was their attire that captured my attention. They were dressed identically, in an extreme fashion, much like members of a gang or secret society. Large and muscular, they wore black vests and their bare arms were almost completely tattooed with tribal symbols of a sort. Metal bands criss-crossed their chests and their legs were tightly encased in leather. Knee high boots and black gloves finished off their ensembles.

As I neared them I felt my flesh tingle and the hairs on the back of my neck come to attention. Gooseflesh erupted and alarms started clanging in my head. I sucked in my breath and as I did, my eyes connected with the apparent leader. I say this because he was in the front of the formation as they plodded along.

Time stood still as our eyes connected. His were an uncanny shade, lavender with hints of indigo and specks of silver. It was a hue I was unfamiliar with but they were intriguing and fascinating. The alarms were still ringing in my ears and the air felt electrically charged around us.

"Halt!"

I turned into stone. I couldn't move a muscle. He cocked his head as his eyes bore into mine.

"Breathe!"

I distinctly heard his command in my mind and I was helpless to disobey him. I felt myself take a deep cleansing breath. I questioned him with my eyes. He flicked his head toward his men and they stepped back several feet.

"Who are you? Why are you here?"

I was confused by the demanding questions swirling in my brain but felt compelled to answer him. I had never used mind reading to communicate, but I was sure he would hear my answer.

"I'm January St. Davis. I'm here working on an internship for college credit."

"You are human?" he asked with incredulity.

I wasn't sure what he meant by that. Why would he want to know if I was human? What a ridiculous question!

"I don't understand. Why would you want to know that?"

"Leave this area and continue on your way!"

He silently shook his head and the intermittent flow of his thoughts was abruptly halted, just as if the internet had shut down. My communication highway had been disconnected—I was now offline. We stood there in silence and I could not break eye contact. I floundered in the depths of their color. I won't deny my fascination with him. He wasn't handsome in the usual way but his compelling looks mesmerized me. I can't say I was attracted to him and yet I couldn't seem to look away. There was also a frightening element to him but I wasn't afraid. It was an erratic mix of emotions.

I abruptly became aware of my ability to move. I gnawed on my lower lip as I continued to stare at him. His eyes raked me over and he slightly shook his head. Then he nodded once, and continued down the corridor.

I felt the urge to run after him and scream at him to stop, but I had no idea why. I eventually began walking again, intending to go home. When I reached the exit doors, I realized I left my purse in the lab. My immediate thought was that maybe I would run into him again. I dashed back down to the lab but the corridor was empty.

Disappointed, I returned to the lab for my purse. As I was moving through the various rooms, I noticed the door to one of the freezers had been left open. It was the freezer that contained the most deadly of viruses. I didn't direct have access to that area, but thick glass walls partitioned off every room, so you could see in each chamber. It was built this way as a security measure. I went to the phone on the nearest wall to call the guards, but the line was dead. I moved back into my area, but that phone line didn't work either.

I found a camera closest to me and waved my arms back and forth in front of it, hoping to catch the attention of the guards. I waited for the alarms to ring, but nothing happened. Exiting my lab area, I wandered the corridor, hoping to run into someone. The whole level seemed deserted. I took the stairs to the next level and it was also devoid of people. Hmmm…this was highly unusual.

I tried the phones on this level, but they were dead, as expected. I grabbed my cell phone and called 911. Ten minutes later, the building was swarming with police, HAZMAT and CDC officials investigating the issue.

It was finally discovered that there had been a brief power outage. That was why the cameras or phones hadn't worked. The lab was investigated thoroughly for foul play, but no evidence was found. The cryogenic container was thought to have accidentally opened when the power outage occurred. All the specimens were accounted for so everyone relaxed and breathed a huge sigh of relief.

My nagging doubt persisted though. Those men I saw in the corridor should not have been there. The video cameras had shut down at exactly the same time of their appearance. Coincidence? Doubtful...at least to me anyway.

And he spoke directly to me...through his mind as though he expected me to answer. How did he know I could read his thoughts?

This troubled me for the next week and I couldn't stop thinking of my encounter with him.

My internship finally ended, albeit on a sour note, and I was taking the weekend to rest up and pack before I headed back to Cullowhee.

On Saturday, I began feeling the beginnings of the illness. After working with the flu virus all summer, I knew I had contracted it. Hopefully, I would make it home before the worst of it hit.

By Sunday morning, my fever was raging. I didn't have a thermometer to take my temperature, but I knew it was high. Every movement put me in torrent of aches and pains. The piercing pain in my head made my eyes water. I kept popping Advil, but it didn't seem to help much. It seemed I couldn't catch a break and that my life was destined to get back on its downward spiral.

Though I felt as ill as ever, I couldn't delay heading back. I had to move out of my room here and I didn't have the extra cash to stay anywhere else. My car was loaded up so I decided to drive back to Cullowhee. I made it up to North Georgia when my vision began to blur. The images on the side of the road took on a wavy appearance. I talked to myself out loud in the hopes of keeping my heavy lids from slamming shut. I pulled off the road to regroup. When I awakened, night had fallen.

My fever raged and I began seeing Tommy and Sarah. My thoughts turned to the fact that they were the only people I ever had loved. My life had been a total twisted mess of unhappiness and maybe if I could find a soft place to lie down, I could go to sleep and peacefully die in comfort. If I were honest with myself, that was what I wanted the most right now. I never would have the nerve to take my own life, but maybe this illness could do it for me. Maybe then I would find that peace and tranquility I had desperately prayed for my whole life.

I was on a narrow road in the forest somewhere. I was hopelessly lost so I pulled off to the side and struggled to open my car door. It was being testy and wasn't cooperating. I gave it a shove and it finally swung open.

I walked a bit and the cool air felt so soothing on my cheeks. The pain in my head was constant and piercing, but it was quiet and somehow soothing out here. I wandered into the woods and reached the point where I couldn't take another step. I was so thirsty…my mouth was as dry as a bone and parched. There's Tommy…and Sarah! As I reached out for them, I tumbled to the ground, but found it to be as soft as my bed. Then my hallucinations began…

Book Two

Rykerian

Chapter One

I *am power. I am strength. I am the wind. I am speed. I am courage. I am faith. I am hope. I am fierce. I am loyal. I am steadfast. I am true. I am protection. I am honor. I am a Guardian of Vesturon.*

Talasi, my human connection, had contacted me. Talasi was the Seer of the Nunne Hi, the Spirit People of the Cherokee Nation. They secretly guarded the Smoky Mountains, keeping humans safe. She possessed the ability to communicate with the living and the dead and often sensed when evil or danger was approaching. She was troubled by a disturbance she sensed in the area. She had the ability to feel a shift of power in the air, both negative and positive. This time she explained it was more of a distressful disturbance...similar to what she felt when someone had been injured. Yet somehow, it was different. She was worried that perhaps someone may be trapped somewhere so she intercepted my thoughts to seek my assistance.

I was in the Command Center of the Compound of The Guardians on Earth when I felt Talasi's thoughts mingle with mine.

"What is it?" my brother Tesslar asked, noticing my momentary stillness.

I shook my head saying, "Not 'what' but 'who,'" I replied. "It is Talasi. She needs my assistance."

"What seems to be the problem?"

I explained her request of me and left the Center to prepare for my departure. As I headed up to my room I communicated with her through telepathy.

"I am sensing a disturbance but the scouts cannot find anything amiss."

"No cause for alarm Talasi. I will be there in moments."

Once in my room I grabbed my gear. I always traveled with the mending device, or the magic wand, as my sister-in-law Maddie liked to call it. It was a medical device that had the ability to heal many injuries.

I strapped my shadars on my hands—the tools that allowed me to communicate, teleport, assess a person's medical status and serve as my weaponry. I performed a quick calibration to ensure everything was working properly.

I tapped the screen and all my information appeared.

Name: Rykerian Tevva Yarrister, Guardian in Command

Location: Guardian Compound, Haywood County, North Carolina, planet Earth

Teleporter Status: Excellent

Communicator Status: Excellent

Locator Status: Excellent

Diagnostic Equipment Status: Excellent

Weaponry Status: Armed

"Please enter your mission," a voice commanded.

"To seek out a reported disturbance in the mountains near Bryson City, North Carolina," I replied.

"Affirmative."

I wondered briefly if I would need food or water and decided on the water. I headed to the kitchen in search of supplies.

"My lord, may I assist you in something?"

Zanna was our housekeeper, cook and general caretaker of everything inside the home. The house sat above ground but below us was the Command Center for the Guardians of Vesturon on Earth. It was here where all of our plans, training, tactics and strategies took place. The Compound itself could house over a thousand Guardians if need be. Zanna only cared for the house above ground.

"I was just getting some water for my mission."

"Will you be gone long?" she asked.

I glanced at her smiling, "I think not. I am running a check of an area Talasi is concerned over. Are you trying to spoil me Zanna?"

"Why my lord, you know I would never do that!" she exclaimed with a devilish look in her eye. I noticed her hand snaking toward a pile of cookies she must have baked earlier in the day. Before I could fill up my water container, she had placed a bag in my hand, filled with her delightful concoctions. She knew I loved chocolate chip cookies. It was an Earthly indulgence of mine.

"Zanna, you are the best and know how to make me happy," I said, kissing her wrinkled cheek. Zanna was quite old but her age did not slow her down a bit. Her bouncy gray curls and elf-like appearance matched her spritely actions as she moved around the house with the speed and agility of someone quite young.

"I am only taking care of what I love!"

Zanna and her mate Peetar had been a part my family since before my birth. She had cared for me and my siblings our whole lives and we all adored her. Peetar matched Zanna in appearance and age defying speed. He took care of the outside grounds and kept everything in perfect order.

I winked at her, placed the bag in my pouch I carried and left the house.

I teleported to the general direction Talasi had provided me. She was convinced whatever I would find would be off the beaten path. Once there, I set off in search of anything that might have set off Talasi's alarms. I skirted the area around Deep Creek in the Great Smoky Mountain National Park, staying clear of any of the main trails.

My feet barely touched the softened earth as I sped along. Using my Power of Speed, I made my way around the dense rhododendron thickets and mountain laurel, as quickly as I could. My eyes darted over the wooded landscape before me, taking care not to miss even the smallest of details. I searched for any clue, whether it be a footprint or a torn piece of clothing, anything at all to indicate the presence of another.

It wasn't long before I began to sense something was amiss, but like Talasi, I could not put my finger on it. As I moved along, my heightened senses were on red alert for anything unusual.

My otherworldly abilities were in overdrive, as I searched throughout the area. I finally noticed a subtle difference in the air around me...an odor that I was beginning to detect. My sense of smell was much keener than even any animal on earth, so I used that gift to hone in on my target. As I moved nearer to it, the odor became recognizable to me. It was the sweet, cloying odor of sickness. Whoever this was emanating from was severely ill. I quickly increased my pace until the scent became overpowering. This could only indicate one thing; whoever was suffering was in need of serious medical treatment.

I navigated around a rhododendron thicket and in the distance I could see a car parked on an old, unused forestry service road. I shook my head, trying to figure this out. Why would someone come all the way out here if they were seriously ill? Maybe they became ill after they arrived. It simply made no sense to me.

When I arrived at the car, I realized it was abandoned. The stench of impending death nearly overpowered me. Whoever the source, they were in pressing need of assistance. I called out to see if I would receive an answer, but there was no response initially. When I first heard the voice, it was so weakened, that even my acute sense of hearing could barely detect it. I followed the sound until I arrived at the source.

I gasped and my heart did a free fall to my knees when I saw who it was. Curled up and lying on the ground was the beautiful young female I had saved from a car collision several months before. She was the one who had captivated me...the one who I had thought of constantly ever since I had laid eyes on her. And here she was...struggling to breathe and fighting for her life. My gut clenched and revolted against what I was seeing. Her ghostly pale skin was covered with deep purple and black splotches everywhere. Her silvery gold hair was tangled and matted and her cracked lips were caked with dried blood. I placed my hand on her forehead and her skin was on fire with fever.

The coolness of my hand on her skin must have awakened her because her eyes fluttered open, only to close again. I aimed my shadar toward her and the holographs appeared. She was indeed extremely ill, but I was certain my shadar was malfunctioning by the reading I was getting. I quickly tapped the communicator and called Julian, our healer on Vesturon, my home planet that was located in a distant galaxy.

"My lord, what can I assist you with today?" he asked.

"Julian, I may have a malfunctioning shadar. I need a diagnosis confirmed on a gravely ill human female. Can you lock in on my location and we can proceed from there?"

"One moment… I have you in my zone now. Hmm, this cannot be correct."

"Julian, what is your reading?" I asked desperately.

"My lord, my scanner is diagnosing her with hemorrhagic small pox."

"Oh no! Then my shadar was not malfunctioning after all. That is the same reading I had."

"My lord, small pox was eradicated from Earth over 30 years ago. And the type she has was uncommon even then. It is a very virulent form of the virus called *variola major*. What is her appearance?"

"As you are aware, her body temperature is 104 degrees. She is dehydrated and has black and purplish blotches all over her skin and the whites of her eyes are deep red. Give me a moment and I will have her hologram available for you."

The image was up and I heard the words I had been dreading.

"I do not have to tell you Rykerian that she may have very limited time," Julian said with hesitancy. "She needs immediate medical treatment if she is to survive this."

"I cannot take her to Talasi because of the risk of spreading this disease."

"You are correct, my lord. You must take her to the Compound."

"Julian, I know not how to treat this. I know it is normally not allowed for you to intervene, but this could have major consequences for the entire human population. I will contact my father so you can gain permission to come to Earth to assist me."

My lord, there is no need for that. "'Under extreme situations, including the threat of disease epidemic, the healer shall be allowed interplanetary travel without first seeking approval by the Council,' and I quote," Julian said. "I shall teleport there and bring the supplies you will need to treat her," he informed me.

I sighed in relief, as I was not completely sure of what I would need to do.

"Bloody hell, I had forgotten about that. Thank you Julian. How can I stop the spread of this virus at the Compound? I do not want to endanger anyone there."

"No need to worry. Vesturions are immune to small pox. My lord, where are Maddie and Rayn?" Julian asked.

I thought for a moment before answering. "I believe they are on Vesturon at the Universal Leadership Conference. Can you confirm that before I take the female to the Compound?"

"Yes, I must. Since Maddie is part human, she could be at risk. She must stay clear of Earth until we find the source of this outbreak."

"Julian, contact my father and Rayn. I need to move the human as quickly as possible."

"I will do that and I shall see you shortly."

I gathered her into my arms and lifted her. Her lifeless eyes fluttered open again and she began murmuring.

"You are so beautiful. Surely you must be my guardian angel. Are you here to help me die?" She whispered so quietly that if I didn't have such acute hearing, I doubt I would have heard her. She tried to raise her hand but it limply fell into her lap.

"I am here to help you. I am taking you somewhere so you can be healed."

"No...you must stop angel. Please...I want to die," she pleaded.

"You are terribly ill; you cannot mean that."

"Oh, but I do. I cannot take my own life and I cannot go on like this. Please angel, stop for just one minute."

Against my better judgment, I did as she asked. She kept staring at me with her unusual soulful eyes.

"Why do you want to die?" I couldn't help asking her.

She smiled wistfully and struggled to say, "It's a long story. Please...sit and hold me for a moment? I have never been held by someone... I like the feel of your arms around me."

I could not believe no one had ever held this beautiful creature before. It must be the delirium of the fever making her say such things. Who would ever allow something like that to happen?

"Surely you have been held by someone...your mother maybe."

"My mother hates me and will be happy when she hears of my death. She won't have to worry about me bothering them anymore. Please...just for a minute...hold me..." she pleaded, her voice weakening further.

I sank to the ground on my knees and leaned back on my heels. I placed her in my lap, holding her close to my chest. She attempted to smile at me and I felt my heart constrict. I couldn't stop myself from delving into her mind and again I felt such deep pain...not just physical but emotional pain. I was mistaken. She was not delirious...she had never experienced the feeling of being held by anyone before. There were no memories of such comfort in her mind. How cruel to live a life with the absence of touch.

"You are in my mind angel...I can feel you there. That's good...you know I am ready to see God now. Thank you for holding me. I understand why people crave this...it is so comforting." She struggled to move her arms again but didn't have the strength.

I took her hand in mine and placed it upon my cheek. Then I heard her mutter, "I never knew my guardian angel would be so beautiful. You remind me of the sun setting...you are glowing. Have I passed? Is that why you are so bright?"

I was shocked by her questions. That made several things she said surprising. First, as a human, she shouldn't have felt my mind probe. Second, now she was seeing my aura. Humans didn't have the ability to do that. No wonder she thought me her angel.

"You are still alive, and I intend for you to stay that way."

"Angel, you must know it is too late for that." She still smiled at me.

I rose to my feet and resumed walking. I went behind the rhododendron thicket and entered coordinates to take me to the Compound of The Guardians where I could mend this lovely creature. Before I had a chance to activate my shadar, she placed her hand on my chest and simply said, "Thank you for holding me. It meant more than I can ever say." Then her eyes closed and she was silent.

I activated my shadar and we appeared in the lawn in front of the Compound. Julian and Zanna met me and we took her upstairs and placed her on the bed in one of our guest rooms. Once she was settled, I teleported back to her vehicle and collected her belongings.

Chapter Two

T he young female had been at our home for two weeks before Julian felt she would make a full recovery. She had hovered at death's door for much of that time. Her fever raged and during those spells, she would scream at some unknown being that seemed to be torturing her. Julian assured me it was the fever causing these spells, but they worried me nonetheless.

Julian had sent a robomedic to see to all of her medical needs. She was given IV fluids and medication such as antibiotics, but the virus was incurable and would have to run its course. We were troubled over how she contracted this disease.

Her name was January St. Davis and she was a college student at Western Carolina University. She had interned as a medical technologist at the Centers for Disease Control and Prevention in Atlanta from June until August and had an employee identification badge that indicated as such. We speculated that perhaps this is where she had been exposed to this horrific virus.

My brother Tesslar, who was an expert in both human and Vesturion technology, had been monitoring the hospitals around our location.

"Rykerian, you need to see this," he called to me one day.

I made my way to the Command Center where he was running checks of hospitals.

"There are reports coming in around Atlanta of humans with this disease."

I checked his screen and saw that indeed, the medical reports showed the same symptoms that the human female originally had.

"Our worst fears are coming to light," I murmured.

"We must contact Father and Rayn. This can be catastrophic for the humans."

"Indeed," I said. *How could this have happened?*

"Tesslar, can you plant some directives into the homeland security and into emergency preparedness programs everywhere?" I wondered aloud.

"Yes…I see where you are going with this. We can get these agencies on Red Alert now so they can start instituting quarantine methods. This may help stop the spread of the disease."

I shook my head, glad to see he was thinking along these lines. I left the Compound, intending to go to the kitchen in search of some lunch when I heard the blood-curdling screams. They were coming from upstairs. *What is happening? It must be the human…*

Using my Power of Speed I made short work of the stairs and burst through the bedroom door. She crouched on her knees in the corner, wide-eyed and trembling.

"Fear not, we mean you no harm," I gently said.

"Liar!" she rasped, scrambling tightly into the corner.

What? Why would she think me a liar?

"I know not why you say such, but I am no liar. I am here to help you," I explained gently.

She looked terrified. Her large eyes were nearly popping out of her head and she held up her hand, palm facing me as if she intended to ward me off.

"It is impossible for me to lie, this I swear."

"That…that thing over there hurt me so that makes you a liar."

I turned and glanced at the robomedic. "Stand down robomedic," I ordered.

"I am programmed to contain the subject and said subject attempted to exit the room," the robomedic explained.

Great! Just great! The bloody robomedic zapped her!

"You're so *bloody* right! That *bloody* whatever-it-is, *bloody zapped* me." Every time she said bloody, she held her hands up and bent her first two fingers. Her gesture confused me.

"Robomedic, alter programming. Remove containment order and stand down," I ordered.

"Affirmative. Programming altered. Robotic Medical Assistant 3279 standing down."

I turned back to the female and apologized. "I am very sorry for that. We only wanted to ensure you were safe, so it was programmed to guard you. I didn't intend for this to happen." She cocked her head and gave me a hateful stare.

"Truly, I am sorry."

She made no attempt to respond or rise as her eyes drilled into mine.

"Here, let me assist you back to bed."

"Stay away from me," she croaked.

She cringed when I reached toward her. *Great day, I am frightening her!*

"Damned right you're frightening me!" she exclaimed.

"How did you...?" It was then I realized she was hearing my thoughts and that clearly baffled me. I immediately blocked my thoughts and then I did the only logical thing I knew to do and delved into her mind.

She is terrified, puzzled, weak and confused.

"Who are you people and what is that thing?" she asked with a jerk of her head.

"Oh, yes well...," I stammered. What should I tell her? Should I tell her the truth? Would she freak out if she knew I was an alien? Would I harm her with the truth? I could not lie so I decided on the honest path.

"Please forgive me but that is what is known as a robomedic or a robotic medical assistant. It can perform all the functions that a live healer can and sometimes with more precision."

I looked into her eyes. The whites were no longer red and her skin only had pale splotches where the hemorrhagic areas used to be. She looked like she was recovering from a mass of bruises. And I had never seen a lovelier female.

"So who are you?" she asked, her voice edged with suspicion. She remained crouched in the corner.

"Please, let me assist you to the bed and I shall answer all of your questions. I promise."

She continued to eye me warily, and I was troubled by her lack of trust.

"Please. I swear to you on my life, I will not harm you."

She inched her way up but remained plastered to the wall to steady herself. I was next to her in an instant, holding her upright. As soon as I touched her, I felt the tension drain from her.

"How is...why am I not scared of you anymore?" she whispered.

I helped her into bed and covered her with the blanket, holding her hand lightly.

"It is my touch that comforts you," I stated.

"Huh?" I saw her eyes cloud with doubt.

"I am Vesturion and I am able to impart that to you."

"What is Vesturion?"

Although I did not relish the thought, she would have to be told the truth about us. She could not go back to her former life, for in all probability it no longer existed. It saddened me for her as I recognized that the world she knew and remembered had ceased to exist. Since I had no other choice, I patiently explained to her that I was an extraterrestrial...and she did not believe me for one minute.

"Okaaayyy. So E.T., how did I get here, and where am I?" she smirked.

"Are you making fun of me?" I asked, slanting my head. I was unsure of how to handle this creature.

"You seem to be the one making fun of me. Do you honestly think I'd fall for the E.T. thing?" She began to chew on her lower lip.

I scratched my head, not knowing what to say or do. I decided to start from the beginning.

"May I begin again?" I asked her.

She nodded, still wary of me. "By all means!"

"I am Rykerian Yarrister and I am a Guardian of Vesturon. I discovered you in the woods. You wandered away from your car and you were gravely ill."

"How did I get there?"

"I do not know. I was hoping you could provide us with those answers Ms. St. Davis."

She shook her head, and furrowed her brow. She began rubbing her neck. I was concerned her fever was returning.

"How do you know my name?"

"It was on your student identification card and your driver's license in your purse. I brought your belongings here. Are you feeling okay? Let me check your body temperature," I said raising my hand to use my shadar.

She immediately began screaming.

What in bloody hell is wrong with her?

"What is that thing?" she screamed.

"What thing?" I asked, confused.

"That thing...on your hand!"

"Oh, this. Forgive me. It is my shadar and I was going to examine your body temperature," I patiently explained. "It is giving me a normal reading of 98.5 degrees. It would appear your fever has not returned as I had feared."

"Who are you?" she asked.

"I am Rykerian Yarrister."

"I know that. I meant who are you really?" She shook her head and rubbed her forehead.

"As I said, I am a Guardian and I am Vesturion."

She blew out her breath in exasperation.

"Are you in need of food or maybe drink?" I asked solicitously. I was at a loss, not knowing how to continue with her.

I delved into her mind again to see how I should best proceed.

"Would you quit poking into my mind? That's very rude you know."

I shook my head trying to clear it. How could she possibly know I was breeching her mind, I mused?

"I just know it okay? I'm a freak. So there! Now quit trying to push your way in. If you want to know something just ask it. Of all the rude things," she murmured.

"Forgive me. I am quite astonished to know that you have telepathic ability. Are you human?"

She gave me a look that spoke volumes. She thought me an idiot.

"You are the second person to ask me that. What do you think I am? A dog? Of course I'm a human!" she responded indignantly. Then under her breath she said, "Of all the idiotic questions!"

"Ms. St. Davis, do you remember anything at all? Becoming ill, or anything?"

"No, not really. I...I was driving home from Atlanta. My internship with the CDC—The Centers for Disease Control and Prevention—was complete so I was heading back to Cullowhee for school. Oh crap, what day is it? I have classes!" She threw back the covers and started to get out of bed. I put my hand on her arm and she was abruptly calmed.

"You cannot go back to school for several reasons, but mostly because you are still not well." She kept trying to pull her arm out of my grasp, but I would not allow it.

"You don't understand. I...I HAVE to go back now," she insisted.

"Ms. St. Davis, it would appear you are the one who does not understand. You cannot go and that is not an option. You are recovering from hemorrhagic small pox, a highly contagious and fatal disease. We do not know how you contracted this illness, but that fact that you have survived it is a miracle in itself. There are reports of people falling ill all over the world and Earth is on the brink of a pandemic. We must uncover how this happened, and we believe you are the key."

Her eyes conveyed everything she was feeling. Shock, sadness, concern, fear...and lack of trust. I kept my hand on her arm and saw her eyelids begin to droop.

"Sleep now," I whispered to her. When I was satisfied she had drifted off, I left the room and called to Julian.

Chapter Three

J ulian assessed Ms. St. Davis and agreed she was out of danger and would indeed survive the horrible virus she had contracted. Now she needed to eat and gain her strength, which I had placed in the capable of hands of Zanna. Hopefully, we would soon be able to put the pieces of the elusive puzzle together to determine how this disease spread.

I heard them before I saw them appear. Rayn, my brother, and his mate, Maddie, were arguing even as they materialized in front of the house.

"I don't care what you say Rayn, I am going in there. That is a human female and I'm quite sure, she is scared half to death," Maddie shouted.

"Maddie, this is not up for discussion. You were there when Julian explained that this female might be contagious for several more days. You are part human and therefore, this presents a great risk to your health. I, for one, will not let you place yourself in harm's way." His love for her was obvious to anyone but he exasperated her as well.

"Ugh! You are so controlling Rayn."

"I must be with anything that concerns you. I make it my duty to protect you at all costs."

This should have been a private moment between them, for the way the stared into each other's eyes made it look extremely intimate. They never were good at concealing their feelings for each other.

Feeling like an interloper, I cleared my throat. "I must agree with my brother. Maddie, you place yourself at great risk by even being here. As leader of the Compound, I must insist you return to Vesturon...Now." I wasn't going to relent on this.

She looked at me, wide-eyed, and I prepared myself for her arguments. To my surprise, she looked back at Rayn, nodded, tapped her shadar and teleported back to Vesturon.

"That was a shock. I had prepared to defend my stance," I declared.

"Yes, we have argued over this all morning. I am glad you used your position of authority with her. I'll have to remember that!" he exclaimed.

I rolled my eyes at him. "You are fooling yourself if you think that will work."

"Hmm...you are probably correct. So, what is the situation on Earth?"

I filled him in on the outbreak of smallpox. Schools were closed, airports had been closed, and cities were quarantined. Businesses had been shut down and everything had come to a screeching halt. The National Guard had been called in and no one was allowed to travel between cities. Hospitals were inundated with the sick and the disease was spreading like wildfire.

The Centers for Disease Control and Prevention wanted to create a vaccine but the virus samples they had stored had somehow disappeared. They were blaming it on a break-in that occurred several weeks prior.

"What steps have you taken in stopping the progression?" Rayn asked.

"Initially, Tesslar was responsible for getting Homeland Security and Emergency Preparedness up and running. Though now, I'm afraid we are stymied. The human casualties are growing so quickly that we cannot keep up. I am afraid of this Rayn. This beginning to look like the plague."

Rayn dragged his hand through his hair and sighed.

"Rykerian, we have to find a way to supply the Centers for Disease Control with new virus samples," he affirmed.

"Yes, that is the only way to stop this. It will take months, however, for the vaccine to be produced in any measurable quantity. So in the meantime, the disease will continue to spread."

My stomach churned with the thoughts of all the suffering that would ensue.

"I've discussed this at length with our scientists and the only way around this would be for us to create the vaccine and slip it into their lab."

"Go on," I said, intrigued.

"I have already ordered them to start work on it using virus samples Julian took from the human female. He had enough to use in cloning for mass production," Rayn explained.

I nodded my head saying, "Yes, he did mention something to that effect but was not forthcoming with the details."

"The scientists are convinced they can have a vaccine produced shortly by using our technology," Rayn announced. He looked at me pointedly.

I cocked my head as his thoughts merged with mine.

"You think to use the human to get the vaccine back to the Centers for Disease Control!" I exclaimed.

"Exactly."

"How?" I wanted to know.

"Julian said she was a college intern there. Surely she knows someone that could help."

"Rayn, I will not allow her to be put in danger." The thought of the lovely human facing harm made my heart constrict in fear.

Rayn gave me a mind-penetrating glare. It was difficult to hide my feelings regarding the female.

"You are involved with her?" he whispered with widened eyes.

I shook my head, my expression anxious. "No, but there is something there," I admitted.

"You have...feelings for her?"

I was sure I did but was dubious about hers. "Yes," I said as I dropped my gaze to my feet. "This is not the first time I have seen this female," I admitted.

"Explain," he demanded. My brother had that commanding demeanor so like my father.

"Several months ago...well it was the night after your official unification ceremony...I came back to Earth and went out on patrol. I saw her car swerving down the highway and I intervened to save her from crashing into the guardrail. Since that night, she has ever been a constant presence in my mind."

"Why have you not said something about this?"

"I thought it was past. I expunged her memory and thought I would never see her again. Admittedly, I have been caught up in thoughts of her but I knew it was useless to be thus as it would be forbidden."

"Rykerian, I understand that more than anyone I can assure you."

"Yes, brother, I know you can, given your past with your mate. I never thought to see her again, much less like this and to have her in such close proximity. It has been...let's just say these past days have been exceedingly difficult."

Rayn nodded and said, "I can imagine. So what are your plans where she is concerned?"

"I have none. Currently, she is not fond of me at all. She is an angry human, but I cannot discern why. Rayn, I must tell you this. She is telepathic. I am sure she can see my aura as well," I muttered.

"And you know this, how?"

I struggled for the words to come.

"Rykerian, I do not understand your reticence with me."

"It is not that. I simply do not know what to say." I shook my head and rubbed the back of my neck. "She saw my aura when I found her in the forest. At first I thought it was her illness. But then she said I resembled the setting sun with my glow and she thought it was the light on the other side. Rayn, it was my aura she described." For some strange reason, I had been afraid to tell this to anyone.

"Hmm, interesting. Have you told Julian?"

"No. With everything else going on, I had pushed it to the back of my mind."

Rayn's eyes showed doubt at that statement, though he did not voice his thoughts on this.

"You understand the importance of investigating this further?" he questioned.

"Of course."

"Good. I must go back to Vesturon and inform Father of the situation here. I will tell our virologists to create the vaccine as well."

I nodded as he dematerialized.

Chapter Four

A nother week passed and the situation on Earth was worsening. The pandemic was in full bloom with humans falling ill on every corner of the planet. The experts at the CDC and the World Health Organization were meeting and conferencing daily. We had Guardians that had infiltrated both organizations so we were keeping abreast of all developments.

We made frequent trips to the city of Atlanta in order the stay current on the latest activity. The city had quickly morphed into something resembling a war zone. Buildings had been torched and turned into rubble. Cars had been abandoned on highways and thoroughfares. Bodies were strewn everywhere and left to rot. The ones who were able had left the city but the ones who remained behind had boarded up their windows for protection from the gangs that had taken over.

Law and order had ceased to exist as the disease had wiped out so many of their ranks. Chaos ruled. And gangs...dangerous and bent on power, they vied with each other for control. They were hell bent on keeping their food and water supplies adequate and would stop at nothing to achieve this goal. The law-abiding citizens of Atlanta lived in fear of not only contracting the disease, but of becoming the victim of gang violence. Humanity had been replaced with fear and the will to survive...and each day it worsened.

My heart ached to see the suffering taking place in front of my eyes.

Worse than that, there wasn't a bloody thing I could do about it. Our numbers were too few and our covenant forbade us to interfere and take over. We would have to wait for another solution to present itself. Hopefully, the plan of creating a replacement vaccine would prove to be the savior we were hoping for.

After returning home from one of these depressing trips, I made my way upstairs to check on January. I had been told she had made vast improvements and was now moving about. When I received no answer from my knock, I went in search of her. I checked all areas of the house and then the back terrace but could not locate her.

I asked everyone and it seemed she hadn't been seen for some time. My heart lurched with fear as I thought about where she might be. I knew she wanted to get back to college in Cullhowee, but she didn't have the means to do so.

I allowed my sensitive sense of smell to pick up her scent. It took me straight out the front door and down the winding driveway. I followed it for about a half of a mile where it veered off into the forest. That was when I kicked in my Power of Speed. Her scent, a combination of citrus and crisp linen, was a stark contrast to the pine and earthy scented forest. It was like a heady perfume to me: a luscious mix of the sweetness of juicy oranges, the tartness of scented lemons and the crispness of tangy grapefruit. I raced along until I spotted her in the distance.

My heart nearly tore out of my chest at the sight of her. She staggered along, walking and then running, her swaying movements an indication of her lack of strength. It was plain to see that she was too weak to carry on a steady run, but she would not allow herself to stop and rest. She resembled a wounded animal, running blindly, desperately trying to flee its predator...and I was that predator. That she thought of me in that regard was what ripped through me, nearly bringing me to my knees.

I must have gasped for she spun around, her eyes darting about, to discover the source of the sound. Our eyes briefly made contact and I felt the fear gushing out of her. She turned back and began to erratically move her way forward. Branches tore at her face and clothing, but she was oblivious to them. She forced herself to continue on until she stumbled over something—a root or rock perhaps. I slowly made my way toward her to lessen the terror I felt emanating from her. She struggled to rise, but lost the battle. It still didn't stop her. That need for survival urged her on as she clawed at the earth and scrambled on her hands and knees in a desperate effort to escape me.

When I reached her side, I could hear her harsh breathing and her heart pounding from her effort. I placed my hand on her shoulder, trying to calm her.

A scream tore through her and she tried to crawl away from me. "Don't touch me! I just want to go home! I have to help my brother and sister!" she yelled in anguish.

I did not succumb to her wishes, but picked her up and began carrying her back to the house. She feebly kicked and pushed me, but in her weakened state, it had only the barest effect on me.

In a ragged voice she croaked, "Why won't you leave me alone or let me go home?"

Gruffly I replied, "You have no home to go to anymore. Can you not listen? This disease you nearly died from has scourged the planet. People are dying by the thousands every day. Life as you knew it no longer exists! We will help your brother and sister when we can but right now there is not much we can do for them or anybody else!" I was angry with myself for speaking so harshly to her. I was angry at whoever was responsible for this pandemic; and I was angry with her because she insisted on doing something so foolish.

Then remorse filled me as I watched the expressions flit across her—shock, denial, horror, self-pity, and sorrow. She hung limply in my arms, refusing to give me any quarter.

Fine, I thought. *Have it your way.*

Knowing my next actions would be construed as childish, I did it anyway. I used my Power of Speed to carry her home, all the while knowing she would hate me more for it. I wasn't one to do this type of thing...my brothers, yes, but not me. I did not care at the time, but I knew I would pay for it later.

I did not stop until I reached her room, where I dumped her on the bed. Her eyes were still widened and I blurted out, "For the love of the Deity, will you cease staring at me like that? You should realize by now I have no intentions of harming you. In fact, it is quite the opposite. If I wanted to hurt you, I would have left you to die in the bloody forest!"

"I wished you had," she spat.

Her comment stupefied me. Why would anyone want to die? I would puzzle over that for days. Not having anything else to say, I turned and left.

The human patient was improving, with Zanna's constant fussing over her and feeding her all sorts of delectables. She still held me in great disdain, and I honestly could not blame her. My contact with her was minimal, as it seemed to cause her such distress.

Late one afternoon, Zanna had set January up on the back terrace. She was resting on one of the couches, with a blanket around her legs, sipping on what appeared to be a cup of tea. I observed her as she sat there. *No one should have the right to look so lovely! What had happened to this female to make her so soured on life?*

I vacillated joining her. My stomach clenched in anxiety as I thought about her rejection. I wanted so badly for us to have a simple conversation. She had occupied my thoughts continually but I felt the twinges of fear inch their way along my spine. *What if she doesn't want me there?*

Before I could lose my nerve, I joined her. Gazing over the splendor of the mountains, I quietly said, "It is magnificent, is it not?"

"It is," she murmured lifelessly.

"Are you comfortable?"

"Yes. Zanna's spoiled me. She's perfect. I've never...er, never mind."

"What?"

"Nothing. She's just great is all."

I nodded. Not wanting to spoil the mood, I gazed into her eyes, and smiled. *Please...please just one smile.*

The corners of her mouth began to curve, but then stopped.

"Why did you bring me here?" Her question startled me for she had not been very willing to converse with me.

"To save you of course. There was no other option since you were contagious. You would have died had I not." I was satisfied with that answer and so proud of it. I should have had a clue that things would turn disagreeable.

"What made you think I wanted to be saved?" she asked, her mood becoming mercurial. The pleasantness had disappeared and the darkness had returned.

"I…because…well, why wouldn't you?" I turned the tables.

"Not everyone has a rosy life, Mr. Happy-go-lucky! You walk around without a care in the world, acting like everyone feels the same. Well, newsflash! They don't. I didn't want to be saved. I've had it with this miserable life of mine and just when I think I've finally…finally gotten to the point where it's over, YOU show up all happy and glowing like you're some sort of guardian angel, swooping down to save me. You, with your stunning looks and…well I'd bet you've never faced a day of adversity in your life. That's the ONLY thing I've ever known. Constantly worried about how I'm going to pay my rent or tuition. Do you know what it's like not to be able to buy a bag of potato chips because you couldn't afford it? Why couldn't you have just left me alone?" She looked up at me and tears were streaking her cheeks. My heart split in two, ripped open by the pain in her words.

I extended my arm toward her but she flinched. I let it fall. My mouth was bone dry with my voice bound by some unknown force. I shook my head and all I wanted to do was comfort this poor creature.

I heard her whisper, "You *can't* comfort me. *No one* can. My life isn't even *worth* comforting. When will I be able to leave here?" She bowed her head and stared at her twisting fingers.

"January, please, let me help you," I beseeched. My heart felt like it was being crushed.

"You. Can't. Help! You *could have* helped if you had left me in the stupid forest!" she yelled.

"I could not leave you in the forest. I am a Guardian. It goes against everything in my blood…everything I stand for." My voice matched hers in pitch.

"You don't understand!"

"Then tell me. I cannot help you if you do not tell me!" My voice was charged with emotion.

She shook her head and dropped it into her hands.

Please talk to me January. Tell me what pains your heart and mind so. I only want to help you. Please…

"Just leave me alone. Please."

My heart was splintering. This ghost of a female was quickly becoming my undoing. I turned and strode from the terrace.

Chapter Five

I was standing in the den, preparing to go down to the Command Center when Maddie appeared, surprising me with her unexpected visit.

"Why didn't you tell me?" she accused.

"I do not know what..." before I could finish, she continued verbally accosting me.

"January. Why didn't you tell me it was January?" she demanded.

I flashed her a bewildered look. "I don't understand."

"January. Upstairs. Sick!" she exclaimed.

I continued shaking my head, baffled.

"Rykerian, January was my roommate in college! Why didn't you tell me?" she persisted.

"I was unaware there was a connection between the two of you." My surprise at her revelation could not have been more apparent.

"I must see her!"

"No, you cannot."

Maddie shot me an incredulous look. "Excuse me!"

"You cannot see her. She is of a fragile mind. I am in charge here and I will not allow it."

"If you don't get your bloody arse out of my way, I'll move it for you!"

"Arse?"

"Yes! I didn't want to call you an ass, but I will!"

"Um, I think you just did Maddie."

Maddie had always been impetuous and used to getting her way, but she had never acted like this toward me. In fact, her heart had always softened with regard to me because at one time I had fancied myself in love with her. I had been terribly mistaken, of course, but since then, she had always treated me with great care. To hear her threats now left me quite speechless.

"I am not kidding Rykerian!"

"But you must listen Maddie. Her mind is very fragile right now."

"Rykerian, you clearly are not listening. I am not asking permission. I am telling you. Now, out of my way."

"I will not allow..." but before I could utter another word, she extended her hand and I found myself plastered to the ceiling. Maddie's Power of Telekinesis was incredibly impressive. I was currently imprisoned by it.

"Maddie!" I yelled. "Put me down, immediately!"

As she turned away, I saw Rayn appearing. "Maddie, release him this instant."

She looked at Rayn and it was evident there was mental sparring occurring between them. Suddenly, I found myself lying in a heap on the floor. I leaped up, intending to intercept her before she could go upstairs when I heard, and then felt, "I Command you to be still!"

The pain was immediate and excruciating. Every cell in my body screamed in agony. I was in Command's clutches and incapable of movement of any kind—my muscles rebelling but in complete and total lockdown. It had been some time since I had been under anyone's Power of Command and Rayn's ability was quite significant. I fought to draw air into my lungs. I knew it was futile to fight against this, but every fiber of my being bellowed at me to do exactly that. It was getting me nowhere, except into deeper pain.

I heard rather than saw my father. "Rayn, what are you doing? Release him now!" he commanded.

I heard the words in my mind, *Release,* and immediately fell to my knees, sucking in as much air as I could. I was still incapable of moving, as I crouched there, recovering. The Power of Command was a talent known only to Vesturions and not everyone had the capability to perform it. My ability with it was only moderate at best.

"What is going on here? I demand an explanation!" my father shouted, his voice reverberating.

"I was protecting my mate, Father!" Rayn exclaimed.

"Against what?"

"Rykerian," Rayn answered sheepishly.

I was still on the floor, regaining control of my body bit by bit. I flexed my hands and arms, testing them to see if they were functional. Finally I rose to my feet, unsteadily.

"Well?" my father asked me.

"I informed Maddie she could not see January, and she used Telekinesis to bind me to the ceiling. Then Rayn came in and she released me but he commanded me to be still." I rubbed and shook my arms, trying to bring life back to them.

"You were threatening my mate!" Rayn snarled.

"Stop! You two are acting like children!" my father exclaimed.

My father just shook his head, assessing the situation. "Maddie, my daughter, you know I have a terribly soft spot in my heart for you, but in this instance, you have no choice but to defer to Rykerian. He is leader here and his decision stands. You cannot see January at this time."

Then he turned to Rayn, and his eyes launched daggers at him. "Do not ever abuse your Power of Command again. Am I clear? Rykerian is your brother and when you enter this Compound, he is your leader and his rule stands. Do you honestly think he would harm your mate? He would give up his life for her Rayn!" Both my brother and his mate looked thoroughly chastised.

They approached me and simultaneously began apologizing.

"Maddie, there is a good reason you cannot see her. As I stated, her mind is very fragile. She is angry with me for saving her life. She will not discuss it and I am baffled by her behavior. But we need her assistance, and desperately so. It is so important that she regain her strength both physically and mentally, because she faces an important task ahead."

Maddie nodded her head in understanding. I could feel her thoughts trying to push their way into my mind and I gave her a dark look. She was not welcome there.

"Down to the Command Center. All of you. Now!" my father ordered.

My father, Rowan, was the Great Ruler of Vesturon. My brother Rayn, the first-born, is in training to someday assume that role. He recently united with his soul mate, Maddie, whom he met here on Earth during her rescue from a serial killer. Their attraction and subsequent bonding was instantaneous, as is common between Vesturions when they find their soul mates. At first, there were issues because at the time, it was believed that Maddie was human. Since then, we discovered she had Vesturion blood lines stemming from both of her parents, who died when she was quite young.

Maddie and Rayn were a perfect match. Their relationship had not been easy for either of them. Rocky best described it. Eventually they learned to work things out between them and were now happily mated. You wouldn't have to know them to see they shared an unbreakable bond of love. Rayn was handsome, with black hair and bright green eyes and his mate was beautiful in every sense of the word. Copper hair and eyes to match, she was a headstrong female. Rayn had met his match in her. His protective instincts went overboard where she was concerned.

We all took our seats around the conference table in the Command Center. My father, Rayn, Maddie, Tesslar and myself were present.

I had two other brothers, Therron and Xarrid, but they were on the planet Xanthus, helping to reestablish a ruling authority. The Xanthians had surrendered to us a few months ago after causing much havoc in the universe. My sister, Sharra, was off commandeering an armada of Star Fighters protecting susceptible planets from Xanthian rebels. It had been a difficult time lately, with all the fighting brought on by the Xanthians.

"As you know, the Xanthian rebels have grown in numbers, to the point where we are deciding on whether or not to abandon creating a new governing authority for them. We are close to pulling Therron and Xarrid off Xanthus, for safety issues," Father informed us.

"It has gotten that bad then?" I wanted to know.

"Rowan, I think it would be a good idea to remove them as soon as possible," Maddie declared. She had dealt with the Xanthians in her role as ambassador and then again when they held Rayn captive. Maddie abhorred the Xanthians. She knew them to be liars and untrustworthy.

"You may be right. But there is another issue blooming before us. Our strategists think there is a connection to this pandemic on Earth and the situation the Brutyns are facing." I raised my eyes in question, as I was unaware with this situation. We looked at my father to continue.

"The Brutyns are having an invasion of a genetically altered insect and it is consuming their gartha crops. If they don't find a way to stop it, the whole planet is at risk. As you know, the Brutyns must ingest a special enzyme daily in order for their brains to function properly. Gartha is the only plant species where this enzyme can be found. This insect is destroying their gartha crops in record numbers and they cannot find a way to stop it. Their entire species faces extinction if this cannot be altered." My father looked at each of us, mentally requesting our input.

"This is terrible news! Who do you think is behind this?" I asked.

"We have no proof, but we suspect it to be the Xanthians. We know they are desperate for Earth's natural resources, specifically their fossil fuels. They have also coveted Brutyna's resources, especially their furrilyum. They have stripped all the fossil fuels and furrilyum from Xanthus and need the aforementioned for their power sources. They realize they cannot continue to power their planet by chemical means, as they too will eventually be depleted. We have begun to think all of this pandemonium is at their hands."

Maddie was the first to react. "I say we destroy their planet. Total annihilation. Don't leave anything behind. Then there will be nothing left to fuel and the Xanthians will no longer be a burr in our behinds."

My father's jaw nearly hit the table while Rayn rolled his eyes and shook his head, trying to disguise his smile. Tesslar burst out laughing and I, well, I did not quite know what to say to that.

"What? I think it's a sound plan!" Maddie stated with conviction, her amber eyes ablaze.

"Maddie," Rayn began but my father held up his hand and interrupted him.

"My daughter, we cannot play the Deity on this. We must rein them in, yes, and perhaps if we find proof we must punish them, but we cannot charge onto Xanthus and annihilate the entire planet. There are innocent Xanthians that know nothing of this," Father patiently explained. He had such a tender heart where Maddie was concerned. If one of us had suggested that, he would have been brutal in his response. I chuckled. Everyone looked my way and I shrugged. No use explaining those thoughts.

"How can we find out the truth?" Tesslar asked.

"We have spies that are working on getting us the proof. In the meantime, we have to find a way to stop this terrible chain of events on both planets."

"What do you propose?" I ventured. I had some ideas I had been toying with in my mind. I ran a finger along the table's edge, my thoughts wandering toward the CDC.

"We have our scientists producing a vaccine for this disease on Earth. The samples that Julian took from January have panned out to be excellent sources for the vaccine. Her blood carried much more virus than is normally found, which lead them to another discovery."

I was not expecting my father to say what he was getting ready to tell us. We all sat there, waiting for him to continue.

Chapter Six

F ather looked at me and then settled his gaze on Maddie. Arching a brow she said, "Well?"

"Your January is Vesturion."

I was the first to jump to my feet, followed by Maddie. "You can't be serious!" she exclaimed.

"Oh, but I am, daughter of mine. Her blood is very rich with her Vesturion heritage. She has two distinct determinants, one human and one Vesturion."

"How can that be?" Maddie asked. Her fair skin had just lightened to an even paler shade of white.

"Quite simple. I do believe one of her parents is from Vesturon."

"Bloody hell, Rowan. I know that. It was meant as a rhetorical question." Maddie knotted her fingers, and lifted her eyes to Rayn. He shrugged. Then her eyes made it to me. I was at a loss.

"Daughter, what can you tell us about her?" Rowan asked.

Maddie was silent for a moment.

"Not much really. January never spoke about her past. I always thought she had some dark, deep secret she didn't want to disclose. She never spoke of her family, except for her little brother and sister. It was all very strange, now that I think of it," Maddie concluded.

Thoughts began pouring through my mind. *She could see my aura. She was telepathic. Her strange eyes had bewitched me. I found them odd for human eyes. Now I knew the truth.* I must have been projecting my thoughts because I lifted my eyes to see all occupants of the room staring at me.

"When were you going to share this?" Father asked sardonically.

"I…I was not thinking. My mind did not grasp it for what it was," I lamely explained.

"Apparently not," he said drily.

My father's eyes bore into mine. Every thought became available for his inspection. I fidgeted with the onslaught of his invasion. My embarrassment over my feelings for January became evident as I felt myself flushing from head to toe. I rubbed my palms on my legs and stood. My eyes darted around the room, looking for a landing site but I was unsuccessful. I had to escape from this room. I strode to the door and made a hasty exit.

I made it as far as the exit of the Command Center when I felt a hand on my arm. I glanced up to see Maddie.

"It's okay Rykerian. Please stop for a minute."

It was hard to refuse Maddie anything. I adored her…in a brotherly fashion. She was dear to me and I trusted her abjectly.

"I am confounded over all of this Maddie." I patiently explained the whole situation to her, beginning with the incident in January's car to her acute dislike for me. "She hates me for saving her."

"I know you don't want me to, but I need to see her Rykerian. Maybe I can find what's troubling her. We were sort of close at one time. Maybe she hasn't forgotten that, and perhaps I can help her with Vesturion heritage. I can help her adjust."

"You may be right."

We headed back to the conference room, me and my ruby-colored face and all. I filled my father in with all the details and we made a joint decision that Maddie would speak with January.

January sat outside on the back terrace, wrapped in a blanket, sipping tea. *This must be her favorite spot. I must remember this.*

Maddie squeezed my hand as we walked toward her. She gazed at the mountains in the distance and didn't seem to notice our presence.

"They're lovely mountains, are they not? My friend Cat and I used to love to camp up there," Maddie whispered.

January slowly turned toward Maddie. Initially I thought I would see her smile. I was mistaken yet again. She stared at Maddie as her narrowed eyes turned into frosted chips of ice. Her frown deepened and her lips hardened into a thin line as she rose to her feet and closed the distance between us. The three of us stood together for a moment before she uttered a word.

"I know I'm not hallucinating. My wits are completely here. I don't have a fever anymore so you're not a figment of my imagination, but reality…here in the flesh. So Maddie, what I would really would like to know is, what kind of cruel game are you playing?" she fumed.

Maddie's face fell, but she wasn't giving up. "No game January. It's me. Maddie. As you said, in the flesh."

"Who in the hell do you think you are?" she asked contemptuously, her voice quivering.

Oh no! No, January, not this!

Maddie was at a loss. I squeezed her hand to encourage her. Her pain was plainly seen in her eyes.

"January…it's me, Maddie. The Maddie you roomed with at Western."

"Like hell you are!" she hurled back, shaking her head. "*That* Maddie would never have let us think she was dead. *That* Maddie couldn't even *walk*! *That* Maddie would have called us to say she was okay. *That* Maddie would never have let Cat become suicidal. *That* Maddie would have shown up at the hospital to help Cat. *That* Maddie would never have let Cat suffer until her life was in shambles. So I have to ask you again. Who in the *hell* do *you* think *you* are?" January was trembling with rage.

Maddie's mouth opened and closed several times but she didn't utter a sound.

I thought I would attempt to help.

"January, Maddie is only trying…" I got no further before she turned her rage on me.

"Shut up! You're just as bad as she is!" she spat. "You couldn't leave well enough alone so you took it upon yourself to make a decision that wasn't yours to make. Who are you despicable people that you can so randomly destroy people's lives? Is this something you enjoy? Do you do it for fun?" Her scathing tone shattered my resolve.

"Stop! Stop it this instant!" I thundered. "I am sick of your accusations. I am a Guardian. I vow to protect. I am sorry it was not known to me you had a death wish. I am sorry I did not realize you would be so ungrateful for what my people have done for you. But most of all, I am sorry you were mostly unconscious and could not verbalize that you wanted to be left in the forest to die. That is not my fault and I am sick to death of bearing the blame for seeing to it that you have life today. As for Maddie, she could not help what happened to her. She was not given the choice to go and visit your Cat and was unaware of what happened to her. She did not do this out of spite or cruelty. It simply happened. Now, if you are finished with your accusations and tirade, we will gladly depart from your presence." I pulled Maddie to me; I placed my arm around her and tugged her toward the house.

When we entered the back door, Rayn was there, pulling a sobbing Maddie into his arms. As I looked out the back window, I saw January's shoulders quivering. She, too, was sobbing. I wanted so badly to go to her, to pull her into my arms and comfort her, but my wounded ego was too bruised and battered to do so. She had pierced my heart with her sharp words and I was ill equipped to deal with it.

Chapter Seven

My feet carried me to the garage where I hopped aboard a speedster, a motorcycle-like vehicle that actually flew. I tore off into the air, praying the wind would wash away my pain. My gut felt like it had been ripped to pieces and my heart felt like a wrecking ball had crushed it. The pain of it all made it difficult to breathe. Higher and higher I soared, until the trees looked like dots along the horizon.

I circled Balsam Mountain but it just wasn't enough. Onward I flew and headed toward Mt. LeConte. The sun was beginning to sink in the distance, but my mind wasn't grasping the beauty that lay before me. I was lost in my anguish and frustration. My hand tightened on the throttle while the other one squeezed the thruster. Faster…I had to go faster. I had to cleanse my mind from the pain.

I can't recall how much time elapsed or when I realized the mountains had disappeared and I was flying over the coastline. My mind finally escaped the grips of pain and I turned my speedster around and headed back to the Compound. I was surprised to see that it was after midnight. As I made my way from the garage to the back door, I heard a sound from the terrace.

It was someone talking. I headed in that direction and I heard a soft voice moaning and crying.

"Why do you hate me so much?" she cried. It was January, caught in a dream.

I touched her arm, in the hopes of soothing her. She kept repeating the questions, "Why do you hate me so? What have I done to deserve this?" Her anguished tone bit me. I gently rubbed her arm, in hopes of waking her.

Why are you bothering with her? She hates you and doesn't want to have anything to do with you? Quit torturing yourself!

I could not stop myself. Something drew me to her, like a magnet. It didn't matter that she did not want me near her. I could not walk away and leave her in pain.

"January! January, wake up! You are dreaming," I murmured.

"No, don't hate me. I promise I'll be good. I swear! Please don't leave me up here!" she begged in a childlike voice.

"January! Wake up!" I gently shook her. Something had caused her pain. Maddie was right. She had buried some awful secret but whatever it was, it was distressing to her. I shook her again and her eyes fluttered open.

They stared into mine. My night vision, that was inherent to my species, was so acute I could see her widened pupils in stark contrast to her beautiful pale blue irises. She parted her perfectly shaped lips and I could hear her as she drew in her breath. I placed my palm on her cheek rubbing my thumb back and forth. She was confused of her whereabouts.

"You were having a bad dream. I heard you as I made my way into the house. Are you okay?" I asked softly.

She licked her bottom lip before she nodded. "I'm fine, Ry…Ry"

"Rykerian," I supplied as she tripped over my name.

"Yeah. Rykerian." She drew a hand across her brow. "Hey, I want to apologize for my behavior earlier. I guess I owe you a 'thanks' for saving me. I'm sorry if I seem ungrateful, but you wouldn't understand."

"I can try, but you have to let me first," I begged.

She silently stared into my eyes.

Before I could prevent it, I heard myself say, "You have a lovely name, January."

She shook her head and made a choking sound, indicating her disagreement.

"I think it is…" She held out her hand to stop me from saying anything else.

"This is exactly what I mean about you not being able to understand." She pinched that perfect little spot between her eyes...that spot that I wanted so badly to touch with my lips. "I was named that because my mother hated the month of January. Cold, rainy, grey skies, miserable, you know. So you see, my whole life is a screwed up mess ever since the day I was born. Bio-daddy raped my mom so she's hated me since I showed up in this world. Every time she looked at me she thought about that gawd-awful night and every day she regretted not having an abortion. Now do you understand?" Her tears streaked down her cheeks as she unsteadily rose to her feet.

"Just because she could not see the value in you does not mean no one else can," I said, wanting more than anything to hold her in my arms, my heart aching for her. She stopped and stared at me and for one brief moment, my heart stopped.

"I'm such a complete and total mess Rykerian. I have issues bigger than that mountain over there. No one with an ounce of sense would want anything to do with me." She gathered her blanket around her and started walking toward the house.

"Then I must not have an ounce of sense January," I whispered.

She stopped, turned around and gave me the saddest of smiles. "Why? You...you have a grand life filled with people who genuinely care for you. You need someone worthy of you and trust me, it's not me." She turned back around and headed in the direction of the house, but her blanket had wrapped around her ankles, causing her to stumble.

My Power of Speed had me scooping her up before her body could reach the stone terrace.

I tried, I truly did, but before I could prevent myself, my lips descended on hers. They were so soft and velvety and she tasted of the sweetest of honey mixed with the salt of her tears. And her scent...all citrus and fresh smelling... *Sweet Deity, please do not ever let this end!* When I felt her arms inch around my neck, my heart soared in ecstasy. At that moment I realized I had been lost my whole life but I had finally found where I belonged—in January's arms.

I tore my lips away from hers, my breath ragged with passion. This ghost of a female had not only stolen my heart but also my soul. I had watched her from a distance, longing for the slightest of touches or the briefest of words, knowing if they ever happened, I would be lost.

Never in my wildest of dreams had I imagined my feelings would be this intense.

Her pale blue eyes beckoned to me in a way I could not describe. I rested my palm on her cheek and whispered to her, "Do you know how beautiful you are? You have bewitched me beyond my wildest dreams. I am lost to you."

I tangled my fingers in her hair and touched my lips to hers again. The current that seared me was electrifying. I gasped with pleasure at the myriad of sensations coursing through me. A thought flew into my mind and that was Maddie had been right all along. I had never loved her. This was far beyond any feeling I had ever experienced.

I reluctantly pulled my lips away from hers and stared into her eyes.

"You're making the biggest mistake of your life. You know that don't you?"

A nervous chuckle escaped from me. "This is the only thing in my life that has ever made sense to me."

She reached her hand to my lips and traced them with her fingers. I closed my eyes in bliss, reveling in the feel of her touch. I had been searching for this for an eternity it seemed.

"Please, don't."

What? No! Please don't say no!

"Please don't close your eyes Rykerian," she whispered.

My eyes flew open to see her staring at me.

"They are the most beautiful and unusual eyes I have ever seen. Your pupils are...different. And your eyes are intense...so impossibly blue and *warm*. I feel as though I can see your soul through them. I want to look into them forever."

I couldn't speak, so filled with emotion I was at her words. I shook my head. No one had ever said such things to me. I swallowed the knot in my throat and smiled at her, then I managed to whisper, "The same could be said for yours."

"You know, you would be smart to put me down, walk away and never look back," she murmured.

How could she think that? I had just found her!

"Like I said, I am a ginormous mess, Rykerian. You need someone who's worthy of you. It isn't me. I'm not worthy of much of anything, but especially you."

I placed my fingers on her mouth. I could not bear to hear her say such things.

"You are more than worthy of me. I should apologize for kissing you as I did, but I will not for I have no remorse for doing so. I am selfish for you January. I have wanted to hold you close to my heart from the first moment I saw you." I shook my head at the memory. "It was a few months ago and you were driving on the highway between Waynesville and Sylva. You had fallen asleep and your car was careening toward the guardrail. I frightened you when I appeared in your car. I had you pull off the road and by that time, you were alert."

"What are you talking about? I don't remember that!"

"I know. I am sorry but I had to erase your memory."

"What do you mean, 'erase your memory?'" How'd you do that?"

"Well, I was hoping we could have this conversation with Maddie present because she could help in providing explanations. As I have said before, I am Vesturion…not human. I know you do not believe it as the truth, but it is so."

"Uh huh. You're gonna have to do better than that." Her eyes clouded with doubt, but her words urged me to continue.

I carried her back to the couch and gently sat down, placing her on my lap and holding her in my arms. I continued, "We come from the planet Vesturon which is in a different galaxy from Earth. We are Guardians and that is why we are here. We pledge to keep all life forms safe from harm and we have protected humans for centuries. Though humans are not the only beings we protect. My father is the Great Leader of Vesturon and he is an integral part of keeping order in the universe."

"Okay. So you're serious about all of this and you're not kidding, right?"

"Not kidding at all."

"Well, I knew there was something strange going on here, but I never imagined it was this," indicating she was trying to process this information. "I didn't believe you before but it all adds up now."

"I never thought I would be telling you this tonight," I said with astonishment.

"Can you tell me more?"

"Does this frighten you?"

"Not really. Well, maybe a little. Okay...yeah, it scares the hell out of me. I kept trying to put the pieces together into something that made sense but I kept striking out."

"Does this mean I am no longer E.T.?" I teased.

A reluctant smile tugged at her lips. "I think you are more like Luke Skywalker. But, can you blame me? This is all sort of farfetched."

I lifted her hand and placed a kiss in her palm, then laced my fingers with hers.

"Oh January, there is ever so much to tell, but I will do my best to appease you. You know how you asked about erasing your memory? Well, Vesturions are gifted with many powers. For instance, some of us have the Power of Speed, which allows us to move extremely fast." I watched her closely for a reaction. Her eyes widened in question at my revelation.

"How fast? Like you did when you carried me back here?"

"Yes, but I didn't go nearly as fast as I could then because I knew it might make you ill. We can move fast enough that I would only be a blur to human eyes. However, that is only the beginning. Some of us are gifted with the Power of Tranquility. Do you remember when I touched you and you felt much calmer?"

"Yes! I thought it was kind of weird when that happened. I was so freaked out by that robot thing, but the next minute I was waking up from a nap. I couldn't figure that one out."

"That was Tranquility. I also have the Power of Obliteration. That is the capability to erase one's memory. That is what I used the night I saved you in the car. And my 'unusual' eyes...my pupils become elliptical at night, allowing me to have keen night vision."

I was feeding her small bits of information and gauging her reactions. I wondered when I should stop, for eventually I would have to tell her of her genetics. I agonized over her acceptance of this.

"What's wrong?" She was very observant. I had blocked my mind so she could not infiltrate my thoughts.

"There is much I must tell you but I would like to wait and have Maddie present. Please don't be angry at her January. Things happened that she could not prevent and hopefully, everything will become clear to you when you hear the full story. I am terribly sorry for how it affected you, but please don't judge her. Maddie's story is hers and hers alone to tell, but I will say this. She is the most unselfish person I

amazement.

"Seriously? I mean do you honestly feel like that? You wouldn't be just saying that, trying to make me feel better about what I told you and all?"

"January, *my* January. I would never say things that are not the truth. You see, it is against my very being to tell a lie. So what you hear from my lips are my own true feelings. If you would like, I can open my mind to you so you can hear my thoughts."

I removed the block and let my emotions show themselves to her. I watched her eyes widened with shock. I was baring my soul to this creature and I stood to lose so much if she rejected me, but I had to do this in return for what she had told me about her past. I knew it was the only way she would trust I was being honest with her.

"How can this be? You barely know me?" she whispered.

My voice was hoarse with emotion as I said, "It is the way with Vesturions. Our souls tend to find our soul mates for us. It has nothing to do with me seeking you out in the physical sense. My soul happened upon yours and I have not been the same since," I smiled ruefully. "I tell you this not to frighten you, but so you will know I will only ever have your best intentions at heart. My feelings are true January. So, that female you see in the mirror is a much different one than the one I see standing before me."

She wrapped her arms around my waist and pressed her body against mine. "Thank you for sharing that with me."

"The hour grows late and I believe it best you get some rest. You are still recovering from your illness and have yet to regain your strength. Come, let me escort you to your room."

She placed her hand on my arm and I walked her upstairs. When we reached her door, I leaned down and whispered in her ear, "Good night sweet January."

Chapter Eight

T he next morning, I woke early and went in search of January's clothing that I had brought to the Compound the day I had found her in the forest. She was in need of something to wear, other than her hospital attire.

I knocked on her door and I heard her say, "Come in."

"Good morning. Did you sleep well?"

"I did. And you?"

"January, I had many sweet dreams, though none were as delightful as you are this morning. I have brought you something."

She glanced at the stack of clothing I was carrying in my arms and her eyes lit up.

"I am sure you are over tired of your hospital clothing so I thought you might want to wear some of these. Zanna has laundered and pressed them. They are yours that I brought here from your vehicle. Maddie and I would like for you to join us in the kitchen for some breakfast. Zanna is making some of her famous pancakes and they are guaranteed to stick to your ribs!"

She smiled and nodded, "I would love that. Let me change and we can go."

Several moments passed and she finally reappeared wearing a pair of jeans that were too large and a sweatshirt.

"I am afraid this will have to do. Most of my things were so big I couldn't keep them up," she said in a small voice. "I guess I must have lost weight from being sick."

"Come here."

When she stood next to me, I tightened her belt a notch and rolled up her sleeves.

"There! Now you look perfect!" I exclaimed.

She made a silly face at me and I laughed. "Well, I think you do and it matters not what you think! Come, let us go and eat."

I took her hand and she followed me into the kitchen where Maddie was already seated and munching on a mouthful of pancakes. When she saw January, she squealed and jumped up to give her a hug.

"Oh January, I am so glad you wanted to eat with us! I have tons to tell you and I hope you will bear with me and listen."

"After my talk with Rykerian last night, I do want to find out Maddie. I'm sorry for the way I acted yesterday too. I don't want to make excuses, but I'm still kind of in shock over all this. You look so different!"

"I know. I'll explain everything. But please sit and eat some of these pancakes. Zanna makes the best ones ever!"

As we sat and ate, I was happy to see January smile occasionally. She gobbled up several pancakes and when she was finished, she sat back sipping on her coffee and listened to Maddie tell her story.

"So January, after I disappeared, I lived here for a time until Rayn went to trial. I was forbidden to contact anyone in keeping with the Vesturion covenants. You see, Rayn took me to Vesturon to mend my severed spine and because of that, I had to break all ties with everyone on Earth. It would simply have been impossible to explain. And that's also why Rayn was imprisoned—because he basically broke Vesturion law when he took me there to be healed. I wanted to contact you and I thought about you and Cat all the time. I hope you understand."

"I can see that now though I wish there had been some way. So what happened after the trial?"

Maddie gave her the long version, but told her how she found out her parents both came from Vesturion backgrounds. January's mouth fell open with that revelation.

"I know, isn't it bizarre?" Maddie asked. "They never got around to telling me either. I found out because, of all things, my mom came to me in a dream and told me about my mark!"

"Your mark?" January wanted to know.

"Yeah, everyone with any Vesturion blood in them has a mark somewhere on their body. It's a triangle with a crescent within it. Anyway," she waved her hand and continued speaking, "then Rayn went to trial and was found not guilty, I moved to Vesturon and became a Guardian and after a few major issues, Rayn and I got married!" Maddie gushed as a blush spread across her cheeks. I don't think she wanted to get into all the complications she and Rayn had to work out before their unification.

As if on cue, the kitchen doors swung open and there was Rayn in the flesh. In his usual manner, he quickly strode to his mate, lifted her out of her seat, and began to feverishly kiss her. She became lost in him, wrapping her legs around him as they carried on.

Every time this happened, and it happened quite often, I felt like an intruder. I turned to tell this to January, but the look on her face was so comical, I found myself shaking with laughter. I reached over and put my hand beneath her jaw and gently closed her mouth.

"I would like to say you will get used to this, but honestly, I find I still have difficulty seeing them. I feel I am locked in their bedroom with them when this happens."

"Is that her husband?" she asked, her voice tinged with shock.

"Oh, most assuredly. That is her mate, Rayn. You better try to get used to this," I added.

"Does this happen a lot?"

"All the time. They cannot keep their hands off each other."

She blew out the breath she had been holding. "Wow. What is it with you all anyway? You are all so...well, you are so imposing!"

"Imposing, are we? How so?"

"Er, you are...well, you are so tall...and," she looked down at her hands before whispering, "attractive."

My heart soared with her words.

Rayn finally released his mate and her feet slid to the ground, but they remained in a tight embrace. They were certainly an attractive couple in my eyes as well.

"Good morning love," he smiled.

"And a good day to you my brother," Rayn said to me and turning to January, he said, "And a good morn to you too."

January was still staring at the two of them, wide-eyed when Maddie said, "January, please forgive my husband. He gets carried away at times." She was grinning from ear to ear.

"I would say it was mutual," January mumbled.

I let out a huge snort and Maddie continued to grin.

"So January, tell me what happened after I left. I know it was awful, but I need to hear it."

January told Maddie the story and when she finished, both girls were crying like babies. I handed January some tissue and Rayn had swept Maddie onto his lap and was comforting her.

"Well, I hope the money I sent you helped. I know it couldn't have made Cat feel better, but at least maybe it helped with the bills," Maddie sniffed.

"What money?"

"I had a sizable sum of money deposited in your bank account. I did the same for Cat," Maddie explained.

"When? I never got any money," January said.

"I had Xarrid, my brother-in-law, deposit $100,000 in both your accounts. You didn't get it?"

"$100,000! Are you kidding me? No! I never got it. Cat never got any money either."

Maddie looked at Rayn in question.

"I know nothing of this my love. When did you do this?"

"You were still imprisoned. I asked Xarrid to do it."

Rayn held up his arm and tapped his shadar. Several moments later, a holograph of Xarrid appeared. He was quite the grump as Rayn had awakened him from sleep. It was the middle of the night on the planet Xanthus, where Xarrid was stationed. Maddie questioned him about the money and he told her, with great discomfort, that he had meant to talk to Rayn about it but had forgotten all about it. It was during the time they had discovered Voldruk Montedelvo's treacherous plot against Rayn and how Voldruk had intended to destroy Rayn. Xarrid was concerned because the amount of money was so large that he thought he should discuss it with Rayn, but when this whole plot was uncovered, all his time was spent tracking evidence against Voldruk and he had simply set the money issue aside. He apologized profusely, but it was over and done and there was nothing to be done about it now.

Maddie told Rayn that she still wanted the money transferred to Cat and January. Rayn raised his brows at that but Maddie responded, "Cat's been ill and can always use it and January can use it for however she sees fit even if she wants to give it to her little brother and sister."

"Maddie, tell me more about this mark of yours. Did you always have this?" January asked.

"Yeah, but I just always thought it was a birthmark. I didn't know it was anything special. It was so tiny I could barely see it. See?" She lifted up her shirt to show January her mark on her back. Then she told Rayn and me to show January our marks. "They have multiples of them because their bloodlines are so strong and pure."

January grabbed my hands and looked closely at them and then looked at Rayn's.

"Okay, this is totally weird, but I have a mark kind of like that on my neck."

"Where is it?" I asked.

She pointed to a place behind the base of her left ear on the side of her neck and sure enough, there was her mark. I couldn't help the grin from spreading across my face. Then I looked up and saw everyone looking at me.

Everyone looked at each other uncomfortably and January asked, "What's going on? What are you not telling me?" Several uncomfortable glances passed between the three of us.

"Rykerian," Rayn said, flicking his head toward January.

I scooted my chair closer to her and took her hand in mine. "January, there are things you need to be told. That is why I wanted Maddie here. When you were ill, the healer came from Vesturon to care for you. He took blood samples to isolate the virus. He wanted to test it to see if it was positive for small pox. He also wanted the samples in case we needed to replicate it. When he took your blood, he automatically ran a genetic test on it and much to our surprise, it was discovered you have Vesturion blood. Your mark is evidence of that as well. Truth be told, I had wondered how you could communicate telepathically and how you could see my aura. Humans do not have that ability."

January stared back at us, ashen-faced and wide-eyed. "B-but h-h-how?" she stammered.

"I am not positive but you know what you told me last night? It must be from your unknown father," I answered her quietly. I could see the wheels spinning in her mind as her eyes frosted with anger and turned to chips of ice.

"So, what you are saying is that the man that *raped* my mother was one of your people? That my father was an alien…a Vesturion?" Her clipped tone indicated her shock and fury.

I took her head in my hands and turned her toward me. "Yes, I believe that is what happened. Like humans, not all Vesturions are good. I am terribly sorry to have to tell you of this."

She jerked her head free of my hands and stood up so fast she sent her chair crashing to the floor. Her eyes darted around the room and I could see her fear mounting in her eyes.

"You are safe here with us January. We will protect you."

"Like you protected my mother? I don't think so."

She ran out of the room. I went to follow her, but both Rayn and Maddie told me to let her go. That she needed time alone to process everything. They asked me how I knew about her mother so I told them pieces of January's story.

"Dear God, I never knew. I always knew there was something so wrong in her life, but I never imagined that." Maddie said, horrified.

Minutes that seem like hours passed and when I could stand it no longer, I went in search of her. I heard her sobs from the corridor outside her room. I tapped on her door, but when I received no answer, I entered to find her curled up in the fetal position on her bed, crying her eyes out.

"January, please don't cry. It will be all right."

"Please don't touch me," she sobbed. "Leave me alone for now. I really need to process all of this!"

"Shh, I know." I was determined to help her. I sat on the bed and dragged her into my arms. At first she struggled against me, but then she relaxed when she felt Tranquility wash over her. I knew I could do nothing but let the storm pass. My stomach clenched as I thought of her agony. I was miserable with this feeling of helplessness. I massaged her back and neck and ran my hand up and down her hair. Her sobs turned to shudders and finally began to subside.

When she sniffed loudly I said, "Here, use my shirt if you need it."

She grabbed the hem of it and lifted it to her face, wiping her tears. She lifted her eyes to mine and my heart cleaved in two with the pain etched in her eyes. I placed my palm on her cheek and turning her face into it, she placed a kiss there. "Thank you. You always seem to do the right thing for me," she said. Her shimmering eyes mesmerized me as I melted into her.

"This is so bizarre. I mean my whole life I questioned myself because I was so different from everyone. The way I look, the way I could hear what people were thinking...and then I always seemed to learn at a faster pace than the other kids. That just added to my freakishness. They would talk about me behind my back and whisper about me thinking I couldn't hear them. And then the way my parents treated me...they knew I was different too." She dropped her gaze as she twisted her hands in my shirt.

"I cannot imagine what you are feeling right now January. Know that I am here for you if there is anything you need." I gently rubbed her back as we sat together.

"Is it weird being able to hear everyone thinking things all the time? I've dealt with it my whole life but I always thought I was crazy."

"You are certainly not crazy but quite the opposite. Humans have an uncanny ability to tag the term 'crazy' onto things they cannot find an adequate explanation for. Being here with us, you will learn how to block your thoughts and those of humans. You will only hear what you wish. Other Vesturions usually block their thoughts unless they want to communicate with you. It can come in quite handy at times. It will be much easier for you January now that you are with us."

"What will happen when I go back?"

"Is that what you want? To go back?" My belly tightened with fear at the thought of losing my ghost girl.

She lifted her eyes to mine and whispered, "I don't know what I want. I've never been anywhere like this before. This beautiful home with all its comforts. And you. But I can't just disappear either."

"We can work on that, but right now, Earth is spinning out of control with this pandemic so you cannot go anywhere until things change. The cities and towns are extremely dangerous places to be. I would not want to put you at risk."

"I didn't think I could get sick again."

"No, you cannot. The cities, however, are no longer safe. People are rioting and the violence has escalated to unprecedented levels. You would not recognize Atlanta for all the destruction that has occurred."

"What about my brother and sister?"

"Right now, Spartanburg isn't as dangerous as other places. It will, however, become so. We are trying to come up with a feasible plan to put in place to help the humans, but for now, there is not much you can do."

She nodded. I brushed the wetness of her cheeks away with the pads of my thumbs and our eyes met.

"I am so afraid for them," she said as I felt her fear radiating from her.

"I know you are. I can feel it pouring out from you. You have had to endure so much January. I wish it could be different. Stay close to me so my Tranquility can calm your fears."

She leaned against me and I itched to brush my fingers through her hair. She was so lovely, even though she had been crying and her nose and eyes were red.

"Your eyes are amazing Rykerian. Last night you told me what you thought of my hair...that it looked like spun silver and gold. Well, your hair is unlike anything I've ever seen. I'm not sure what color I would call it but it's...well, don't be mad at me for saying this, but it's incredibly gorgeous! Why do you and Rayn wear a braid?"

"Ugh! It is awful, is it not?

"No, not at all. It's different, but I sort of like it. Do you mind?" she asked reaching out her hand. At my nod, she took it in her hand and examined it. It was quite long, reaching well past my shoulder. Then she began playing with it, wrapping it around her hand and sliding it between her fingers.

"It is something I complain about all the time. All Guardians must wear them and we are only allowed to cut them every ten years."

"Is that why Rayn's is much shorter? Has he cut his recently?"

"No, he was captured and held by the Xanthians last spring and they cut his off then."

"Oh, that sounds awful."

"It was a terrible time for my family. Had it not been for Maddie's daring attempt at his rescue, I am not sure what would have happened."

"Maddie rescued him?" Her voice was tinged with a mixture of shock and awe.

"Uh hum. You must get her to tell you all about it sometime." During our conversation I found I could no longer stop myself from weaving my fingers into her hair. It was the silkiest feeling and I leaned in to inhale her fragrance. "Ah January, your scent takes away all coherent thoughts in my mind."

I began to nuzzle her neck and I lightly trailed kisses from her neck to her ear, where I whispered, "You have completely stolen all of my thoughts."

"Rykerian I...you, um..." she breathed.

Her fingers left my hair and moved back to my shirt when suddenly I felt her lifting it up and then her fingers were dancing across my torso eliciting a gasp from my mouth. She scrambled around and straddled my lap and took possession of my lips. She tasted of honey, maple syrup and January and I felt her tongue tracing patterns across my lips. I was weak and helpless to stop her. Our ragged breaths were mixed and I knew she felt the passion, as did I. My fingers were still braided in her silken tresses and I held her head with my hands. Her fingers continued to make their way along my torso and up to my chest. They finally withdrew and started a new journey across my face and into my hair again. Her moans were telling me she was on fire as I was.

I pulled away to gaze upon her passion filled face and my breath caught in my throat. Her lips were swollen from crying and kissing, and her face was flushed with desire. I had never seen her look more lovely.

"Sweet Deity you are beautiful!"

I saw her swallow and her throat was working to say something. She finally said, "Rykerian, I want to...you know. I want to be with you."

I slid one hand down to her hip and said, "You are with me. I am here and I am not going anywhere."

"That's not what I meant. I want to...I want us to...you know. I've never been with a boy before and I want my first time to be with you." Her long, pale, eyelashes fluttered over her eyes, shielding them from me.

She wants to be with me! I felt my heart surge with joy at her words as a smile burst upon my face. I placed her hand over my heart so she could feel it beneath her fingers. "Ahh, I see. I would love nothing more, but I am afraid I am not allowed to do that. On Vesturon, we all swear to uphold that until we are unified or married as you say here on Earth."

She raised her brow and asked, "Seriously?"

I nodded. "I am afraid so. We take a vow of celibacy."

"What? Celibacy? You're joking?"

"No, I am not joking. I wish I was."

"So you've never…?"

I shook my head saying, "Never."

She cocked her head and her eyes drilled into mine. I think she was gauging whether I spoke the truth. I did not want her to feel thus, so I opened my mind. I took her hands into mine and looked into her eyes. Her eyes immediately softened and a smile tugged at the corners of her lips. She leaned in and ever so gently touched her lips to mine.

"It would be my luck! I finally find the one I want to…well, you know, and I find out he's taken a vow of celibacy!" she exclaimed as she rolled her eyes.

"Is that a bad thing?" I muttered.

She snorted, "No, unless you are feeling frustrated, like I am right now."

"So, are you saying that you are disappointed?"

"Well, yeah! How can I not be? Rykerian, you are the first boy I've ever kissed much less want to *be* with. How can I not be disappointed?"

My heart tripped in my chest. I was unsure of her comment. I closed my eyes before whispering, "I do not ever want to disappoint you."

"Please open your eyes," she pleaded.

I lifted mine to hers and she gently said, "*You* don't disappoint me. Your rule about, well you know, is what disappoints me." The corners of her mouth turned up.

"I see. It has a strong purpose though. On Vesturon we mate for life. Divorce does not exist. We take this vow very seriously," I murmured.

"Tell me something. You all seem so honorable. What do you think happened with my mom? I mean, how could she have ended up being raped by one of you?"

"I cannot say. As I said earlier, there are bad Vesturions as much as there are bad humans. The only thing I can deduce is that somehow their paths crossed. Are you sure of your father...or the man you know as your father?"

She nodded, "He was totally different with Tommy and Sarah, my little brother and sister. So I am sure he is not my biological father."

"What of your mother's background?"

"She is from Charleston, South Carolina but she didn't have a close relationship with her parents. She never spoke of them and I only remember meeting them once."

"Hmm. She must have encountered a Vesturion at some point. And you are nineteen years of age?" She nodded and I continued, "Do you know anything of her background? Did she go to college or leave Charleston for any reason?"

"She went to Clemson University in South Carolina, but she never finished because she got pregnant. That's all I know."

"Hmm. Do you want to know who he is January? We can trace your lineage. It is a relatively easy thing to do on Vesturon."

"I don't know."

"You do not have to make a decision now. When you are ready, you can tell me. If you do not ever want to know, that is fine too." A random thought popped into my head. Thinking she was in need of a change of scenery, I asked, "Would you care to go for a ride?"

Chapter Nine

When we reached the garage, I headed for the bay that contained the speedsters. I placed a helmet upon her head and wrapped her in a cloak I had carried from the house.

"Up you go," I said, assisting her on the seat.

Her mouth formed an O and she cocked her head. "What *is* this thing?"

"It is called a speedster. You will see how it operates momentarily."

I leaped up in front of her and instructed her to hold tightly to me. Her arms came around me and she hugged herself to me. I gave her arm a squeeze and tapped a few buttons and the speedster came to life. I programmed it for a tour around the national park and up we went. While we were lifting in the air, I instructed her to communicate with me telepathically.

"I'm not sure I can."

"Yes, you can. Whatever you want to say, just tell me with your thoughts. You are doing it right now. The more you do it, the better at it you will become."

"Okay, can you hear me?"

"Loud and clear!"

I took her around the highest mountains, Mt. LeConte, Mt. Guyot and Clingman's Dome. We zoomed over the majestic peaks and vales, soared above cascading waterfalls and over rushing streams and came to rest on my favorite mountaintop near the Compound. Throughout the trip I heard her constant intake of breath and multiple "oohs" and "ahhs" and I felt myself smiling in response.

As I climbed off the vehicle, I uttered, "Well?"

She yanked off her helmet and I was treated to a dazzling grin.

"That was…incredible…awesome! I've never seen anything like it!" she exclaimed.

I lifted her up and she threw her arms around me and gave me a loud smack on the cheek. "Thank you! Thank you! Thank you! That was wonderful!"

January's excitement was contagious and I had caught it. I beamed.

Her arms were still wrapped tightly around me and I was returning her embrace. Before either one of us could stop it, we found ourselves locked in a kiss that took my breath away. She ran her tongue along my lips, exploring my mouth, and I mimicked her actions, tasting of her sweetness. I felt her fingers twist in my hair and I was like putty in her hands. I leaned away from her so I could look into her eyes. With the pads of my thumbs, I massaged tiny circles on her cheeks.

"You are so lovely, with your eyes bright with excitement and your cheeks rosy from the cool mountain air. What am I going to do with you January?"

"What do you want to do with me?" she breathed. I was shocked by her question. I hadn't expected that and there was only one thing I wanted to do with her, but I was afraid if I told her, she would run away, frightened by the seriousness of my thoughts.

"Don't look so wary Rykerian. I didn't mean that the way it sounded." My actions were betraying me.

"January, if I told you what I truly wanted to do with you, I fear that you would run away from me, never to return," I confessed. *What possessed you to say a thing like that?*

"Never. You would never frighten me," she said with conviction.

"What happened to that ghost of a female that was so unsure of herself only a day ago?" I wondered aloud.

"This may sound quite weird, but I've never trusted anyone before. I trust you Rykerian. It has been liberating in a sense." She beamed at me again. Her smile warmed my heart and soothed my ragged soul. I had observed my ghost female for several months now, not ever daring to get close to her. And here she was, smiling and kissing me, and asking what I wanted to do with her. Do I dare tell her? My conscience screamed that it was too early, but once the idea took root, it began to blossom and I couldn't control myself.

"Promise?" I whispered.

Her face screwed up with confusion. "Huh?"

"Promise me you will not run away. Promise me I will not frighten you off with my words," I pleaded.

"Rykerian, you have only been kind to me. I've lived in some pretty bad circumstances so why would I run from you when you've been nothing but kind?"

"Because you have unwittingly stolen my heart and it would be a simple thing for you to crush it." *There, I said it.*

"I...you...what did you just say?"

"Most assuredly you heard me correctly, but to reiterate, you have stolen my heart January. Somehow, my heart has become yours...your possession to do with as you please. As I told you before, my soul has chosen yours. Where my soul goes, my heart follows. It no longer belongs to me, but to you. What I am most desirous of is to have you by my side always and forever." *Well, you definitely did it now! You deserve whatever she decides to dish out.*

"Rykerian, I don't quite know what to say. This is a bit fast, isn't it?"

"For humans, I suppose it is, but not for Vesturions. May I ask you something?" When she nodded, I carried on, "Do you feel any kind of attraction toward me? I do not speak of my looks. I speak of something deeper, like a magnetism or an electrical current?"

"Yes," she muttered without hesitation.

One simple word and my heart nearly leapt out of my chest with joy. My smile was radiant. I felt myself glowing, from inside out.

"That is the Vesturion in you feeling my soul touching yours. Our souls have met January, and they determine where our hearts go. I believe your heart will be with mine soon."

Her brow was furrowed again and her mouth opened and closed several times. She was confused, of that I was certain. She stepped back from me and twisted her fingers together. My heart clenched with fear, as I was not sure where her thoughts were taking her.

"Please talk to me January. I do not want you to be afraid of what I have just told you."

She lifted her eyes to mine and her uncertainty was reflected in them. "I don't know what to say. I am flattered that you feel this way on one hand, but on the other, my mind is screaming that this is too soon. Rykerian, you're the first boy I've ever kissed. No other boy has even given me a second look. Not that I would have encouraged it or anything. I was always too busy for anything like that, but I wasn't blind to the way boys looked at and treated me." I opened my mouth to interrupt her...to tell her how lovely she was, but she held out her hand halting me.

"Please, let me finish before I lose my nerve. Then you show up, swooping down like an angel from heaven, rescuing me from certain death, when that's what I had been praying for. My life had become such a tattered mess that I couldn't see the light at the end of the tunnel. I wanted to die; it was that bad. When I first saw you, I really did think you were an angel. You carry this glow about you...even now I can see it."

"My aura. That is my aura, January. As a Vesturion, your eyes have the ability to detect it."

She shook her head as though she were trying to dislodge something. "Then there's this whole Vesturion thing. Not to mention everything else...Maddie, my bio-dad, everything. And then you take me on the ride of my life. I'm still in awe over it. Now here we are, you telling me we are soul mates and all. When I asked you that question, I thought you were going to tell me you wanted to have sex with me. Instead, if I heard you correctly, you just declared your love for me! I...I'm so confused!"

I reached for her saying, "January..."

"No! Please, I can't think straight when I'm in your arms. I need to figure all this out," she cried out, dropping to the ground and hugging her legs with her arms. I leaned back on the speedster, stretching my legs out and crossing my arms. I wanted to relieve her of her troubled mind but I also understood her confusion. I gave her the space she needed and watched her.

Sweet Deity she is lovely. When she wrinkles up her brow, I want to kiss the little creases that form. And her mouth...her lovely lips scrunch up in cadence with her brow. It makes me want to taste them. Her fidgeting hands, twisting and turning... I want those fingers dancing across my torso again!

As my frustrations over not being able to touch or comfort her mounted, I pushed away from the speedster and began to pace. I raked my hands through my hair and struggled with the varying thoughts pouring through my mind. My feet carried me to the place on the mountaintop that afforded the magnificent views of the Blue Ridge Mountains, as they lay in splendor before me. I stood there, my body tense with emotion. Suddenly, I felt hands wind their way up my back and come to rest upon my shoulders. Her fingers began to sink into my muscles, massaging out the stress.

"Don't be so tense Rykerian. You whole body looks like a piece of wood."

"Ahh, that feels divine." Her deft fingers were melting away the tension. I closed my eyes, enjoying the sensations she was producing in me. When I could stand no more, I reached up and grabbed one of her wrists and spun around. I did it with Speed and she gasped when she found herself in my arms.

"Is this okay?" I inquired.

"More than okay. It's wonderful. I do love being in your arms." My heart was dancing again yet her mercurial moods were puzzling to me.

"Ms. St. Davis, your ever-changing moods will be the death of me!"

"I don't know what you mean, Mr....I don't even remember your last name!" she huffed.

My body shook with laughter. "It is Yarrister. May I present myself? My name is Rykerian Tevva Yarrister and pleased I am to meet you."

She had joined me in laughter and suddenly we fell silent our eyes locked on each other's. "I believe what you tell me Rykerian Tevva Yarrister, but I am still in shock over everything that has happened. I can't promise you much, but I can promise I won't run away," she breathed. "Will that be enough for now?"

"It will have to be because if you run away, I will have to chase you and beg you to return to me," I admitted and I closed my eyes, not able to bear the thought of that.

"Please don't do that."

"Chase you?"

"No...please don't close your eyes to me. They are so perfect I want to see them always. I don't think I've ever seen eyes so blue."

As I looked at her, for whatever reason, my face flamed with embarrassment. I know not if it was my declaration of feelings or if it was the moment, but it did not go unnoticed.

As she pulled my lips to hers, she said, "Your face is beautiful when you blush." Then I was lost in her kiss.

When we finally pulled away from each other, she was smiling.

"Is this really happening to me?"

"Yes, but I feel the same as you and keep asking myself the same question," I said.

"So what happens next Rykerian?"

"That will be up to you. You know where my heart lies January."

"Yes, and I would like to take things a bit slower Rykerian. So much has happened to me in the last few weeks that I cannot commit to anything right now. Are you angry with me?"

"Why ever would I be angry with you?"

"For not returning your feelings."

I shook my head saying, "No. I cannot be angry with you for that, but I would ask you one thing. Please always tell me your feelings. I do not want to seem pushy or to make you feel forced in this in any way."

She nodded and said, "I promise. And Rykerian, just for the record, you have blown me away in a good way." She gave me a radiant smile and I felt myself grin in return.

"We should probably head back to the house," I told her. I assisted her up on the speedster and in moments we were soaring through the air.

Chapter Ten

January and I came in from our ride to find Rayn and Maddie seated in the den. They were listening to the news and by the looks on their faces, it was dire. The hospitals were overflowing with cases of small pox and the death toll was growing exponentially daily. It had become the worst-case scenario. However, the horrific thing was most of the medical staff in the hospitals had succumbed to the disease, leaving them empty handed and uncertain of how to care for the patients.

"We cannot delay. We must act quickly. January, how are you feeling? Has your strength returned?" Rayn asked.

"I think so. I have felt pretty good these last few days."

"Rayn—I do not think she is ready," I stated. "She has been through a great deal in the last two weeks. She needs more time."

"We are out of time Rykerian. Look at the news. People are dying all over the world now. This is beyond epidemic and now in the pandemic stage and if we don't step in fast, we risk losing at least fifty percent or more of the population. I will go to great lengths to ensure January's safety. We will take every precaution. She is now immune from the disease so she will be fine."

Suddenly January jumped to her feet and started ranting. "Yes, we have to do something Rykerian. Tommy and Sarah are out there, and as much as I hate to say this, so are my parents. If something happens to them, Tommy and Sarah won't have anyone to take care of them."

"That is an example of why we must move and as quickly as possible," Rayn stated.

Rayn looked at me and gave a quick jerk of his head, indicating where he wanted me. I moved to January's side.

"Rykerian, I need to go to Tommy and Sarah. Can you take me there?"

I quickly averted my eyes, trying to avoid hers. I glanced at Rayn, willing him to answer her for me.

"January, that isn't possible right now. We need you to do something for us...something that can alter the outcome of this disaster we are facing," Rayn explained.

January cocked her head to the side and asked, "What are you talking about?"

"You know where the lab is at the Centers for Disease Control and we need you to get virus samples and the vaccine itself into the CDC."

"But how? Where did the vaccine come from?"

"Our virologists on Vesturon produced it from the virus samples they extracted from you during your illness. They replicated the virus and using our technology produced the vaccine. We had to do this because the methods of producing the vaccine on Earth would have taken much too long. We are trying to stem the illness as best we can and we felt this would be the most effective way. Our biggest issue at hand is that the scientists at the CDC would recognize they weren't able to produce something this fast. This is where you fit in," Rayn explained.

She nodded and said, "Go on."

"You are familiar with the area the vaccine would be stored, correct?"

"Sort of. I was shown the area but never really entered it until the day of the break-in. I noticed the door was open and that's when I entered, but, I never had access to that area. It was under strict security. The day I saw those men was when my suspicions grew. Then when I called security and they examined the area, they determined nothing had been taken."

"What men?" I asked.

"Oh, I was leaving work late one Friday evening. Most of the employees had left and I was headed out when I saw six men walking down the hall leading to the lab. They were dressed in completely bizarre clothes...totally out of place for the CDC."

"What do you mean?" I questioned.

"They wore leather vests with no shirts; their arms were covered in tattoos... I mean their tats were almost completely covering their arms and they were all identical. And they had these weird looking straps that went across their chests. They reminded me of men that were in a motorcycle gang. I guess if I had seen them on the street I wouldn't have thought much about it, but it was strange seeing them in the CDC. Most of the people that work there are pretty geeky and would never dress like that."

I looked at Rayn and we briefly exchanged thoughts. I nodded and urged her to tell us more.

"Yeah, but some other weird things happened," she said.

"Explain," Rayn gruffly commanded. I shot him a cross look, indicating my displeasure at his harsh tone.

"Well, when we passed each other I stopped...it was like I couldn't move. I heard this voice in my mind. He wanted to know who I was and then he asked me if I was human. I thought that was pretty strange at the time."

Rayn looked at me and mumbled, "This is not good. Worse than I imagined."

"What do you mean by that?" January inquired.

"This male is telepathic. In our experience there are very few species that possess this talent. He may have been Vesturion," I explained.

"I don't think so," January said, surprising all of us.

"What makes you say such?" Rayn asked harshly. Once again I felt my eyes darken at his tone.

"I'm not sure I can explain it. One thing though—their leader had the most unusual eyes. And when I got close to him, it felt like the room was electrically charged."

"What?" I yelled. My instincts did not respond well to this. I felt the first stirrings of jealousy begin to take root, something I had never experienced before.

"I told you Rykerian. I'm not sure I can explain it. It was totally strange. When we passed each other it was like there were sparks flying." She was looking at me when she spoke and noticed my reaction. She rolled her eyes at me. "Not *those kinds* of sparks. It felt like there was static electricity everywhere. It made me wonder if my hair was standing straight up in the air."

"Oh," I muttered. A tremendous feeling of relief washed over me.

"Anyway, the whole thing was bizarre and none of it was captured on the video off the security cameras. After a while, I thought I had imagined everything."

Rayn had stepped closer to January while she was talking and reached out and placed his hand on her face. Her eyes widened and he immediately said, "Do not fear me as I would not ever harm you. However, I find it necessary to reach into your mind. I must capture all of your memories on this situation. May I?"

January nodded and Rayn began his mind search. Minutes passed before he stepped away. He looked at Maddie first and then me. I could immediately tell he was deeply troubled.

"Are you going to share?" I asked, my voice dripping with impatience.

"She speaks the truth," he stated bluntly.

"Of course she speaks the truth. Why would she do else?" I asked in frustration.

"That is not what I meant. I should have said that her words accurately described what she saw. She did not imagine it. These men are the ones responsible for this travesty and we must find out who they are," Rayn stated.

"What would you suggest?" I wondered.

"At the moment...nothing. We must first focus on getting the vaccine to the CDC so we can bring an end to this epidemic. January, do you have enough knowledge to get us to the correct place this vaccine would need to be stored?"

"Yeah, but I can't get you in. As I said, it's under the strictest security."

"That will not be a problem for us. We need you to get us there and we can proceed from there." Rayn looked at me and said, "Rykerian, tell Father we require his presence in the Command Center immediately. Meet us there in fifteen minutes."

After Maddie and Rayn departed and I sent the missive to my father, I looked at January. I felt the beginnings of fear creep up my spine. I knew something was about to go dreadfully wrong, but I didn't know what. "I am afraid to let you take part in this," I admitted to her.

"Will you be joining me?"

"I cannot say at this time. I will know more after we meet with my father."

"Am I to go with you to that?" she asked, her voice tense.

"Yes, I think it best as we need your knowledge. Since you will be joining the Guardians in this mission, you will need to know what it all entails. Are you okay with all of this? Tell me true January, because if you are not, I will not allow you to participate."

"Rykerian, people are dying everywhere. If there is something…anything I can do to help, I am willing to do it. Besides, I have a brother and sister that will benefit from this too. When we finish, can you take me to them? I must see Tommy and Sarah…I need to know if they're still…" her voice trailed off as tears prevented her from saying more.

I gathered her into my arms to calm her. When trembling subsided, I told her that we would go to her brother and sister. "We will take some of the vaccine with us to ensure they receive it. Hopefully, they are safe and sound, but we will know more in a few days."

"How long before we leave for Atlanta?" she asked.

"My guess is later today or tomorrow. Come, we must get down to the Compound."

Along the way I explained how the Compound beneath the house was the Command Center for all the Guardians on Earth. It was a massive complex that on any given day had hundreds of Vesturions moving about performing their various duties.

I snorted when I looked at January's expression. I put my hand beneath her chin and gently closed her mouth.

"I've never…I mean, how big is this place? What are those things over there? How many people are down here?" The questions continued to tumble out of her mouth.

I gave her a brief description of what took place here but by then we had reached the conference room where everyone waited for us.

As we entered, I looked around. Rayn and Maddie were present, along with my father and Kennar who was a Guardian that had at one time been second in command at the Compound here. My other brother Tesslar was also present, as well as five other Guardians.

I pulled January to my side and introduced her first to my father and to the rest of those present.

After we all were seated, Rayn began explaining what he thought was our best option to get the vaccine in the right place.

"January has consented to assist us in the mission. She spent several months at the CDC working in the lab. While she did not have access to the secure part of the lab where the *variola major* virus was stored, she knows the location. We can teleport to the CDC and she can lead us to the storage area. We will need to go when some of their virologists are present so we can plant the information into their minds to make it look like they've developed the vaccine themselves. We will also take virus samples so they can have them on hand to produce more vaccine. We have produced enough vaccine to inoculate all of Atlanta. We can leave them with the vaccine in various stages of development so they won't immediately run out."

"That's a ton of vaccine. How do you intend to get it there?" January asked.

I answered, "That's the easy part. Once we know where the storage facility for the vaccine is, we will teleport it directly there."

"I only know where the virus samples are kept for that and for the flu. I don't know where they stored massive amounts of the vaccine." Her words were laced with anxiety. I quickly reached for her hand and watched her tension dissolve.

"Do not be concerned about that. We can discover that when we have contact with one of the scientists. We will find everything we need to know then," I explained.

"Why don't you just go to them directly and tell them you have the vaccine? Why all this subterfuge?"

All eyes in the room glanced at January then honed in on me. They all waited expectantly for my answer.

"January, I suppose I have been remiss in not telling you that we cannot disclose our identity or existence for that matter. It is against our Covenants. There is sound reasoning behind this. Our species is so much more advanced than here on Earth that if humans were to discover even one of our technological advances, it could alter the future of this planet. We swear not to ever interfere in the development of any species or society."

"I see. Even when half of humanity is at stake? That seems like a stupid rule to me!" she exclaimed.

January's face had flushed and her eyes were shooting sparks. I glanced at my father to see him scowling. Rayn pushed his way into my thoughts and all but ordered me to get my hands on her and keep them there. We didn't need her attention to be diverted as it was.

I put my arm across her shoulders and she glared at me. Eventually my Power of Tranquility calmed her and diffused her anger. "Are you using your Power on me?" she wanted to know. I nodded in response. She licked her lips and stared at me for a second before nodding in return. We finally pulled our eyes away from each other and I noticed everyone was staring at us.

"Shall we continue? Rayn asked.

"Yes. As I was saying, the difficult part will be for us to identify the researchers that we can pull into our circle and fill them with the appropriate information. It should be relatively easy to find the depository where the vaccines are stored. Once this task is complete, we can also get this vaccine distributed to various pharmaceutical companies here and abroad to get as much out to the public as we can."

"Other than show you where the lab is, what else would I have to do?"

"That is the most important part. That and identifying the researchers that we can plant the vaccine information in so they will know of its existence," Rayn said.

"Well, that all sounds relatively easy," January replied.

"Our biggest concern is that all the virologists that know how to formulate the vaccine will be gone...as in..."

"Dead." January filled in the blank and then the silence was overbearing. "What are we waiting for? Let's go!" she exclaimed.

We all sat for a while discussing and finalizing our plan. We would go that afternoon. As soon as we had the location, the vaccine would be teleported there. It should be a smooth operation, proving we could find the virologists to carry out the rest of the plan.

Book Three

January

Chapter One

W e arrived near the side entrance of the Centers for Disease Control and Prevention. I still had my ID card, which would gain us entrance; after Rykerian had found me in the woods, he went back to my car and gathered some of my belongings. I was feeling disoriented from the teleporting, but Rykerian assured me it would quickly pass. It was a strange sensation having your body converted to energy and back to mass again. I shook my head, trying to clear it.

Moments later I was feeling close to myself again so I motioned for the group to follow me. Rykerian held my hand and Rayn, Tesslar, Kennar and four other Guardians followed him. They were to guard the vaccine, as there were many crates in which it was contained. Maddie had been furious, as Rayn was adamant about her staying behind. Since she had human genetics, she was susceptible to the virus and he would not take any chances on her falling ill. I didn't blame him and told her as much.

I began leading the group inside. I was baffled at how deserted the area was. Normally, since the Centers for Disease Control was located at Emory University, this area was bustling with students. It made my skin break out in goose bumps when I realized why there wasn't anyone around.

"Rykerian, this is bad. There should be tons of people around here now."

"It is the pandemic. Martial law is in effect so no one is supposed to be out and about, and of course, the University has closed down due to the quarantine."

When we reached the door, I used my ID card and we were able to enter. I was worried about whether it would still be activated. That was a relief; although it never occurred to me that we could simply teleport inside. I immediately took the stairwell down and we were soon in the corridor that led to the lab area. There was absolutely no one around. It was eerily quiet. The corridor wound around and soon we found ourselves outside of the glass partition, which the lab was located behind. I saw no one inside.

"This is the lab area. Behind this glass wall is where we need to be. I don't see anyone though."

Rykerian cocked his head and then said, "Someone is back there. At least two people as I can hear them conversing."

"How can we get back there? To gain entrance, we need retina scans and fingerprints, and that's just the first chamber. Behind that wall back there," I pointed, "is where the cryogenic storage vaults are and where all the virus samples are stored," I indicated with my hand.

"No worries...we will teleport inside."

Rykerian looked at Rayn and he nodded. The four of us were soon materializing inside the lab, to the astonishment of the two people inside.

Rayn immediately approached them saying, "Do not fear us as we mean you no harm. Which one of you is in charge?"

The first one who spoke was a woman who looked to be in her mid-thirties. "I am. Who are you and how did you get in here?" she asked, alarmed.

"Who we are matters not nor does how we got in here. We are here to help you put a stop to this pandemic," Rayn began.

"I wish I could believe you, but I'm afraid there's no hope. It's not safe here either. You should leave immediately," she responded.

Rayn advanced toward her and placed his hand on her arm. Her eyes opened slightly and then she closed them. He continued to hold her arm when Rykerian went to her companion who was a younger man. He began to do the same to him.

I tried to poke into Rayn's mind to see what he was discovering, but I was unable to, as he must've blocked any thoughts.

After some time he stepped away from her and Rykerian followed suit. The man and woman both found chairs and took a seat in them. They leaned their heads against the wall and immediately appeared to be taking naps.

I looked at Rykerian with raised brows.

"We have told them to sleep and before we leave we will erase their memories."

"Did you find out what you needed?" I asked.

He nodded and glanced toward Rayn who was making his way toward another door.

"Come," he ordered.

We followed Rayn and in seconds I felt myself swirling through a vortex again. It lasted a millisecond, or so it seemed. That disoriented, dizzy feeling hit me again. I looked up to find we had reappeared within the secured part of the lab. The cryogenic storage area was directly in front of me.

Since Rykerian, Tesslar and Kennar carried the containers with the virus samples they headed toward the opening of the vault and entered. I thought it was odd that it wasn't locked, but Rayn supplied the answer.

"The female said they hadn't found it necessary to keep many of the areas locked since there were not many people in here anymore."

I cocked my head as I looked at him and he gave me a sheepish grin. "I apologize January. I read your thoughts as they were quite loud," he explained.

I snorted saying, "I guess I'm going to have to get used to this mind reading thing. I keep forgetting about it."

"Yes, I suppose you are. As a rule, we try our best not to invade others' minds, but sometimes their thoughts can be so loud that we cannot help ourselves."

"Oh, don't I know that. I've been hearing thoughts all my life but always thought I was a freak of nature. I didn't know..." I trailed off.

Rayn looked at me with a dark glint in his eyes. "You are anything but a freak January. You are very special indeed to have such a strong grasp of telepathy without any training. It is a most impressive thing," he said, his face a mask of seriousness.

I stared at him thinking how easy it must have been for Maddie to fall in love with this man. When I saw his brows lift and the corners of his mouth turn up, I knew he "heard" me loud and clear. His response baffled me though.

"January, you have no idea. Maybe someday my mate will share our story with you. I will leave that decision to her."

I nodded, not knowing what else to say or do.

"So what next?" I blurted out. I was slightly uncomfortable in his intimidating presence. He was as tall as Rykerian, well over six feet and his dark wavy hair fell across his forehead and slightly over one eye, giving him a rakish appearance. Where Rykerian had eyes like the bluest of sapphires, Rayn's looked like brilliant emeralds. These men had the most amazing eyes I had even seen. Rykerian was much more polished in his appearance as well, but they both had this commanding air about them and power seemed to radiate from each of them.

Again, Rayn must have discerned my thoughts because he chuckled, saying, "Do not tell my brother I shared this with you, but we jokingly refer to him as Fifth Avenue. Let us say he has a penchant for dressing the part."

"I think I understand what you mean. Please don't take this the wrong way, but he definitely looks more into fashion than you! He always looks like he stepped out of a photo shoot or something."

That elicited another hearty laugh from Rayn.

"We always give him a hard time about his fondness for that. But getting back to your original question, as soon as Rykerian has placed all the samples in the vault, we will go back outside and join the other Guardians, at which point we will make our way to the storage facility."

"So you were able to get that information from her?" I was curious to find out what he had learned. "Is it far from here?"

"No, she said it was east of here...maybe three miles or so. It will not be difficult to find."

"Rayn, did she say anything about what's happening around Atlanta?"

He eyes darted around the room, hunting a place to land.

"Rayn?"

"It is bad January. The hospitals are overflowing with the sick and dying and there is no one to care for them. People are dying in record numbers. Gangs are taking over the city, looting, tearing down buildings and setting fire to things. Atlanta has turned into hell and it is a very dangerous place to be."

"How are we going to get the uninfected people vaccinated?" I wondered.

"My father is sending in troops of Guardians to take care of this. Once they institute some semblance of order and get the inoculating underway, they will move across the globe. It is the only way, but we understand how devastating this will all be. We will be taking some of the vaccine to our Guardians in Europe, Asia and Africa to get things moving in the right direction. The first group of Guardians will be arriving soon and will go directly to the pharmaceutical companies that produce vaccines and get that operation up and running. They will speed up the manufacturing process, and the Guardians will remain here until we see a positive turn of the disease cycle, as well as a sufficient amount of vaccine. We will not pull them back until everything is in order. Only then will we let the humans carry on with their usual order of business. I hope this all makes sense. It is the soundest plan we could institute quickly."

"Rayn, how can this all be accomplished without the people here knowing it was you that did it?" I didn't understand how this would be possible.

"It will be necessary to use our Power of Obliteration. They will think they developed the vaccine themselves. It is a relatively easy thing for us to do," he explained. "It is much like your hypnosis, except it goes much deeper into the mind. It becomes part of the long term memory so it seems it was always there."

"When can Rykerian take me to my family so I can see if they're...?" I knotted my fingers as my stomach careened, but I couldn't make myself voice those dreadful words. I couldn't bear the thought of anything happening to Tommy or Sarah.

"After the vaccine supply is delivered to the storage facility, he is planning on taking you directly there."

I rushed to him and gave him a hug saying, "Thank you!"

"What is going on in here?" Rykerian had entered the room as I was hugging Rayn.

"Not to worry brother. January was just thanking me for I told her you were going to take her to her family to inoculate them. Do not tell me you are jealous!" His tone was laced with humor.

Rykerian's stance immediately relaxed and then he flushed upon hearing Rayn. I looked at him and his eyes softened at once.

I ran and threw myself at him. I felt the tears on my cheeks before I realized I was crying. He cradled me in his arms and whispered, "It is going to be okay January. We will go to them when we are finished here. Please do not cry."

"Rayn said it is terrible here. I am so worried about them Rykerian. I can hardly think straight."

"I know." He stepped back so he could look into my eyes and said, "I promise we will do all we can for them." His eyes bore into mine and I heard his thoughts...how he swore to help and care for them if necessary.

I reached up and put my palm against his cheek, "Thank you. I owe you for this, you know."

"No, you owe me nothing January. I do this freely for you and you know exactly why." He turned his head into my hand and kissed my palm. I swallowed the boulder that had formed in my throat and nodded.

"I know and I feel the same Rykerian." His eyes widened at my words and I felt his surprise, but at that moment I did care for him, as much or more than I had ever cared for anyone before.

The four of us made our way back to where the other Guardians were waiting. Rykerian leaned over to me and said, "This delivery should not take much time and then we will be on our way to your family."

I nodded as I felt myself, again, swirling and spinning. When everything stopped, I saw we were in a warehouse district of sorts. I realized that this time I only felt slightly dizzy from the teleporting, so at least that was improving.

The Guardians began teleporting all the vaccine into the refrigerated storage facility and completed that task in short order.

We bid farewell to Rayn, Tesslar, Kennar and the other Guardians. Rykerian looked at me and said, "Are you ready?" lacing his fingers with mine.

"I'm so scared. What if they're all...?"

"Do not think those thoughts. Can you tell me exactly where the house is so I can locate it with my tracker?"

I gave him the necessary information and he began tapping his shadar. He looked at me in askance and I nodded. He grasped my hand in his and off we went.

Chapter Two

We materialized in the backyard of the house I grew up in. In the three years I had been gone, nothing had changed. Everything was completely silent. There wasn't a trace of sound from cars or people. I felt the hairs on the back of my neck rise and I rubbed my sweaty palms together.

I ran to the back door and pushed it open.

"Mom, Tommy, Sarah! Is anyone here?"

I ran though the kitchen and came to a screeching halt in the den. They were all sitting there, staring at me like they were seeing a ghost.

"January?" It was Tommy who spoke first.

"Tommy! Are you okay? Sarah!"

I turned to look at my mom and she sat there with a look of horror upon her face.

"How did *you* get here?" she demanded in a scathing voice.

"Do NOT speak to her in such a manner or I swear I will..."

"Rykerian! Stop! Please!" His face was flushed with anger.

I turned back to my mom and saw that she and her husband were staring at Rykerian, wide-eyed and mouths agape. I briefly wondered if they saw what I did...an impossibly gorgeous man with brilliant blue eyes and hair that looked as though each strand had been individually hand-painted a unique shade of bronze. Impressively tall, and broad shouldered, he looked like he could take down my father with a slight flick of his wrist.

They kept gaping, looking as if they were struggling with whether to say something.

"We've come to vaccinate you against smallpox," Rykerian said, bringing me back to the present.

Rykerian pulled out the vial, along with the syringes and prepared to give them the injections.

"Wait a minute. First of all, who are *you* and second of all, there is no vaccine. Do you think we're stupid?" she asked, her tone accusing.

"Mom, shut up! I'm not going to answer that last question, because you won't like my response. You have no clue of what's going on. Yes, this is a vaccine and it *will* save your life. Now, I'll be happy to walk away and let you die a horrible death, if that's what you want."

I swung my head in my father's direction and the look on his face would have been comical in any other situation. He was still staring at Rykerian and he looked like he was badly in need of a toilet. All the color had drained from his face and his hands were fisted so tightly I could see his white knuckles from where I stood. He was either going to hurl or mess himself, and I really didn't care to witness either.

"How do I know that what's in that stuff won't kill us?" Mom asked.

"Seriously! Do you honestly think I would ever harm Tommy or Sarah? I love them more than my own life!" I said fervently.

"No, I know you won't harm them, but I wasn't asking about that. I want to know if you intend to harm me and your fath..." her voice trailed off.

"I would never do that. Do you know so little of me that you think I could be capable of that?" I was astonished she would think such horrid thoughts.

"You must hate us for what we did," she said bitterly.

"You're the ones filled with hatred, not me!"

I turned to Rykerian and he nodded.

"Tommy and Sarah come here please," I said softly.

They were both crouching in the corner holding each other. They looked at my mom and she nodded. They slowly rose and walked to me. Tommy was trembling and Sarah was crying. I raised my eyes to my mom.

"What have you done to them? What have you told them about me?" I cried. I knew in my heart she had filled their heads with lies. They were scared to death of me.

"I told them the truth is all," she snarled.

I turned back to them and knelt down. I opened my arms and they stood back from me. I gave them a shaky smile. It was becoming unbearably difficult to hold back my tears. I didn't want to hurt them, but I wanted them to know the truth.

"Tommy, Sarah," I began in a whisper, "I would never ever in a million years hurt you. I love you with all my heart and would do anything for you. I'm here because...well you know how everyone is getting sick? I am here to give you some medicine that will help you not get sick like everyone else. Does that make sense?"

They both stared at me with their huge eyes and beautiful little faces and I broke down. I felt Rykerian lift me into his arms and walk to a chair where he sat down with me in his lap.

"Sshh. It is going to be okay love. We will take care of things here...I will take care of things here and make it right." He whispered to me as he rubbed circles on my back and ran his fingers through my hair. My sobs finally subsided and I was able to speak.

I lifted my head and looked him in the eye. "I feel like a roller coaster of emotions right now. Sorry about that," I sniffed.

He gave me one of his disarming smiles and said, "No need for apologies. Let's get this taken care of so I can have a nice little chat with your parents."

I stood and turned back to Tommy and Sarah and called them over.

"Tommy, Sarah, we need your arms so we can give you this medicine, okay?"

They glanced to my mom and she nodded. They rolled up their sleeves and Rykerian quickly injected them. Sarah cried a bit while Tommy scrunched up his face, trying to be the tough guy.

Rykerian looked at me and his thoughts passed to me. I was startled at the extent of his anger. He was asking for my permission to confront my parents. I was so weary I didn't have the strength to say no.

He walked to my parents and they had to crane their necks to look at him. My father's scowl vanished, as did my mom's.

Rykerian began addressing my mom first. "You have been the most pitiful excuse for a mother that I have ever encountered. To blame what happened to you on your daughter is reprehensible. If I had my way I would cut you down and walk away without remorse, but your beautiful daughter would never allow that."

"You don't know what you're talking about," my mother retorted.

"Cease your prattle female!" Rykerian thundered, causing the walls to vibrate.

"Don't you speak to her like that," my father shouted.

Rykerian turned to him, venom spilling from his eyes and thundered, "I Command you to Silence!"

My father's eyes widened and his mouth attempted to form words but no sound came out. His body went absolutely rigid and he looked like he had turned into a stone statue.

What is happening to him? Why is he acting like that?

Rykerian looked at me with guilt in his eyes and shook his head. He raked his hand through his hair, then extended it toward my father and said, "Release."

My father fell forward onto his knees and rolled into the fetal position, drawing deep breaths into his lungs.

I ran to Rykerian and grabbed his arm. "What..."

He cut me off saying, "I will explain later."

He turned back toward my mother and said, "If you two *ever* do *anything* to hurt January again, you will regret it for the remainder of your life. Now, you will sit down with your children and tell them that January is not the evil demon you have made her out to be, but a wonderful, loving female."

My mom just stood there, immobile.

"Now!" Rykerian shouted.

She scurried to Tommy and Sarah and the words started to spill forth. She explained to them how she had done me wrong. She confessed she had never given them the letters I had written and that I loved them dearly and wouldn't hurt them for anything. She also explained to them that it was okay for them to love me back. They looked at me, and I had tears pouring down my face. I held out my arms and they ran to me, crying as well.

The three of us hugged and I couldn't stop telling them how much I loved them. We were all on the floor, me in the middle and they were crawling all over me.

"You two have grown up so much since the last time I was here. Tommy, remember that day I came here and you two were playing outside? Did you keep your promise and take good care of Sarah?"

"Yeah, I think so January."

"Sarah, how about you? Did you take good care of Tommy?" She nodded her head vigorously up and down.

"Good! I knew I could count on you two! Now I'm going to be leaving in a few minutes, but I want you to know something. I love you with all my heart. You are always right here," I said as I pointed to my head, "and right here," as I pointed to my heart. "I'm going to write you letters and if for some reason you ever need me for anything...anything at all, you just think serious thoughts about me and I'll come to you. Okay?"

"Do you gotta leave?" Sarah asked.

"Yeah, I do sweetie, but don't forget what I said, okay?"

"We won't," Tommy said.

I hugged them both again as hard as I could without squishing them to death. Then I kissed them both and stood up.

While I had been talking with Tommy and Sarah, Rykerian had given my parents their vaccinations. Then he looked at my dad first and his eyes glazed over and then closed. My mom was next, and then finally Tommy and Sarah.

"What did you just do?" I wanted to know.

"I erased their memories of us but left the good ones of you with your siblings. They deserve to know what a loving sister you are."

I gave him a watery smile and hugged him, my arms around his waist.

"Thank you!" I said into his chest.

"Come, take my hand sweet thing and we will depart from here."

I tightly held onto his hand and Rykerian tapped his shadar. Moments later we were back at the mountain house.

Chapter Three

When we took form back at the house in the mountains, I felt my head spinning. This time it was different. My vision seemed distorted and I felt like I was going to throw up, but before I could say anything, my legs crumpled beneath me and everything went dark.

Vague voices in the distance infiltrated my mind. It sounded like several people were whispering. I wanted to open my eyes but they felt like lead. My attempts at speaking failed; my tongue felt swollen and my mouth was like sawdust. I drifted back to unconsciousness.

I'm not sure how long I slept, but I awakened to see golden streaks of sunlight softening the room. My eyes darted around, searching for something familiar, not recognizing where I was. The room looked similar to the one I had been staying in at Rykerian's, yet this one was different...more masculine.

The furnishings were massive...a large chest of drawers, a beautiful armoire and a gigantic bed. I felt I was lying on the softest cloud ever and I was swathed in silken bedding. I lifted my head to gaze around and sitting in a chair next to me was Rykerian. He must have felt me move for he sprang to his feet and his eyes shot around the room before landing on me.

A grin immediately spread from ear to ear and he sat down next to me and began to tenderly brush the backs of his fingers across my cheek.

"What happened to me? Where are we?" I croaked. My throat felt sore and scratchy.

"You are in my bedroom at the house. You fainted when we returned here and you have been unconscious for a time."

"For 'a time?' How long of a time?"

He glanced down before answering. "Five days," he muttered.

"Five days? I have been unconscious for five days? What happened?" I squeaked.

"As soon as we teleported back here, I looked at you and your body simply collapsed. I carried you up here and called our healer, Julian. He has examined you every day. He is certain you suffered from a combination of shock and exhaustion. I was furious with Rayn. I told him you were not ready to undertake this mission." Rykerian stood and dragged his hand through his hair. He began pacing next to the bed.

"Hey. Rykerian. Is anyone in there?" He kept pacing. I sat up and threw the covers back, intending to stand. I didn't get very far before the dizziness hit me. That seemed to get his attention.

"January, what are you doing?"

"I was trying to grab your attention. I thought I'd stand but I guess I'm too weak or something."

"Deity! Do not do that again. You have been here for five days, completely unconscious. Your mind and body have suffered a great shock. You must take time to recover and regain your strength!" he was nearly bellowing by now.

"Rykerian! Please, lower your voice. You're upsetting me!" I was trembling now.

"Bloody hell! Forgive me," he said as he sat next to me and took me into his arms. He pulled me across his lap and cocooned me, using his Power of Tranquility to calm me.

"Thank you. Please don't yell at me. It upsets me when you raise your voice like that. It's a throwback you know."

He drew back to look at me and I could see the regret in his eyes.

"Please forgive me. I never want to upset you in any way January. I've been so distraught over your collapse that I haven't been myself lately. Forgive me, please?"

I nodded. "Okay. Do you think it was seeing my family again because I can tell you it really upset me? I was a wreck Rykerian," I confessed.

"I know. I could see you were. I could feel it radiating from you. I had every intention of comforting you with Tranquility when we returned here, but I never got the opportunity. I am sorry for the way your parents treated you. It was disgraceful."

I thought for a moment and then said, "I don't know why I expected any different. I guess I thought that maybe since I was bringing them the chance to live they would be grateful. I must be a slow learner," I admitted ruefully.

"Seriously January? That was your mother. Every child wants one thing and only one thing from their mother and that is love and respect. Well, I should have said two things. In any event, you received neither. It will always be something you hope for."

"No...not any more Rykerian. I think it took this one last time to make me see something. She is not worthy of me or my love. There... I've finally said it and I mean it this time."

He looked into my eyes and I could feel him poking in my mind.

"Hey, you don't believe me, do you?" I asked.

He gave me an utterly disarming smile and said, "I do now!"

I shook my head. "Yeah, but you had to poke my mind first?"

"Okay," he admitted remorsefully, "Yes, I did have to see for myself, but only because I would imagine it would be an exceedingly difficult thing to accept. I do believe you. Trust me when I say this: they are not worth your time January."

"It totally killed me when Tommy and Sarah were afraid of me. I thought I would die."

"I know," he whispered as he nuzzled my ear. "It nearly destroyed me to see you so upset."

We sat together, tangled up in each other, for a long time. I felt myself drifting when a question popped into my head.

"Did Julian say how long I would remain this way? You know, weak from the smallpox?"

"He thinks you will improve every day, providing you eat well and rest. No more excitement for a while."

We heard a slight tap on the door and Maddie stuck her head inside. Her eyes lit up when she saw I was awake.

"How are you feeling?"

"Tired and hungry!"

At my words, Rykerian was off the bed so fast, it made my head spin.

"I will return shortly," he said as he dashed out of the room.

I crinkled my forehead and Maddie shrugged.

"So did he tell you what happened?"

Maddie nodded. "I never knew how it was for you January. I'm so sorry."

"Forget it. I never talked about it because it was so awkward and embarrassing. Who wants to tell their friends about parents like mine? I mean Carlson would blather on about how her parents bought her this and that, and there I was struggling to find the money to buy a stupid hot dog for dinner. And it wasn't Carlson's fault. She didn't have a mean bone in her body. She was just totally clueless. She'd get these calls and texts from her mom telling her how much she missed and adored her and couldn't wait to see her. And there I'd sit, thinking about how I got ousted out of my house the night of my high school graduation." I had gotten on a roll and didn't realize all I said until I looked at Maddie and saw her stricken face.

"I thought you...you didn't know all of this, did you?"

She shook her head and I could see her working her throat, trying to hold back her tears.

"Hey, Maddie, I thought Rykerian told you everything. I guess I shouldn't have run my mouth."

Before I knew what was happening, I found myself wrapped in her arms.

"January, I am so sorry. I never knew. I wish I had, I really do. I could have been there for you somehow."

I could feel her trembling with her tears.

"Maddie, it's water under the bridge now. I didn't want anyone to know, so that part is all my fault. Don't be upset about it now. Please?"

"I'm sorry. I just can't imagine how hard it must have been. And then I just added to it all with my disappearance." Her voice was edged with emotion.

I leaned away from her and said, "Look, none of this was your fault. You couldn't help what happened to you, but the thing with my parents was out of anyone's control. So don't waste your tears on it. In fact, I've decided after the other day that they just aren't worth my time at all. They have tried everything to destroy me, but I won't give them that satisfaction anymore. I guess it took me seeing how they had turned my little brother and sister against me to understand that they are evil people."

The bedroom door burst open to Rykerian carrying a massive tray filled with all sorts of food.

"Anyone hungry?" he asked. Then he noticed our faces and thundered, "What has happened?" He set the tray down and rushed to my side. "Are you okay? Have you become ill again?"

The whole situation hit me as funny and my slight chuckle quickly turned into a roaring laugh. Maddie began laughing as well and Rykerian looked at us like we were both insane.

"Females! Who can figure them out?" he asked, scratching his head.

The bubbles of laughter tapered off and I explained what had occurred, but he couldn't find the humor in it.

Instead of belaboring the point, I said, "I am starving and would love some food."

He was only too happy to comply. When I was finished eating, I said, "I have one request." They both looked at me in question. "I would love a bath!"

Rykerian glanced at Maddie and gruffly said, "Leave us please."

"I hardly think that..."

"Maddie, I care not what you think. I can remember a time when you..."

"Okay! Okay, I'm outta here!" Maddie said as she darted out of the room.

"What was that all about?"

"Nothing that should excessively concern you January. I will go and run you a bath."

He left the room leaving me perplexed over his exchange with Maddie. For whatever reason, my apprehension began mounting over this bath thing. Did he think he was going to bathe me? If so, he had a big surprise waiting for him! It was one thing to be in the heat of the moment, hormones raging, and passion burning through our veins. At that point I probably would have run straight through the streets of Atlanta, buck-naked. But this? Now? That was another story. There was no way on God's green Earth I was going to strip down, naked as a jaybird in front of this Greek god! Uh huh...absolutely no way.

When Rykerian returned, I was finishing up the last of my tea.

"Are you ready?" he asked.

I twisted the coverlet in my hands and licked my suddenly bone-dry lips. I knew his intentions would always be above board but yet I had this gnawing feeling of awkward embarrassment in my belly.

I looked up at him and he recognized it instantly for what it was. I wondered at this uncanny ability of his. He was at my side in a blur of motion, something I speculated if I'd ever get accustomed to.

"What is it? What has distressed you so?"

"I...er, I don't know." I lied. I knew exactly what had distressed me.

"January, it is not necessary to hide your feelings from me. I can discern them on my own but I do not want to do that. I want to hear it from your lips."

I dropped my gaze to my knotted my fingers, unsure of this shyness that had descended on me.

He took my chin in hand and lifted it so he could look into my eyes. "Tell me please," he softly implored.

"For some reason I feel incredibly self-conscious and awkward right now," I admitted.

"Is it the bath that has made you so?"

I nodded.

"I do not intend to do anything other than escort you to the bathroom and show you where everything is located. I will remain outside the door and you only have to think my name if you need me."

"Okay," I whispered, relief etching my voice. *Phew, my inner brain screamed. I feel like a ton of bricks has just been lifted off my chest.*

He leaned in and planted a feathery kiss on my lips and helped me to my feet.

"You did not think my intentions were to join you, did you?" His eyes were filled with mirth.

"Well, yes I was sort of thinking along those lines." I'm sure my cheeks were flame red. They felt like they were on fire.

Laughing, he said, "Not that it hasn't crossed my mind, among other things, but have no fear on that account."

"Okay...honestly, that's a relief. I was a bit worried about that I guess. I don't feel lightheaded anymore. It must have been the hunger or something," I mumbled, taking a stab at changing the subject.

"Maybe so."

We walked into the sumptuous bathroom and I felt like I was at an elite spa...the kind you read about in magazines. The jetted tub looked large enough for four and the vanity, located in a separate room, had two sinks and went on forever. There was all sorts of storage space, a huge linen closet filled with stacks of white fluffy towels and shelves and drawers everywhere.

What in the world does he have stowed in here?

I heard him chuckle so I turned my eyes to him and crinkled up my brow.

"Many of them are empty, but feel free to look around and inspect their contents," he snorted. "I know, it seems a bit ostentatious, doesn't it?"

"It's quite beautiful Rykerian. I've never been in a bathroom like this. Very luxurious." I ran my fingers along the smooth marble vanity, feeling its coolness against my skin.

"Please make yourself at home. I thought you would prefer a bubble bath, but there is a shower in here as well," he explained as he indicated the shower with his arm.

My curiosity got the best of me so I went to examine the shower. It was an amazing thing. There were water nozzles everywhere...on three walls and the ceiling. It looked like an upright Jacuzzi tub.

"I can show you how to operate it if you'd like," he offered.

"Maybe some other time. Right now, I just want to sink into that water over there." It looked totally tempting.

"As you wish. I shall be right outside in the event you should need something. Just think my name and I shall be right here. And January? Take all the time you want. I want you to enjoy this. If you press this button over here," he said pointing to a chrome button on the tub, "it will turn on the jets. Enjoy!" Then he was gone, leaving me to savor this chance and to spoil myself.

Chapter Four

I emerged from the bathroom feeling like a new person. I felt clean and refreshed and energized. I was wrapped in a humongous fluffy black terry robe that dragged on the floor.

When he heard to the door open, Rykerian turned to look at me and a huge grin spread across his face.

"I can see that we will need to get you your own bath robe. That one is a might too large!" He chuckled.

I joined him in his mirth and added, "Yeah, I didn't know what I was going to put on until I found this. It's so soft though! I love the feel of it," and as I lowered my eyes, I whispered, "and it smells so good. It smells exactly like you."

His eyes widened and he pulled me to him and took possession of my lips. At first he was gentle as his lips grazed mine but then I felt a current of electricity rip through me and his kiss became demanding and possessive. He lifted me until our heads were level and continued to pour his passion into me. I wrapped my arms and legs around him and let my fingers slide through his hair. I felt his tongue seek entrance and it danced around mine until we were both breathless. When he pulled away, I could feel his harsh breathing on my neck. His thoughts rained down on me letting me know how I took his breath away. It took me a moment before I could speak as I was having a bit of a problem breathing myself. Gawd I loved how he made me feel!

"You take *my* breath away Rykerian. Does kissing feel this way all the time?"

He smiled and shook his head and admitted, "Never like this before you January. You own me. Do you understand what I am telling you?"

"Yes," I murmured. "I do, even though it frightens me."

"Why does it frighten you so?"

"I didn't think I had to ability to feel this way about anyone. It scares the crap out of me that I even trust you. I'm damaged Rykerian. I was never shown love so I guess I'm not sure how I should feel about it."

"Hmmm, I can understand that. Not the way you feel because I was lucky to be born to two wonderful parents. Love was abundant in our home, but I can understand why these feelings frighten you."

I could only nod. That huge lump had returned to my throat.

"January, I promise you I will never hurt you or play you false. I am yours whether you want me or not. If you decide you do not want me, then say the word and I will go. But know this; you will always be mine, no matter what path you choose."

"I don't understand what you mean by that."

"Vesturions are a strange lot, we are. As I've told you before, we mate, or unite for life. When our souls find each other, there is no going back. So what I am telling you is that if you decide to choose a path away from me, our souls will always be joined."

"That's kind of creepy Rykerian. What happens when someone dies?"

"The link is broken and the soul of the deceased enters another plane. It is a difficult thing for the one remaining behind to deal with, but that is the way of things. One other thing—Vesturion males may seem highly possessive of their mates. It is because they hold them in the highest esteem. They have the utmost respect for their mates. I am talking out of turn here, and I should be getting her permission to say this, but you can ask Maddie about this. She had a difficult time adjusting to Rayn's possessiveness at first. We only want to protect our mates and sometimes it comes across as controlling."

"Hmmm. I have no experience with boys so I have nothing to compare any of this to, but I don't think I want someone telling me what to do."

"It is not that at all. We do not tell our mates what to do. In fact, we encourage them to follow the dreams of their hearts with everything.

However, where their safety is concerned, we become quite...brutish," he explained. He turned a delightful shade of pink at this admission.

"You know, you really should blush more often as it's such a lovely shade and goes very nicely with your tanned skin!" I joked.

"Are you toying with me Ms. St. Davis?"

"Maybe!"

With that, he threw me over his shoulder and carried me to the bed where he gently tossed me. Then he grabbed me and started tickling me unmercifully.

I was laughing so hard my sides were cramping. I begged him to stop repeatedly and finally he did saying, "That will teach you to poke fun at me!"

These Vesturions were strange people, but I needed to stop comparing them to humans since I was, in part, one of them. That was a sobering thought and Rykerian recognized immediately that my thoughts had turned serious once more.

"No need to worry about your genetics now January. I think you will find that being Vesturion has its advantages. Once you learn how to use your Power of Telepathy to its fullest, you will quickly discover how lucky you are. We will explore whether you have inherited any other Powers as well. For instance, Maddie's Power of Telekinesis rivals just about anyone's I know."

"Seriously?"

"Uhhum." He was staring at my lips again and I was hit with a sudden flow of thoughts coming from him.

For the love of God! Does he genuinely think that about me?

"I absolutely, one hundred percent think you are the most beautiful creature I have ever had the pleasure of laying my eyes upon."

My heart was tripping over itself. My breath caught in my throat. I ran my tongue across my lips and he grabbed my chin and started kissing me again. His lips trailed across my cheeks, over my eyes and descended to my neck. I found that there simply wasn't enough oxygen in the room.

Okay, we need to stop this before I come apart at the seams.

He pulled away again, sighed deeply and said, "How would you like to walk down to the terrace out back and take in the view for a while?"

"Yes, I'd love that!"

Chapter Five

I n seconds I had taken off the fluffy robe and threw on some clothes and we were heading outside. The day was beautiful. It was late September and the weather was changing. The sky was bright Carolina blue and the sun was warm on my skin. The mountains in the distance rose before us and I ironically thought I had never been happier in my life. It scared me though because the last time I said that was right before things went south at work and I ended up becoming deathly ill. But in the whole scheme of things, if I hadn't contracted smallpox I would never have met Rykerian. Fate has a strange way of showing itself sometimes.

"It was meant to be January. You do realize that don't you?"

"Were my thoughts that loud again?"

He nodded, smiling.

"How can I keep them quieter?"

"There is a shield within you that needs to be activated or turned on, if you will."

"Okay, now I'm totally confused."

"Let me explain. Deep within your mind there is a shield. It is not something you can feel unless you seek it out. You need to recognize its presence and then put it to use. But first you must concentrate."

We made our way to the back terrace and he indicated that I sit.

I took a seat on one of the sofas and he sat next to me.

"Close your eyes," he said. "Now envision a shield like maybe a glass partition or a window. You can see out but it is totally soundproof. Now raise the partition bit by bit. Hold it steady there. Keep your eyes closed. Can you feel that?"

I nodded. "Yeah, it feels like a filter or something."

"Exactly! Now relax, yet keep the partition up."

I sat there with my eyes closed when I began feeling something probing the filter. I felt tentacles moving around, much like a soft tickle. I angled my head, trying to grasp what it was I was feeling when I heard Rykerian chuckling. I opened my eyes to see him grinning and shaking his head.

"What's so funny?"

"Not funny at all. I am amazed at how quick you were able to accomplish that."

"Accomplish what?"

"I've been tele-communing with you...or at least attempting to for the past few minutes with no response from you. You completely tuned me out. I landed on a blank slate. Tell me, what did you feel?"

"Do you mean I was blocking you?" I asked incredulously.

"Oh yes. And very effectively I might add. Could you feel anything?"

"Yeah, I could. It was like more of a soft barrier or something. I felt the brush of something moving on the opposite side, but didn't know what it was."

"January, you were feeling my thoughts...my mind trying to probe yours."

I looked at him as my chin dropped to the ground. "Seriously? Is that what that was?"

He nodded, beaming, "Oh yes. I was very insistent too, yet you allowed me no quarter. That was excellent!"

"Rykerian, how can I do that though without concentrating so hard?"

"Ah, that will come with practice and experience. Once you master the technique it will be much like...how do you say it? Oh yes, it will be much like riding a bike. You will do it like second nature, without thinking about it," he explained.

"Will that take a long time?"

"That depends on several things. First, how strong your ability is. Second, how much you practice. And third, how badly you want it."

"Do you think my ability is very strong?"

"Most definitely. You have been hearing thoughts your whole life. Most telepaths don't develop until they are appropriately trained. That you managed to block me after one attempt is undoubtedly impressive. The other thing that is extremely spectacular is over the years, you have learned to tune the thoughts of others out. Albeit they were human thoughts, and even though humans don't have the ability to probe, you accomplished that without being taught. You are very talented where Telepathy is concerned."

He sat there grinning at me and I felt myself smiling in return.

It was surreal sitting there with Rykerian, looking at the beautiful scenery when people were dying in massive numbers across the globe. I told him as much because I couldn't get the feeling out of me that we should be doing something.

"Yes, but do not forget, the Guardians are currently implementing their tactics. They are getting the vaccine where it will benefit humanity the most and in doing so, will stop the pandemic from worsening. Besides, you need to recover and regain your strength before you can do anything. I do not want you to have any more episodes like you recently had."

I nodded, agreeing with him.

I was looking at him, admiring him beneath my lowered lids, when I heard the first strains of music reach my ears. Rykerian began smiling, and when he did, it felt like the sun shining down on me, with his amazing aura, coupled with his unreal looks. It felt weird describing a boy as beautiful, but that's what he was. I don't think I'd ever seen anyone that could come close to matching him in the looks category.

"Maddie must be at the helm of the sound system," he remarked.

"Why do you say that?"

"Because she loves Adele, and that is what is playing now. January, dance with me."

"Uh, I don't know how to dance," I said as my face flushed with embarrassment. "I never learned."

"Oh, it is easy if you let me lead. Come, I can teach you," he said excitedly. He held out his hand and I had no choice but to take it. He pulled me to my feet and took my left hand and placed in around his neck. He held my right hand in his and encircled me with his left arm, pulling me close against his body.

"Mmmm, you smell so wonderful," he said as he bent to nuzzle my neck.

"So do you," I replied as I laid my forehead against his chest. We swayed to the sounds of Adele as she sang, "One and Only."

He moved with the grace and rhythm as if he had been born to dance. When he bent his head and began whispering words to me, I didn't initially recognize them. I lifted my head and our eyes met and then I realized he was whispering the lyrics of the song.

You've been on my mind I grow fonder every day
Lose myself in time just thinking of your face
God only knows why it's taken me so long to let my doubts go
You're the only one that I want

My eyes widened at the realization of what he was saying as the song came to an end. This man, who looked like a Ralph Lauren model, was telling *me* that he wanted me to be with him always. He, who could have anyone in the universe, wanted *me*. I bit my lip and tasted blood as I struggled with the emotions rolling through me.

We still swayed together as if the music were still playing and a sad smile tugged at his lips.

"Don't be sad," I whispered.

"I am not sad January for the reason you may think. I am sad for the life you have led until now. It grieves me to think of you as a small child with no one to love you. My heart swells when I am near you and I cannot fathom how anyone can be near you and not feel the good that emanates from you. You are a very special person, my dear sweet girl and as long as there is breath in this body of mine, you will never feel as such again! My most fervent desire is for you to 'forget your past and simply be mine.'" His voice was filled with so much emotion I felt my eyes tearing up.

My heart sang when he said those words. I knew deep in my heart I was lost to him then only I wasn't quite ready to admit it.

"I did not intend for my words to make you cry, love."

"Oh Rykerian, they are not sad tears, but happy ones. You've touched my heart with your sweet words." I placed my palm on his cheek and smiled. He placed his hand over mine and turned his face into my palm to place a kiss on it.

Right at that moment, as we stood in each other's arms, Maddie bounded down the stairs of the back entrance.

"Rowan is on his way to give us an update on the status of things. He's asked for you to join us January."

"Me? Why me?" I asked. Maddie shrugged and Rykerian shook his head indicating he didn't know either. He grasped my hand and gave me a gentle tug and we followed Maddie down to the Compound.

Chapter Six

T he Command Center was massive—like an underground city. We went through corridor after corridor and ended up in an area that looked like a loading dock of sorts. It was filled with all sorts of crazy looking things, including what I believed to be space ships. The last time I was down here was such a blur. We were in a hurry to get our plans underway that it wasn't possible to take all this in. Now, I didn't know if I should laugh or scream.

"It is quite a bit to comprehend and yes, you are correct in your assumptions, January."

Rykerian spoke to me through telepathy.

"Depending on their size and function, they are known by several names: Space Transporters, Space Travelers, Star Fighters and Star Freighters. We normally use them for long-term visits or when we need to get large amounts of supplies somewhere. Please do not be afraid."

He looked at me and grasped my shaking, sweaty hand, lacing his fingers with mine. I immediately felt comforted. I gave him a tentative smile in return and I watched his eyes soften as he stared back at me.

"Why do you think they want me down here?"

"That I cannot answer but I think it will be to thank you for helping us. Please do not worry."

I kept thinking how unsuitably dressed I was.

"Do not be concerned about that. It is unimportant."

"I suppose I'm not doing such a great job of blocking my thoughts, am I?"

He winked at me and Maddie turned to me and said, "Isn't this place unreal? I can remember the first time I came down here. I was shocked because I had been living in the house for months and never knew any of this existed!"

We finally came to a room with a set of double doors and we went inside. Seated at the table were Rayn, Rowan, who was an older version of Rayn and Tesslar.

Rowan rose to his feet and hugged Maddie, and next approached me. He was tall, like Rykerian and Rayn, had those unbelievable emerald eyes so like Rayn's and was wearing a full-length white robe belted with a gold rope.

The last time I was down here, I didn't pay as much attention to Rowan, but now I was immediately aware of the man's power and commanding presence. He bowed to me and held out his hand. I rubbed my palm on my pants before placing it in his and smiled.

"Ms. St. Davis, it is nice to see you again. I would like to thank you for assisting us in getting the vaccine transported to the proper locations. We owe you a huge debt of gratitude for what you have done for us in our attempts to curtail this pandemic we are facing on Earth. Consider the Guardians at your service for all time. If there is anything at all that we can do for you, please let me know," he said with a flourish.

"I was glad I could be of help, sir. And please call me January. May I ask you something?"

"By all means," he responded.

"Will I be able to travel to Vesturon?"

"Certainly and anytime you wish, our Space Transporters or teleporters are at the ready. Have you an interest in going to Vesturon?"

"Someday I think I would like to see it," I said.

"Then I hope it will be sooner rather than later," he said as his eyes lit up.

I turned to Rykerian and he had a goofy little grin on his face. When I saw it, I couldn't stop a tiny bubble of laughter from escaping.

"What is so humorous?" he wanted to know.

"Rykerian, you're an open book for all to see," I whispered as I leaned into him. His smile grew even bigger.

As we sat around the conference table, Rowan explained the decision he and the Council of Elders, the governing force of Vesturon, made regarding the Guardians on Xanthus. Apparently the situation had become critical and it had escalated to the point where everyone's safety was at stake.

"We are underway with our evacuations as we speak," he concluded.

Maddie jumped to her feet all but screaming, "Are Therron, Xarrid and Saylan okay?"

Rowan calmed her by saying all was fine and that by the month's end, everyone should be safely back on Vesturon.

"Whew, I've been so worried about them," Maddie exclaimed.

"As are we which is why we made this decision," Rowan concluded.

Rykerian had leaned toward me and explained that Therron and Xarrid were his brothers and that Saylan was a Guardian that gone through the Academy with Maddie and was one of her closest friends.

"Father, what will happen on Xanthus if no one is there to establish a new government?" Rayn asked.

"The rebels have caused such extreme chaos we fear that this will advance to another war," his voice edged with dread.

Rykerian was shaking his head as he further explained to me how the Xanthians had been attempting to raid other planets for fuel resources. They were a species of ruthless abusers for not only did they abuse each other, they had also stripped their own planet of most of its natural resources, leaving Xanthus at the mercy of other planets. But instead of trading fairly, they would invade other planets and cause great annihilation in order to obtain what they wanted.

Maddie looked toward me and said, "January, they are a disgusting bunch of creeps and I wish we could blow them into oblivion!"

I was mortified by her vehemence. "Maddie, I've never heard you spout such hatred before."

"Yeah, well I have good reason. They abducted Rayn and tortured him and I don't take kindly to them for that. But even before that happened, I served as an ambassador to Xanthus. They are nothing but a bunch of lying, cheating scoundrels. Rowan, I told you we needed to get rid of them all!"

By this time Rayn had walked over to Maddie and placed his hand on her shoulder in an attempt to comfort her. They looked at each other, Maddie stood up and Rayn turned to his father and said, "Please excuse us, my lord," and they left the room.

"Neither of them have any use for the Xanthians," Rykerian said. "I am talking out of turn here, but this is a very difficult subject for them."

"I can understand why!"

Rowan shifted in his seat and rubbed the back of his neck.

"We are heading into very difficult times I am afraid. This pestilence on Earth, the gartha situation on Brutyn, and now the rebels on Xanthus just to name a few. I fear our safety during space travel. I have ordered all travel, other than teleporting, to be closely scrutinized," he concluded. Rowan's brow was furrowed and his eyes had darkened with worry.

He turned to Rykerian saying, "I am pulling everyone out of here other than you, Kennar and the rest of your team. I need Maddie and Rayn, as well as Tesslar back on Vesturon. You are to remain in charge here. Keep close tabs on the pandemic and I expect daily reports on the progress. Watch for any shifts. The vaccine is in the proper hands and we must leave it to the humans to take care of the rest...restoring order and so forth. Step in where and when you need to, but only if necessary."

Rowan rose to his feet, looking worn and weary, and we all followed. "Be safe my son and take care of January." He smiled before continuing, "But I do not think I need to tell you that do I?"

"No, my liege, you do not," Rykerian answered with a smile. "Please give Mother my love."

"I always do, my son." They embraced and Rykerian led me out of the room and back up to the house.

Chapter Seven

I needed to speak to Maddie before she left. I excused myself from Rykerian telling him I wanted to find her. I searched everywhere except her bedroom. I didn't dare go up there for I had a feeling she was locked inside with Rayn.

My feet carried me to the large den and I plopped down on one of the many cushy sofas that dotted the room. I couldn't help but think how incredible this house was. It was comfortable yet elegant but had that mountain feel at the same time. The vaulted ceiling in the den was made of gigantic timbers and the massive rock fireplace only emphasized the height of the ceiling even more.

I was sitting there, lost in my thoughts when Rayn flew down the stairs with Maddie on his heels.

"You can't go alone Rayn. Please listen to me!" she begged.

"It is just a routine mission Maddie. I am only staying here—no intergalactic travel. I must check out that rogue space traveler they've tagged."

"But that's what you did last time and they captured you! Please... I'm begging you. Don't go out there alone," she urged in a tearful voice.

Maddie was visibly upset, wringing her hands and her voice was constricted with fear. I sucked in my breath when I saw her face and they must have heard me as they both looked my way.

"I'm sorry. I didn't mean to eavesdrop, but I couldn't help it."

"January, where is Rykerian?" Maddie wanted to know.

"I don't know but he is around somewhere."

As soon as I was on my feet, Rykerian was walking across the room.

"Rykerian, please talk some sense into Rayn. He wants to go out alone to investigate a rogue star traveler and I want him to take someone." Maddie was trembling and still wringing her hands.

After a brief discussion, Rykerian agreed with Maddie so he gave the order that Kennar would accompany Rayn.

When they left, Maddie ran to Rykerian to hug and thank him. "I couldn't bear for anything to happen to him again. I owe you Rykerian."

"No Maddie. I couldn't agree with you more. He should know better than to charge off without discussing this with anyone."

After Maddie left, I wondered why Rayn would even think of doing anything like that.

"Because he is Rayn and that is what he does. He doesn't want anyone else to take unnecessary risks yet he thinks nothing of putting himself in harm's way," Rykerian answered.

"How long will he be gone?"

"Maybe a couple of hours or so."

I had a million questions about how everything worked and Rykerian started to fill me in little by little. The biggest question I had was how they could go into space undetected by radar. He explained that they used a system that shielded them, making them invisible to radar or other detection devices.

"We have the capability of putting up a veil or a power shield of sorts. It is an invisible form of protection that rearranges the radio waves and other detecting devices and deflects them, making it seem like nothing is there. It is somewhat like your Stealth technology here, only better. A lot better," he said smiling.

It made me wonder about all the cool things that Vesturon had. Would I ever travel there? And what would that be like?

"As soon as it is safe to do so, I will take you there myself in a Star Transporter. I think you would enjoy the ride. We also have the option of teleporting there if you'd like. You could even go with Maddie and Rayn later today," he suggested.

"Oh no... I don't think I'm ready to go just yet. But I do want to someday."

Out of the corner of my eye, I saw Maddie heading toward the back of the house. I needed to speak with her...I needed to confide in someone about my confused feelings concerning Rykerian, I mused. Again, I had forgotten about his ability to hear my thoughts.

"I urge you to speak with her January if it will make you feel better."

I felt my face flaming and I was stricken with a severe case of shyness. I would have to practice shielding my thoughts, as it was a huge embarrassment for me when he heard my deepest darkest secrets.

He was at my side before I could blink. He tilted my head back and our eyes locked.

"Please don't ever be embarrassed about your thoughts of me, no matter what they are," he whispered. "There is nothing to be ashamed of or embarrassed about."

I could only shake my head in response before he claimed my lips for the briefest of kisses. Then he said, "Go and speak with Maddie. I believe you need each other right now."

Rykerian had such a tenderness about him and he always seemed to say the right thing. I made my way to the back terrace in search of Maddie. She was sitting in my favorite spot looking up at the sky. "I pray for his safe return," she said as she heard my approach.

"I know you are going crazy right now."

"Oh January, if you could have seen him when I pulled him out of the Xanthian prison, you would have a better understanding. It was a horrible time for us. I had done some incredibly stupid things, like going to the Academy for Guardians behind his back. I was afraid to tell him for fear he would pitch a fit. Then I had a run-in with another student there who was insanely jealous of me and intent on getting rid of me. She abducted me and left me for dead. It's a long story, but if it hadn't been for Saylan, and then Xarrid who found me, I wouldn't be here right now. When Rayn found out about that, he totally flipped out. We didn't speak for a long, long time. It was his capture by the Xanthians that brought us back together. He went to investigate a rogue Star Fighter and it was a trap. They took him to Xanthus and it was weeks before anyone told me. I was serving as an ambassador at the time and was stationed in the farthest sector of the universe. Anyway, it was an awful time and I just worry to death about him in times like these," she concluded.

"Well, it's not like you don't have good reason to."

"So tell me...you and Rykerian, huh?" she said with a conspiratorial smile.

I could feel my cheeks flushing. Why did this always happen to me, I pondered?

"Yeah, and I'd kind of like to talk to you about that," I mumbled.

"Sure thing, but let me say this first. Rykerian is top-notch January. He is also the most sensitive guy I've ever been around. I mean, he is so tenderhearted, I sometimes feel sorry for him."

"What do you mean?"

"Well, you can see how easily he blushes. Sometimes he's so quiet and introspective. He's told me he feels like people are constantly judging him. I also think he gets tired of all the girls that try to smother him. It's obvious why, but he honestly hates all that attention. When I first came here, he was so shy...painfully so. I thought he didn't like me. But he's extremely loyal and would never do anything dishonorable. He is true January. And so attractive, don't you think?"

"You're kidding, right? Attractive is an understatement. I mean look at him! That hair, those eyes, that smile, and that body...gah! He couldn't be more perfect. But I don't know...I'm really scared by all of this. It's happened so fast. And I have zero experience with boys. Maddie, I've never even been on a stupid date! I'm a total dork."

"January, I was exactly the same way. I guess I had dated a few boys, but nothing major. Then this unbelievable guy comes barreling into my life, sweeping me off my feet and nothing's been the same since. But I wouldn't change it for anything. If you only knew..." she said as a far-away look came into her eyes.

I was trying to process everything she was telling me. It seemed we were on the same track but at different times.

"Listen to me January. I'm not ever going to tell you what to do because I'm a firm believer that you have to make up your own mind about this type of thing. But Rykerian is good...I mean oh-my-gosh good. He will never do anything to hurt you and your safety and *your* happiness will always come first for him—before *anything* else. Vesturions are weird when it comes to relationships, trust me. They're totally different than humans. Humans take everything lightly. Not Vesturions. They bond with each other. Their souls unite, as well as

158

their hearts and minds. Once they're in love, there is no falling out of it. It is a lifelong thing for them. But it's a good thing. They cherish their mates and respect them. Rayn says it best...he says they hold their mates in the highest esteem and with the greatest of reverence. It's totally *epic* January. I'm not trying to sway you in any way, but I know exactly the kind of turmoil you are facing. I would gladly walk through the fires of hell for my mate and wouldn't trade my life with him for *anything in the universe.*"

I tried to digest what she was telling me but I was still having difficulty believing in myself, much less that someone like Rykerian had a serious interest in me.

"I just don't feel like I deserve him Maddie. I mean I'm such a failure. Everything in my life has been such a tortuous mess. And look at me! I'm a gangling, gawky, strange looking thing," I insisted, my hands gesticulating in front of me.

Maddie grabbed one of my hands and gave it a squeeze. "Look January, first of all you're not a strange looking thing. You're beautiful, but you don't see that. Most nineteen year olds are uncomfortable with their appearance. I know I was and so was Cat. The only one I've ever known that wasn't was Carlson and that's because her mother told her a million times a day how wonderfully perfect she was. I can tell you this too: Rykerian doesn't see you the same way you do. I know this by the way he looks at you. He smiles constantly when you're around too. And you're most certainly not a failure!" she insisted.

"I have to disagree with you on that one. I almost flunked out of school Maddie. I lost my scholarship. I had to change my major because there was no way I would ever have gotten into medical school with my grades," I confessed.

"Let me ask you something. How many hours a week were you working when all this started happening? Thirty or forty?"

I nodded saying, "Yeah, something like that."

"And how many hours were you carrying? Fifteen or eighteen?"

"Yeah, I took eighteen the last two semesters."

"So you were working two jobs at about forty hours per week and taking eighteen hours and you say you failed because you lost your scholarship?"

I nodded again.

She snorted and said, "You're nuts January. No one can burn the candle at both ends like you did and come out unscathed. Not to mention what you were dealing with as far as your family was concerned. I'm surprised you were able to retain any semblance of sanity!"

Maddie sprang to her feet and stated pacing. She came to a stop in front of me and grabbed my hands, pulling me to my feet. Then she dragged me to the edge of the terrace and pointed to the mountains in the distance.

"Tell me January, what do you see out there?"

"The mountains...well, one in particular."

"Yeah, and you know what? How do you climb a mountain like that?"

I looked at her and shrugged. I puzzled over where she was headed with this.

"The way you climb a mountain is one step at a time. But you weren't able to do that and do you know why? Because someone kept pushing you back down. Every time you made some headway, someone was in front of you forcing you back to the bottom. It was either your parents, your job, your classes, your finances...but there was always something or someone pushing you backwards."

I thought about what she was saying to me for a second. "But Maddie, I don't think I'm capable of making it to the top. I did at one time. I really thought starting all over at Western would be my big chance, but I failed at it too."

"That's the biggest wad of malarkey I've ever heard! You're brilliant January. You graduated from high school when you were sixteen years old. You were the class valedictorian, you made a perfect score on your SAT's and you made straight A's all the way through school. You're the only one I know who scored a perfect five on all her AP courses too. I would even go so far to bet that if your circumstances had been different, you would have made straight A's at Western. If things had been different I know your grades would have been perfect. But think about this. If your grades had been perfect, would you have done that internship in Atlanta?" I wondered where she was going with this.

"I really can't say. But in all probability, no."

A huge smile spread across her face and she said as she put her arm around me and squeezed, "Then you wouldn't be standing here with me right now. You wouldn't have contracted smallpox when you did and in all likelihood, you wouldn't have met Rykerian. And do you know what else?"

I nodded. I seemed to be doing more than my share of that in this conversation.

"You would never have discovered your Vesturion background. If you only knew...only realized what that means. January, once you get to Vesturon, you are going to be so amazing!"

"What do you mean by that?"

"Well, first off, Vesturon is magnificent. There's not an adequate word that can fairly describe it, but it's perfection. If you combine all the beautiful places here on Earth, they still can't compare. I don't know what Rykerian has told you but some people refer to it as the true Eden. I can't tell you how much I love it there."

"He never mentioned any of this. So it's like a paradise of sorts?"

"Not 'like' but is. It's unreal. I can't wait for you to go there. You'll love it." Maddie's face was literally glowing as she spoke. "But that's not even the best part. You know how Vesturions have special abilities? When you get there and stay for a while, yours will develop to their fullest potential. It has something to do with being where you belong. At least that's my opinion." At my puzzled look, she continued, "Remember how clumsy I used to be? Julian, the healer, thinks it had to do with my human side warring with my Vesturion side. Once I hit Vesturon, it started diminishing and then it disappeared altogether. I love my new self and my new abilities. I promise you're going to love yours too."

I began to walk around the terrace, thinking about everything she was telling me. I'll admit I was beginning to feel the first stirrings of excitement.

"You have so much to look forward to January. I know it's difficult to take in, but I'm telling it to you straight here. And then there's your Rykerian," she said grinning.

"He's not mine Maddie," I corrected.

Her eyebrows nearly shot off her head and she began shaking her head and said, "Oh yes he is...one hundred percent yours. You just haven't figured that out yet. He *has* and I can tell you he's done a one hundred eighty degree turn."

"How can you say that?"

"Because I've been there and done that. As I said before, the way he looks at you, you'd have to be blind not to know how he feels about you. Before you came here, he was brooding all the time. Not sad, but certainly not happy. He was always so serious too. I told you already how much he smiles now. I think he's smiled more in the last week than in the whole time I've known him. Seriously...I'm not even kidding here. Let me ask you one thing. What does Rykerian tell you?"

"He thinks I'm the most beautiful thing he's ever seen," I said in the quietest of whispers.

Maddie grabbed my hands again and smiled. "And there you have your answer, my friend."

"I still don't know about all that."

"Oh I do. And you will too one day. In fact, if you don't ask me to be your matron of honor, I'll just have to kill you," she said laughing.

I rolled my eyes at her and said, "I think you're jumping the gun a bit."

"We'll see," she said winking. "One other thing. On Earth we have this thing about time in relationships. Like we need to know someone for months or even years before we might feel comfortable enough to want to get involved with them, right?"

I nodded.

"Well, throw everything you've always heard out the window and unlearn what you know. It's totally different with Vesturions."

"Why is that?"

"Well, first off, they cannot lie. So when Rykerian tells you something, believe it. If he says he loves you, he does. If he tells you that your souls have connected, they have. Vesturions share this bond that is an incredible force that binds you together. It doesn't exist between humans. On Earth, you can spend ten years with someone and you wouldn't have what you and Rykerian already have between the two of you in the brief time you've known each other. So, if it feels right, go with it and don't worry about the time thing."

"Is that why I feel this? I don't exactly know what to call it. Maybe a current or something...that flows between us?"

"Yes! You can tell if he's in the room or not! You can FEEL his presence before you can even SEE him. I swear to you January, go with your feelings here. You won't regret it. I promise!"

I did feel better about things. I wanted to get to know Rykerian better. I wanted to learn as much about him as I could.

"Who helped you once you got to Vesturon? Was it Rykerian's family?"

Maddie nodded and said, "Yes they did some but my grandparents worked closely with me until I had surpassed the point where they could help me."

"Your grandparents are there?" I asked, shocked.

"Yeah, crazy, huh? I'll tell you all about it sometime. I hate to break this conversation off but I want to see if there's been any word from Rayn." She started walking back toward the house.

"Hey Maddie!" I called. She looked back and I said, "Thanks for listening and for all the advice. I really do appreciate it."

She grinned and nodded and headed to the house.

Chapter Eight

Maddie had certainly given me a ton to think about. Rykerian for one. I knew his feelings were over the top for me. I also knew I felt something for him I had never felt before. I just wish I had more experience in this arena. I was such a loser in the boy department so I had nothing on which to base my feelings. It was so frustrating because I wanted to run to him screaming out how giddy he made me feel. I was also frightened out of my wits. If something happened and he decided he didn't want me after all, I'm not sure my fragile psyche could handle that.

For the first time in my life, I was feeling like I belonged somewhere. I never felt this way growing up—even in my own home I had always felt like an outsider. I didn't here, which struck me as extremely strange. So did this mean something? Did this mean I belonged here with Rykerian? Or was it just because I was half Vesturion?

Maybe I was over thinking all of this. Maybe I needed to take it all in stride and not be overly concerned about everything. As I glanced over at the stunning mountains in the distance, their magnificence took my breath away. Maddie's words came back to me when she said I needed to climb the mountain one step at a time. Perhaps that's where my focus should be...taking it one day at a time and one step at a time. Perhaps I needed to stop looking at the whole picture and start focusing on each of the components, bit by bit.

As I sat there, lost in my thoughts and feeling myself relax for the first time in ages, I felt his presence. Glancing over my shoulder, I saw him staring at me intensely. His magnetism beckoned to me and I felt myself rise. My feet carried me to his side and I was barely conscious of what I was doing, so lost in his eyes I was.

Speech became impossibility. My desire to stand there and stare at him forever was overwhelming. His lips parted and a slow, inviting smile lit up his face. There was only one thing I wanted at this moment.

He took one step forward, placed his hands on my waist and continued staring into my eyes. My breath left my body in a whoosh and I suddenly felt lightheaded. He moved his right hand from my waist to my cheek, and his thumb began tracing the outline of my mouth. He mesmerized me as his thumb continued to brush against my lips. I wanted him to put his lips there instead.

As soon as that thought popped into my head, he cocked his head slightly and bent toward me, murmuring against my mouth. "Is this what you want?"

"Oh yes," I whispered against his lips. At first the kiss was soft and his lips lightly danced across mine. Then that familiar electric current raced through my body and his lips turned demanding, as they took possession of mine. He moaned into my mouth and then quickly pulled away, his breath rasping.

"I am sorry January. I...I should not be doing that. It is becoming exceedingly difficult for me to control myself around you," he admitted ruefully.

"Did you...did you feel that too?" I asked softly, hesitantly.

"Oh yes. It is very powerful!"

"What is that? I've felt it before when we kissed, like a strong current of energy."

He laughed under his breath and said, "I believe it is our souls meeting and uniting. I am told that is how it feels...like a surge of energy coursing through the veins."

A piece of the puzzle had fallen into place. There was some unimaginable force binding us together...more than his feelings for me and mine for him. I saw him nod in agreement.

"It is the way for Vesturions. Remember when I explained that our souls find each other before our hearts do? That is part of the bonding for us. January, it is undeniable. Try as one might, it is impossible to ignore. I understand your hesitancy, but it is my hope that you will realize and accept it sooner rather than later," he finished as the corners of his mouth turned up.

"Well, it's impossible to ignore, I'll say that." I smiled back at him.

"Tell me about your talk with Maddie."

I fidgeted a bit because this was a girl thing and I wasn't sure of how much to share.

Luckily, he came to the rescue. "If it is something you do not wish to share, I understand."

"It's sort of a personal thing but it was all really good. I feel so much better about things...about, er, about us."

His aura brightened immediately at my words. It took me by surprise. My eyes widened as I stared at him. He was literally glowing and looking quite like an angel standing before me, though that was nothing compared to when he added his smile. I thought then that if it had been dark outside, he would have lit up the entire terrace. Would I ever get used to his astounding beauty, I mused?

"Whoa!" I exclaimed.

I watched a flush spread across his face as he lowered his eyes.

"Okay, now it's my turn to say something. Please don't be embarrassed Rykerian. And please look at me. You know how I adore your eyes. I've already told you how I love to see you blush. Add to that your aura and...well, I'm not sure there are words that can describe it. You are...er, quite attractive," I said boldly. And that was even an understatement.

His smile grew even more with my words and then he said, "As are you January."

We were still standing facing each other, lost in the moment when we heard Maddie calling to us.

"Hey you two! I hate to interrupt you but Rayn and Kennar should be teleporting here in a moment and they are bringing in a prisoner."

"What?" Rykerian shouted in surprise.

"Yes, you heard me correctly. He said they came upon the Space Traveler and they locked onto it and are conveying it to the dock in the Compound. The three of them should be here in a moment," she explained.

My eyes darted between them as Rykerian said, "Let's go to the front and meet them. I wonder who they have captured."

"I'm not sure. He didn't elaborate. I was just happy to hear he was okay," Maddie replied.

As we began walking towards the house, three melon-sized shapes of light flew toward us.

"Here they come," Maddie said with excitement.

The three balls hovered for a second then elongated and morphed into the shapes of three men. I had never witnessed this process before so I was quite fascinated.

"Wow! No wonder you feel all goofy in the head when you do this," I commented.

Rykerian chuckled at my statement.

Maddie flew to Rayn and hugged him. I turned to look at the men and suddenly felt my head spinning. The breath flew out of me and before I knew what was happening, I screamed, "You! It's you! You're the one I saw at the CDC!"

I spun around to Rykerian, yelling and pointing, "It's him! He's the one that stole the virus!"

The same man I had passed in the corridor that day was standing before me. He was dressed as I remembered but he was alone.

I shouted to him, "Where are your buddies? The ones who were with you?"

Before anyone could move, Rykerian asked, "You know this male?"

"He's the one I told you about!" I exclaimed.

Then the prisoner surprised us all by saying, "I knew you weren't human. Why did you deny it?" his tone demanding and accusing.

I stood there, my mouth agape.

"Do NOT speak to her as such unless you are given permission!" Rykerian shouted.

"Oh please," the stranger said with derision.

"Silence!" Rayn demanded.

"I didn't know I wasn't totally human at the time. That's why I said I was," I shouted back to the strange man.

Rykerian turned to me and said, "There is no need to explain anything to him. He is our prisoner."

"I am *NO ONE'S* prisoner!" he said disdainfully.

"No?" Rayn asked.

"No! Especially not yours!" the stranger insisted.

"Who *are* you?" Maddie wanted to know.

"I am Jurek Herdekian."

"Why are you here?" Maddie continued to question him.

"Because this *Guardian*," Jurek jerked his head toward Rayn as he spoke, "brought me here!"

"You've got to be kidding me!" Maddie said to herself. Then she continued, "That's not what I meant and you know it!"

"Answer my female!" Rayn demanded.

"Oh, so now you want answers. Make up your mind Guardian. I attempted to supply you with some but you would not listen earlier."

"Do not speak to him thusly!" Rykerian shouted.

This was turning into a "he said, she said" and I was quickly getting frustrated. I stepped closer to this Jurek person and spread out my arms yelling, "Stop! Will everyone stop? If this bickering continues, we'll never learn anything!"

Maddie stepped next to me and said, "January's right. Let's do this one by one. I'll go first."

I glanced up at Rayn and saw him roll his eyes. I couldn't stop my giggle from escaping. That caught everyone's attention.

"Sorry, but this whole thing is becoming sort of funny now," I said.

Everyone, including Rykerian gave me an exasperated look.

Maddie began speaking once more.

"Let's start at the beginning. Why were you in your Space Traveler near Earth?"

"It is a long story, one that I attempted to explain earlier but the Guardian wouldn't listen."

"He's listening now," Maddie said. "Go on."

"I was hired by the Xanthians to steal the virus samples and infect Earth with smallpox. I believe the Xanthians want to claim Earth as their own. They're a disgusting species," he spat out.

"You'll certainly get no argument from me there," Maddie said, "but if you hate them so much, then why are you assisting them?"

"Good question," I said. Everyone looked at me again and I saw some eye rolling. "What?" They all shook their heads and looked back at the stranger, Jurek.

I guess that was my cue to keep my mouth shut. So I stood there and listened to them all.

Jurek Herkekian answered, "That is a long story."

Rayn jumped in and said, "We have all the time in the world prisoner!"

"I am no prisoner. I *allowed* you to capture me. I have been trying to get your attention for days and it took this long for you to even notice me. You Guardians think you are so smart and savvy," he finished with a snort.

"What do you mean by that?"

He gave us an exasperating look and as we stared at him, the energy bands that bound his wrists together vanished into thin air. That even surprised the Guardians.

As the stranger Jurek stood before us he began to move toward Maddie.

Suddenly, Rayn extended his arm and shouted, "I Command you to stop!"

I had seen Rykerian use this technique on my stepfather and it literally paralyzed him. I looked at Jurek and he just stood there, unaffected.

"Your Power of Command is useless on me Guardian as are all your other Powers," he stated nonchalantly.

Everyone was speechless. Rykerian's mouth hung open, Maddie's eyes were like saucers and Rayn's jaw was clenched.

"How can this be?" I finally asked. "I didn't think anyone was immune to these Powers." I had intended this question to be answered by Rykerian, but Jurek started speaking first.

"The arrogant Vesturions think they are omniscient and omnipotent. They and their Guardians think they control the universe, though there is so much they do not know. Take me for instance. They have no knowledge of the existence of my species. Yet, they go around and try to rule everyone and every planet with their outdated Council of Elders. They would be wise to go back to their ancient ways when they were seeking out new worlds and new forms of life."

"What *are* you?" Maddie asked.

"I am a mercenary by trade. My work goes to the highest bidder," he said with a deprecating smile as he bowed at the waist.

"So you were paid by the Xanthians to release the virus that would destroy humanity?" I shouted.

"Not exactly."

"Well?"

"The reason I wanted you to find me was because I recognize the errors I made with them. I should have driven a harder bargain with the Xanthians, but it is too late for that."

"I'm confused. You're here because you regret not making a more substantial 'bargain' as you called it?" I asked.

"No. I am here because, believe it or not, I *do* regret releasing the virus upon the humans. However, I had no choice in my actions."

"No choice? Would you care to explain yourself?" Maddie asked.

Jurek Herdekian looked directly at Rayn before he answered.

"It is a long and complicated story, but the short version is I had no choice but to comply with their demands. They hold my father and sister captive and have threatened to end their lives if I did not do as they said."

We all looked at each other. I wasn't sure if I believed what he said and as my eyes held Rykerian's, I was positive he didn't either.

Maddie broke the silence by saying, "So what do you expect from us?"

"I came to see if you could find a way to get my father and sister out of their prison. I know you succeeded in getting your mate released a few months ago. You have knowledge of how their security system works. As primitive as the Xanthians are, they have a highly sophisticated method of securing their prisoners."

"I am quite aware of that," Maddie said, her tone clipped. She glanced at Rayn and I knew they were speaking through their thoughts.

"You can speak out loud. I have access to all your thoughts. Your blocking methods are useless where I am concerned."

"How are you able to circumvent our powers?" Rayn ground out between clenched teeth.

Maddie placed her hand on his arm, intending to calm him. He looked at her and his eyes softened, but when he turned back to Jurek Herdekian, they again turned stormy.

"I asked you a question," Rayn barked.

"My species is capable of things you cannot even begin to comprehend."

"If your species is so powerful, then why don't you rescue your father and sister yourself?" Rayn ground out. It was apparent he was having great difficulty controlling his temper.

"Yes! That's a good question," Maddie added.

"I cannot because as you are well aware, and as I stated earlier, the Xanthians employ a very sophisticated method of security. I know how sophisticated it is because I designed the damned thing myself. Now do you understand?" Jurek asked.

Maddie looked at Rayn first and then at Rykerian.

"He's correct about the complexities of their force shield. Remember Rykerian when we were devising our plan to get Rayn out?" she asked.

Rykerian nodded and said, "Yes. Our ship's teleporters were useless as were our shadars. Their systems can detect any weight changes and motion. Even if the prisoner jumps and leaves the ground for the briefest of moments, the cell implodes."

"That is correct. However, what you do not know is that it also can detect various life forms. For example, if you wanted to substitute one prisoner for another, the two of them would have to have identical DNA. And then there is heartbeat modulation, body temperature, composition and brain waves. As I said, I designed the bloody thing so I know it's impenetrable. The only way in and out is to shut the system down," Jurek said.

"Why should we help you? You have done nothing but wreak havoc here on Earth," Rayn said bitterly.

"I am aware of that and I have regrets over it, but you misunderstand why I am here."

We all looked at him in confusion.

"We thought you came to ask for our help," Rayn's voice still taut with anger.

"I do apologize for the misunderstanding. I am not here to ask. You have no choice in this matter," Jurek said arrogantly.

We all looked at each other and then Maddie said, "I think you are the one who is mistaken. We *do* have a choice and in my opinion, I think you need to leave."

Jurek's unusual eyes, which were that odd blend of lavender and indigo, suddenly turned black. The flecks of silver that danced in his irises began to glow. One minute he was standing there and the next minute he was gone. I saw Rayn's and Maddie's eyes widen as they looked at me. Then I heard Jurek's voice coming from directly behind me.

"As I said, you have no idea of the things I am capable of...of the powers I have."

I jumped at his words and Rykerian's head whipped around toward Jurek.

"Now, either you devise a plan to free my family, or you will live to regret it."

"And what if we don't believe you about this power you say you possess?" Rayn asked icily.

One minute I was standing on the terrace, the next minute I was on the roof standing next to Jurek. He had his hand around my wrist and I felt like my arm was on fire. I tried to tug it out of his grasp, but he tightened his hold on me.

"Release her!" Rykerian demanded.

"In due time. As you can see, I have no need for a teleporter or a weapon for that matter."

I watched as his eyes turned black again and a single beam of light shot out from one, and made contact with a tree on the other side of the yard. In a millisecond, the tree had vanished, leaving behind a small mound of dust.

"*What are* you?" Maddie inquired.

"In your world, I am known as a shapeshifter, but most shifters take the form of another being. I am an energy shifter. My body transforms into energy not mass. I can harness this energy and use it in any way I see fit. What you just saw was a tiny demonstration of my powers. Now, if you would like for me to continue to destroy things here, I would be happy to comply. Or perhaps I can give you another type of *demonstration*, if you will."

He looked directly at Maddie and she fell to her knees and began screaming. Her hands were on her ears as if she was trying to stop some kind of noise. Rayn was instantly by her side and had his arms around her. Her screams stopped as quickly as they started and she fell to the ground, lying on her side.

"What did you do to her?" I screamed.

"I gave her another example of what I am capable of. Would you care to experience it as well?" he asked.

Rykerian burst forth and started shouting hysterically, "Leave her be. Do not touch her!"

Jurek Herdekian smiled wickedly and said, "Oh, and how do you think to stop me Guardian?"

"Enough!" Rayn bellowed. "We will do as you say. Give us the information and we will find a way to get your family released."

"I thought my little demonstration might persuade you to change your mind!"

I turned and looked at him saying, "I still don't understand. If you have all this power at your fingertips, why can't you use it to get your family out?"

"Because as I told you," his voice etched with irritation, "I designed their damned system and I did it to restrain all life forms, including my own. It also prevents all forms, including my own, from entering."

I looked at him and I don't know if I was stupid or brave when I said this. "So you come here spouting about your special abilities and powers and look at us with great disdain and condescension. Then you admit that even you, the almighty energy shifter, can't get your family out, so you coerce us into doing your dirty work! Have I gotten it right?"

His eyes had turned black again and sparks were literally popping out of them. My remarks must have hit home.

"Are you quite finished?" he ground out.

"You're a disgusting creep!" I shot back.

Jurek ignored that statement and turned to the others and said, "In case you have second thoughts, this annoying female will accompany me as my hostage."

My vision turned hazy and I heard voices in the distance, but I couldn't comprehend the words before everything turned black.

Chapter Nine

W hen I awakened, I was lying on a platform bed. My confusion evaporated as I remembered the recent events on the back terrace. Jurek Herdekian had somehow transported me to this place using his power of energy.

Everything surrounding me was white...furniture, coverlet, walls, floor, etc. The sparse furnishings, which only amounted to a platform bed and small nightstand, were ultra-modern. I sat up to get a better look at things. My head swam a bit, but only momentarily.

The walls were plain and held no pictures or any kinds of decorations. Small glass panels that resembled built in iPads were scattered across one wall. I wondered if they were supposed to be some kind of decoration or if they actually served a purpose. It was all very unusual.

There was a large glass window that looked out into a star sprinkled darkness. Was this outer space? I didn't know for I had never been, but it looked like what I had imagined outer space to be.

Where was the door, I wondered? There didn't appear to be one anywhere. I thought that perhaps this chamber was somehow hermetically sealed. My heart began to thrum as I pondered where I might be. Maybe this was some type of prison and this Jurek Herdekian planned to keep me here until the task of rescuing his family was completed. My eyes jerked around, frenetically searching for some kind of sign of safety. I found none.

I charged over to the wall to investigate the iPad look a-likes. Perhaps they held my answers. I roughly touched them to see if they came to life but nothing happened. I pounded them with the backs of my fists but nothing happened. Even though the bed had been comfortable, the starkness of it all made me feel anything but that.

I ran my hand along the walls wherever I could reach to uncover any hidden areas that may indicate a door or an entrance. No such luck. I dove back down on the platform bed and tried to figure out a plan. I wrung my hands in frustration as I lay there. When I could no longer sit still, I arose and began pacing the small room. There had to be some way out of here and I aimed to figure it out.

I headed toward the giant window to look out at the stars, hoping they would help me think. It was an amazing view. There must have been a million stars winking at me and under any other circumstance, I would have been giddy at the sight of them all. It made me think about how I wished Rykerian was here. He was the one that should be showing me this...not some cruel stranger. The thought saddened me...that this had been stripped from us by some strange being intent on forcing the Guardians into a rescue they wanted no part of.

I closed my eyes, leaned in and fisted my hands against the window, more in anger than anything else. That's when I heard the voice.

"Is there something I can help you with?" a tinkling voice said.

I lifted my head and found myself staring at an unusual looking girl. She seemed quite young and had large, almond shaped eyes that resembled Jurek's. They were that unusual mix of violet tinged with indigo and I saw the same flecks of silver in them. When I looked at her closely, I thought her to be quite beautiful. At odds with her whole appearance was the fact that she was completely bald...but it did not deter her beauty in the least. In fact, it enhanced it.

"Where am I? What is this place?" I shouted.

"That is not for me to answer. Do you require food?"

"No, I am not hungry! But, maybe something to drink." My throat was so parched it ached.

She turned her head slightly and I noticed she had a series of multicolored markings that ran from her temple to her jawline. They reminded me of some sort of tribal symbols, as they were somewhat geometric-like in their appearance. She smiled then and she was stunning.

"I shall see to it." The screen returned to its array of stars.

I stared at the view before me, not knowing if it was all an illusion. The questions pounded in my brain. Where was I? How long would I be here? What would they do to me if the Guardians failed?

I closed my eyes, massaging my throbbing temples. When I heard the pop and felt the hairs on the back of my neck rise, I knew he was in the room with me. Instantly I began trembling.

I turned around and he said, "I will not tell you the exact location of where you are for no one knows of this place beside the few that reside here. It is my home and it is a safe house for us. I hope you find that my room meets your approval."

His appearance initially left me stupefied. His tousled dark hair was long, brushing his shoulders as he moved. His arms bore the same tribal symbols I had noticed earlier on the beautiful woman. He was dressed in tight black leather pants, but instead of the leather vest and criss-crossing bands, he wore a crisp white shirt. The sleeves were rolled up to his elbows and the top three buttons were undone. Lean, muscular and confident, he wasn't handsome in the traditional sense, but he exuded magnetism and a masculinity that was difficult to ignore. He was the epitome of what I would consider the "bad boy" to be.

He cleared his throat, bringing me back to the conversation, while telling me he knew where my thoughts had been.

My face spontaneously flushed. "Your room?" I asked in confusion.

"Yes, these are my quarters. I thought you would be more comfortable here since it affords much more privacy."

"How kind of you," I retorted sarcastically.

"I can imagine how you must be feeling right now."

"I doubt it and don't patronize me. How long do you intend to hold me hostage?" I didn't know from where this foolish courage had come.

"I hardly doubt that you are living like a hostage here."

"Liar! You took me against my will and now I am locked in this room like a prisoner," I shouted, slamming my fist into my open hand. Oh how I wanted to punch him.

"You can try, but you will fail," he calmly said.

"Tell me something I don't know. Do you enjoy flaunting your power?"

"I am not..."

"Liar! Is your super awesome species also known for telling constant lies?" My anger had become palpable. Unfortunately, my stupidity had tagged right along.

He was at my side, grabbing my arm before I could even detect his movement. His touch sent a searing pain down my body and I screamed, attempting to free myself from his grasp. I failed. His power coursed through me, and I supposed it was like being electrocuted. It was agonizing. It brought me to my knees, but his ironclad grip remained in place. I was no match for this.

My lungs burned as I fought for oxygen and begged, "Please, let me go. You're hurting me!"

"I am highly aware of that." The cruel twisting of his lips made me think he was enjoying my pain.

"You could not be further from the truth. I am simply attempting to teach you some manners Ms. St. Davis. Keeping your annoying mouth shut would be a good place to start," he snapped, reading my mind.

"Okay!" I whimpered. "I'll be quiet. I promise. Just let me go...Please!"

He regarded me critically but then released me. I tumbled forward slamming into the cold hard floor. It felt wonderful against my burning body. Pure abject fear then took over, flooding every fiber of my body. Then, violent trembling began and I thought my heart would explode. I felt the tears flooding my eyes. My emotions were going haywire. One second I was angry then I was contrite, now I was terrified. What was happening to me?

"You are reacting to my power. The pain of my touch has caused this cascade of emotions. It can have a psychological as well as a physical effect. It will pass."

I couldn't speak. My throat had constricted to the point I was worried about breathing. He continued to assure me it would pass. All sorts of horrible things were happening at once. I was mortified, in pain, frightened and sad. It was overwhelming.

"Breathe Ms. St. Davis. It will pass," impatience echoing throughout the space. If that wasn't enough, I suddenly became violently ill, throwing up all over the place.

He bent down and reached for me, but I cringed and tried to crawl away. My body still wasn't cooperating.

"No!" I tried to scream. "Don't touch me." My voice was raspy.

"Fear not," he said gruffly, "I have repressed my powers. You will feel no pain."

He scooped me up in his arms but I was shaking so badly I hardly noticed. He placed me on the bed, wiped my face and brow with a soft cloth and wrapped me in the coverlet. I still had no control over my body. My face was wet with tears and I was struggling to breathe normally.

"Be still," he said harshly.

"I'm trying," I sputtered.

He placed his palm on my forehead and I began to feel pleasant warmth spreading throughout my limbs. My shaking subsided and my breathing returned to normal.

"What kind of creature are you?" I whispered, blinking excessively.

He took the back of his index finger and moved to wipe my tear-streaked cheeks. I cringed again, and tried to scoot away from him. My muscles acted like they didn't know me.

"Do not fear, I will not hurt you with my touch," he said, his voice softening. He went to the iPad things on the wall and a light beam appeared which must have somehow cleaned up the mess I had created.

His gentleness was at odds with his behavior from moments ago.

"I gave you a small demonstration of my powers because you would not listen to me," he said as he read my thoughts. "You were acting the childish fool."

I felt the blood drain from my face. If I didn't do exactly as he said, he could do that to me again. The thought of experiencing that turmoil again made my stomach contract into a tight ball.

"I will only do that to you if you become exceedingly unreasonable, as you were then. Contrary to what you are thinking, I do not make a habit of torturing creatures nor do I enjoy it," he informed me.

"What kind of being are you?" I could barely hear my own words as I spoke.

"As I told you on Earth, I am an energy shifter. My kind is a rare species so we try to keep our existence a secret. I am known as a Praestanus. I am comfortable in both of my forms. I can communicate without speaking...as can you. I can suppress my powers so I can touch others without inflicting pain. I can exist in any environment, as I do not require the need of certain elements to survive. It is difficult, yet not impossible to destroy or kill us. You are now thinking that if we are so powerful and difficult to destroy, why are we so secretive about our existence? The answer to that is my species has great difficulty in reproducing. Our infantile survival rate is dismally low."

"Why?" I don't know why I should give a rat's behind, but I was somewhat intrigued by him.

"Because at birth, we can only sustain life in physical form, but we cannot control our strength or power. You may think that it would be greatly diminished in an infant, but it is the opposite for our species. Our infantile powers are so great, yet we cannot control them. Therefore, it is nearly impossible to care for our infants. They are often the cause of their mothers' deaths."

I looked at him saucer-eyed, trying to take all this in.

"How cruel to those mothers."

"Exactly. They want nothing more than the survival of their young but it is often paid for with their lives," he said with a rueful smile.

"So let me get this straight. You have a baby that doesn't know how to control or suppress its power and the poor mother tries to care for it and ends up getting killed in the process."

"That is correct."

I spoke before I thought. "Maybe that's God's way of telling us your species shouldn't survive."

His eyes turned black and his voice was laced with menace as he said, "If I were you Ms. St. Davis, I would not verbalize comments such as that. There are others here that would quickly extinguish your life for even thinking such."

"I apologize," I quickly said in a strained voice. "I don't know why I said that. It just popped out."

"I would highly recommend you curb even thoughts such as that from 'popping out' while you are here. Unless of course you have a death wish. I understand from reading your memories that you did at one point. Oh, and Ms. St. Davis, this is not a warning...it's a threat."

I nodded as my throat worked convulsively.

I did not wish to die. I realized that now and it slammed into me in full force making my head reel. My experience with Rykerian had changed all of that.

He cocked his head at an unnaturally weird angle. It brought home exactly how "alien" this man was.

"So this Rykerian means a great deal to you then?" He read my thoughts again.

I knew there was no use denying it to him. He could pull anything out of my head if he chose.

I nodded saying quietly, "Yes, he does. He saved me. Literally and figuratively. I wanted to die at one point. Fortunately, I was never brave enough to take my own life. Rykerian's made me realize quite the opposite now; he's made me aware of how much I want to live," I admitted.

A smile spread across his face. "That is good."

"How so?"

"He will be most eager to accomplish this mission of rescuing my family."

I giant hand seemed to wrap itself around my stomach and squeeze. The thought of Rykerian putting himself at risk made me want to become violently ill again.

"Ahh, you truly do love him, don't you?" he asked in awe.

"No, I don't...well, I think I...oh, I don't know what I feel! I'm so twisted up over him!" I exclaimed, throwing my hands up in the air.

He angled his head again and I saw a band of light project from his eyes. I immediately drew back in fear, but this band enveloped me and I felt no pain. Images of two people began dancing before me. Then the voices came. It was Rykerian and Maddie talking at the house on Earth. He was moving around like a mad man screaming about my disappearance. Maddie was trying to calm him down...trying to comfort him. He was frantic, his eyes wild. He stopped and looked at her and exclaimed, "If something happens to January, I want you to destroy me. If you don't, I will. I cannot live without her. She is the sunshine to my rain, the light to my darkness. She is the comfort to my pain, the joy to my sorrow. She is everything to me Maddie." The images and voices began to fade.

I looked up at Jurek.

"Please let him know I am okay. Please?" I begged. I even reached my hand to his arm and held onto it. The resulting shockwave of pain made me jerk, but I didn't let go. I only squeezed tighter. His widened eyes informed me of his surprise. He nodded and disappeared. I was left standing there, holding onto to nothing but air.

Chapter Ten

T he lights in the room had dimmed, as if they were on an automatic timer. I took that as a cue to try to get some sleep. My body had not healed completely from my brush with death so I fell into an exhausted dream-filled sleep.

I saw all the Guardians sitting around the conference table trying to devise a plan, but coming up empty-handed every time. Rykerian kept tearing his hands through his hair and the look on his face brought tears to my eyes. If I hadn't known completely before this, his actions were convincing of how deep his feelings ran for me. The fingers of fear inched along my spine as my mind raced with all sorts of unacceptable outcomes.

What if they couldn't figure out a way to get Jurek's sister and father released? What if someone was killed in the process? What if Rykerian died? I awakened, dripping in sweat and tangled in the bedding. My heart was pounding and I was panting with fear.

The star filled picture captured my gaze so I dragged my enervated body out of bed and walked toward the large window. Was this all an illusion or was I looking out at the universe? As I stared at the view, I saw a light in the distance moving toward me and as it came closer, I realized it was some kind of space ship, much like the ones I saw at the Compound. Was my mind playing cruel tricks on me or was I truly seeing such a thing?

I began to doubt my sanity. I threw my hands against the window and started pounding it.

The screen lit up, but this time it was a male that looked much like Jurek. In fact, he could have been one of the men I saw at the CDC that day.

"Cease your pounding of the screen!" he ordered. "If you require something, you need only to gently tap it!"

"It would have been nice if someone had bothered to tell me that," I muttered angrily.

"What is it you want?" he asked curtly.

"I... I don't know! I mean, where is Jurek?"

"He is busy. He is not at your beck and call!"

"Ugh," I said under my breath.

"If there is nothing you need, please stop disturbing us," he said through clenched teeth.

What is it with these people, I thought? They expect me to sit here calmly, like I don't have a care in the world?

"You are a prisoner here. What did you expect?"

"I... I just want to know what's going on! Ugh! Will somebody tell me something?"

That feeling of electricity struck, and I was beginning to recognize it for what it was. I whipped my head around and there stood Jurek.

"My men are busy. What is it you need?"

"I'm... I'm so, I don't know. I'm frustrated. I can't just sit in here and wait. I can't sleep. It's driving me nuts!"

Unexpectedly, he started laughing. Not a chuckle or a brief snort. He was downright laughing, bent over at the waist.

"What? What's so funny?"

He lifted his eyes toward mine and I sucked in my breath. Gone were the silver flecks and shades of midnight blue. His eyes were completely lavender, a soothing, most beautiful shade of lavender and they were stunning.

They were soft and gentle and I felt them tug at my heart. He seemed...nice. Not harsh and unbending but kind.

His head slanted to the right as he stared. Then he surprised me by saying, "Do not get used to this. It is rare that something makes me laugh."

As I stared at him, his eyes changed back to the color I had become accustomed to.

"Make no mistake Ms. St. Davis. I am no gentleman nor do I intend to be. So do not allude yourself into thinking I can be changed. I am what I am and it has served me well all my years."

I numbly stared, not quite knowing how to respond. His words shook me out of my frozen state.

"Is there something else you wish? I am busy and have no time for dawdling."

"Er...right. Well, I need to use the restroom." I could feel my cheeks flaming.

His head flicked up and down once and he turned to the iPad looking things scattered on the wall. He tapped the first one on the left and the room immediately transformed into a bathroom.

"Seriously. This is incredible." I turned to look at everything. There was a shower, sink and what I thought was a commode, but it wasn't attached to anything. I bent down to take a close look. I put my hands on it and pushed down to see if it would move.

"May I ask what you are doing?"

"How does this thing work? It's not attached to anything?" I kept pushing on it.

"You act like you want to hop aboard and take it for a ride. Just use it and do not worry about the mechanics of the thing. It is too complicated to explain."

I looked at him and stuck my tongue out. Okay, I know it was childish, but I couldn't think if anything else to do.

He burst out in laughter. Again. That's right...he who never laughs, has now laughed twice in one day.

The whole situation struck me as comical so I found myself giggling along with him. He must think I'm dorky as all get out. Trying to push the commode around like a piece of furniture!

Our laughter finally subsided and he gave me the oddest look.

"You have quite an unusual effect on me, Ms. St. Davis."

"It's January. My name."

He formally bowed to me and said, "January."

I giggled again because I found that action to look comical.

He raised his brows and chuckled. "Enjoy the bathroom, January." He was gone.

I rapidly took care of my needs when a thought hit me. *What if they're watching me?*

I should've expected it but I was, nevertheless surprised when I *heard* his voice.

Have no fear. No one is watching.

How do I know?

First off, I do not lie. Second, my species does not approach a female unless they are invited. So unless you are inviting me January, you have no need to fear you are being watched.

Oh, okay. And just for the record, I'm not inviting you.

I never thought you were.

I stripped and stepped into the shower and...stood there. There was no water nozzle, no knobs or handle to turn on the water...here was nothing but a series of buttons. His voice came to me again, laced with laughter.

It seems I am destined to find humor today.

Yes, at my expense, I thought drily.

Humor is humor January. The top buttons on the left turn on the water. Tap them both simultaneously. The left is hot and the right is cold. The ones beneath them control the strength and type of flow. Play with them if you like. The second panel of buttons are body wash, hair wash, and so forth.

I tapped the two buttons to get started and the water appeared from everywhere...above, behind, in front and on the sides. It was like being in a water park. I couldn't help but twirl around and laugh. I found the soap and had a bubble of a time. I tapped the next button and started to wash my hair. My guess was the third button would be conditioner and I hoped I was right, because that's what I used it for. Then the fourth button threw me. I tapped it and at first nothing happened. Then I felt my arms being raised by an invisible string and next I saw my body glowing and surrounded by light. Seconds later, my arms fell to my sides and the glowing went away. I was momentarily confused until I looked at my skin and realized I was totally devoid of any body hair, save the hair on my head. I stood stock still. The hair must have melted off of me. My fingers quickly touched my face, inspecting it for eyebrows and lashes. It was a relief to find they were still there.

I should have warned you about that last button January.

His *voice* was laced with laughter.

I can't tell you how thrilled I am that I can be such a source of amusement for you!

My eyes darted around in search of a towel but I quickly realized I didn't need one. I was completely dry, including my hair. I stepped out of the shower and wondered about my clothing. My eyes landed on a neatly folded stack of white garments. I stepped into a soft pair of leggings and wrapped myself in the accompanying tunic, which was equally as soft.

Tap the first screen on the left when you want to return to the bedroom.

I followed his instructions and I found myself back in the white bedroom.

The large window beckoned me so my feet carried me there. Leaning in to get a better view I tried to imagine how I could possibly be standing and overlooking this glorious arena of stars. *Is it real or an illusion?*

It is as real as you are.

The felt room become charged with his presence. Every time he came to me, my fears lessened.

"As I said, you have nothing to fear from me January."

"I am learning that," I responded, though I was still wary of him.

"Was your time in the bathroom enjoyable?" he asked with a smirk.

My face flamed with embarrassment as I thought about my hairless body. I swiftly turned away.

"Perhaps I should have warned you," he said.

"Yes, perhaps. Can we please change the subject?"

"Indeed we can. I came to inform you that I will be leaving in a while."

"What? You can't leave me here!" My apprehension mounted and I broke into a sweat.

"So you enjoy my company that much?" he teased. "Wait until your Rykerian hears of this." He laughed under his breath.

"He is not 'my' Rykerian!" I shouted.

"You think not?" he challenged. "Have you learned nothing from the silly Vesturions and their ways?"

"They aren't silly! Besides, when you insult them, you insult me."

"Even so, you must face the facts January. Like it or not, Rykerian is yours. What you need to decide is what you are going to do with him. Vesturions connect for life."

"I'm fully aware of that!" I snapped. Why was it that every time I thought of Rykerian my stomach did a flip-flop and my heart began racing?

"Because you are not being honest with yourself and your feelings," Jurek answered my question aloud.

"That's rude you know! You should stay out of my head!" I yelled.

"You are angry because you do not want to admit the truth. You know I am correct, and if you are truly Vesturion, you will stop lying to yourself and others."

He had me there. My mouth opened and closed several times in my quest to formulate an adequate response. No such luck.

"Why are you so unwilling to admit this?"

"Why are you so nosy?" I bit back.

His eyes lightened and we stared at each other for a moment.

"I cannot explain this but I somehow feel linked to you."

He just gave me the shock of a lifetime. My mind started to spin with this information.

"Do not mistake me January. When I say connection I do not mean that in any sexual or romantic way. There is something that flows between us that I cannot name and it puzzles me. Make no mistake though, this does not mean you are in any less danger here."

I blew out my breath in relief and chuckled nervously.

"Well, I'm certainly happy you cleared that one up! I didn't know how I was going to handle that. I have enough issues in dealing with Rykerian."

He jerked his head in that strange angle of his and smiled...really smiled at me then.

"Do you care to discuss it with me?" he asked kindly.

"I'm not sure." I gave him a wary look. This man was a huge mass of great contradictions.

"What are you not sure about?"

"No, I didn't mean exactly that. I meant..." I stopped because I didn't have an appropriate answer. "Well, I'm not sure if I want to discuss it with *you*."

Jurek moved closer to me and said, "January, has he done anything dishonorable?"

"No! He would never..."

"Has he shown you anything but respect and love?"

"No!"

"Then I do not understand."

"It's me, not him," I murmured. "It's hard to explain."

"May I?" I was very aware of his intention as I gave him the go ahead. He lifted his hand and placed it on my forehead. Several moments later he stepped away, his eyes stormy.

"This woman, your mother," he spat, "did you great harm. I should like to destroy her!"

"Stop that. Getting rid of her doesn't solve my problem. Besides, I think I am incapable of being in a relationship."

"That is incorrect. I can feel your emotions and I have witnessed the strength of them. This female did you great damage but you are most capable of a relationship. You must trust yourself January and you must trust the Vesturion. I have seen his reaction to your disappearance. He cares a great deal for you. You must give him the chance to show you how much!"

He was so emphatic I could only gape at him. Eventually my tongue came back to me and I responded, "Why do you care so much? Besides, it's a bit difficult being held prisoner somewhere in the middle of outer space in no man's land!" My tone was dripping sarcasm.

His left brow lifted and then his booming laughter filled the room. Talk about ever-changing moods!

He was still shaking with laughter as he headed toward the iPad looking things. His fingers raced across the middle one and I immediately found myself standing in the middle of a living room, fully equipped with sofas, tables and the like. Now what?

"I thought it might be more comfortable if we had a place to sit," he answered between chuckles.

"By all means. I was wondering when we could have a little fireside chat!" I retorted.

When would I learn to keep my mouth shut? My last comment brought out another round of guffaws. I was rapidly becoming exasperated with this man.

I collapsed onto one of the sofas and did my best at giving him a perfected eye roll. It had no effect, except for adding to his humor.

"Would you stop already?" I was exasperated with him.

"Forgive me. I find myself enjoying our repartee. You are quick witted January and highly intelligent."

"Okay, first off, a repartee involves two people conversing. This is not a conversation. It's me saying something and you laughing at me. Second, did you expect me to have the brains of a rock or something?"

Don't ask me why I said that because he was now slapping his hand on his thigh, in complete hysterics.

My mouth clamped shut and I decided my best course of action was to keep it that way until we could have a normal conversation again.

He finally ceased his howling and dropped himself next to me on the sofa.

"Oh January, I suppose I need to beg your forgiveness but I cannot remember when I laughed so hard as to make my body ache." He threw his arm around me and gave me a squeeze and a hug.

"Okay...who is this man and what have you done with Jurek?" I should have known better.

The snickers began again. Maybe he'd lost his mind. The stress of having your family imprisoned could totally mess with your mind.

"No, I assure you I am not losing my mind." His face became serious again.

"I have not found much to laugh at in a very long time."

"I'm sorry I've turned out to be such a great source of entertainment!" I said a bit harsher than I had intended.

"I am not. I will tell you what I *am* sorry for," he said softly as he turned to face me and took my hands in his. "I am sorry I had to steal you away from your new found love. And do not dare to deny it for it radiates from you. I am also sorry I have done such a terrible deed on Earth. I regret those actions more than I can say. I am sorry that the Xanthians are holding my sister and father hostage and that I have had to seek out your Guardians for assistance. I am sorry that some will get hurt or even die in the process. I am sorry I did not meet you under different circumstances." His penetrating glare threw me over the edge.

I'm not sure how it happened, but I found myself wrapped in his arms, crying my eyes out. My sobs ebbed and I sniffed loudly, saying, "Now it's my turn to apologize for turning into a blubbering mess."

He pulled away from me, and those intense violet eyes bore into me.

"What's going to happen?" I asked in a raspy voice.

"I cannot say. I am hoping your Guardians can pull off the coup of a lifetime." He wiped me tears away with his thumbs.

I whispered my next question, partly because I was afraid of his answer and partly because I wasn't sure if I wanted to know. "What if they can't do it Jurek?"

"Then that means some will die." His response was so matter-of-fact I had difficulty processing it.

"You have to call them back. I'm begging you."

"January, oddly enough, I like you. I do. It is rare for me to feel this way, but this is my father and sister I am trying to free and for them I would do anything."

"I see." This was no game. This was real life. The wonder of the view from the window was replaced by a deep sense of dread.

"I must leave for a time. That is what I originally came to tell you," Jurek said ruefully.

"Where are you going?"

"I have business to check on. I should not be away for too long. You need not know more than that."

"I am afraid here," I whispered, admitting it to myself as much as to him.

"There is no need to be. You are safe with my men until I command them otherwise."

"They don't look safe. They look at me like they want to kill me."

"That they do."

"Then how can you leave me here with them?" My voice rose with panic.

"Because I trust them to follow my orders. I pay them handsomely for what they do. I offer them a secure place to live. You are safe here. They have strict instructions to make sure you are well cared for. Anything you want or need...just ask and you shall receive."

Doubt dripped from my eyes.

He grasped my hands in his and explained, "January, I am a mercenary. Do you understand what that is? I am a hired gun. I sell my services to the highest bidder. I am not the good guy here," he explained roughly. "My men are well compensated for what they do. They have been with me for a very long time. They follow my orders to a T. Do not waste your energy on worrying about your safety. In fact, for the time being, you are safer here than anywhere else in the universe."

"May I ask you something?"

He nodded.

"If the Guardians can't get your family, will you kill me in return?"

"Yes, I will do what I must."

"If you kill me, will you feel remorse?"

"Yes. I have felt great remorse, though, for many other deeds I have committed so it will not be something new for me."

"Will you at least be a bit sad?" My voice trembled with emotion. I should hate him for this, but strangely, I didn't. I was more confused than ever.

"Yes, it would sadden me to have to kill you," he replied in anguish as he rubbed the back of his neck.

I wasn't comforted in the least by his words, and he knew it. He shrugged, rose to his feet and disappeared.

Chapter Eleven

J urek had been gone for several days, each of them seeming to last a week. His words came back to me over and over. I had no doubt he would kill me if it came to that. I stretched out on the sofa in an attempt to get comfortable. Rykerian's words came back to me about shielding my thoughts. He said I needed to practice to become more adept at it. Deciding to give it an honest try, I began concentrating on that place deep within my mind.

I relaxed and let my mind roam. When I found that place before, it was with Rykerian's coaxing. He said to hunt for the partition that I could raise. I remember it feeling more like a soft filter than a partition. I let the tendrils of my mind wander and sure enough, I could imagine the thing so vividly, it was like pulling a blanket over my brain.

It was a bit more difficult this time because I was alone with no one to test the strength of it. I forced myself to keep at it though. Knowing I was at least doing something that could potentially help me in the future kept me satisfied for a short time.

When I couldn't take another minute of practicing, I arose and began to pace around the small room. I was as restless as I'd ever been. I stood for a moment in front of the iPad things. I really did need to find out what these were called.

Now that I knew one didn't have to pound on them, I wondered what else they could do. I ran my fingers across the last one on the right, tapping gently on the surface of the screen.

Nothing happened at first but then the room was converted into a dining area, complete with a full meal sitting on the table. The food looked strange...it consisted of multicolored items that I didn't recognize. The utensils were also odd. They weren't the traditional knife, fork and spoon, but they looked similar.

I wondered if the food was edible for my consumption. What if it was poisonous to humans or Vesturions? I hadn't thought of it before, but Vesturions and humans must eat the same things. At least they did when I was in their company at the Compound.

My curiosity got the better of me as I bent over and stuck my nose next to the food.

"Eww, that stuff smells nasty!"

No sooner had the words left my mouth, I felt the hairs on the back of my neck rise and I heard that familiar popping sound.

I spun around, grinning, and said, "Jurek! I'm glad you're..." It wasn't Jurek standing there. It was one of his men.

"Oh! I thought you were Jurek." Then my anger sparked at his intrusion. Did these people never knock?

"Please make yourself at home," I said sarcastically.

"Your tone does not match your words," the man said gruffly.

"No kidding," I replied under my breath. "Is there something you want? Do you guys never use the door? Have you ever heard of knocking before entering?"

He scowled saying, "You forget your place female! You are still a prisoner here and shall be treated as such."

He radiated hostility and my palms quickly became damp with sweat. Did I dare think that he wouldn't harm me?

"Fear not female. I know when and how to follow orders. I am Tak and I have come to offer you sustenance. I do not believe you should eat what you have brought forth using the transmuter."

"Huh?" I was lost in the weeds here. Transmuter?

"Yes, transmuter," he said, indicating the iPad look a-likes.

"Ah, I didn't know that's what they were called. Yeah, that stuff looks pretty disgusting. What is it?"

His faced turned a mottled shade of red before he answered in a scathing voice, "That 'disgusting stuff' is considered a fine delicacy to my species!"

"Geez, I'm sorry. I didn't mean it as an insult. It just smelled bad to me."

"As you smell bad to me, human!"

I smelled bad? I just took a shower. How could I smell bad?

"You cannot wash away the odor of your species, human," he spat. "It is inherent to you...like that of a stinking beast!"

"What? I smell like a stinking beast?"

"That is correct! A stinking beast of the worst kind."

"Of all the rotten things...well I don't think you smell so good yourself. How can you with that rotten food you eat?"

And so it went. We continued to insult each other until I gave up.

"Will you just get me something to eat that won't kill me?"

He moved to the transmuter and ran his fingers across the screen so fast, I could barely track them. The nasty food on the table vanished and was replaced with a yummy looking pizza. My stomach immediately growled and I wasted no time in diving into it. It was delicious. For aliens, they sure could make an awesome pizza.

"Mmm, thanks," I said around a mouthful of food. He stood like a statue, not even blinking. After a few minutes of that, I finally uttered, "Would you stop looking at me like that? It's completely rude you know."

"I care not." That was it. No more explanation.

"Don't you ever blink?"

"It is not necessary."

"But why not?"

"We are energy beings. This form is simply a variation of ourselves so blinking or even breathing for that matter is unnecessary."

I'd never get use to this stuff. Just when I thought I had my brain wrapped around something, I'd get hit with another curve ball.

"What is this 'curve ball?'"

I shrugged. "Nothing. It's just a saying. It means something like a surprise."

He grunted.

"If you're just going to stand there and stare, you might as well have a seat."

He cocked his head in that strange, jerking way that Jurek did all the time and his eyes drilled into me.

"Why would you invite me to your table when you dislike me so?"

Okay, I so wasn't expecting that.

"I don't know. I guess because it's the polite thing to do."

"Why do you want to be polite?"

"What is this? Fifty questions? Either sit down or leave. You know you can join me if you'd like. I'll never be able to eat all of this."

When I looked at him, I nearly died laughing. The look on his face was so comical I couldn't help myself.

"Why are you laughing at me?"

"Because you look like you just swallowed an entire lemon!"

"I do not understand."

"No doubt. Look, have a seat and share my food, okay? It's very uncomfortable for me to eat with you staring at me like that."

His movements were stiff and awkward, as if he was unfamiliar with sitting at a table.

"You are correct. I am unfamiliar with this. My species eats in private, as we do not think it is something to be shared. Much like bathing. It is a bodily function that is done alone."

"You all think eating is like bathing? That's the weirdest thing I've ever heard." I stuffed my mouth again with another huge bite of pizza.

I picked up another piece and offered it to him. "Here, try some."

He scrunched up his face in distaste, like the pizza was something putrid and disgusting.

"I'm telling you, it's the greatest. You don't know what you're missing."

He continued to shake his head in disgust.

"So, why did you pop in? Was it to feed me?"

"That is correct. I was left in command with orders to care for you and when I saw you had created sustenance, I knew you could not eat it. So here I am."

Interesting. How did he know I created this meal?

"It is easily seen when you activate your transmuters," answering my thought.

"So what else can these things do?"

"Mostly what you have used them for already. We are short on space here so each room has transmuters to enable one room to become many."

"Are we really in outer space?"

I looked at him and almost fell out of my chair when I noticed his response.

"Tell me you did not just roll your eyes at me!"

"You are exasperating. Why do you ask such silly questions?"

"They are not silly. I have never been anywhere in my life besides South Carolina, North Carolina and Georgia before a week ago and you say I'm being silly. What did you expect? I'm sorry I'm not acquainted with space ships and fancy space stations or whatever this place is!" Okay, I was back to feeling like I was twelve again and having a bickering contest with another twelve year old.

Silence stretched between us and he eventually nodded sharply once and said, "Yes, we are in deep space, in our headquarters. I cannot tell you more due to security reasons."

I stared back at him when his actions shocked me. He extended his arm and pulled me by my hair. He took his hand and twisted his fingers around it, rubbing my hair with his other hand. Then he pulled it to his nose and smelled it.

"What are you doing?" I asked suspiciously.

"I had a desire to touch and examine your hair." He said it like he would if he wanted to touch a piece of wood. This was a highly unusual man.

"Why?"

"The females of our species have no hair and I wanted to satisfy my curiosity. I have never touched this before. It is very interesting. I can understand why your males like it so." As soon as the words left his lips, he released me.

"You people are very strange."

"You are replete?"

"Huh? Oh, yes. The pizza was great. Thanks." I looked at the remaining pieces and when I lifted my head, he was gone.

Chapter Twelve

These strange beings were beginning to evoke feelings and emotions in me I wasn't sure if I wanted to examine. I was beginning to like them. Really like them. That scared the wits out of me since they wanted nothing but to kill me. It also made me positively nuts...as in insane. How could I like a group of weird mercenaries that would kill me whenever they wanted?

Maybe because even though they were a gruff bunch, they had been almost kind to me. Jurek certainly had. And this Tak...while he was intimidating, he had odd softness about him. Like the way he looked at me when he was touching my hair.

Dear God, I hope I wasn't falling victim to Stockholm syndrome. I bristled at the thought while I examined my feelings and emotions. No... I didn't think that was it. I didn't feel a deep emotional bond with them; I simply *liked* them. They were unusual and totally weird, but they interested me. 'Kindred spirits' came to mind. All the kids in school would often tell me how weird I was or talk about me behind my back. I felt connected to these strange beings because of that. Like me, they didn't fit in.

One week later my mindset had made a one eighty degree turn. I was going stir crazy. Jurek hadn't returned and I had walked the floors for hours on end. Everyone who answered my call had denied my requests for permission to leave my quarters. I tapped the giant window repeatedly but they had all ignored me. That I was being a major pain in the butt was an understatement, but it was cruel to leave me hanging in here, with no communication from anyone. The last time I had tapped the screen I was told they would only respond henceforth in the event of an emergency! Of all the...

I caught myself running my hands through my hair and stopped. The action itself was so like Rykerian, my thoughts immediately turned to him. Who was I kidding? I had done nothing *but* think of him.

The gravity of my situation slammed into my gut. I prayed the Guardians would be successful at freeing Jurek's family. I couldn't bear to think of the alternative. After becoming quite fond of Jurek, I wondered if he could go through with his threats. I knew he was very fond of me, but his family's lives were at stake. He did say he would stop at nothing to see them released.

Oh how I wished I knew more about this whole ordeal. The information I pieced together was that Jurek had been coerced by the Xanthians to release the virus on Earth. I wasn't sure how his father and sister had been captured. He did mention to me that his father was not Praestanus, but from a different planet. Therefore he had no special powers and his sister had no special powers either. I knew Jurek was a mercenary by trade and that was how his association with the Xanthians had developed. Maybe the Xanthians discovered where Jurek's family lived and kidnapped them. But Jurek never mentioned his mother. Where was she and why didn't she help? Maybe she was similar to my mother. Maybe she hated him.

I threw myself across the bed. All these random thoughts were making my head spin. I closed my eyes and rubbed my temples and felt myself drifting.

"Do you plan on sleeping your life away?"

I groaned as I rolled over to look at him. "I'm mad at you!" I grunted as I rubbed my eyes, trying to get them to open.

"And here I thought you would be pleased to see me!" Jurek said as his eyes crinkled.

"You told them to keep me locked up in here! I've been trapped in here for days!" I said, pouting.

"January, need I remind you that you are still a prisoner? They were merely following my orders. Did Tak not stop in for a visit?" he asked with a smirk.

"Yeah, a most unpleasant one too. Why did you send *him*? He was like talking to a five year old!"

The room was filled with Jurek's rumbling laughter.

"Now what's so funny?"

"Your description of Tak! I wish I could have seen the two of you. Who won?"

"What do you mean?"

"You and Tak are of like minds. Very argumentative. I was wondering who won the argument."

"Honestly, I think it was a tie," I scrunched up my face and stuck my tongue out at him.

That only brought another round of guffaws from him.

"Well, I wondered how you would deal with Tak's grumpiness. He can be testy at times."

His expression turned from jovial to serious, reminding me of his volatility.

"What? What's happened?" Without stopping to think, I dashed to his side and grabbed his arm. The immediate burning pain made me flinch, causing me to increase the pressure of my grasp. Jurek's eyes flashed silver, but I didn't care. I needed to know what was happening.

"Your Rykerian is safe. He is unharmed and as healthy as ever."

I hadn't realized I was holding my breath until it rushed out of me when I heard his words.

"Oh, thank God! And the others?"

"Some have not fared as well. They sent in a team of three to try to infiltrate the power generating station. Two were able to safely escape but one was killed in the process."

My heart fell to my knees. I felt a torrent of grief wash over me.

"Who? Do you know who?"

"I believe his name was Kennar. Not one of your Yarristers, so have no fear."

"I knew him," I mumbled.

I lifted my eyes to his and said, "He was a good man. He died for your family. I hope you are happy."

"Need I remind you he died for you as well?" he retorted acidly.

"What?"

"He was following the orders of his leader, your Rykerian. Yes, January, your Rykerian will go to any lengths to save you, including putting himself and those closest to him at risk. He will stop at nothing to save you. I know this for he has told me. He is much more honest about his feelings than you are."

I opened my mouth to dispute him but he cut me off before I had the chance.

"Cease with the lies January! When are you going to admit your feelings for him? You are only lying to yourself. Do you think others cannot see how you feel? I am no youngling that I cannot recognize what it is you are doing. Do you think I cannot hear your heart beat faster when you say his name? Do you think I cannot see how your face softens and your eyes light up at the mere mention of him? Do you think I do not recognize when your belly tightens with fear when you think that something has happened to him? When will you pull yourself out of your cocoon and acknowledge these things? You cannot let fear rule your life forever."

"You don't know anything about my feelings!" I screamed. "You don't know what it's like to be a scared child and the only thing you want is to feel your mother's arms around you, but instead, you feel her hatred pouring out. You don't know how that rejection feels. You don't know what it's like to lie awake at night, locked in the attic, frightened out of your wits with no one to turn to. You couldn't possibly understand why I'm afraid to take this leap!"

"And that is your biggest misconception," his voiced edged with steel. "You are so blinded by your own self-pity and misery; you cannot see the truth of the world around you. You are the one who knows nothing about this. Your mother may have hated you, but at least you weren't responsible for her death, when the only thing she was trying to do was to nurture her very own infant child! And yes, I know rejection too. I was rejected and hated by my father for killing his one true love. So stop with your self-pity. You are not the only one who has been dealt a horrible hand in life!"

Sweet holy heaven! The blood drained from my face as I reeled in astonishment. His words came rushing back to me when he told me how his species was close to extinction...when he explained how the Praestani infants were so powerful that they often killed their mothers. It had happened to him! My heart was filled with his pain and I had the deepest urge to comfort him. I looked into his eyes and I sensed his power diminishing. I knew he understood my intentions.

I rushed to him and my words tumbled out, unbidden, "I am *so very sorry*. I didn't know. Dear God, I didn't know. What you must've gone through your whole life, trying to deal with this. Oh Jurek, my heart hurts for you." My arms were wrapped tightly around him, my face buried in his shoulder in my attempts to comfort him.

He whispered back raggedly, "You could not have known. It is not something I speak of to many. The fact that I have even told you has me baffled."

I looked up at him and his eyes were that beautiful shade of lavender, soft and lovely. I reached up and put my hand on his cheek, my heart pouring out to him.

We were standing there, me embracing him, and it turned into one of those awkward moments. Eventually my gaze fell to the floor as I stepped away from him and knotted my fingers. The silence expanded between us.

His voice startled me. "January, you must open your heart to Rykerian. Do not live your life in fear of being hurt because you will find you are not living at all. I know this because that is what I have done. For many years I have buried my feelings and it has turned me into something I am not very proud of. Do not let this happen to you. Your Rykerian is a very honorable man. He will never betray you; let yourself love him."

"I am so afraid," I admitted.

"Your fears are misplaced. What you should fear most is life without him."

His words turned on the light in my brain. My arms fell to my sides and I turned away from him, contemplating his words. He was dead right. My fears of living with Rykerian made no sense. I should be more scared of living without him.

"How is it that the one who holds me captive sheds so much light on my life?" I mumbled, more to myself than anything.

"We are often blind to the truth of ourselves. Sometimes it can take an outsider to bring that truth to light."

"I suppose you're right. I want to see him. No, I *need* to see him Jurek. When?"

"I have no answer for you. My hopes are that it will be soon."

I thought for a moment. What was Rykerian doing now?

"Can I send him a message? Please?"

He nodded his head in that abrupt way of his and reached for my hand. In seconds I was in Rykerian's mind, experiencing his grief over the loss of Kennar, and the fear over my well-being. I communicated with him. I poured my heart out to him, telling him I was okay and that no harm would come to me. I knew this for the truth it was, although I couldn't explain it to Rykerian. I was so deep in his mind, that my body began reacting to all of his emotions. My heart was racing, my pulse quickening, my blood was rushing through my veins scorching me; my belly was on fire with fear. I poured my soul into him and tried to ease his discomfort. We were so deeply connected, that when I released him, the emptiness of his absence made me physically hurt.

Jurek had to carry me to the bed for I didn't have the strength to stand, much less walk.

"Are you feeling okay?" he gently asked as he lay me down.

"Yeah, just weak." I grasped his arm, squeezing. "Thank you. For doing that. And for..." For some reason, I was shy about Rykerian now.

"It was noth..."

"Don't say that. It was way more than nothing. This is totally nuts, but I owe you Jurek. I really do. I have to say this though. This is downright strange...this thing between us. I've never been very close with anyone. I only had a few friends but never ones I could tell my troubles to, but with you it's different. I'm not sure how or why this happened, but thank you."

"I do not understand myself January. I feel like you are a lost sister. There is some reason for this and perhaps we will discover it one day."

I was so sleepy I couldn't hold my eyes open any longer and I fell into a deep, dreamless sleep.

Chapter Thirteen

A nother week passed. I was becoming more anxious about returning to Rykerian. I drove myself and everyone else crazy with my questioning.

Any news yet? What's the progress? Is everyone okay? How much longer? Can I go out for a walk? Have you seen Rykerian? Have you communicated with him? Has he asked about me? What did he say?

The list went on and on.

I practiced my mind blocking every day. I wish I knew what else I could do. I often thought about what other Vesturion powers I might possess. The thought of having them sort of freaked me out. If someone could teach me about them, I would feel more comfortable.

Jurek popped in one day and commented that my ability to block thoughts had grown significantly.

"Seriously? You can tell?"

"Most assuredly. Although you cannot block them from me, I sense the barrier you have erected. Against the weak Vesturion mind, it should prove to be very effective." The corners of his mouth turned up as he said that. He certainly knew how to goad me, and he did it so well.

I punched him in the shoulder as hard as I could. The only problem with that was any contact with him was usually more painful for me than it was him.

"When will you learn, my friend?"

Jurek had been unsuccessfully trying to teach me to control my temper. He wanted me to stop and think before I reacted. I had a tendency to speak my mind and he said before doing that, I needed to bide my time. I wasn't a very strong adversary if I ran my mouth for all to hear.

"I don't understand what the big deal is!"

"You will someday when you are mated to your Rykerian and are the subject of those who want to hurt or even destroy you."

"I think you are overreacting." I flung myself on the couch.

"You do not understand. The Yarristers are a very powerful family. Rykerian's father is the Great Leader of Vesturon and is a controlling figure in Universal Rule. I am not terribly familiar with Earth and its governing policies, but the Yarristers are royalty, January. You must learn how to protect yourself."

"Maybe you should teach me how to fight instead!" I blurted out.

That comment was met with gales of laughter. I should have expected as much.

I walked up to him and swung with all my might, landing another blow on his shoulder. It stung but I couldn't have cared less.

Rubbing my hand I stormed, "Stop laughing at me! I'm serious. You talk about learning to defend myself. Then Buddy, put your money where your mouth is. Teach me how!"

Eyeing me skeptically, he questioned, "You are serious, are you not?"

"Dead serious!"

"Well then Ms. St. Davis, are you prepared to take some mighty hard blows?"

Hmm, I hadn't thought about actually getting hurt. I guess if I were going to properly learn to fight, I would have to take some hard knocks.

"Yeah, I am," I assured him, and myself as well.

"You are certain about this?"

"Absolutely."

"How much do you know about your own powers?"

I explained how I could hear thoughts from the time I was very young. But that was it.

"It makes me wonder what else you are capable of achieving."

"Can you teach me that as well?"

"I do not know. It usually takes someone that has mastered a certain power to be able to teach it to others. Since you and I are two different species, and since I have never tried to teach your species before, I do not know if I am able. But, I am willing to try."

"Now?"

"Now is as good a time as any."

"What can you tell me about that Command thing?"

"Command is the most potent of the Vesturion powers. As you know, it is completely ineffective against the Praestani. However, I believe we are the only species like that. It is a Vesturion's greatest strength, if they have that ability. Like most species, the powers can vary from one individual to the next. I do know that Command is especially rare and the most difficult to master."

"How would one go about seeing if they have it?"

"I would imagine it would take great concentration, but January, I think it would serve you better if you began trying to learn a lesser power, such as Telekinesis."

"Okay, then let's give it a go."

"You understand how Telekinesis works."

I shot him a look that said, "Duh!"

"Right then. How about we start with something very small. Like that small pillow on the sofa?"

I went to retrieve it but he stopped me saying, "Leave it be. You will attempt to move it from there. Concentrate on it now. There will most likely be a place in your mind you can go. My guess is that it is the same place where you find your barrier to block your thoughts. Seek out that place now and focus on nothing but that," he instructed.

I sat with my eyes closed and found my blocking blanket, as I had come to call it. I let my mind wander around it, touching it, feeling it glide though my thoughts. I slid along it, enjoying the comfort it brought to me...like my very own security blanket.

"Now use your thoughts to visualize what you think you would need to move a physical object. Maybe your hand, or a device of some kind. Let yourself get comfortable there. Relax your body and wrap your mind around whatever it is you are visualizing."

My thoughts envisioned a long handled gripper of sorts, the kind of thing an elderly person might use to pick up an item off the floor. I wrapped my mind around that device, ran my imaginary hands up and down it, examining how it might work.

"Now try to use it January." Jurek's voice had become so soft, I had to strain to hear it. It was soothing to me and I didn't want to move. He had to coax me again.

"January, use whatever your mind has conjured up to try to move the pillow. Reach across the room and retrieve it for me. Go ahead, the pillow cannot run away from you."

I put my little gripping device to work but it wouldn't cooperate with me. I tried to use my arms but they would stretch out and contact with the pillow, but my hands wouldn't close around it. I kept repeating these actions, but nothing worked.

"Ugh, this is *too* hard. I'll never get it."

"You have to practice every day, just as you have practiced blocking your thoughts. Keep trying this every day."

"Is that it? Is that all we're gonna do today?"

"January, in case you have not noticed, I have a business to run and a station to see to. I have duties and obligations. I must go."

"Let me go with you! Please! I need a break from this room! Please Jurek, pretty please!"

He snorted and said, "Let me see what I can do. No promises though. My employees do not see you as I do. They only see a prisoner January. At least when you are in here, I know you are safe."

"Humph," I grumbled under my breath.

"Perhaps I can talk Tak into coming in here to teach you how to spar."

"Tak! Ugh! Why can't *you*?"

He rolled his eyes at me. "Tak is better than I and would be better equipped to knock you around."

"No doubt," I said sarcastically.

There was a crackle, then a spark and he disappeared.

Chapter Fourteen

T rue to my word, every day I practiced trying to learn Telekinesis. After days of major concentration, I had a breakthrough. I moved the pillow a hair. Literally, it shifted. That's it. Nothing more. I was disgusted with my lack of progress.

I started ranting and raving out loud, not recognizing how loud I was.

The electrical charge surged through the room and I knew Jurek had popped by. I was disappointed to see it wasn't him, but Tak instead.

"I have been sent to fight you," his voice haughty.

"Don't you mean 'teach me'?"

"I was told to come here to fight you," he spat.

"Obviously, there won't be a fight. Look at me Tak. I am half your size. I barely weigh a hundred pounds soaking wet." I laughed at him. Come on, like I'd think he'd seriously fight me.

I never saw it coming. I felt a whoosh of air and I found myself sprawled on the floor on my backside, attempting to get some badly needed air into my lungs. He had knocked the wind out of me and my diaphragm was in spasms, putting me in a dead panic.

My throat convulsed as I struggled to breathe and my heart turned into a jackhammer, so high was my anxiety.

After a million years or so, the ability to breathe returned and I sucked in as much air as I could hold. Inhale, exhale, and repeat. I slowly returned to normal.

The blood rushed to my head and I could hear it pounding in my ears as the anger diffused throughout my body.

"What the hell do you think you're doing?" I bellowed, my lip curled in disgust as I flew to my feet.

"I am fighting you," he replied nonchalantly.

I was now beyond furious. A red haze descended over my eyes. Before I knew what happened, Tak was plastered to the wall. My arm was extended and I was panting with the effort, but I had pinned him to the wall with my telekinesis.

Through gritted teeth I shouted, "Jurek, if you can hear me, you'd better get in here fast. I mean it!"

I heard the electricity crackle, followed by the biggest, brawniest howl I had ever heard.

My anger had just kicked up a notch and I could feel the muscle twitching in my jaw. "Get him out of here now," I ground out through my still clenched teeth.

Jurek was beside himself with hysterics. He continued to slap his knee and wouldn't stop with the guffaws. I'd had quite enough when before I could even ponder my actions, my arm flung itself out and Jurek was now pressed against the ceiling.

"Well done January. Release us now."

"No!"

"Oh January, you know you have not the power to restrain us. We can convert to our energy forms and go where we want."

"Ugh, you two are the most inconsiderate, horrible, cruel, and...and, well, *mean* people I've ever known. How could you? And *you*," I said moving toward Tak, "you're nothing but a giant bully. Throwing me around like that! You *hurt* me!"

The flash lit up the room and Jurek was standing next to me with Tak on the other side.

"It worked January. I told Tak to come in here and do that, just to see if anger could propel you to unleash your Power of Telekinesis and it worked. We now know you have the ability, you simply have to find and harness it."

"Yeah, well, easy for you to say. You weren't the one *he* beat up, knocking the breath out of you. Of all the..."

Tak vanished and Jurek continued, "Isn't this what you wanted? To learn how to do this? I've been listening to you try every day knowing it would take something to push you over the edge. And I am not sorry I had Tak do this January. Now work on controlling the Power we know you were gifted with!"

With a pop, he was gone.

Chapter Fifteen

I practiced daily on this newfound gift I had unleashed. It took a while, but I finally understood the method I needed to use to pull it forth. Like my blanket, it was there but instead of pulling it up and encasing me within it, I had to push it outward, expanding it *away* from me. It was the complete opposite of blocking.

Jurek had warned me about trying to move large things, as he said it could be very dangerous. I could lose control and could hurt others or myself if I wasn't careful. He was right. One day I tried to lift the dining room chair. I did it with ease. So, being the idiot I was, I stupidly assumed the table would be just as easy. I had it in the air when something outside the window distracted me and the table went hurtling across the room, banging into the wall. It almost nailed me in the process. I was flattened on the floor when Jurek appeared.

"What's going on here?"

I sat up, shaking my head, rubbing my cheek where it had hit the floor.

"You were right, as usual," I explained begrudgingly. "I tried to move the table and I think I would have been okay if that thing outside the window hadn't made me lose my concentration."

"Are you injured?"

"No. Not physically. Only my pride." I chuckled.

He gave me a look that spoke volumes. "January, the irony is not lost on me. I could and would still kill you if it becomes necessary. I would not like it though but that does not mean I want you to walk around with an injury."

He headed toward the window asking, "What thing outside the window?"

"I dunno. I thought maybe it was a space ship or something." I massaged my face as it still throbbed from the impact with the floor.

He took a look around and then tapped the window. The beautiful woman's image appeared and he ordered, "Make sure all our shields and blocks are secure. I think we have just been probed by a space scanner."

"Yes, sir, I will see to it."

"What's a space scanner?"

"The Vesturions use them to see if there is life on undiscovered planets. They are robotic devices that travel the universe and report back to the Command Center on Vesturon," he elaborated.

"Would it be bad if they knew where this is?"

"Very." He looked at me and sighed. "There is a great deal about us you do not know and I must keep it that way. The same goes for the rest of the universe. We do not want this location disclosed."

"Can this place, whatever it is, be moved?"

"Yes. And we do it often."

It made me wonder how much danger he was in every day.

"More than you care to know or experience January. Have a care with your practice and please, do not try to move such large objects. Let me take a look at you." He took my chin in his hand and gently inspected my face with his fingers before declaring I would survive.

I was alone again. Dragging a chair to the window, I unceremoniously deposited myself in it and began to star gaze. I chuckled when I thought about this whole thing. Only a few months ago I thought stargazing was looking through a telescope or laying on your back on a blanket looking at them. Here I was, deep in space, a gazillion miles away from Earth no doubt, really and truly stargazing.

It was amazing!

As usual, my thoughts turned to Rykerian. I hoped he was doing okay, amidst all this turmoil. I sure did wish they would hurry up and complete this mission so I could go home to him. Funny thing...a couple of weeks ago I never would have thought about him this way.

A few more long, miserable boring days dragged on, second by second. I was stepping out of the shower and wrapping myself in a robe when I felt the room take on what was now that familiar charge.

"This better be good as I'm nearly naked having just finished my shower," I said sourly.

"Get dressed. We are going."

"Going?"

"Yes, now hurry!" he said impatiently.

"And just where is it we're going?" exasperation pouring out of my mouth.

"I am taking you home. Now *hurry!*" he commanded.

"Home as in Earth?" I screeched, jumping to attention.

"Yes! Now hurry January!"

"Well, if you'd pop out for a second, I might be able to get dressed."

"Do not worry about that. I have no desire to see you naked," he said with distaste as he turned his back.

"I don't care, go! Out!" I yelled. His eyes darkened as he popped back out.

It took me all of, oh maybe three seconds to throw my clothes on. I quickly tore a brush through my hair, thinking how great these showers were that dried you too. He was back.

"Shall we?" he asked, extending his hand toward me.

"I'm scared," I said in a small voice.

"What are you afraid of?"

"What if he doesn't want me anymore?"

He angled his head in that odd way if his and then shook it. "Are you insane? You occupy his every thought. He thinks of you every waking moment. His soul is wrapped up within yours. You are his, whether you want to admit it or not. Come, we are wasting time." His voice was urgent.

"Wait. What was the outcome?"

"He would not say. I could have forced it from him, but I decided against it."

"Why?"

His eyes softened as he said, "Because of you, my friend. Now let us go!"

"Wait, one more thing! If for whatever reason he doesn't like me anymore, can I come back here with you? Wherever it is you go? I mean," I twisted my hands as I spoke, "I don't have anyone that gives a damn about me and you're the closest thing to family I've ever had!" I looked up at him and his eyes were that wondrous soft lavender. I smiled and he smiled back. It lit up his whole face.

"Yes, I will keep you with me for as long as you wish. However, if he doesn't want you anymore, I will also kill him," he said seriously, but then he gave me a big wink and stuck his tongue between his teeth and grinned.

"Do you think he'll still want me?"

"Stop! Your lack of self-confidence is beginning to annoy me January."

"Will you still kill me if you have to?"

"Well, I might kill you anyway, simply because you are annoying me so much! But to answer you, yes, if it comes to that, then I would kill you," he said, but then the corners of his mouth turned up, ever so slightly.

"Oh you," I said, elbowing him in the side. "You never were really going to kill me were you?"

"Of course I was. You were my perfect pawn."

I stuck my tongue out at him, and raised my hand to him, giving him a perfectly obscene human gesture.

"Are you quite finished or are you going to stand here all day and ask more irritating questions?"

"We can go," I whispered. He took my hand and gave it a reassuring squeeze. Then everything turned black.

Book Four

Rykerian

Chapter One

S he was gone. I watched in numb horror as Jurek Herdekian disappeared and took January with him. The numbness lasted only a minute and was replaced with a blinding panic, and then outrage. My eyes darted around the terrace, hoping to see her reappear at any second. Bile rose in my throat and adrenaline surged through my veins. My hands fisted in my hair, nearly pulling it out by its roots.

I screamed her name over and over but only vaguely remember that now. Maddie and Rayn were quick to approach me but I pushed them away. I was frenetic in my movements, not knowing where to go or what to do. For a moment, my sanity slipped away from me, leaving in its wake a raving maniac.

It was Rayn who finally broke through my pattern of hysteria.

I focused on his face as he screamed my name. My chest heaved as I pulled air into my lungs and my hands clenched into fists, my nails tearing through the flesh of my palms, as I tried to regain control. My bones felt like they were exploding within my flesh, ripping me to pieces.

I squeezed my eyes shut, willing the pain to disappear. It didn't, nor would it. I knew I would feel this way until I had January safely back. My nostrils flared with the intensity of the breaths I drew and my mind, ever so slowly, returned to me.

"Rykerian, stay with me! Focus on my eyes!" Rayn was pulling me into himself, passing Tranquility into me. His hands were like steel grips on my shoulders. I stared into his eyes and felt the panic and fury easing away.

"That's it, brother. Breathe deeply. Slowly. Yes, that's it."

Reason began drifting back but so did the abject grief.

My eyes drilled into Rayn's, seeking comfort. I wanted to hear him say that it was all a mistake and that January was still here.

I knew I was trying to convince myself of a falsehood, but I needed something to hang my last shred of sanity on.

"Rykerian, we will make this work. We will get his family out. I know we can do this, but I need you brother. I need your help and knowledge. You must pull it together for January. Do you understand?"

"Yes, I need to be strong for January," I repeated.

"That is correct. Stay with me now."

The Tranquility descended upon me and I drew it into myself. It took every ounce of resilience I possessed to bring myself around, but I finally became more coherent with each passing minute.

"Rayn, what if..."

My brother interrupted me, saying emphatically, "Rykerian, you *cannot,* under any circumstances, allow yourself to think that. January is fine. This Herdekian will not harm her. He knows she is his bargaining chip, but we must get to work immediately on getting his family out. You understand?"

I nodded, "I understand."

Rayn looked at an ashen faced Maddie and told her to get our father, Tesslar and any other available Guardian here immediately. She sprinted off to the house as Rayn pulled me to a seat on the terrace.

I sat on the edge of the sofa and dropped my head into my hands.

"I need your focus Rykerian. I cannot stress this enough."

I leaped to my feet yelling, "Bloody hell Rayn, do you not think I am trying? I am still trying to process the fact that my...my..."

"Say it Rykerian. We all know how you feel about her. Just say it already," he urged.

"All right then! My mate, damn it. I am still attempting to understand that my mate just vanished before my eyes. With the enemy in control. An enemy we know absolutely nothing about! What *was* he?"

"Clearly he is a being we know nothing about."

"I *know* that damn it. Bloody hell Rayn, do you think I am in idiot?"

"Okay...okay. Just calm down my brother."

"Stop it this instant! I swear to the Deity Rayn, if you tell me to calm down one more time I am going to kick your bloody ass!"

"Yes, right then," he said, completely chastised and shocked at my foul language. "Let us think for a moment. We know the Herdekian needs his family released and he cannot do it himself."

"Bloody hell, if *he* cannot do it, how in the universe do *we* expect to?"

Rayn grabbed me by my shirt, got right in my face and said savagely, "Because we have accomplished it once before. Or rather Maddie has. When she saved my life! We are going to pool our knowledge and come up with a plan."

The situation on Xanthus had deteriorated to the boiling point. All remaining Guardians and ancillary personnel were currently being withdrawn in an effort to keep everyone safe. We needed to evacuate the place, but instead we would be landing in a hornet's nest and attempting to extract a father and his daughter from an impenetrable prison.

Maddie ran back outside and explained, "Rowan and Tesslar should be here any minute."

"Thank you love," Rayn said as he pulled her to him. "Can you remember exactly what you did when you broke me out of the Xanthian prison?"

"The Herdekian is right Rayn. The only way out is to shut down the main power generating station. I used Command and the prison guard shut down the system so I could enter your cell. If you recall, I was dealing with Counselor Druaha before we imprisoned him. The security is as tight as a drum there."

"Then that is exactly what we will do. We will have Father tell Therron and Xarrid where to meet us and they can assist us in infiltrating the station."

"Rayn, after I got you safely to a Space Transporter, remember that Sharra and I went back and I destroyed most of the existing power generators on Xanthus. That generating station no longer is in operation. What are they using to power it now?"

"Therron and Xarrid will have to fill in the blanks for us on that.

We will need to get our hands on the blueprints so we can see exactly where we need to go in the prison."

I listened to their conversation, but my heart was shredding to pieces. It felt as if someone had reached into my chest and tore my heart out of my body, so deep was my pain. What frightened me even more was that it was quickly being replaced with a deep consuming savagery that would fuel my actions until I had January back here with me. I wanted to wake up from this ridiculously horrid nightmare, but that would not happen, as it was reality I was facing.

I lifted my head from my hands and saw my parents, along with my brother Tesslar headed to the terrace.

"Rykerian, my son, I am terribly sorry." My mother pulled me into her arms and held me tightly. "We will stop at nothing to see her safely returned to you."

"Thank you Mother."

At her advancing age, my mother was still stunningly beautiful. Most children did not feel their parents were attractive, but it would be impossible not to say so about my mother. Her hair was still worn long and it was as blond as it had ever been. Her face bore no wrinkles and her blue eyes had the clarity of someone less than half her age. She was the rock of the family and her love for us was her first and foremost priority.

She stepped away from me and pulled Maddie and then Rayn into her embrace.

My father immediately jumped into his leadership role.

"I have already contacted Therron and Xarrid and they are at the ready for your command Rykerian. We must devise our tactics and strategy on how we will proceed."

Rayn glanced at me and seeing I was still unable to process, he replied, "Yes then. Shall we head to the Command Center?"

Chapter Two

W e made our way to the "War Room" as we sometimes called it, and began discussing our next steps.

"Father, do you know anything of this species?" I wanted to know.

He indicated he did not. "I have our researchers investigating it at present, but we have never encountered a being like this Herdekian."

My heart sank at his words. I had hoped, beyond hope, that he knew at least a tiny bit about these creatures.

"Maddie and Rayn, and you too Rykerian, I think it imperative you three stay here on Earth while this mission is being executed," my father said.

"No," I yelled out as I exploded to my feet. "I must go to see this mission accomplished."

"You cannot Rykerian. You need to remain here. I cannot risk having all of my children on Xanthus. It is too dangerous. Think of the consequences if you are captured or worse than that.

"He is right Rykerian. It would be unprecedented for all of us to end up as prisoners on Xanthus. The Xanthians would eagerly put us to death, if nothing else, simply to make a statement to Father." Rayn was, of course correct, and his logic was inarguable.

I nodded in agreement. I would abide by this even though I did not like it.

"I knew it! I just knew we should have destroyed them all. They have been nothing but a huge pain in everyone's bohonkus ever since...well probably since the beginning of time!" Maddie was shouting now.

Rayn let loose a monstrous sigh and my father shook his head at her.

"Maddie, stop already," I with a deep sigh. "You are well aware of the fact that it would be an impossibility to go in and destroy the whole planet of Xanthus. We are the peacekeepers of the universe, not the destroyers." Everyone's jaw dropped as they turned to stare at me, in shock over my response.

Then Rayn grinned, as did everyone else, except for Maddie, who just grunted at me.

"Rykerian is correct Maddie. Now you must stop this train of thought...it is unhealthy to continue to harbor such severe hatred toward them."

"Rowan, forget about that. It ain't ever gonna happen!" she retorted.

"Enough." Rayn spoke softly, but with intent. He leaned into his mate and laced his fingers with hers before saying, "We know and understand how you feel love, but right now, we need to focus on the problem at hand. We need your expertise and knowledge of the prison area and the layout of the structure, as well as that of the power plant. Can you do this? For me? For Rykerian?"

They were engrossed in each other for several moments when she nodded and began explaining how the power plant was designed.

"Therron has said most of their power now is through auxiliary sources, mainly solar and chemical. The sources are scattered throughout various areas, which will make it a bit more difficult to execute," Rowan explained.

"Or maybe not," Maddie piped in.

"How so?" Tesslar asked.

"If we can coordinate several parties to teleport in simultaneously, we could have a sort of systematic destruction take place. It would very be helpful if Therron or Xarrid could figure out which area was specifically responsible for powering the security system at the prison. We could destroy others first, using that as a decoy. Then we could hit the prison security system. Hopefully, with everyone occupied and distracted by the first outage, the prison break would be less notable."

We all piped in saying how that sounded like a great plan. I'm not sure who beamed brighter, Maddie or Rayn.

We all went to work devising the specifics of how this plan would be executed.

In the meantime, Xarrid's holographic image came to us. He had been investigating the power sources and their locales and had identified which one did what. So that part of the equation had been solved.

Next, we handpicked several Guardians that would man the team for the operation. Kennar was chosen as their leader, for he had the most experience in this type of covert mission.

A thought struck me and I asked, "Do we know anything about the father and daughter? We need their names and descriptions, else we will not be able to identify them."

"How will we contact Herdekian?" Maddie asked.

I quickly responded, "I do not believe we will need to contact him. I have a strong feeling he is monitoring our activities and will contact us."

We formulated our plans but the only missing piece of the puzzle was the information we required to recognize the ones we were to rescue.

Chapter Three

Hours later I lay on my bed, trying to get some rest. My mind was a hive of activity, thoughts zinging through my brain like lightening. My attempts to shut it down were unsuccessful, so I simply stopped trying.

Stretched out on my bed, my arms crossed beneath my head, I was suddenly impacted by a series of visions. January was sitting in a stark white room drumming her fingers on a bedside table. Her frustration was obvious by her erratic movements. She would sit, then stand, then pace, then repeat the process. She appeared to be physically fine and I felt my tension release through my breathing.

As the vision remained, I heard *his* voice clearly. "As you can see, your January is unharmed. She will remain that way unless you renege on our agreement. My father goes by the name Boland Herdekian and my sister is called Zulietta Herdekian. You will find them located on Level 4 of the prison."

His voice faded away and then the vision disappeared.

Dashing to Rayn's room, I pounded on the door. A disheveled looking Rayn opened the door and I fell into relaying the information I had just gained.

"January is well, even though she is a bit frazzled!"

I was relieved by my vision. It had given me a new sense of purpose, but it also reignited my anger I had tried to suppress.

"I learned the names of his father and sister as well as their location in the prison."

Rayn mumbled something but I didn't pay attention. My bed was calling to me, as sleep had been so evasive. With this news, my excitement turned to exhaustion so I spread across my bed and was instantly asleep.

She was home! January threw herself into my arms and we spun around and around as I held her high in the air. Her radiant smile sent tingles up and down my spine. My eyes drank in her lips and they ignited such a need in me I had to taste them.

I let her slide down my body until her head was level with mine. Her lips curved into a knowing smile as her eyes smoldered with passion. I could wait not a second longer and my mouth slanted across her, tasting her honeyed lips. It wasn't enough. My tongue traced the outline of her mouth and then sought entry. I felt her response as her tongue met mine and did its own special dance.

Her heart pounded against my chest and I could hear and feel her blood rushing through her veins. Her heated response increased my boldness as my invasion of her mouth intensified. With one arm around her slight body, holding her tightly to me, my other arm crept up to her neck where my hand encircled it. My thumb gently massaged her pulse until I heard her moan. I pulled my mouth away from her so I could mimic the motion of my thumb on her neck. I kissed her gently there at first but I heard her mumble, "More, please."

I drew back to look at her loveliness when her face began to blur. The edges grew less sharp and began to fade. I tried to hold on to her but she disappeared. I screamed her name and when I did, I woke up, drenched in sweat, and tangled amidst damp sheets.

My breath heaved in my chest as my heart pounded. The dream had been so real; I could still taste the honey of her kiss.

Feet were pounding down the corridor and my door burst open.

"Are you all right? Is everything okay in here? I heard you screaming and I feared something happened."

Rayn was there, and Maddie came in behind him.

"I am fine. It was only a dream," I croaked.

"Are you sure you're okay Rykerian?" Maddie asked in a disbelieving voice.

"Yes, I am fine. It was but a dream."

Maddie placed her hand on my shoulder. "Dreams can be very disorienting Rykerian. Give it time to pass."

I nodded as they left the room.

The next morning everyone was sitting around the breakfast table as I joined them. Rayn had already explained how I had garnered the information on the prisoners.

We were set to brief the rescue team later that morning. Kennar would lead the team as planned and they would be heading there tomorrow.

We finished eating and my mother requested a moment alone with me. She took my hand and walked me into the den.

"How are you feeling my son?"

"I will survive."

"You are sure of her...your January? There have been many before her that you paid no interest in."

My eyes bore into hers as I replied, "I have never been more sure of anything in my life."

"I see. Rykerian, you were the one I worried about the most."

"Why me mother?"

"Oh, my son." She reached up and pushed my hair off of my forehead. "You have always been so softhearted and introspective I feared you would pass up an opportunity because you were so shy amongst the females."

"Yes, well, I have never been comfortable around them but it is different with January. She makes me feel strong...and powerful, like I have this deep need to protect her."

"It sounds like you have found your *amashan* Rykerian...your one true soul mate. Have you told her of your family's prominence and of the role she is to assume if she accepts you as her mate?"

I sighed, "I have not. I did not have the opportunity before she was stolen away from here."

"Rykerian, I only ask because of my love for you. I do not want her, or you, to have false illusions of what may lie ahead for the two of you.

She must be willing to give up her place on Earth if she is to be by your side always, and she must learn of the Vesturion ways."

"I *know* that Mother and I will explain that to her when I am with her again."

"Have you bonded with her?"

"I do believe we have connected Mother. It is like nothing I have ever known. A current of energy flows between us that is something I cannot begin to describe."

"From your glowing aura, I believe you have my son. Well then, I look forward to meeting this female of yours." She graced me with one of her beautiful smiles that lit up her face.

My stomach churned as I thought of January and if she would make it back to me.

"Do not think such thoughts. She will be yours in every way one day. My hearts sings for you Rykerian." She hugged me and turned to leave.

"Thank you Mother. You know you have my love as always."

"As you have mine, my son," she smiled.

I was left standing alone in the den, haunted by thoughts of life without January. My dream had disturbed me more than I cared to admit. The fact that she had vanished before my eyes made me tremble with fear. I was close to a full on panic attack, with my heart thundering in my chest. Sheer will power was keeping it in check. I felt my brother's presence as I turned to him.

"Besides the obvious, what has you in such a foul mood."

"The dream I had last night. It was about January; she disappeared before my eyes."

"Do not over think it...it was a dream and only a dream Rykerian."

"What if it was a prophecy?"

"It was not, but if you want to know the truth, ask Talasi. She is a seer and can tell you. Perhaps she can put your mind at ease."

It did not take any more persuading for me to seek her out. I decided against teleporting, as I needed to expunge my adrenaline. I changed into my Guardian uniform of black trousers, black shirt and black boots. I placed my shadars on my wrists and moments later I was using my Power of Speed to race through the forest. The feeling of the wind on my cheeks was exhilarating and freeing. I ran as hard as I could, stopping for nothing. When I reached the caves of the Nunne Hi, my tension had disappeared.

Talasi and the Nunne Hi were our kindred spirits. We were here on Earth, North Carolina specifically, to protect them. We had formed an unbreakable bond with them many years ago and her people were my people. She was like an extension of my family.

Talasi was by my side in seconds. Her ability to see the future warned her I was on the way. We sat outside the caves as I told her what she already knew. I needed another set of ears as well as her wisdom.

"Your female is fine and will remain so. Her captor has grown fond of her."

I bristled at her words and jealousy tore through me.

"It is not what you are thinking," she covered my hands with hers. "He is fond of her in the way you are of me. A sister or dear friend, no more. It will however, ensure her safety."

I was a tangled mass of emotions. One second I was raging with jealousy and the next I could feel relief surging throughout my body.

"It is understandable as you feel she belongs to you."

"Talasi, does she return my feelings?"

"Her heart is filled with you, but she is unsure of how to respond. Give her time Rykerian. She is unfamiliar with love, unlike you. She has faced rejection and hatred her whole life. What she feels for you is as alien to her as are you. In time, she will understand the depths of emotions such as these."

Her words made sense and I felt myself breathing easier.

"Can you tell me anything of this Herdekian and his species?"

"I am sorry but I cannot. I feel he has faced great difficulties in his lifetime and I am of the mindset that he is not a wholly bad individual. However, that is all I can tell you."

My hand reached for hers and I squeezed it. "Thank you Talasi. You have eased my fears somewhat and for that I am grateful."

She graced me with a smile. Her curtain of black hair reflected the light of the sun, creating hints of blue. Her smile conveyed the warmth of the sun and her eyes were a rich coffee-colored hue that softened when she spoke. "Have a care Rykerian. Things will work out for you but you must have patience."

My spirits were uplifted as I raced back to the Compound. The heavy burden had been somewhat lessened. The run had also eased my restlessness. When I reached home I headed straight for the kitchen and some of Zanna's food, for I suddenly found I was starving.

Chapter Four

The team of six arrived safely on Xanthus and met with Therron and Xarrid. They dispersed to their assigned duties. The news was sketchy at first, and then everything went completely chaotic. We weren't quite clear on what happened, but something went terribly wrong and we suffered a grave casualty. Kennar had been part of our team on Earth for years and we all mourned his loss.

Our communications with Therron and Xarrid were sparse now for they feared for their lives. We ordered all Guardians off of Xanthus immediately. Freighters were waiting in the safe zone outside of Xanthus controlled space where the Guardians could teleport to safety. The Rebels had somehow stolen spacecraft from other planets and refitted some of their own, making them quite a dangerous presence. We had greatly erred in our dealings with them by underestimating their tenacity and quest for power.

Maddie was in turmoil. Her distress was palpable. She hadn't heard from Saylan, her best friend, in days. Our communications had been cut with Xarrid and Therron so she was out of luck. All thoughts went unanswered. We put tracers on everyone, but Saylan's went undetected, as if she had dropped off of the face of the planet.

Rayn and I were seated at the kitchen table as we had just finished lunch when Maddie barged in the door and made a beeline for her mate.

"I'm going home. To Vesturon. I have to go to the Command

Center to see what's going on. I'm too far removed here," she said her face haggard with worry.

Rayn's arms reached for her, pulling her into his lap.

"I understand Sunshine. Anything you need, anything at all. Does Father know?"

"Yes, he's meeting me at the Center in about a half hour."

"Any word from anyone at all?"

"Nothing. Not even Xarrid. Something is dreadfully wrong Rayn and I just can't sit still anymore and do nothing."

"No, I understand completely. You need to go." He wrapped his hand around the side of her neck and kissed her. "Go now and be safe. Let me know first thing when you hear something."

"I will, I promise," she said, standing. "Rykerian, you have my prayers." I nodded as she turned to leave.

Rayn's words reached her before she made it to the door. "And Maddie...I love you."

"I love you too," she said kissing two of her fingers and holding them out toward him. Then she placed her fist over her heart for a second and held her arm out to him. It was a gesture of love that was common to Vesturions.

"I know how she feels...utterly helpless," I said. Rayn nodded in agreement.

Days passed before we heard something from Therron. Xarrid was in turmoil for he hadn't heard from Saylan. They were supposed to have met up at a prearranged location, but she never showed. At first he was not too concerned because they were trying to get all of their equipment out for they didn't want to leave anything behind the Xanthians might use against us. They were all assigned an abundance of tasks so Xarrid figured she had fallen behind in getting her list of things accomplished. That turned out *not* to be the case. Saylan had simply disappeared. No one could recollect seeing her anywhere.

Xarrid and Saylan had become quite close. We even speculated they were romantically involved, though they did not speak of it to anyone. To those watching or hearing him now, it was clear the two of them were much closer than mere friends.

We could not count on Xarrid now to help us in our mission of freeing Jurek Herdekian's family. He had his hands tied with the evacuation and the investigation of Saylan's disappearance. It was now up to Therron to coordinate with our next team we were sending in.

The information we had initially received on the power generating stations had been incorrect. A Xanthian spy that had infiltrated the Guardians had supplied us with the wrong information. Therron now had the proper locales of where our men needed to go. We faced a more challenging task however, because after our last attempt, the Xanthians had now doubled their sentries. Getting to the stations would be much more difficult.

The team opted to use drones as decoys. The devices could be programmed to do just about anything. They would send in groups of them at different locations for a distraction. When the Xanthian guards would be dealing with the drones, the Guardians would slip in and destroy the generators.

If it didn't work this time, we would be out of options.

Therron sent us all the coordinates for the specific locations and our men began their mission. The only form of communication allowed was Telepathy. The team would take no risks. Xanthians did not possess that ability so that wouldn't pose a threat.

Rayn and I waited at the Compound for news of success. It was several days before we heard that they were only partially successful, but again suffering great losses.

Evidently things went smoothly until it came to retrieving the prisoners. They found both the father and daughter, but as they were getting ready to teleport them to safety, a team of guards reactivated the security beams surrounding their location. They were out of their cells but they were trapped within the walls of the prison. The two Guardians with them could only stave off four of the five Xanthians. The elder Herdekian threw himself at the final Xanthian to allow his daughter to escape. He perished in the skirmish, along with another Guardian.

Therron was able to whisk Zulietta away and they were now in hiding somewhere. We waited to hear from Therron with some sort of news, but nothing. The only thing we could surmise was that something must have malfunctioned with his shadars.

"But that would not account for his silence. He should have reached out to us by now using Telepathy," I stated.

"That only affirms that something has not gone as planned," Rayn commented.

"What do you think it is?"

"Perhaps he does not trust who he is involved with. Maybe it is one of the Guardians there and that is why he will not use Telepathy."

"Excellent point. It would have to be a Vesturion for Xanthians have no telepathic abilities."

"Exactly."

Upon hearing this, the fingers of fear tightened upon and squeezed my gut. What would this mean for January? How could we get her back if we had to explain to Jurek that his father died and was not here?

"At least we know that Zulietta is safe with Therron. He will protect her life at all costs," Rayn said. That thought comforted me somewhat.

"Rykerian, we need to get some rest. It has been nearly twenty four hours since we have slept."

"I know. Go to bed Rayn. I will try to get some sleep, but I doubt I will succeed."

Knowing Zulietta was safe with Therron, I fell into bed in an absolute state of exhaustion. Despite the fact I still harbored fears for January's safety, I found I could no longer stay awake. I slept for fifteen hours straight, until Rayn came in my room to awaken me.

"I wondered if you would ever get out of your bed at all today. Come, we have work we must do before we contact the Herdekian and fill him in on what has occurred."

"Any news?

"Not yet."

I forced myself to get up and shower. My head was groggy from the long hours I slept, but the shower was helping to clear it. When I walked out of the bedroom, there was a tray of food waiting for me.

I ate an enormous fluffy ham and cheese omelet, a bowl of creamy buttered grits, two large biscuits and a large bowl of mixed fruit. I drank a large glass of ice-cold milk and two huge mugs of coffee. I was feeling much better as I made my way down the steps.

I made my way into the kitchen where I deposited my breakfast tray on the counter.

Zanna was cleaning up the mess made from the morning meal. I grabbed her shoulders from behind and thanked her for leaving the tray in my room.

"Ah but you should be thanking your brother. He is the one who brought it to you."

I turned to Rayn to thank him when he said, "If I had not woken you up, you would still be sleeping up there. I have never known you to sleep so many hours Rykerian."

"Too true. I have not been sleeping much these past weeks and it must have caught up with me. I finally feel clearheaded though."

I took a seat across the table from him.

"So, what do we need to do before we contact Herdekian?"

"I fear his reaction when he discovers his father did not make it out alive and that we know not where his sister is."

"As do I. Any news from Therron? If anyone can get her to safety, it is Therron. I only wish he would contact us."

"The sooner we notify Jurek the better," I mused.

"Thesta will be meeting us in the War Room in a few minutes. Since he was Team Commander, he will thoroughly brief us on all the details."

I nodded then asked, "What about Saylan? Any news?"

Rayn shook his head, "Not a word. Maddie is contacting everyone Saylan may have been in touch with but so far there is nothing."

"And Xarrid?"

"He is as you were when January was first taken."

"Shall I speak to him?"

"You can try but I doubt he will answer at this point. He is tracking all of her last moves, hunting for some kind of clue. He is in deep water too for the Xanthians have closed ranks on us. If he does not leave soon, he may be trapped. Father is beyond upset over this whole debacle."

"Nothing has gone as planned, and that it the truth!"

I absently rubbed the back of my neck, trying to ease the tension Rayn's words brought. I hated that for Xarrid. I didn't know at what state his relationship with Saylan was, but if he had any feelings for her he must surely be going mad right now.

"Agreed. We better head over to the War Room where Thesta will supply us with all the facts."

Chapter Five

T hesta was waiting on us as we arrived at the Command Center. We determined there was nothing the team could have done to prevent the turn of events. They were moving to leave the prison when two armed guards halted them. Boland Herdekian told the Guardians to get his daughter to safety while he intervened. It was just enough time for the last Guardian to get Zulietta to Therron, but Boland sacrificed his life in the process.

Rayn and I decided to call Jurek here to the Compound and relay the information as such.

My heart thrummed in anticipation as we waited for their arrival. I stood stock still, my fists by my side, clenching and unclenching them. Even though Talasi assured me January had been well cared for, a million questions still zinged through my mind. Had he treated her kindly? Or had he been cruel to her? What would her mental state be? Or her physical state?

A few minutes passed when we heard a popping sound and they appeared across the terrace.

My expectations left me unprepared for what greeted me. January was...*glowing!* I had expected her to be distraught and haggard, but instead she was beaming.

My eyes quickly darted to *him* and I noticed a much more pleasant look on his face than the last time he was in my presence.

What is going on between them?

I tried to mind probe her but nearly staggered when I found she was totally blocking me! As I stared at her, her smile began to fade. She still clung to the Herdekian's arm but what was nearly my undoing was when he patted her hand with his! *What the bloody hell was going on here?*

Jurek Herdekian's eyes drilled into mine as he said, "Calm down Guardian. Your female here is fine and you have nothing to worry about!"

My brows shot up so high it felt like they left my head altogether. I could not have been more shocked by the interaction between them. I shook my head and stalked over to January. I latched onto her free hand and began towing her inside the house when I heard, "If you harm even one hair upon her head, I will destroy you and your family!"

My body froze and without turning I released her hand and between clenched teeth I gritted out, "Go to him. If he is what you want... Go!" I burst into the house, and didn't slow down until I reached the den.

"Rykerian, stop!" she called. "You are wrong about this. You are *so* wrong. It's not what you think!"

I spun around and spat, "Then, by all means, why do you not enlighten me?"

"I... I..."

"Go on! I am waiting. I am waiting to hear an explanation from the female I have fallen apart at the seams over because I thought she was in danger. I am waiting to hear why, when she finally arrives here, she is *glowing* and behaving as if she were attending a bloody garden party. I am waiting because I want to hear from her lips how she can be having such a grand time when LIVES WERE LOST AT HER EXPENSE!" My voice had reached a thunderous level that I felt the floor vibrate. I was way past furious.

Her eyes had become saucers and her lower lip began trembling. The blood had drained from her face leaving behind the ghost girl I had fallen in love with. I was so angry I could not stop myself from going in for the kill...the kill with hateful words.

"Do you even realize what has taken place here? Do you know that Kennar, our most loyal Guardian whom I had trusted with my life many times, was killed? He was like my brother January! Do you know how my family contrived to retrieve you and that...that *creature's* family? Do you know how much pain you've caused us?" I knew every word was a knife to her heart but I could not stop myself from inflicting more.

"I thought I knew you. I thought you were a *good, kindhearted and loving* female, but I must have been wrong about you." I tore my hands though my hair as I screamed out my frustrations.

I heard her mumble in the smallest of voices, "I didn't ask to be taken. I didn't do anything wrong. I thought I was going to die and for the first time in my life I didn't *want* to die anymore. Because of *you*. *You* made me love life and I had never loved it before. I thought about *you* every minute I was there. I didn't know how much I..." I saw her throat working as she swallowed convulsively, unable to say another word. She looked down at the floor and in a rush she spoke again, her voice gaining strength and momentum. "I didn't know how much I love *you* until *he*," she jerked her head toward the outside, "made me look deep into my heart and admit the truth. I was afraid to admit it because I was," she cleared her throat several times, "because I *am* so afraid of losing you when I just found you! I know it looks bad but I can explain if you'll just give me a chance."

Then she lifted her eyes to mine and I noticed her cheeks were streaked with tears.

"I am not falling for that 'pity me' attitude. You have no idea what my family has been through and the lengths they have gone for *you*," I said in a scathing tone. "Do you even know how *sick and twisted* this all is? Ugh, I cannot bear to be in the same room with you!"

I turned to leave when she screamed hysterically, "You can't just walk away and leave without giving me a chance to explain!"

"On the contrary. I can and I will." I turned to leave.

"Stop Rykerian," she called. I did not dare answer for I was still seething inside.

She called my name again and I continued to make my way to the front door.

Then I heard her voice change, grow deeper, more intense, and thundering as she said, "I said stop!"

Her Power of Command plowed into me, gripped me in its clutches and I turned into a heap of stone, unable to so much as twitch a muscle. I tried to breathe but it was impossible. My lungs were trapped in a vise. I was locked in Command's grips...and then I became truly frightened. It was not fear of Command, but it was fear of her ability, or lack of it, to release me.

She screamed my name, "Rykerian! Oh my God, Rykerian!"

She was shouting at the top of her lungs, trying to release me, without success. I was no fool. I knew she didn't know how and I knew this could spell disaster for me.

I heard Rayn and Jurek rush into the room, questioning January. Then I heard Jurek's booming laughter.

"It serves him right, the pompous ass. January, shall I kill him for you?"

"Shut up Jurek! Just make it stop!"

"January, you are the only one that can do that," Rayn explained.

Jurek was still laughing. I wanted to murder him...slowly and painfully.

"Herdekian, can you please be silent?" Rayn asked with annoyance.

Oh how I wanted to scream out to Rayn, "Kick his ass! Kill him!" but I could not breathe, much less speak.

"January, calm yourself. I cannot help you if you are wailing in hysterics!"

"What! Wailing in hysterics? Are you crazy? Look at him!"

"My vision is as clear as ever, so I know what he looks like. I am trying to guide you but you are in such a state, I cannot accomplish that."

Now I wanted to punch Rayn for his ability to remain levelheaded. Did he not know I was in acute agony here? *What is wrong with you people? Help me!*

"Oh for the love of God, just *DO SOMETHING!*"

Since my back was facing them, I could only assume Rayn was using Tranquility on January for the room was suddenly silent.

"January, pull from within," Jurek told her.

I wanted to jump in his face and break his nose! I wished he would just shut his mouth!

"Yes, January. Go to your place that you use for Telepathy," Rayn instructed. "It is much the same with Command. You must access that part of your mind."

"I'm trying," she said, "but I can't seem to make it do anything."

"Extend your arm and perhaps it will flow from within."

Nothing happened. Command's clutches made me want to writhe in agony, but I was frozen in my own body.

"January, remember when you learned Telekinesis and you had to do the opposite of what you do for Telepathy? Maybe it is similar to Command," Jurek suggested.

Okay, now my mind was over the top reeling. *January knows Telekinesis? How? When?*

Rayn's thoughts must have mimicked mine for I heard him exclaim, "She knows Telekinesis? How?"

"I taught her!" Jurek said with unabashed pride. No doubt his chest was now so bowed out it would be near to exploding.

I wanted to grind my teeth in frustration. It should have been *me* that taught her.

"You did not teach me. You tried but failed. It was Tak who taught me!" January stated.

Now I wanted to scream. Who the bloody hell was this Tak? Teaching *my mate* Telekinesis? UUGGHH!

"No, you learned it on your own when Tak attacked you! But it was all my idea so technically, I was the one who taught you," Jurek said smugly.

No doubt about it. I was going to kill him. As soon as I was released from this, I was definitely going to kill him. I would find a way and I was going to make it a slow, tortuous, drawn out process. When I was finished, I would kill this Tak next, for attacking January. No...I would kill him just because he had looked at her!

Rayn finally piped in, sarcasm lacing his comment, "I find it very disconcerting that you allowed someone to *attack* her when she was supposed to have been under your protection!"

Thank you Rayn!

"Oh, it wasn't like that Rayn. Jurek did it to get me to harness my powers."

"Oh, I certainly am happy you cleared that up January, as that makes me feel so much better. It is comforting to know your species, Herdekian, treats their females so kindly," he finished acidly.

Could you please just shut up and get me out of this, I longed to scream?

Jurek jumped in and said, "We need to get her angry. That's what worked before. That's why Tak did what he did. You know how hot tempered she is!"

No, I didn't know how hot tempered she is...because she's been spending all her time with you, you bloody ass! Sweet Deity, get me out of this and soon. I do not know how long I can retain my sanity!

The room became quiet again. Then I heard a crackling pop right before the booming laughter shook the walls.

Another creature, that looked similar to the Herdekian walked around me and got directly in my face, his guffaws, following him.

"I think we should just kill him Jurek, so ripe for the taking he is." He had the nerve to poke his finger into my chest.

"I do not think January would be pleased with you Tak if you killed him. For some obscure reason, she is in love with this *Guardian!*" he spat.

"Jurek, you underestimate your manly charms. You could easily make her forget him."

Okay, wasn't this supposed to be making January mad, because right now I felt the greatest gust of anger roaring through my veins? I was sure they must have heard it too for it was booming in my brain, threatening to detonate at any moment. If I was not released from Command soon, I was positive I would explode.

"Or better yet Jurek, let me be the one to make her forget!"

Next I heard scuffling noises and then January screech, "Get away from me you *dog!*"

In my head, I heard the most glorious word, *"Release,"* and my body crumpled beneath me.

In the background I heard rumbles of laughter but I couldn't focus on anything except the immense feeling of relief coursing through every fiber, every nerve ending, every cell in my body. I gulped gallons of air until my lungs were satisfied and I was unmindful of everything save the sensation of being agony-free. I lay on the floor, knees to my chest, until my senses returned.

That is when I noticed my cheeks were wet. Curious, I brushed my fingers across the damp areas, for I did not know where the moisture came from. I gradually opened my eyes and she came into focus. Her tears ran freely down her face and pooled onto mine. Her wrinkled brow formed a frown and her eyes were awash with sorrow.

She tugged her sleeve over her hand and used it to blot her tears from my cheeks. "I am so sorry Rykerian. I didn't mean to do that. I didn't even know I *could* do it. I...I'm so sorry," she sniffed.

Her fingers gently moved through my hair and made their way down to my arms. I suppose she thought to comfort me somehow. All I wanted to do was kill those vile creatures and then run away...like the wind.

As my body regained its control, I lost control of my emotions. They were a volatile mass churning inside of me, ready to burst forth. I had to get out of there.

I brushed her arm aside as I wobbled to my feet. Without a word, I stumbled out the front door. Each step was an improvement over the last until I knew I was able to run. I heard her calling my name but I paid her no heed. Escaping her presence was more important to me than life right now.

My first stop was the terrace, where Rayn stood with Jurek and Tak. I came very close to plowing into them but stopped myself at the last minute.

I took a step forward, until I was nose to nose with Jurek and said through clamped jaws, "Stay away from her. Forever. Do not *ever* come near her again and if you do, I swear I will kill you."

"You can't kill me Guardian," he taunted.

"Then I will die trying." I turned and sped into the forest.

I broke into a run and urged my legs on. As I gained speed, the wind beneath and around me began to reveal the hurricane of emotions brewing within me. Anger at January and those disgusting creatures, resentment, shock and awe at her abilities, sadness, despair, love, hate. They were a violent cascade thundering throughout my core and I wasn't sure if I was capable of controlling them.

My thoughts churned with how this emotion of love had been nothing but a huge pain in the ass. Did everyone experience these issues? It was becoming painfully clear that it could be more trouble than it was worth. I looked at my life as two separate chapters: before January and after January.

Before January, I was miserable, but in a different way. Well, maybe miserable was too strong a word. I was not completely happy. I had always been the object of female attention. They would declare I was the Adonis, when I would have preferred to crawl in a hole, unnoticed.

My shy demeanor was not suited to the attention that was bestowed upon me. It frustrated me and as a result, I withdrew from situations I knew would present a problem for me.

With the exception of my family and my work as a Guardian, I had a lonely existence. Then January bursts on the scene, like a meteor shower lighting up my life, and ever since I've been a crumpled mass of erratic emotions, not knowing which way to turn half the time. I've vacillated between extreme joy, sorrow, misery, hate, frustration, angst, worry...just about everything. Could I handle much more? Or did I *want* to handle much more?

My feet continued to carry me through the forest. My heightened senses began to notice things around me. The air was crisp upon my face and my nose was filled with the scents of the forest...earthy pine, moss, and...*citrus?* How could I be smelling citrus?

My eyes scanned a three sixty pattern and I glimpsed a slight movement in the distance behind me.

Impossible. She could not move fast enough to be able to follow me.

Ghost girl was on my tail and she had clearly pursued me. I could not stop the unwitting grin from spreading across my face. I admired her moxie...not to mention the fact that she had used her Power of Speed. I decided to make a game of this...a game of hide and seek.

I took off again with a blast of velocity. Let's see how fast she can move. I knew I was testing her ability, but that was the point after all. If she wanted to catch me, she was going to have to work at it.

Skirting rhododendron thickets and sailing over fallen trees I hastened on. Before long, I found myself on the mountaintop. I waited, my chest barely moving as I breathed. I lifted my head and inhaled deeply. I could detect her scent getting closer and closer. The snap of a distant twig, the whisper of a cluster of pine needles were the only indications of her progression. She was good...fast and quiet in her movements.

Seconds later she was by my side. I could hear her heart wildly beating in her chest and could only assume it was her anxiety and not exertion, for she did not look the least bit winded.

She craned her neck to look at me, trying to read me. My mind was guarded, and I had no intentions of letting it slip.

Sweet Deity, she looked more beautiful than ever. Her gold and platinum tresses were in wild disarray and her cheeks were like pink roses blooming in the summer. She was attired in white from head to toe—soft leggings that hugged her slim legs and a soft tunic that graced her lean body. Her ruby lips were swollen and lush and my desire to taste them as I drank in her loveliness was nearly unbearable.

I wanted to hate her at that moment for making me feel as such. I once heard that there is a fine line between love and hate. I knew that to be a fact for right now I straddled that line, teetering back and forth between the two.

Viciously, I jerked my mind to the present issue at hand. Her eyes had misted and her lower lip trembled. She took a deep breath and began speaking.

"Before you tear off again, I have to tell you what happened. Please hear me out. Then if you want me to go, just say the word and I swear you won't ever have to look at my face again. Okay?"

Chapter Six

My head flicked up then down once, indicating to her to continue. And so she did.

She relayed everything that had taken place between the time she left and today.

There were moments I wanted to scream at her to shut up...my mood swinging from love to hatred back to love. Jealousy raged in my heart. I should have been the one to teach her how to use her powers, not HIM! I should have been the one to show her the stars and moons...not HIM!

Perhaps I was being childish, but those precious moments had been stolen from me and I was incensed over it.

"Rykerian, it *WASN'T MY FAULT!*" she screamed in frustration. "It just happened!"

Those words crashed into me with overpowering clarity. It wasn't her fault. *It wasn't.* She had asked for none of this. My blame was misplaced. I could be angry and jealous until the sun burned out, but was it fair for me to hold *her* responsible?

My chest was still heaving with my inner chaos but heavens above, I *needed* to feel her in my arms. It was like the first time I had ever kissed her. I had tried so hard to resist but could not. I was now in the same predicament. It was the only thing I could think of. Unable to stop myself, I took one, then two steps toward her and suddenly we were in each other's arms and I was devouring her, kissing her lips, her cheeks, her eyes, much like a man lost in the desert greedily guzzles down water, desperately attempting to quench his thirst.

"I want to hate you!" I said between kisses.

We tasted each other and lost ourselves in the moment. We couldn't touch each other fast enough. Her hands moved over my body like she had never touched me before. They danced through my hair, across my shoulders and up to my face. She tenderly stroked my cheek and then I pulled away.

"I hate you not for what happened, but for how you were acting with *him*," I gritted.

She winced, then ran her tongue along her lips and whispered, "I *love you*...more than anything Rykerian. I know things looked awful back there, but it's *you* I want...it's always been you. Only I didn't know it. Or maybe I did but wouldn't admit it. Because I'm so scared. I'm scared of losing you. I'm scared of life without you. I'm scared I'm not good enough for you...that you'll get tired of me in a couple of years and think you made a mistake. I'm scared you'll wake up one day and say, 'What the hell was I thinking?' I'm scared you'll walk away from me right now and we'll never know what could have been. I'm scared of *everything* because I've never gotten anything right in my life. I've failed at almost everything I've tried. I'm only nineteen years old, I'm inexperienced and I'm scared to death over all of this. I didn't mean for that Command stuff to happen. I'm even scared of that! I'm so sorry I hurt you I..."

Her words forced their way into my soul. I could stand it no longer so I cut her off.

"Stop. Let me speak," I said against her lips as I briefly kissed her.

She nodded, her eyes imploring.

"I still want to hate you, though it seems I cannot. However, I cannot stand the thought of you with *him*, seemingly enjoying his presence. That is intolerable to me January."

I stopped and took a deep breath.

"I'm sorry for everything Rykerian, but I didn't choose that path. It was forced upon me."

"You looked as if you enjoyed being with him!" I insisted.

"Because I *do*! But not in the way you think!"

"I want to kill him January...and that other one too. So fierce is my anger."

"I don't want you to kill him. I care for him."

"WHAT?"

"Not in *that* way. You are so aggravating! He's like an older brother. Like the way you feel about your brothers."

"Bloody hell January, you've only just met him. I have known my brothers my entire life!"

"It doesn't matter. There is something between us. Not like what's between you and me. It's different. Besides, I've only just met you too!"

I stared at her shaking my head.

"You do not understand our ways January. Vesturions are dominant males. I am not sure if I can accept that."

"I can't give him up. We are *friends*...nothing more. I am not asking you to give up any of your friends or the close relationships you have with your family. I won't accept you demanding I give him up."

I ran my hand through my hair and looked up at the sky. The question wasn't whether I loved her. Undoubtedly I did. The question was whether I could live with Herdekian in my life.

"My instincts are urging me to kill him January. For taking you prisoner and holding you against your will. You are asking something of me I am not sure I am capable of doing. I want you January, always by me side. I want to hold on to you forever."

"Rykerian, love isn't always about holding on. It's also about letting go and trusting each other. That may seem like an impossibility for you, but sometimes you have to stretch as far as you possibly can to achieve the impossible."

"You are my 'impossible.'"

Her fingers traced my lips as I kissed them. They touched my cheeks, nose, and eyes and ended in my hair.

"As you are mine. I never thought in a million years I'd ever find someone like you. You are so beautiful Rykerian. I missed you so much."

I lifted her in my arms, wrapping her in them and kissing her as if my life were ending. I didn't want to let her go for I was afraid of losing her, yet I wasn't sure I how I could live with her demands. I would have to find a way.

I felt her wrap her legs around me as we continued our exploration of each other. I leaned against a tree and slid down its trunk, not wanting to let her go. Her hands were all over me, finding their way under my shirt, stepping across the planes of my chest. I sucked in my breath at the myriad of sensations I was experiencing.

"Don't leave me Rykerian."

"I am not going anywhere."

"We can make this work. I know we can. Please trust me."

"Yes," I said into her mouth.

She pulled away when she heard me.

"Really?"

"Yes! I don't want to live without you in my life. I want you beside me, every single day. I will *never* tire of you or wake up thinking, 'What the hell have I done?' It will ever be quite the opposite. I will always be amazed that *you* wanted *me*. I was a bloody ass...a complete idiot. I apologize for that. I said some hateful things to you that were unforgivable and I scratch my head when I think of it. I normally do not act so childish. I was extremely jealous when I saw you with *him* and I acted like a complete and total bloody fool. So it is I that needs to beg for forgiveness. I am begging now. January, will you please forgive me?"

"Yes! I was so afraid Rykerian. I was afraid that when I got back here you wouldn't want me anymore. I was so..."

"Sshh. I think we've said enough. Let's go home, shall we?" I said against her lips as I sought them out once more.

"Yes, let's," she whispered against my lips. We briefly explored each other again.

"Would you like to teleport or run?"

"Let's teleport. It's faster," she grinned.

I tapped my shadar and in seconds we were on the front porch. I turned to her and she charged me, flying into my arms. Her lips took possession of mine and the familiar current of electricity tore through me, setting me on fire.

I lifted her to where our heads were level and carried her up the steps, kicking my bedroom door open, and then kicking it closed behind us. I threw her down on the bed and my body followed hers. Alarms were ringing in my ears and I knew I should stop but I had to drink in my fill first.

Her arms were around my neck, pulling me into her. I had never felt such ecstasy before and I was reluctant to stop. Her lips were soft and sweet and her tongue met mine, as we tasted of each other. I groaned into her mouth and spread my hand across her cheek as my thumb massaged circles on her neck. I rolled over and pulled her on top of me as we continued to caress each other with our lips.

By now, the alarm bells were accompanied by flashing lights and sirens so I physically forced myself away from her mouth.

I kissed her face, her cheeks, taking the last traces of her tears away. I softly pressed my lips to her eyes, and traced the shell of her ear with my tongue. I moved to her neck and found myself becoming intoxicated by her scent. My hands fisted in her hair, feeling the silken strands sliding around my fingers.

"Heaven help me you are so beautiful. Your skin is flushed with desire and your lips are so soft I can barely keep from kissing you."

"Rykerian can we," she put both of her hands on either side if my face and asked, "Can we, you know, make love?" Roses bloomed in her cheeks when she asked me, but she didn't look away from my eyes. I could relate to her shyness regarding this subject so her attempt at boldness warmed my heart.

"I would love nothing more and heavens above you push me to the edge, but you know of our ways. We cannot until we unite."

"Then let's do it! Get married I mean! Tonight!"

"Wha... what? Are you serious?"

"Yes! We can do it however you want...here or on Vesturon. I don't care. I just want us to be together forever!"

"January, you are not just saying this are you? Because you are afraid of losing me? If that is the case, have no fear. I am going nowhere without you."

"No! That's not it. Well, I would rather die than lose you, but I want us to be married. I want to spend the rest of my life with you so why not just get married? I don't care about a fancy wedding or anything about that. I just want us to be together."

"My family is...well we are the First Family of Vesturon and therefore we must have a public ceremony, announcements along with all the formalities."

"Let's do what Maddie and Rayn did. Let's just get married and then have all that later!"

"You are sure about this?"

"Absolutely sure."

"Come with me." I pulled her to her feet and guided her into my bathroom. I took a cloth and moistened it with warm water and wiped her face and eyes. I then filled a glass with water and handed it to her to drink.

"Thank you," she smiled as she handed it back. I should not have looked at her because she was so beguiling my arms automatically reached for her and we found ourselves kissing again.

"Hmmm. When we are united, this may present a huge problem for us."

"What do you mean?" My comment had puzzled her.

"I will not be able to keep my hands off of you for any reasonable length of time." She must have been happy with my explanation because when I looked at her she was beaming.

Chapter Seven

When we arrived back on the terrace, the green monster of jealousy had crept its way back into my gut, and I felt myself bristling even before Jurek Herdekian came into view.

January smiled at him and the green monster nearly engulfed me. The feel of her hand squeezing my arm was the only thing grounding me.

I leaned into her and placed my arm around her announcing to all present that she was mine.

Rayn was detailing to Jurek the events of what had taken place on Xanthus. He showed no signs of anger or remorse about the death of his father, which was quite puzzling to me.

"Well, then, it is imperative we contact Therron immediately. Should I go to Xanthus?" Jurek asked.

"I do not think that would be wise. It could compromise our entire operation there. Let's wait to hear from him. Knowing Therron, he will contact us as soon as he possibly can. He knows the importance of this mission," Rayn informed Jurek.

"I understand."

"We should go to Vesturon in the hopes of hearing from Therron soon. Then you can be rejoined with your sister there," Rayn was saying.

"Really?" January asked me. "Are we going to Vesturon?" Her eyes were bright as she spoke.

"Yes. We thought it best to have Zulietta sent there until Jurek can collect her. We have yet to hear from Therron though since the situation is so terrible on Xanthus. You also need to be introduced to Vesturon," I said, the corners of my mouth turning up. It pleased me to see how excited she was about our upcoming voyage.

"When? When do we leave?"

Jurek interrupted our conversation saying, "I would prefer to travel by my own means and Tak and my men will accompany me."

"As you wish," Rayn responded.

"When and where shall we meet up?"

"We can meet tomorrow afternoon at the Guardian Headquarters in Aurora. Do you know it?"

"Yes, I am familiar with the city so finding the headquarters should be an easy thing. Until tomorrow then."

I thought he would immediately flash himself home, but instead he approached January and bowed deeply to her.

"All is well with you?" he asked, giving me a scathing look. "The Guardian was kind to you?"

"Yeah... I'm fine Jurek. I'll see you tomorrow."

Then I received the yet shock of a lifetime. January all but threw herself at him and said, "Take care of yourself. I'm gonna miss you!"

He grumbled something back in her ear and right before he vanished, she stuck her tongue out at him.

When she spun around to face me, I knew she could see the storm clouds brewing in my eyes.

"Rykerian, *please* let me explain things. I don't want to fight about this but you have to let me tell my side of the story. Please?" she pleaded with me.

I nodded curtly and looked at Rayn, silently telling him to leave us.

"One thing before I leave you two alone, do you wish to teleport or travel by Space Transporter."

"Space Transporter. I wish to show January the universe."

"Very well. I shall make the arrangements. And January, it is good to see you again. Welcome back."

January took a seat on the couch and I pulled up a chair so I could face her. Then she told me this incredible story. I didn't know if I wanted to thank this Jurek or if I should kill him.

"You don't really feel like you want to kill him do you?"

"Oh January, I am at great odds. On the one hand, how can I not be grateful for what he has done for you? And for me? But it has come at such a huge expense. And if he had not abducted you in the first place, we would not be having this conversation."

"I know, but his story is such a sad one. We related on that level and when he told me about his species, I felt so sorry for him. And then the whole thing about how he made me confront my feelings for you. We just sort of became friends. I don't expect you to understand nor do I expect you to like it, but there is some kind of connection between us that neither of us can deny nor explain. Before you get all mad at me again, it's not *that* kind of connection. It's more like friendship or even family." She rose to her feet and started wringing her hands.

"I don't want you to be upset by any of this. I swear my heart and soul lie with you and always will."

"But January, can you not see how twisted this whole thing is? He destroys half of humanity on Earth, then comes here and threatens us and abducts you. He holds you prisoner for weeks with demands of saving his family and if we fail, he says he will kill you. Yes, he allowed us to communicate twice, but other than that I didn't know if you were alive or dead. Can you try to understand how I feel about this? I assure you I am having great difficulty in tempering my thoughts of him."

She came to me and knelt between my legs as she grasped my hands. Her pale ice blue eyes held mine as she spoke.

"I know it's completely strange. I'm not sure how I'd handle it if the shoe were on the other foot. I am so mad at him about what he did here on Earth, but he also protected me. He did what he had to do for his family. He felt he was given no other choice. I was not harmed at all while I was there. I really don't think he would have killed me. He was just saying that. And he forced me to look deep within myself confront my own demons. He understands how I couldn't let myself open up to you because he's been through much of the same things. We are so much alike in that regard. I'm not asking you to like any of this, but I am asking you to accept it for what it is."

"Where did he take you January?"

"I honestly don't know. He wouldn't tell me but it wouldn't have mattered anyway. We were somewhere out in space in some kind of space station or something. I stayed in one room that would convert itself into whatever room I needed it to be."

I nodded, trying to digest everything she was telling me.

She hadn't moved from the place between my legs and her beautiful face was imploring me to understand.

"I missed you so much." It was the first thing I thought to say.

"Not as much as I missed you," she whispered.

I picked her up and set her in my lap, refusing to let her go. She laid her head on my chest and spoke again.

"I want you to get to know him Rykerian. He could be a great ally for us in our war against the Xanthians."

I smiled at her words, saying, "Spoken like a true Vesturion."

She sat straight up, looked at me and said, "I know, right?"

"Look, I will do my best to have an open mind concerning your friend, but I cannot promise I will like him."

"That's more than fair, and more than I can ask."

Chapter Eight

January and I decided we would finalize the issue of Jurek's sister before we would approach the idea of getting married—as she called it. We didn't want to add any more stress than necessary to my family.

The next day we boarded the Space Transporter and headed for Vesturon. Rayn was at the helm, which allowed me to explain all the sights to January. Other than the usual first time side effects of space travel, January was seemingly intrigued by it all. She couldn't stop asking questions.

When we made the jump to hyper propulsion, her curiosity presented itself.

"What happened to all the stars?"

"Oh, they're still there. You can't see them because we are traveling faster than the speed of light."

"Okay, where I come from that would be an impossibility."

"That is correct. But where we come from it is a way of life."

"How so?"

"Rayn, would you care to answer? I let him answer this kind of thing as he's the family genius," I joked.

"I'll do my best. January, we learned a long time ago that you can cheat astrophysics."

"How can you do that?"

"Okay, cheat may be too strong a word. How about this...we take shortcuts."

"Can you explain?"

"Let's see...well the shortest distance between two points is a straight line, correct?"

"Duh! Yeah!"

"Hang on a moment and this will all make sense. What we do is take the space-time continuum and fracture it into sections, much like your string theory. If you bring the ends of the strings together and move from end to end, in that fashion, your distance is shortened significantly, correct?"

"Yeah, but..."

"Stay with me for a moment. We bend the trajectory on which we want to travel in a loop formation—much like a switchback on a mountain road. Except for a major deviation. We don't follow the road."

"Huh? You lost me on that."

"Okay. Imagine a straight path, but take it and bend it like this," Rayn said, taking his finger and drawing an imaginary curved line.

I went to the screen and using my glove, I drew the line that Rayn was describing.

"Like this January. We start with this and change it into that."

"Okay, but you still have the same length, except it's not straight."

"Ah, you are correct. But there is a big difference. We don't follow that trajectory. We leap from one section to the next using a sort of loophole method," Rayn finished.

I gestured with my hand at the line I had drawn saying, "Like this. We jump from point A to B to C and so forth. So in a sense, it is a shortcut because we cheat the space-time continuum. If you were to stretch the trajectory out, it would be the total distance traveled, but our method makes it only *seem* much shorter. Does that make sense?"

"Yeah, in theory. But how does it really work?" January persisted.

"Now that is a question for our astrophysicists and engineers! I can only describe the theory but not the mechanics," Rayn said.

"Do not believe him January. Rayn could build this Space Transporter if he wanted. He is brilliant and the brains in the family," I quipped.

No sooner had the words left my mouth when the ship's screen lit up like a Christmas tree.

"What was that?" January asked, her eyes popping out of her head.

"Rykerian, strap yourselves in, and fast. We have company...and not the good kind," Rayn shouted.

I threw January into a seat and fastened her harness and barely got myself strapped in when Rayn threw the ship into an evasive maneuver. Unfortunately, we were in a Space Transporter and not a Star Fighter, so our capabilities were limited.

"Rayn?" I yelled.

"The ship has Xanthian markings. I'm getting Xanthian readings from my probe too."

"Can we outrun them?" I inquired.

"Doubtful. Start stripping the ship's data but be careful. Our ride is about to get very bumpy!"

"Can I help?" January shouted.

"No!" we both retorted simultaneously.

"Stay put. I do not want you to get injured," I told her as I moved toward the ship's compsys.

My fingers flew across the board commanding the compsys to transfer all data to my shadar.

"How long?" Rayn asked.

"A few minutes. How much time do we have?"

"About that much. We will be cutting it close."

"Your veil is up right?"

"Yes, but they tracked our heat trail. They cannot see us but they know where to fire."

"Fire? What do you mean fire?" January asked.

"They are preparing to fire on us," I told her. "Rayn, teleport her to the space dock right now. I would feel better knowing she was there."

"What about you?" she asked.

"We will follow as soon as we strip all the data on board. It cannot fall into Xanthian hands. We can sacrifice the ship but not the data."

"I'll stay," she said.

"No! I want you out of here. Rayn, teleport her now!"

I watched as she disappeared and did not breathe until the

commander on Vesturon informed us she had arrived safely and was in his care.

Rayn bellowed, "Brace yourself, incoming annihilator beams!"

The blast hit the ship and I crashed against the main console, wrenching my shoulder and snapping my forearm. I screamed with the initial break, but forced myself to go to that place in my mind where I could control the pain.

"Are you okay?" Rayn shouted.

"No! I broke my bloody arm! Just get us out of here!"

"Impossible. They are all over us. There are five of them and they have us covered like icing on a cake. How much longer before the strip is complete?"

"Soon! Can you do anything at all?"

"Incoming!" he shouted.

This time we took multiple hits that sent me airborne. I collided with the main screen, bones crunching and flesh tearing. The impact left me dazed. My ribs were broken; of that I had no doubt. Breathing was sheer hell. My midsection quickly became saturated with what I could only assume was blood. My head throbbed as the back of it had also slammed into the screen. My leg was awkwardly contorted, but I couldn't stop. If I did, we would die.

"Rayn!"

No response. I heaved myself upwards and saw Rayn slumped in his chair. The whole of it had been torn from its bolts and it was lying sideways in the aft of the ship. Using my good arm and leg, I pitched myself toward him. Tapping our destination into the teleporter, I got us out of there.

We materialized at the space dock and then everything faded to black.

Chapter Nine

I heard faint voices in the background and a constant whirring. My eyelids felt glued together. Every muscle felt leaden and when I tried to lift my head, it was locked in place. Where was I? What in the world happened?

I dug into the recesses of my mind and I recalled boarding the Space Transporter, but then...nothing. I engaged my senses in an attempt to understand what was happening.

The voices became clearer, but not enough to interpret their meaning.

Then it hit me like lightening. The Space Transporter...the Xanthians...taking multiple blasts...getting injured...Rayn! How was Rayn?

I was instantly assailed with her scent as it penetrated my soul...citrus with a crisp freshness to it. It reminded me of floating on a warm sea. I could taste the tanginess of the citrus mixed with the salt in the air. Oh how it soothed me. I inhaled deeply, letting it infuse and permeate throughout my body.

At first, her touch was so light, I barely felt it. Then I felt cool, soft fingers weaving their way through my hair, beginning at my forehead and moving back to the crown. Oh it felt so nice, that soft massaging motion.

Why couldn't I open my eyes? I wanted to see her. I opened my mind instead. Her anguish engulfed me. I wanted to hold her in my arms. I willed her to put her face next to mine. It wasn't that I wanted her there—I *needed* her there. We spoke through our minds...she telling me how worried she was and I telling her I was glad she was here. Her love washed over me like a cooling rain...a balm to my torn and battered body.

"Why can I not move?"

"You were badly injured Rykerian."

"How is Rayn?

"In about the same shape as you, but he's going to be fine too."

"What happened?"

"You mean on the ship?"

"No...me. What happened to me?"

"Only a broken arm, a broken leg, fractured neck vertebra, crushed ribs, punctured and collapsed lung...not to mention the countless lacerations."

"Are you trying to be humorous?"

"No...I'm totally serious here. Like I said, you were injured...critically, in fact. Luckily, you got here in time and they did a decent job of patching you up."

"Lay next to me."

"There isn't room."

"Please!"

"I'll hurt you. I don't want to cause you any more pain Rykerian."

"You are causing me a great deal of pain by refusing *to lay with me. Please...I* need *to feel you...all of you January."*

"Okay...but will you let me know if this makes your pain worse?"

"It won't. Trust me."

The bed moved slightly as she climbed on it.

She gently rested her hand on my chest, being so very careful not to apply any pressure. Then she moved it up to my neck and then my cheek, and finally my lips. She traced the outline of them and I felt the bed move a bit. Her lips touched mine ever so briefly. I moaned in the back of my throat, wanting more, but knowing I could not.

"Take my hand in yours January," I barely croaked out.

The soft yet firm fingers laced with mine and I felt a peace descend over me, as sleep reclaimed my body.

Time passed. I knew not how much, nor did I care. I was healing and that was all I focused upon. The day finally came when I could open my eyes and move my arms. Julian had kept my body in a semi-unconscious state for several days. Knowing me well, he understood I would not be willing to lay quietly, hence the major sedation.

January stayed by my side continuously, refusing to leave for anything. She slept next to me every night, holding my hand and murmuring words of love to me. She had lightened up my life and my love for her rooted itself deeply within my soul and spread throughout every part of me. I was madly in love with her, bound by heart, mind and soul, and could not ever part from her again.

Chapter Ten

I t took January a bit of time to get over her shock of her first view of our home. My family resided in a palace of sorts, as we were much like royalty on Earth. It had been built over a thousand years ago and looked similar to the Biltmore House in Asheville, North Carolina, albeit much more grand and ancient. It was constructed mostly of a variety of stone and had weathered beautifully over the ages.

The interior was luxurious by any standards. Masterful oil paintings and hand woven tapestries graced the walls while the polished marble floors gleamed.

The palace consisted of five levels. The main level contained all the formal areas...the grand dining room, greeting rooms, music room, ballroom, and so forth. It was where all high level entertaining took place.

The kitchens were all located on this level as well. The lower level beneath the palace housed the laundry facilities, and all the other working areas of the palace.

The second floor was where the family resided for the most part. The informal living areas, kitchen, dining room, entertainment room, exercise area, and the like were all located here.

All the bedroom suites were located on the third floor, other than my parent's. Theirs was on the fourth floor, where they each had an expansive office, along with their own private living quarters. Their personal staff was located on that level as well.

On the third floor, the spacious bedroom suites were divided by the main staircase. All of my siblings stayed on one side, leaving the other side for guests.

Each floor had a gallery that contained artwork and marble busts of Vesturon's past rulers, my ancestors.

My mother, being the perceptive individual that she was had given January the room next to mine. I showed her where she would be staying and during the brief tour, she barely spoke a word.

"Why didn't you tell me about all of this?"

"Would it have mattered?"

She looked pensive then blurted out, "Nope. I don't think anything could keep me away from you. It's just insane to me when I think about it all. I mean how long ago was it when I was scrounging around for change to buy a hot dog? And now this! It's a bit over the top and all, but it's not gonna run me off if that's what you're thinking."

I must have been looking at her oddly for she asked quietly, "Was that the wrong answer?"

"It could not have been more right. I was thinking that most females would flock to this lifestyle and you were thinking the opposite."

"Well, I'm glad you finally figured that one out! I'm not most females!" she winked. "Don't you think it would be a good idea if you took it easy...you know, chilled for a bit. You still have some major recovering to do."

"I am tired, but I should like to talk with my family first. Come."

"Geez, always the demanding one, aren't you?"

"Me? I'm the most mild-mannered one in the family. Wait until you've spent more time around Rayn and my father!"

We joined my family in the den. Rayn, Maddie, Tesslar and my parents were present. I quickly made the necessary introductions and we launched into the status of the Xanthian situation.

"They're demanding the release of Counselor Druaha. They are also demanding control of Earth," my father began.

"What?" I was shocked.

"All space travel is suspended unless you are part of an armada. No Space Transporters are allowed to go unescorted. That was a blatant attack on you and Rayn. They knew you would be heading to Vesturon. They were tracking all space traffic to and from the Milky Way."

"What will happen to Earth?" January asked.

"We will do what we can but we make no promises. It is the beginning of a terrible time for our universe. The Xanthians are trying to garner support from other planets. There are enough unsavory ones out there that they are sure to gain numbers."

"Father, what of Xarrid, Therron and Sharra?" I wondered.

"Sharra should be here soon. She is coming back with a team of fighters and she will be training others here until we can build up our forces again. Therron and Xarrid are the ones I fear for the most. Xarrid will not leave Xanthus until he locates Saylan. We finally heard from Therron a few days ago. A Xanthian spy posing as a Guardian compromised his position. Therron has no idea how much information the spy had passed to the Xanthians before he was caught and dealt with. Therron's shadars both malfunctioned, so he was trapped for a time. Therron will not leave Xanthus without Xarrid." My father rose and began pacing. The creases around his eyes and mouth and deepened since that last time I saw him.

"What about Zulietta?" I asked.

"She arrived safely here and other than being shaken up, she was fine," Father explained.

I lifted my eyes to Rayn and his look matched my father's.

"Rayn, how are you feeling?" I asked.

"About the same as you. Glad to be here, thanks to you," he grinned ruefully.

"So what can we do?" I wanted to know.

"You two need to rest up because you are going to need your strength in the days and months ahead," my mother suggested.

"I assume the Herdekian claimed his sister?" Rayn questioned.

"Yes, and all went as we expected. I think we should engage him as an ally. January could help us, could you not January?"

Anger diffused through my body at the mention of his name and I said, my voice tinged with menace, "I do not want January within one hundred light years from him."

"Rykerian, you are taking this the wrong way. Anyone could see they have formed a friendship of sorts and he will not harm her. It would help our cause if she was there."

"I could not care less about our cause or any cause for that matter. I do not want January near Jurek Herdekian!" I bounded to my feet and began pacing.

My father looked at me intently and then asked, "January, how do you feel about him?"

"He is my friend," she said softly.

"Elucidate," he demanded.

"We've faced a lot of the same issues during our lives and I think it's kind of thrown us into a friendship type of thing. It sounds strange and convoluted and all but there is nothing between us but friendship. I could ask him whatever you want. And I wouldn't feel unsafe around him. I'm sorry Rykerian."

My father stared at me and I felt the fingers of his mind probe, making their way into my head. There was no use in denying him for he was extremely powerful and would find a way to accomplish this. I granted him entry and waited for him to finish.

He sat back and gave me a look that I recognized. His eyes softened as he spoke. "You have no reason to fear this if it is as she says. I know this is something you do not desire, but the greater good of the people is at stake here. I am sorry my son, but we must have January contact him. His kind may be the key to keeping the Xanthians from wreaking havoc on the universe."

The muscle in my jaw twitched furiously as my anger intensified. My family was betraying me.

"No, we are not betraying you Rykerian. We would not be doing this if we were putting anyone in harm's way," my father stated, tersely.

I jerked my head in mimicking a nod, and headed up to my room.

Chapter Eleven

T he situation continued to deteriorate on Xanthus. Xarrid teleported to the Guardian Command Center for a briefing on the situation. He only agreed to come because we dangled the proverbial carrot of our potential alliance with Jurek Herdekian.

I could not contain my shock at his haggard yet hewn appearance. He had lost weight and his skin was stretched tightly across his taut muscles. His face was now chiseled, having lost all his youthful appearance. The light had been extinguished from his eyes, but in its place burned an intense fire that alarmed me. His usually neatly trimmed hair was now long and scruffy, as was the beard on his face. Although he had never had much interest in fashion, he was always smartly attired. The Xarrid of old seemed to have been replaced by one that dressed with purpose. He not only wore his shadars, he also carried daggers attached to his belt and had one strapped to his thigh. There were all sorts of deadly throwing devices attached to various parts of his clothing. An air of danger surrounded him. He no longer bore any resemblance to the brother and Guardian I knew from a short time ago.

"Have each of you seen enough?" His impatience rolled off his tongue as his eyes flicked around the room. "I am quite aware of my appearance so either put a cork on your thoughts or leave this room."

Maddie ran up to him and threw her arms around him, but he shrugged them off and backed away from her reach.

"Xarrid!" Rayn admonished curtly.

"Look, I didn't come here for a little social gathering or love session. I took a huge risk leaving, and I'll take another one when I return. I'm not sure any of you get it! Xanthus is a pressure cooker right now and it's not getting any better!"

"I believe you underestimate our intelligence brother. We have been most concerned about you and Therron and Maddie can hardly sleep at night due to her concern over you and Saylan's disappearance," Rayn said.

"How touching. Now quit wasting my time and get to the point. Why did you call me here?"

"There is someone...or rather an entire species that you are unfamiliar with that may be interested in furthering our cause in stopping the Xanthians," Rayn began.

"Go on."

"We have recently been introduced to them. They are known as Praestani."

"What's so special about them?"

"You shall see," Rayn said.

"Okay, well, this has been great, but I have things to do, places to go...you know the line."

He held up his shadar but was interrupted by a popping noise. The room became electrically charged as Jurek and five of his men appeared.

January immediately ran to him and all but threw herself at him. His entire demeanor changed when she reached him. His face lit up and his eyes even changed color.

And so did mine. I could feel them darkening as each second passed.

"Stop fretting Guardian. You have nothing to worry about where January is concerned. She is your female through and through."

All eyes swung to me and I could feel my face burn. I was sure it was a mottled shade of purple by now.

Jurek whispered something to January that I did not want to hear or speculate on, and then she was back by my side, squeezing my hand.

Xarrid's eyes were fixated on us and I noticed the muscle in his jaw twitching.

"Xarrid, this is January, but the way," I introduced them.

He nodded curtly, and then swung his head to Jurek.

"Who are they?" Xarrid demanded.

"I am told your rear end is in a sling and we are here to help you get it out. For a large fee of course," Jurek smirked.

That male had the most irritating way about him.

"Jurek!" January admonished.

"I speak only the truth."

"Well, aren't you full of yourself?" Xarrid mocked.

"No. Just honest."

"What makes you think you can help?"

"Because we are powerful, nearly indestructible, and know how to properly treat the Xanthians."

"Okay. Rayn, this has been an amusing little diversion, but I cannot afford to waste any more time. It's been nice..."

Xarrid had gone to use his shadar to teleport, but before he knew what happened, Jurek was holding it in his hand. Xarrid was staring at his own naked wrist.

"Looking for this?" Jurek wanted to know.

"What the..." His eyes bounced between his wrist and Jurek several times. "How did you do that?"

"As I said, we are powerful. You cannot stop us. You cannot kill us."

Xarrid stretched out his arm and boomed, "I command you to your knees."

Jurek looked back at him and smiled. "Your Powers are also useless on us, even Command."

"How can that be?"

"Accept it Xarrid for it is the way of things," I said. "Jurek and his people are gifted, in a much greater way than Vesturions ever dreamed."

"How so?"

"Would you care for a demonstration?"

No sooner had the word, "Yes," left Xarrid's mouth, he found himself stretched out and suspended in midair, trapped and unable to move. Jurek hadn't moved so much as an inch.

"Enough!" January shouted. I arched a brow at her, interested in her rescue of my brother.

Jurek shrugged, "No worries, friend, he is in no pain," and Xarrid was back on his feet.

"How do I know that's not the extent of your so-called powers?" Xarrid questioned.

Jurek instantly shifted into his alternative form and brushed against Xarrid, dropping him to his knees, sending him into fits of agony.

It only lasted a second, but it was enough to convince Xarrid of Jurek's powers. After he recovered from his brief contact with the Praestanus, Xarrid was ready to strategize on how Jurek's men could take out and destroy key areas on Xanthus. Even though Xarrid was livid when he discovered it was Jurek and his men who were responsible for the pandemic on Earth, we persuaded him to accept the Praestani's help on ending this war sooner.

Hours later, Xanthus' weaknesses were bared to the Praestani and plans were established to disable all their power generating stations. Ten teams of Jurek's men would go in and disable all available ships in their docking stations so they would have nothing to transport them to other planets. They would be effectively stranded on Xanthus.

They were targeting the Xanthian rebel headquarters to gain information on the allies they had established so they could initiate a breakdown of those relationships. They would sabotage everything the Xanthians had put into place thus far, making the Xanthians appear to be even more untrustworthy than they were.

Jurek would send a contingency of his men to Earth to make sure the Xanthians there were rounded up and sent back to Xanthus. We did not know how many of them had infiltrated Earth, but we wanted to make sure we didn't give them an opportunity to establish any kind of strong hold.

I observed Xarrid and Jurek interact and it struck me as odd, but they reminded me of each other. Xarrid's tough persona was a new experience for me, but Jurek seemed to get him. It was amazing to see these two warriors planning covert missions and they even laughed a few times at shared remarks.

I still had trouble wrapping my brain around Xarrid's transformation. As I stared at him he caustically remarked, "Look pretty boy, if you don't stop staring at me, I'm going to start thinking you have a thing for me." Jurek sputtered at his words.

I, on the other hand, gave Xarrid a scorching look and fumed, "That is disgusting Xarrid and you well know it. What in the bloody hell has gotten into you? What has happened to the brother I knew so well?"

Xarrid threw his shadar down and thundered, "I'll tell you what the bloody hell has happened to me! I've been trying to survive in a bloody war zone for the last several months, while you've been living the high life, chasing your mate around laughing and carrying on. I'll tell you what the bloody hell has happened to me! I've been existing on the barest hours of sleep, trying my damnedest to find Saylan, searching every possible corner of Xanthus and coming up empty handed. I'll tell you what the bloody hell has happened. The love of my life—my mate—has fallen off the face of the planet and no one seems to know a bloody thing!" By the time he finished speaking, he was in my face, poking me in the chest with his finger, and screaming in anger.

I wrapped him in my embrace and he struggled at first to break free, but I held on, not allowing that. The harder he fought me, the tighter I held him, until I felt the fight flee him and he returned my embrace.

"Bloody hell Rykerian, what am I going to do?" he sputtered onto my shoulder. "I've searched everywhere and I've done everything I know to do. It's like she simply vanished into thin air. Even her tracer came up blank!"

The pain in his voice tore me apart. I know exactly how he felt, for I had been there with January.

"We will find her Xarrid. Dead or alive, we will find out what happened to her. She didn't just vanish. She is *somewhere* and we will find her. I promise!"

I glanced across the room and Jurek caught my eye. My mind was instantly infused with his thoughts.

"I need a description of her along with her last location, living quarters, complete name and history with the Guardians. I will send one of my men right away to begin a search for her. We will locate her."

I nodded back at him and he left the room.

"Come. Let's get out of here for a break."

"Yes, I could use one. Sorry for being such a jerk to you. I have no excuse except I *am* a jerk. Please forgive me?" he asked.

"There is nothing to forgive, brother. I know exactly how you feel. Trust me." We made our way back to the palace.

Chapter Twelve

L ater that day, January and I sat on the terrace overlooking the Vesturion mountains. I knew she would love it here—I just hadn't realized how much.

"I want us to get married right away. I don't want to wait. I know this may sound selfish and this is a terrible time for your family, but we could do it right here with just us. If we don't do it now, it may be forever, with the situation being what it is." She stopped talking and took my hands in hers and asked, "Rykerian, will you marry me?"

"Yes!" I kissed her quickly then said, "Follow me."

We went up to the family living quarters. Rayn, Maddie, Tesslar and my parents were all sitting there.

"I'd like to discuss something with you please. January and I have decided to have a private unification ceremony."

Everyone did their obligatory "Oohs" and "Aahs" and patted me on the back and congratulated us.

"This is a terrible time for Vesturon now and it does not look like it will improve anytime soon. So we thought a private ceremony with just us on the back terrace would be appropriate."

Everyone was smiling and happy. My mother asked when.

"Tonight."

You would have thought a blaster went off. It was total silence and then a million questions.

"Please. Hear me out. There will not be a good time for this in a very long while. We don't want to wait. Our souls are bound together so why not tonight?"

"Well, why not indeed?" my father asked.

"Exactly!" I said.

"I second that!" Rayn said.

"So, can you get a clergyman?" I asked my father.

"What time?"

Several hours later, dressed head to toe in traditional Vesturion formal white attire, I stood at the edge of the terrace waiting for her to appear. My father, Rayn, Tesslar and Xarrid stood beside me. Across from us stood Maddie and my mother. Victus, the clergyman stood with us as well.

January had insisted on three things: Jurek escorting her down the aisle; Pachelbel's Canon in D playing when she walked down the aisle; and finally, carrying a bouquet of freshly cut flowers. That wasn't normally done here, but she was so fond of them, and to her point, Vesturon had stunning flowers, she had gotten her way.

Jurek swelled with pride as he held her hand on his arm, and as he did so, my thoughts flew back to the day I discovered her at death's door. My how she had changed! Gone was the timid, ghost girl of the past and in her place was a stunningly beautiful golden princess. Everything ceased to exist but the two of us as I gazed at her while she made her way toward me. Could this truly be happening? Was this ethereal nymph going to be my mate...now and forever?

My mother and Maddie had helped January decide on what to wear. She had no interest in donning the traditional wedding attire Earthlings commonly wore, so they had settled upon Vesturion garments...and they could not have been more perfect for her.

She was dressed in a white fitted tunic that stopped above her knees, showing off her shapely legs. The tunic was trimmed in silver and gold and had hints of those threads woven into it, which set off the magnificent color of her hair. The neckline plunged into a deep V, allowing her bare neck to be adorned in rows of beautiful sapphires, intensifying the unusual hue of her eyes. Her hair had tiny braids intricately twisted throughout it. She was exquisite. The bouquet she carried held a multitude of shades from, blues and greens to bright pinks and purples. The complete effect was perfectly gorgeous.

She beamed as Jurek handed her to me, and her hands clasped mine, indicating to me she would never let me go.

The ceremony was simple, yet meaningful, as we had written our vows to each other. They were filled with promises of hope and love and we vowed to walk side by side for the remainder of our days. Her eyes shimmered as she spoke them, but I knew she was filled with joy. When we were pronounced as true soul mates, I lifted her in my arms as my lips sought hers. It took Rayn's elbow in my ribs for us to break apart, so engrossed in each other we were.

When our lips separated, everyone applauded for us and we both grinned unabashedly.

We celebrated afterward with a delicious meal and toasted with champagne. I couldn't help noticing the amount of time Xarrid was spending with Jurek. The two of them seemed to have become fairly close within the brief time they had known each other. January had remarked on this as well.

"Maybe it will be for the best when the time comes for them to go to Xanthus and do what they're planning to do."

"Perhaps. It is strange to me though."

"I think it's because you don't like him Rykerian, so you don't want anyone else to."

"Most likely you are correct."

"Uh hum," she said as she placed a kiss on my lips. "That's my goal you know."

"What is?"

"To get you to like him."

"Hah! It will be a cold day in hell before that will happen, my lovely bride! Have I told you how beautiful you look my love?"

"Only about a hundred times!"

"Well, that is certainly not nearly enough. I will have to make a point to tell you more often!"

"I think you're trying to spoil me!"

"You have no idea, January. It starts today and will continue for the rest of your life," I told her, kissing her.

Maddie came up to us and said, "Well, Rykerian, I suppose hearts will be breaking all over Vesturon today when news of your unification breaks."

"Do not count on it. It was Rayn who broke all the hearts when he took you as his mate," I countered.

"Yeah, well, whatever, but I have it on good authority, that all the women here will be heartsick at the loss!"

I shook my head. I put my arm around January and steered her into the corner. "I have waited so long for this day. I am not sure how much longer I can wait to be alone with you."

"Well then, why don't we just leave?" she asked.

"Do you truly want to?"

"Are you kidding? I've been nothing but a heap of combustible hormones since I've met you. Of course I want to leave!"

I latched onto her wrist and tugged her down the hall. When we were away from all eyes and ears, I picked her up, kissing her, and carried her up the stairs to our room, where I placed her on the bed. Lying next to her, I continued my exploration of her with my lips. I kissed her neck, running my tongue along her pulse point, feeling it beating beneath me.

I sat up and looked at her in awe. She was a glorious vision...braided hair fanned out across the bed, and cheeks like summer roses. Her lips were lush and pink from our kisses and her eyes smoldered with passion.

"Sweet Deity, I thought when you walked down the aisle that I had never seen you look more lovely. I was wrong. Lying here, with your eyes on fire and your lips swollen from our kisses, I have never seen a more beautiful female...and you belong to me, body and soul."

"Yes...always and forever yours Rykerian."

Her arms encircled my neck and drew me to her. Then she pushed my shoulder and rolled me to my back. Climbing on top of me, she began her exploration of my body. Her fingertips gently touched my arms, then my shoulders. She made her way to my shirt where she began to undo the buttons, locking onto my eyes as she did so. I was absolutely dissolving into her.

January always seemed to render me into nothing, turning my bones into liquid gold. This time, however, I began to feel a surge of intense heat as it made its way through my veins. Every cell, every molecule in my body responded to her touch. We always had this connection, this awareness of each other. But now, it was overpowering, almost as though I was feeling what she was and vice versa. Her eyes widened as the same realization hit her.

"I had a conversation with Rayn after he and Maddie united," I began, "and he told me it was unimaginable. I suppose this was to what he was referring," I whispered, breathlessly.

"I never thought it would be like this Rykerian."

"Neither did I," I grabbed her and kissed her, not wanting to spend any more time chatting.

When the last button was undone, I could barely shrug out of my shirt as my breath caught and her hands continued their journey across my chest and down the planes of my torso. When I could take no more, I grabbed her hands and brought them to my lips. It was the most world shattering experience of my life.

"My turn," I whispered brokenly.

She looked at me with her doe eyes and nodded.

"Are you frightened January?"

She shook her head. "Frightened? Never. Not with you. On the other hand, I am a bit nervous."

"Ah, my love. Please do not fret. We will go slow and if at any time you want me to stop, just say the word and I will. Okay?"

"Okay. I love you Rykerian."

"As I love you January. Always and forever." I knew exactly what I wanted to do with her but I would do it with care because I wanted this to be the most special night of our lives.

I sat up and wrapped my arms around her and began my own exploration of her lovely body, beginning with her lips. It brought me back to the very first time I had tasted them...honey, sweet, luscious honey.

"You are more than anything I could have ever hoped for January," I said against her lips and then I lowered my head to nibble on her alabaster neck. I ran my tongue along its length until it met her collarbone, where I allowed my fingers to play lightly across its ridge. I leaned away from her and was treated to an exquisite view—her head was thrown back, her lips were slightly parted and her chest was swelling with her every breath.

I laid my hand across her chest for I had an urge to feel her heart beating beneath my fingers. She looked at me at that moment and then placed her hand on top of mine, but surprised me when she moved it to the swell of her breast.

I gently nudged her backwards until she was lying on her back, and softly breathed, "Don't fret love, there will not be one tiny inch of your loveliness I won't be touching or kissing before the night is over." Her breath caught in her throat at my words and she tugged me to her and kissed me fervently.

I would commit to memory the picture she made forever. She was lying there in her bridal tunic with one arm over her head and the other stretched out, her hand clutching the satin sheets. Her eyes were focused solely on me, her lips were slightly parted and she was making the tiniest of moans that nearly drove me mad with desire. I slipped my hands beneath the hem of her dress and slid them along her silken skin, as I slowly removed her garment. I heard a whiff as she quickly inhaled.

"Tell me I'm not dreaming Rykerian. Tell me I'm not going to wake up to find this was all not real." Her voice was husky with desire.

"I believe it is I who should be saying that as I behold something as beautiful as you." I had to pause before continuing, for she was simply breathtaking. "I promise you love, this is very real, and what you will soon feel will prove to you that it is so."

Our senses were heightened with desire as currents of heat ran between us. We were linked by our souls and the waves of passion ignited and burst forth as we discovered each other through our touch, hearts and minds. We fell asleep in each other's arms, exhausted from our hours of lovemaking.

We awoke the next morning, tangled up in sheets and limbs, I was grinning and she was smiling shyly.

"Nothing to be shy of, love." I ran my thumb along her bottom lip as I cupped her cheek in my hand. It was impossible not to caress this lovely mate of mine.

"I guess I never thought that it would feel quite so...well, so *good*! And it was so *wicked*!"

I roared with laughter at her response. "Of all the things I expected from you this morning, 'wicked' was not one of them."

"I didn't expect that either! When can we do it again?"

"Um, is now a good time for you?" I asked as I grabbed her, pulled her on top of me and picked up where we left off the night before.

Chapter Thirteen

"I thought we promised to be by each other's side always, Rykerian. I thought that's what our vows meant."

"Listen to me love, I cannot have you on Xanthus with me. I would not be able to do my job with you there. I would be incessantly worried about your safety. It is a very dangerous place."

"But I won't be able to stand it here without you. Please," she pleaded.

We both heard the pop and felt that current flow through the room.

"Are you insane? Do you think for one minute either of us would allow you to be there? I know your mate is adamant about this January, as am I. You *cannot* come. If we have to put you on the space station to ensure your safety, so be it," Jurek said.

For once, I completely agreed with him.

"Look love, I hate leaving you as much as you hate it. I do not want to go, though I must. It is my duty, not only as a Guardian, but also as a brother. Therron needs us and so does Saylan. I promised Xarrid we would stop at nothing to find out what happened to her and I meant that. Now, does Jurek have to take you to the station or will you stay here?"

They both looked at me like I had lost my mind. I rolled my eyes at them.

"You did not just roll your eyes at me, did you?" she asked.

"As a matter of fact I did. However, you did not answer my question."

"I will stay here of course. Jurek, will you stay by his side?"

"If I must," he said sardonically.

She flung out her arm and bashed him in the shoulder saying, "Yes you must!"

Then January flung herself at me and wrapped herself around me like she would never see me again.

"Hey, it is all right love. I will be fine. I promise," I swore to her, hugging her tightly to me and inhaling her essence. "I take you with me everywhere I go. You have my soul as I have yours." I pulled back a bit so I could look at her. I saw the tracks of her tears so I took my gloved thumbs and swiped them away. Then I kissed her face where they had been and moved my mouth to her lips. She clung to me like I was her lifeline. I tore off my gloves and placed my hands on either side of her head, willing Tranquility into her.

"Better now?"

"Yes," she murmured huskily. "I love you so much. Be safe."

"You know I will and do not forget, I have a babysitter." That made her lips curve upward so I felt better as well.

Xanthus was a changed place. It literally looked like a version of hell, complete with the fires. Destruction ruled and so did the rebel fighters. They had grown to such large numbers; they had taken over what had formerly been the Xanthian governing facilities.

Smugglers were in and out as the planet could not supply all the necessary items for survival. There were rumors of a secret sect that had ties to a unified superpower of sorts. It was said that this unity consisted of various planets that never would join the Universal Free Rule of which Vesturon was a part. Vesturon and the Free Rule believed that all creatures had a right to exist freely and equally in the universe and could do so as long as they were willing to work hard and live according to the democracy. Its people were not dependent on any form of government nor did any government own the people.

The Unified Superpower, on the other hand, wanted control over everything, including finances, property and rights for all. It was a tyrannical rule, one that went against everything Vesturon and the Free Rule stood for.

There were other rumors that Unified Superpower was starting to amass an army of vast proportions in an attempt to take over the universe. There were reports of Xanthians already on many planets, infiltrating their governing bodies, so when the appropriate times came, they would rise and over take everything.

My father had been right all along. For years he had tried to convince the council that turning a blind eye to things was not the way to solve problems. They had not heeded his advice and recommendations and we would be paying for it in the years ahead.

Jurek, Xarrid, and I were to rendezvous with Therron and his allies. We crept through the darkened streets on our way to the assigned place, with Xarrid leading the way. Jurek's men were to follow on his command.

As we neared the place of the meeting, I felt an impending sense of doom descend upon me. It felt like it was smothering me.

"We have to get out of here. Something is dreadfully wrong," I whispered.

"I agree, but we cannot leave Therron. He is expecting us to be here," Xarrid answered.

"You two go on and I will remain behind," Jurek suggested.

"That will be of no use. Therron does not know you."

"There he is!" called Xarrid.

I looked up to see Therron zig-zagging his way toward us. Suddenly, the night air lit up with blaster beams. We were surrounded on all sides.

I shouted to Xarrid, "Hit the deck!"

Jurek converted to energy and began taking out the enemies.

Xarrid screamed, "Don't kill them all! We need a hostage. One of them may know something!"

I lifted my shadar and began firing in the opposite direction of Jurek. Out of the corner of my eye, I could see Therron making his way closer and closer to us.

Xarrid and I had crawled behind a pile of debris left by some previous skirmish, or so it seemed. "Keep your head down Xarrid!" I yelled.

"I'm trying, but I can't get a good shot!"

"Any shot is better than having your head annihilated!" I screamed back at him over the ruckus.

Therron was getting closer and closer and I was beginning to breathe a sigh of relief. Once he got here, we could teleport out. I didn't want to do it without him because his teleporter wasn't functional and I could not leave him behind.

I turned to order Xarrid to cover me, for my intention was to distract the firing away from Therron so he could make a break for us. The words never left my lips. The air suddenly lit up with a huge flash and I saw Therron's body burn brightly for a brief second and fade away into nothing. I shook my head in disbelief. The blast was so forceful, the aftershock threw my body backwards and then everything began to fade. I heard someone screaming Therron's name when a subtle warmth covered my arm. It silenced the screams, but a numbness descended over me. I wasn't even aware Jurek held my arm until January's face came into focus.

Book Five

January

Chapter One

After Rykerian, Jurek and Xarrid left, I could do nothing but chew my fingernails. My stomach roiled and my body felt reminiscent of the day my dad kicked me out of the house, but this was much worse. I feared for Rykerian's life. I was no fool. Xanthus was anything but safe and Jurek could only do so much.

Maddie tried to comfort me. I swore I was going to become a Guardian so I could accompany him wherever he went. I did not ever want us to be separated for any reason. I had never felt so helpless.

"Come with me," Maddie said.

"Where?"

"Just come on," she said.

I followed her outside where we hopped in a car—except it didn't have wheels. It flew—not high like a jet or anything, but more like one of those Speedster things that Rykerian took me on. We were chauffeured by someone to a building called the Academy of Sciences. When we arrived, Maddie took me by the hand and pulled me inside. She stopped by a glass case filled with awards.

"The first time I ever came to Vesturon, Rykerian brought me here to show me Rayn's awards. That's not why I brought you here, although I did want you to see Rykerian's. Our spouses are terribly modest January and would never talk about themselves. So I am going to tell you. They are brilliant. I mean, total geniuses...amazing. So check out your Rykerian's awards. They're bound to put a smile on your face."

And did they ever. There were awards for everything that he had attained throughout his life. The entire Yarrister family was represented... Rayn, Therron, Rykerian, Xarrid, Tesslar and Sharra.

"They're all super smart, aren't they?"

"Seriously! January, I think you'll fit right in with them. I've decided that it's a Vesturion thing!"

I looked at everything but paid special attention to anything with Rykerian's name on it. He truly was extraordinary.

"Hey, are you interested in seeing the Academy for Guardians?"

"Yeah!"

"Come on. You said something about wanting to be a Guardian. Were you serious?"

"I dunno. Honestly, I just want to be with Rykerian, Maddie. I was only running my mouth because I hate it when he's away from me."

"Well, if you could do anything you want in the whole universe, what would it be?"

"Oh, that's easy. I'd want to go to medical school!"

"Then come with me!"

Maddie took me to see Julian, the healer, and we talked about what it would entail for me to go to medical school.

"January, this is something you would need to discuss with Rykerian. It is a huge commitment, as you know, and now that you are mated to him, you may not want to spend that much time away from him," Julian explained smiling.

"Point well made! Thanks for taking the time to speak with me about it Julian. I appreciate it so much."

"Anytime and congratulations on your unification!"

We headed back to the palace where Rowan and Annalise were waiting with Rayn for some word from Rykerian and Xarrid.

"Rayn, what do you think is going to happen on Earth?" I wanted to know.

"That all depends on whether the Guardians can regain control and whether the Xanthians have gotten any kind of following yet."

"What if they have?" Maddie piped in.

"I don't know Sunshine. I guess it depends on the extent of their infiltration. The gangs in the cities will always vie for power. Without law and order, they will rule."

"The Xanthians will love that Rayn. They hate law and order of any kind," Maddie fumed.

"No Sunshine, they love law and order when it's their own. They will try to persuade the gangs to join with them, telling them lies of how they will rule together. You and I both know once the gangs join up, the gangs will be stripped of their power and forced to bow down to Xanthian law. Then the gangs will rebel and well, I don't have to go on. My concern is for the innocent people who will get caught in the crossfire."

"Oh no! Tommy and Sarah!" I cried out, leaping to my feet.

Maddie and Rayn exchanged a look and Rayn said, "January, we have discussed this with Rykerian and when he completes this mission, we think it best if you bring Tommy and Sarah to the Compound."

"Yeah, I think you're right. What about them finding out about us?" I wondered.

"Earth is no longer the way it was. I'm not sure it matters so much anymore," Rayn answered.

"Maddie, what about Cat? Is there anything we can do for her?"

"While you were unconscious after your visit with your family, Rayn and I went and vaccinated Cat and her family. They are safe from disease. We also deposited money for them and teleported in a hefty supply of food. Rayn erased their memories so that's about the most we can do, other than check on them from time to time to see if they're safe."

"Okay, and thanks for doing that. Is there one more favor I can ask? Well, maybe two?" I looked at Rayn more than Maddie.

"What are they?"

I explained my relationship with the Campbell's and with Lou and Diane from the restaurant in Waynesville. I asked if they could be vaccinated and looked after.

Rayn shook his head saying, "I do not think that would be a problem at all."

"Thanks Rayn."

Hours later we were still sitting and waiting for some kind of news when I felt this searing pain tear through my heart.

"Ugh," I fell forward and my body slammed to the floor. I vaguely heard wailing in the background and then shouts of, "NOOOOO!" and "Deity, please *no*! This cannot be!"

I was on the floor, making every effort to drag air into my lungs without it feeling like a knife piercing my heart. Then his voice came to me.

"NOOOO... Therron! Answer me! Bloody hell Therron. Answer me. I know you're still here. This cannot be happening. NOOOOO!"

Oh dear God! Something happened to Therron. I was finally able to open my eyes, but I could still barely breathe. I looked around the room. My ears were ringing. Maddie was lying on top of Rayn and he was screaming Therron's name. Rowan and Annalise were making guttural sounds and moving around the room erratically. Their minds seemed to be gone. I somehow made it to my feet and staggered to them, forcing them down onto one of the couches. I awkwardly lay between the two of them with my arms flung around them both. My goal was to keep them in one spot until someone could help. I think my actions jolted them into reality because Annalise began sobbing and curled into Rowan who clung to her like a vine. In the meantime, I had yet to dislodge that intense, knife-like pain shooting straight into my heart. I absently rubbed my chest in the hopes of making it disappear.

Rykerian. I must get to Rykerian. I sat back on my heels and my eyes darted around the room, looking for what, I had no idea. I *had* to get to him somehow. He needed me. That's the pain I was feeling. I felt it throughout my entire body and soul. It was *his* pain.

What the hell had happened? What had gone so impossibly wrong? Where was Therron? Was he injured or worse yet, was he...? I couldn't force myself to even think those dreadful words.

"JUREK! JUREK, where are you?" my mind screamed.

It was mere minutes later, but it felt like years when I heard the popping noise and felt the current fill the room. My head jerked around until my eyes landed on them. Jurek had Xarrid on one side and Rykerian on the other. Jurek's eyes latched onto mine and he sliced his head in Rykerian's direction. I needed no other indication. Rykerian's face told me everything—it was a twisted mask of pain.

I ran to him as swiftly as I could. Helping him became paramount. I wrenched him to me and he numbly followed me to our room. I did the only thing I knew to do. I removed his shadars and boots and then peeled every thread of clothing off of him and pushed him into the bed. I went to the bathroom and grabbed a washcloth and moistened it with cool water and cleansed the dirt and soot from his face, neck and hands. My clothing fell in a heap on the floor and then I curled up next to him and tried to infuse my strength into him.

"Oh God, I'm sorry. I. Am. So. Sorry. I don't know what else I can say. I wish there was something...anything I could do to make this whole thing go away." The words kept tumbling from my lips. I wanted nothing but to ease his pain. I didn't possess Tranquility. I didn't know what else I could do for him.

I kissed his eyes and his tears. I slid my hands into his hair, massaging his head. I lay across his chest, heart to heart, trying anything to comfort him. I knew Vesturions were bound by some unseen force and that he was in the throes of agony right now.

I ran my hands along his arms to his shoulders and down his chest to his abdomen. I brushed his hair off his forehead and then took one of his hands and kissed each of his fingers. I felt his chest rise and heard him inhale deeply and then I saw he had opened his eyes. He was staring intently at me. His normally sapphire eyes were nearly black with pain.

"I need you January...badly. Right now, I need you more than the air that I breathe. I need to feel your soul wrap around mine and I need to feel your heart beating beneath my hand." He placed his hand over my heart as he spoke. "I need to feel your flesh beneath me and around me. I need to bury myself within you, mind, body and soul and I cannot promise I will be gentle. You may not want me like this, and if that is the case, please say the word and I will leave," he rasped, his voice raw with pain.

I held his face in my hands and said urgently, "No! I am yours Rykerian, through good times and bad, to walk by your side, to share your joy and your pain. We are one for now and forever," I repeated some of our unification vows.

When the last word left my lips, he took possession of my mouth like a drowning man in need of oxygen. I felt him shudder as his tears poured freely down his cheeks. His eyes never left mine, reaching into my soul, feeding from it, finding strength in it.

"Don't ever leave me. EVER!" he groaned.

"Never. I'm here. I'll always be here for you," I said against his mouth before his lips claimed mine again.

His hands were everywhere at once, gently at first and then urgently, desperately trying to prove to himself that I was here and not leaving. I don't know if he was even aware of what he was doing. His grief penetrated every cell of mine and I cried right along with him. I didn't know what to say or do so I just rode his terrible wave of torment with him. True to his word, it was a dark night for him. Somehow, my body seemed to ease the tempestuous storm raging within him and our lovemaking was the only solace for his tortured soul.

Hours later, we awoke, entwined in each other's arms, stiff and achy.

I wanted to see into his eyes, yet I didn't want to disturb him if he was sleeping, so I rose onto my knees and straddled him. He was awake and looked into my eyes. The pain reflecting back to me from his normally stunning eyes was so fierce and utterly profound, I gasped. I quickly flattened myself against him and attempted to cover him with my body, willing with all my might for his anguish away.

"Ah, love, that will not work you know," he said brokenly.

"Then Rykerian, please tell me what will," I begged. "Take me again, if it will help. I'll do anything for you, anything at all! Do whatever you need to do."

"Oh, love, you have already done so much, but the truth of it is I am not sure if anything will work. Most likely nothing will. Time maybe. I do not know for sure. I wish I had an answer for you."

"You must know I would take it away from you if I could."

He wrapped his arms around me and said, "The only thing that could take it away would be to bring him back," his voice constricted with pain. "I keep reliving it January. He was getting closer and closer. Blasters were firing all around us; annihilator beams coming at us from everywhere. I told Xarrid to keep his head down because he kept lifting it trying to get in a good shot. Then I told him to cover me because I was going to distract the enemy so Therron could make it to us and all of a sudden there was this huge blast that lit everything up. One second Therron was there and the next he was gone," he finished, trembling, his face pallid and wet from his tears.

I cupped his face with both hands and tried to wipe his tears away.

"I fear it is useless January. I do not think the tears will ever end." He wrapped his arms around me tightly and bent his head into my neck. "Thank you for being here for me."

"Don't ever thank me for this. I wouldn't want to be anywhere else. The truth is I couldn't bear to be anywhere else. A minute away from you is torture for me, and I'm here for as long as you need me. I love you so much Rykerian."

"And I you. I am lost without you my love."

"You will never be without me, Rykerian."

We passed the entire day wrapped in each other's arms, alternating between talking, crying and making love, but mostly making love. I think he had to prove to himself that I wasn't going anywhere and I would always be here for him. He wouldn't let me out of his sight for anything. Our touch seemed to ease his pain somewhat. When I had to use the restroom, he insisted on standing right outside the door, but that was the only time there was any distance between us. He was a desperate man in need of his mate for peace and comfort, and I was a very willing partner.

We ordered food from the compsys in our room—a computer system that allowed you to specify what you wanted. It was an awesome invention—humans had no idea what they were missing on this one.

I fed him chicken sandwiches and chips in bed and he told me stories of Therron when they were growing up. I wished I had met him because he seemed like an amazing person.

"He would have really liked you. He was the one that had to deal with Maddie when she nearly destroyed our house on Earth. He was always so patient with her."

"What do you mean?"

"I never told you?"

"Huh, uh."

"Well, Maddie used to be extremely clumsy."

"Oh, yeah, I know about that!"

"Julian says it was her body fighting itself. Her human side warred with her Vesturion side all her life. When she finally came here to Vesturon, the Vesturion side took over and defeated the human side— sort of anyway. So now, she is not clumsy in the least. In fact, she is quite the opposite."

"She did mention something about that. But what does that have to do with destroying the house?"

"When Rayn was awaiting his trial and she was staying with us, she was trying to be helpful, but everything she did resulted in a catastrophe. For example, she tried to cook and started the kitchen on fire. She tried to help Zanna one day and put regular dish soap in the dishwasher and bubbles were flying everywhere. One day, she wanted to drive Rayn's Lamborghini and ended up driving it through the garage. She was a walking disaster and Therron was the one who calmly dealt with her."

"Sweet God in heaven! How did you all put up with her?"

"It was a true test of will I think, but an honest testament of Therron's patience."

I picked up our plates and returned them to the compsys.

"Can I get you anything else?"

"Yes," he said huskily. "Shower with me." The bold look in his eyes told me it was more than a shower he needed.

An hour later, we emerged from the luxurious bathroom, showered and feeling a bit better. We decided it might be a good idea to see what the rest of the family was doing.

Rykerian dressed in a pair of black slacks and a black shirt and I put on a light turquoise dress and sandals.

"You comfort me immensely January. I have no doubt I could not have survived this tragedy without you here. We are truly one, are we not?"

"For now and forever. I love you and I wish so much there was something I could do to make all of this disappear."

He roughly pulled me into him and lifted me until our eyes met and he vowed, "January, I was lost before I found you and yesterday confirmed that. You are my light and I know the days ahead will not be easy ones, but I also know that with you by my side, I will without a doubt, make it through this. Therron was one of the best males I have ever known and when he died, a part of me died as well. But you give me a much more meaningful reason to live. So, on one hand, you have done so much more for me than you can ever imagine. Although on the other, I am not sure I want the pain just to disappear because in some way, it would lessen the way I felt about Therron and that would not seem right in my heart. I suppose my grief is a necessary evil, but you, my love, are a soothing balm for my weeping soul." He kissed me gently and then set me back on my feet. He laced his fingers with mine and we went to seek out his family.

Wow. The urge to pinch myself was overwhelming. Where did this man come from and how did I get this lucky?

When we reached the family quarters, there wasn't anyone around. Rykerian led me toward the stairs and we went down to the back of the house. Was it just a few weeks ago when we stood here and vowed our love for each other? It seemed like eons had passed.

"I feel the same, love, though not with respect to you."

"Oh of course not. Though it seems so much has changed."

As we neared the terrace, seated were Maddie, Rayn, Rowan and Annalise. When they became aware of our presence, Annalise flew to her feet and into Rykerian's arms. His hand dropped mine as his arms engulfed his mother in his embrace. I walked to Maddie and she and I hugged. Her eyes were red and swollen and it was evident she had been crying a lot.

It was particularly awkward for me because I didn't know what to say. "I'm so sorry for your loss" just seemed so inadequate.

Maddie spoke first. "It's okay January. There isn't anything anyone can say. I, for one, am sorry you never got to meet him. Therron was awesome."

"So I hear. I'm sorry for that too. Rykerian has filled me in on so many things about him and I'm so disappointed we never met. I'm so sad for you because I know the two of you had gotten pretty tight. I still can't believe this has happened."

"I know, right? I'm still numb I think." Rayn was absently rubbing circles on the inside of Maddie's wrist. For some reason, he made that simple gesture seem impossibly intimate. Maddie's cheeks turned pink. She must've heard my thoughts so I immediately put up my blocks.

Rykerian and Annalise joined us and Annalise gave me the tightest squeeze for a hug. "Thank you for being there for my son."

I looked her directly in the eye and said, "Annalise, you don't ever have to thank me for that. There is nowhere else I would ever be, and I am at a complete and total loss for words at what to say to you over your loss. Please accept my sympathy." I hugged her tightly. She gave me a watery smile and went to sit with Rowan who had greeted me earlier.

Rykerian pulled me to him and took a seat on an oversized chair, pulling me into his lap. My brows shot up but he just nestled his arms around me, holding me tightly. He bent his head into my neck and said, "I refuse to be anywhere away from you. When I say that, I am talking mere inches, love. I *have* to touch you. I need your strength."

"Oh, okay," I muttered in understanding. I would give him anything he needed...anything at all. If he had to touch me constantly, then so be it. As I looked around the terrace, I noticed the other couples were sitting in much the same fashion.

"Rykerian," Rowan said, "we will have a memorial service for Therron the day after tomorrow for the immediate family. Then the day after that, the public ceremony will be held."

"Yes, my lord. What time?"

"The private one will be at sunrise here. The public one will be at high noon at the town central."

Rykerian nodded. "January hasn't any formal garments for the service."

"Your mother has taken care of that. They will be delivered tomorrow.

Chapter Two

A sadder event I had never attended nor did I ever want to for as long as I lived. Never having met Therron, after the morning's service, I felt I had known him since birth.

All the siblings spoke of their memories of him and as I watched Rowan and Annalise, I wondered how they withstood the grief. Parents were not supposed to outlive their children.

Sharra, Rykerian's only sister arrived last night and she could barely remain standing. Maddie supported her on one side and Rykerian on the other. Everyone stood linked together, drawing inner strength and fortitude from each other.

There was one female in attendance that was not a family member. Her name was Athyna Monteveldo and she barely said a word. She looked like she had turned to stone. She clung to Tesslar for dear life. There was something odd about her though...something I couldn't put my finger on.

I asked Maddie about her later and she told me that Athyna had always loved Therron. Athyna's father had been Rowan's best friend but had tried to ruin Rayn because he wanted Rayn and Athyna to be mated. When Rayn showed no interest, Voldruk Monteveldo committed treason and ultimately took his own life. Athyna was so angry with him because she never had eyes for Rayn, only for Therron. Everyone always assumed they would be united one day.

My heart went out to this Athyna. How sad to lose her only true love.

Later that night, Rykerian and I were talking in bed and I told him how sad I was for her.

"Yes, Therron was always a blind fool where Athyna was concerned and we told him so. I think they had worked things out when this idiotic war broke out and pulled Therron away. The Xanthians have caused us way too many problems."

"Rykerian, what are you thinking?"

"What do you mean?"

"Don't be hedgy with me. I can see your wheels spinning. I don't want you to go back there. You could have died and I would be the one mourning *you* now. I can't even go there."

"The Xanthians must be stopped January. We must figure out a way to do that."

"Fine! Get someone else to go. Let Jurek and his men go. They can go in their energy forms. They can't die then!"

"January, you don't understand."

"No, Rykerian! *You* don't understand! This is exactly what I meant when I told you I was scared. Do you remember that conversation we had when I came back from Jurek's space station? I told you I was afraid of losing you! This is what I meant! I couldn't survive losing you! I mean it Rykerian. If anything like that would ever happen to you I wouldn't be able to...I couldn't..." I had worked myself into tears, and I was shaking and my voice had become overwrought with grief.

"Okay...sshh. It is okay. I will not go to Xanthus love. I will not leave you. Okay?" His hands were gripping my shoulders, his eyes boring into mine.

"Do you promise? *Swear to me!*" I sniffed. I took his face into my hands and my eyes implored him to promise me. "Swear to me Rykerian because *I couldn't live without you in my life!*" Suddenly the events of the day crashed into me and I was an uncontrollable sobbing mess.

"I swear to you my love. I will not go to Xanthus."

I buried myself in him, trying to stem my flow of tears and regain control of my emotions. The thought of going to a memorial service for Rykerian simply threw me into a fit of hysterics and I just sobbed like an idiot.

I finally seemed to get it out of my system. "I'm sorry I went all emo and geeked out on you," I said, taking in a big gulp of air.

He tangled his fingers in my hair and looked me in the eye, "Do not ever be sorry for telling me how you feel. Do you understand me? I do not ever want you to hold that back from me."

"Okay," I nodded.

The next day the family made the procession to the town central where the final service was to be held. Thousands of people lined the streets. Flowers had been placed everywhere with notes and tributes.

We were all attired in black. The men wore black robes with black ropes at their wastes and the women wore black gowns with similar ropes on our wastes. They were very simple with no adornments. We wore no jewelry and our hair hung straight down our backs.

The ceremony was formal with the Council of Elders presiding. The Guardians of Vesturon were present, dressed in their formal uniforms, and they did a formal greeting to the family and then a formal send off to Therron. Finally, three council members eulogized Therron. The first one talked about his years at the Academy. The second one talked about his years in servitude as a Guardian. And the third one talked about Therron as the outstanding male he had grown to be. It was a very moving, uplifting and emotional ceremony.

Afterward, the family processed back to the palace, where we greeted various Heads of State and Council members. I was ready to collapse by the time I saw Jurek and his men enter the palace. As they neared us, I felt Rykerian tense a bit, but much less than he normally did. The Praestani were dressed much more formally than usual. Gone were the leather pants, vests and criss- crossing straps across their chests. Their hair was neatly trimmed and they had no signs of facial hair what so ever. I saw the corners of Jurek's mouth turn up so he knew where my thoughts were. I bit my lip to keep from grinning and Rykerian looked at us with a raised brow. I just shook my head, not trusting myself to open my mouth.

Jurek bowed to Rowan and Annalise first, and then to all of us. His men followed suit. In his deep voice he offered condolences from himself and his men and spoke about Therron's courage and bravery.

I was impressed by the seriousness of his tone. Gone was his sarcasm and hardened nature. In its place was a proper gentleman. Even Tak stood at attention, bowing to my in-laws in deference.

"They are most impressive when they want to be," Rykerian

observed.

"I know, right?" I agreed.

Finally, Athyna Monteveldo walked in. Her grief was palpable and my heart nearly leapt out of my chest when I saw her. I felt this inexplicable attachment to this bereaving young lady...why, I had no idea. Then the strangest thing happened. She headed straight for me and threw herself into my arms, sobbing.

I held her tightly against me as I didn't know what else to do. Rykerian looked as though he would lift her away from me, but I shook my head indicating otherwise. Athyna needed this for her own reason and I would do whatever I could to help her.

Eventually, she lifted her head and said, "I find that I need to be near you and I must beg you for your forgiveness for overstepping my bounds."

"Please don't say that! You are a part of this family Athyna and I know how much you loved Therron. There is no need to apologize. And besides, I find this strange attachment to you as well."

I caught Rykerian staring at us both, looking back and forth.

"What?"

"It is nothing. Athyna, please, will you join us upstairs?"

"Yes, thank you."

Athyna and I walked arm in arm up the huge staircase to the family quarters, where refreshments awaited us. I couldn't wait to get off of my feet for I was exhausted. We plopped down onto one of the sofas and Rykerian brought us some drinks. He kept staring at us strangely. Athyna and I made some small talk, mainly trying to fill the awkwardness that had fallen between us. Jurek and his men came in and he pulled me to my feet and gave me a huge hug. Then he did his awesome energy thingy by placing his hand on my forehead and I immediately felt his warmth flowing through me, followed by a surge of energy.

"Where were you an hour ago? I thought I was gonna collapse down there!"

"Sorry your highness," he smirked.

I just stuck my tongue out at him and he laughed. I don't know why I insisted on repeating that childish gesture with him, but I guess it was because he always thought it was funny, and admittedly, I liked making him laugh.

"Oh, Jurek, this is Athyna Monteveldo. Athyna, this is Jurek Herdekian."

They exchanged greetings but Jurek kept looking at us strangely, like Rykerian had.

"What?"

"Nothing."

"No. What are you looking at?"

"You and Athyna. You look alike is all. Your eyes are exactly the same color."

My eyes swung to hers and hers to mine. We both stared at each other and our mouths formed huge O's. She was about my height but a bit larger framed. Her hair was blond, but more golden than silvery, but her eyes were definitely a very pale ice blue, *exactly* like mine.

By now, everyone in the room had joined in the "Let's all stare at January and Athyna contest." The silence was deafening.

"Rykerian," I said in a monotone, not taking my eyes off of Athyna. He was holding my hand in the next second.

"You told me Athyna had no siblings, correct?"

"That is correct."

"What does it feel like when one of your siblings enters the room?"

"It feels like your heart is attached to theirs by a string of sorts. It is different than how it feels for you and me. For us it is a current that blankets us. For siblings it is more of an attachment."

"Yes. Do you feel their pain?"

"Yes. Not as much as I would yours, but yes."

I turned to Athyna and said, "You are my sister."

Chapter Three

T he room erupted in bursts of chatter, coming from every corner. "How?" "When?" "Where?" And so it went.

I turned to Athyna, saying, "Did your father ever spend much time on Earth?"

Before she could respond, Rykerian shouted, "Father!"

Rowan immediately joined us, along with Annalise, Maddie and Rayn. We were all standing in a circle. Behind us stood Xarrid, Tesslar and Jurek.

"January, Athyna's father did indeed spend time on Earth. In fact, when Athyna was a young girl, Voldruk went rogue for a time and roamed the Smoky Mountains. It was difficult period for us as well as Athyna and her mother."

"Yes, I remember my mother crying all the time," Athyna said. "I don't really remember much else because I was at the Academy then."

"I went after him several times trying to talk sense into him. Voldruk and I were friends since childhood. He was always the one who bucked convention. We remained friends for life, until..."

"Yes, well, as we all are aware, he wasn't the most upstanding of males," Athyna finished.

"In any event, he did spend time in North Carolina January."

"Then that must've been when he raped my mother."

Maybe I shouldn't have been so blunt about it, but I had come to terms with it a while ago and didn't think about it before I said it.

Athyna's face lost every bit of remaining color, which hadn't been much to begin with. Then she crumpled to the floor.

I smacked myself on the head and said out loud, "Excellent work January. Just what the poor girl needed. First, she loses the love of her life. Then she finds out she has a sister and now I tell her that her dad's a rapist. Sweet God in heaven I'm such a friggin' idiot!"

I was on my knees trying to wake her up but Rykerian picked me up instead and carried me upstairs.

"Wait, where are you taking me? Rykerian, put me down! Stop!"

Of course, he completely ignored me and didn't stop until he dumped me on the bed. He joined me there and sat back on his heels, rubbing his neck.

"Heavens, what a day!" he sighed.

It was the first time I had a chance to *really* look at him all day. Gawd, he was impossibly gorgeous. Would I ever get used to this boy—I had to quit saying that? He was no boy. This was a *man*...or a male as the Vesturions said. And he was pure male through and through. And no, I doubted very seriously I would ever get used to looking at him.

Before I could stop myself, I sat up and faced him, and stretching out my hand I laced my fingers though his oh-so-pretty hair.

"Have I ever told you how amazing you are?"

His eyebrows lifted, most likely at my shift in thought, but I didn't stop.

"I know I'm drastically shifting gears on you, but I need to say this here and now. Your hair is the most extraordinary color I have ever seen. It baffles me when I try to describe it. I've laid awake at night trying to come up with the perfect name for it, but no can do. It looks like every single strand was individually hand painted. And then there are your eyes." I moved my hand from his hair to his face, cupping his cheek with my palm and tracing his eyebrow with my thumb. "They are the color of the most magnificent cobalt sapphires that have ever existed. But the fact that they send currents of heat through my body when you look at me is what thrills me the most. And those lips of yours—sweet heavens Rykerian, I so love your lips. Soft, yet demanding and oh so *knowing*. Mmmm...and yummy." I leaned into him and kissed him and traced the outline of his lips with my tongue.

"Yeah...just as I remembered. Totally yummy lips." The corners of his lips curved upward, but I didn't stop...I couldn't stop. This male was pure perfection.

My fingers danced down his neck across the spot where his pulse beat. I could see it picking up its pace as I bent my head to run my tongue around and around it. I heard him suck in his breath and I smiled. There was only one thing I wanted now, but our robes were in the way so I tugged viciously on his.

I felt his laughter deep in his throat and he put his hand on mine saying, "Are you trying to destroy these?"

"Maybe."

"May I ask you something?"

"Anything."

"Does it bother you knowing that Athyna is your half-sister?"

I froze briefly and thought for a moment. "Not at all. Your family obviously loves her. Therron loved her. You've known her your whole life and I imagine you love her. Her father...my father..and your father were close at one point, so no. It's actually kind of cool that I even have a sister. Well, two sisters. But a Vesturion sister."

"You couldn't have a better one," he said, pulling me to him, crushing his lips to mine. He somehow managed to remove our robes and finish what I had begun earlier.

Later, as we lay entwined together, I breathed, "I meant what I said earlier Rykerian. You really are the most beautiful man I've ever seen. And I didn't get close to finishing describing you."

"I appreciate the compliment, love. But..."

I cut him off by placing my fingers over his lips. "My turn. You've complimented me over and over but now I want to tell you some things. Sometimes, like right now, I am so filled with love for you, I can't express the right words. I know it sounds so lame but..."

He took his fingers and placed them over my lips. Suddenly I felt his mental blocks fade away and our minds merged. All of our emotions flowed between us—love, happiness, sorrow, pain, joy, etc. It was the most mind-blowing and extraordinary thing I've ever experienced.

I hadn't even realized I was crying until he took the sheet and wiped the moisture from my face.

"Why didn't you tell me we could do *that?*"

"I thought it best for us to take things one step at a time. You know, sensory overload and all."

My breathing was still uneven and my trembling hadn't subsided, when I said, "So we don't ever need to speak, do we?"

"Um, not really, but then I would be cheating myself from hearing your lovely voice," he finished as he grabbed my chin and placed his lips on mine. It didn't take long before the flames of passion consumed us and we were lost in each other again.

Chapter Four

Something kept tickling my nose and every time I swatted it, it came back with a vengeance. I was getting totally annoyed now. Then the darn thing moved to my ear. It was tickling it, nibbling on it and then blowing in it. Wait a minute!

I opened my eyes and Rykerian's face came into view. "I did not think you would ever open your eyes sleepy head. I was wondering whether you wanted to go and chat with your *sister*."

"What?" I rolled over and then, "Oh my gawd! My *sister*!" I jumped out of bed and tripped on the rug, stumbled into the chair and crashed on the floor.

"January! Are you okay?"

"Owww! My toe! I stubbed my darn toe!"

Rykerian, of course, was there in a millisecond. He gently inspected my wounded toe and declared I would live.

"Well, duh! I knew that! The darn thing just hurts!"

"Would you like for me to kiss it for you?" he chuckled.

"No, but I have something else I'd like for you to kiss," I suggested.

Before I knew it, we were rolling on the floor, doing those wickedly naughty things to each other. I guess we were both making so much noise, that at first we didn't even hear the pounding. When it sounded like the door was going to be torn off its hinges and split in two, Rykerian yelled, "Do *not* even think about entering this room or you *will* regret it."

"If the two of you could pull yourselves away from each other for several minutes, there are guests here that would like to speak to you," Xarrid's voice came through the barrier.

"We will be down shortly," Rykerian answered curtly.

We quickly dressed, washed our faces and brushed our teeth and headed down to the kitchen, where everyone had congregated for breakfast. As we made our way to the stairs Rykerian started chuckling.

"What are you laughing at?"

He reached over and began to pick carpet fuzz out of my hair.

"Holy moly, I forgot to brush my hair!"

He was biting his lips to keep from laughing.

"It's not funny!"

"I have never seen you look more...er...sexy!" he said, flashing a wicked grin.

"Whatever! I don't want to look sexy right now! Give me a hand."

We both made a feeble attempt at restoring order to my uncooperative, straw-like, and now slightly matted and fuzz-covered hair.

When we made it to the family kitchen, I knew we had failed miserably by the looks everyone cast our way.

Then came the remarks. Of course, with Jurek in attendance, I should have expected as much. I guess we deserved it. After all, it was ten o'clock in the morning!

Rykerian leaned into me, nuzzled and kissed my neck and softly said, "Thank you, love."

"For what? Carpet fuzz?"

"Hmmm. For giving me one of the best nights of my life, when it should have been the worst. For giving me a morning to always remember and for making me laugh when just a day ago I did not think I would ever laugh again." He smiled and kissed the corner of my mouth.

Whoa! Oh how this man had a way of making me melt right into my shoes!

I slid my hand to his cheek and said, "I think I should be the one thanking you. If you hadn't persisted in your belief that I was the one for you, we wouldn't be standing here today." I brought my lips back to his.

"I think you two may need to go back to your bedroom!" Jurek suggested. My faced burned with embarrassment and Rykerian's turned that wonderful shade of pink that looked so great on him. Then everyone laughed.

Athyna came up to me and hugged me. Immediately I launched into an apology. "Oh gawd Athyna, I'm such an idiot. I can't believe I just blurted that out last night. I guess I got so used to hearing it from my nasty mother I didn't stop to think about how it would sound to you. Please forgive my rude behavior."

"It is okay January. Maddie and Rayn told me everything and I am sorry about all of that. I also wanted to congratulate you and Rykerian on your uniting. I know Therron would have been happy for you."

That comment brought all conversation to a screeching halt.

Trying to break the uncomfortable moment, I blurted out, "Athyna, I am happy to know I have a sister. Rykerian tells me I've lucked out with you."

"Yes, well he would say that," she smiled.

Rykerian handed me a plate of food as we made our way to the table to eat.

The room began to grow a bit noisy again, not so much with jovial conversation, but chatter nonetheless.

Xarrid and Jurek were in close conversation, I suppose discussing their next move over how best to get control of the situation on Xanthus. Xarrid's intentions of going back had been clearly made. He would not stop searching for Saylan until he found her and Jurek had agreed to help.

The day wore on with various people coming and going. I had met so many friends of the family over the last two days my head was spinning.

Rykerian, Rayn, Tesslar, Xarrid and Jurek were going to be meeting at the Command Center in the afternoon to formulate a plan on how next to proceed.

Sharra and Maddie were discussing plans for Sharra's redesign of the Star Avengers. With the expansion of the war, the number of pilots needed was growing so Sharra was in charge of the entire Star Avenger program, including recruiting and establishing space bases in strategic locations. They were deciding how to best implement everything.

I was feeling quite useless so I began wandering around the house and ended up in the library, where I discovered ancient books written in a language I didn't remotely understand. As I walked along, I started paying attention to the artwork on the walls. It was beautiful. Portraits, still life, and scenery all done in beautiful oils. This was such a lovely place, I felt like I should pinch myself or something.

I sat down in a chair and reflected on the last few months of my life. It had gone from sheer hell to absolute heaven. I'm sure I walked around with a goofy smile pasted on my face. I felt giddy most of the time now. Really, how couldn't I? I was married to hawtness on a stick! He was ridiculously smart, had this awesome family, he made me feel like I was the center of his universe and...just shut up January! I'm gonna make myself hurl if I don't stop it already!

"Don't worry, you will get used to it," Maddie barged in. "You had that look on your face. I remember feeling exactly like that when I first came here."

"I know. I keep wanting to pinch myself."

Maddie laughed. "In no time flat, you'll feel right at home."

"It's crazy, because I already do."

"That's because your mate's here. You'll always feel at home wherever he is. And when you're away from him, you'll feel a part of you is missing. It's painful not being with him."

Rayn barged into the room then, "Sunshine, I've been looking for you." In his usual manner, he wasted no time in making his way to Maddie and gathering her into his arms. That was my cue to disappear.

I headed back to the den and was intercepted by Rykerian. "I've been looking for you," he said as he picked me up and carried me upstairs to our room. One thing was certain, these males were certainly...er, well, energetic!

"You have this thing about carrying me around, don't you?" I asked him afterward.

"I had not thought about it, but I guess I do. Does it not please you?"

"Oh no! It pleases me very much. As a matter of fact, I haven't found anything about you that doesn't please me. I'm the luckiest girl on Earth. Or on Vesturon. Or I should say the universe!"

He twirled a piece of my hair between his fingers and for whatever reason, my stomach lurched a bit.

"What's going on?"

"We have made our plans January. Rayn wants to go with Xarrid and Jurek back to Xanthus to try to retrieve Saylan. I think they will also take Maddie."

"Seriously? Maddie?"

"Maddie is a formidable fighter and she abhors anything Xanthian. Besides, she is a trained Guardian. She graduated first in her class which is a most difficult achievement."

"What will you do?"

"You and I will go back to the Compound on Earth. We need to retrieve your family and bring them to the Compound for safety."

"My parents too?"

"Yes."

"I don't think I want them there," I said as I looked down at my knotting fingers.

"I knew you would say that, though love, you cannot bring your brother and sister and not their parents. It would be something you would hate yourself for later." He tucked a piece of my hair behind my ear.

"I know, but..."

"Sweetheart, if you leave them behind and they die, Tommy and Sarah will blame you for that. Are you willing to live with that? They love their parents, no matter how much you dislike them."

"How come you make so much sense?" I lifted myself up on my elbows and kissed him softly on the lips. "When do we leave?"

"Next week."

"Good. Then let's take advantage of this night shall we?"

Chapter Five

I t was sad as we said our goodbyes to everyone. I made Maddie promise to keep me informed of what was going on with them. I was so frightened for her. I had never gone into a war zone but as Rykerian reminded me, we were getting ready to go into one ourselves.

I got terribly nervous thinking about what Spartanburg would be like, so much so, that I ended up losing the breakfast I had just eaten. I was totally mortified over that.

"Look love, there is nothing to be upset about. You are the one that reminded me the night of Therron's death that we are in this for better or worse. Do not worry yourself over this little incident, okay?" he said, wiping my face for me.

"Thank you. I think I want to brush my teeth."

After I finished, I told him about how I could barely keep food down the year after my parents had booted me out of their house.

"It was like this every time I ate. I would eat a little and hurl. It was so gross. Everyone thought I was anorexic because I wouldn't eat and I wouldn't talk about it. You remember how God awful skinny I was when you first met me? Ugh! I was disgusting."

He brushed my hair back from my face with his fingers and said, "You were beautiful. You were always beautiful, even when I found you dying in the forest, covered in those horrid bruises. You were beautiful when you thought you hated me, when you were so angry with me for saving you. You have never been disgusting, my love."

I did the only thing I knew and that was I let my love flow to him from my mind. His eyes widened and he gasped. His fingers dug into my shoulders as our souls merged. It was one of those defining moments. I knew we would always love each other with an intensity unmatched by anything I could describe or explain. He was mine as I was his, always and forever.

We teleported to the Compound and arranged for my old family's arrival. I was hopeful that it would go smoothly. Zanna handled the preparations. They would be staying on the upper level. There were four bedrooms up there so they could have their privacy. Rykerian and I would go first thing in the morning.

That night, we ate dinner in the kitchen. I was rather sleepy so we headed up to bed early. Before we fell asleep, I told Rykerian stories about Tommy and Sarah. I was worried about how they had fared during the past few months. He rubbed circles on my back and it wasn't long before I was fast asleep.

I heard the click of the door and lifted my head to see my husband carrying a tray. He flashed me a smile when he saw me watching him as he set the tray down. He poured me a cup of coffee and lifted a lid off a plate to a beautiful stack of fluffy pancakes. I inhaled their aroma and when it hit me, my stomach roiled in protest. I flew off the bed and barely made it to the bathroom in time before I threw up all over the place.

"Are you okay?" Rykerian was by my side.

"Please, go away. I'm so embarrassed."

"I thought we covered this yesterday, love."

"I know, but that was yesterday. I don't know what's gotten into me."

"I'm calling Julian," he said, tearing his hand through his hair.

"No, you're overreacting. It's probably just nerves. I told you yesterday. Seriously, I was like this for three years."

"I do not want to take any risks."

"Let's wait until we have my family here. If it's not better then let's call him."

"Okay."

I brushed my teeth and was suddenly hungry. So I ended up having a couple of pancakes and a cup of coffee.

"Are you ready?"

Their backyard was overgrown with dead kudzu vines. It was February so all the greenery was dormant. Even so, you could tell, no one had been keeping up their yards. They weren't doing any maintenance either. It was amazing how fast something could turn to disrepair.

The back screen door hung off its hinges. I turned the door knob and it didn't turn at all. You could just push the door open. I walked into the house. My mother had always been a neat housekeeper. While we never had fancy furniture or fine things, our house had been tidy and clean. Things had gone seriously south.

The house was filthy. There were piles of trash everywhere. Dirty dishes were strewn across every spare inch of counter space. I kept walking. The den looked like a disaster area. The furniture was ripped and torn, like someone had plunged a knife in it with the sole intention of destroying it. Stuffing had been pulled out and the upholstery was torn everywhere. Pictures were lying on the floor, their frames broken into pieces. As I moved further into the house, I began to realize they couldn't be living here.

I looked at Rykerian. He brought his fingers to his lips, signaling for silence. He ran his fingers across his shadar and then looked at me. He held up four fingers and pointed down.

A basement? This house didn't have a basement that I recalled. I sent my thoughts to him.

"January, this is a danger zone. We need to get out of here ASAP."

"This house doesn't have a basement that I'm aware of."

"Then they have created one. Look for a trap door under a carpet, rug or a piece of furniture."

We went from room to room and I finally found it in Sarah's room beneath her bed. Rykerian pushed it aside and lifted the door. I heard my father say, "Don't come any closer or I'll shoot."

"It's me, January. You can't harm us anyway. We're wearing protective clothing that repels gunfire." Thank heavens for Vesturion technology!

"January, is that really you?"

"Yes, Sarah, it's me! I've come to get you all out of here and take you somewhere safe. Come on up, but you have to hurry!"

"How do we know we can trust you?"

"Come on Mom, do we have to go through this again?" I wanted to tear my hair out!

Rykerian put his hand on my arm and I immediately felt better.

I heard feet scrambling up steps and saw Sarah's head pop up. Her face was filthy and she was super skinny.

"Come here sweetie!" She threw herself at me and I lifted her in my arms. The rest of my family followed.

"Listen, I don't have time to explain this now, but I will in a couple of minutes."

"Rykerian, get us out of here."

His fingers tapped his shadar and seconds later we materialized at the mountain house.

I still held Sarah in my arms and I asked her if she was okay. All I got was a nod. Tommy yelled, "Wow, that was cool!"

My parents were speechless.

"Come on, let's go inside. I imagine you're hungry."

After they ate an unbelievable amount of food, they filled us in on what had taken place. Even Spartanburg had been taken over by gangs. Everyone feared for their lives. There was no food or water. Cars were inoperable because there was no gas. Electricity was nonexistent. Nor was there natural gas. If you didn't have an adequate store of nonperishable food, you were in serious trouble and if you did, the gangs would find out about it and come and raid your home.

Then came the fun part. We had to explain where they were, who Rykerian was and who I was by way of my father. At first my mother sputtered, but after repeated reminders that we could always send her back to Spartanburg, she finally shut up. Tommy and Sarah thought the whole idea of aliens was totally awesome, making me laugh.

The day flew by and I'd forgotten how much energy little kids had. By dinnertime, I could barely keep my eyes open. Rykerian suggested I head upstairs and he promised to show them where everything was. I never heard him slide into bed, for I was fast asleep.

In the morning, he woke me up with nibbles on my neck, but I groaned because I didn't want to get up.

"Shall I fetch you some breakfast love?" he wanted to know.

The thought of food turned my stomach into a heaving mass of bile. I flew out of the bed and hugged the porcelain goddess again.

What was wrong with me?

"I intend to find out love," Rykerian said softly, but in a tone that told me he would entertain no argument.

When I exited the bathroom, Julian was waiting for me. Smiling, he greeted me saying, "Do you wish this to be private?"

For a second I was lost but then I figured it out. "No! Of course not," I answered, reaching out for Rykerian.

Julian led me to the bed and had me lay down. He took out his abracadabra wand and images started appearing everywhere. Obviously, I was amazed, but had no idea what was going on. His smile kept getting bigger and bigger, so I looked at Rykerian and he shrugged.

"Well? Is she going to be all right?" Rykerian wanted to know.

"Why yes. In approximately ten more weeks, her nausea and vomiting, along with her fatigue should disappear."

"Ten weeks!"

"Oh, but then in about twenty nine weeks after that you will be extremely tired again!"

"What? What is wrong with me?"

"January, you are going to have a baby," Julian said gently. "Here, let me help you up."

"Huh? A baby? What do you mean?" I asked as Julian helped me off the bed. My head was spinning with the news.

"A baby?" Rykerian asked. He had a silly lopsided grin on his face.

Julian was chuckling now. "Congratulations you two. You will make magnificent parents. Now January, get plenty of rest, make sure you eat well and you must take these vitamins every day." He handed me a bottle of pills. "I'd like to check you again in a month."

"Okay." I couldn't speak. I was numb. Me? A baby? What was I going to do with a baby? I just got married for heaven's sake!

I stood there in shock as Julian left. Rykerian came and wrapped his arms around me like I was the most precious thing in the universe.

"Sweet Deity! We are going to have a child."

The look on his face was one of pure enlightenment. Not because he had just found out he was going to be a father. It was something altogether different. Something I never expected in a million years.

"We're going to have a boy January. He was conceived the night Therron died; the night you showered me with your love and protected me with your soul." He put his hands on either side of my head and kissed my forehead and said, "It is Therron's way of speaking to us. He always said that when the Deity takes one soul away, another is sent to take its place," his voice was filled with wonder and amazement. That was the last straw. I broke down and sobbed.

His arms lifted me and carried me back to the bed. It seemed he was forever doing that, for one reason or another. He kept me wrapped in his arms and I kept sobbing. When there was nothing left to cry, he asked, "Is it that bad then?"

"Oh Rykerian, it's not that. I just wanted to have you to myself for a while. I never in a million years ever thought I would get pregnant so fast. I'm only nineteen and I thought we could wait. Well, the truth is I never even thought about it at all. I always knew I wanted children, but..." I sniffed. "And then I had thought about going to medical school and becoming a healer. I even spoke to Julian about it. I was going to discuss it with you but then Therron was killed and I never got a chance."

"A healer, huh? Do you not want to keep it then?" he asked it a very quiet voice.

"*WHAT*? What do you mean? I could never...no! I mean *YES*! I want to keep it. Oh God! Rykerian, *we made* this child *together*. *You and me!* With our *LOVE* for each other. I could never...and if it *is* Therron speaking to us. Oh God Rykerian, how could you even *think* that?" The thought of what he was suggesting sickened me.

"Sshh..." he put his fingers on my mouth. Then he kissed me and spoke against my lips. "I love you January and I have loved *every single* moment we have spent together and this child to me is a celebration of that love. It is tearing me apart to see you unhappy over this. That was why I asked."

Since we were still wrapped around each other, to say I threw myself at him wasn't quite accurate. However, I did hug him with quite a bit of force, landing on top of him. My hair formed a curtain around us as we dissolved into each other.

"I love you so much Rykerian. But I'm *scared. Really, really* scared. I'm such a loser. I'm always telling you that. But I. Am. So. Scared. What if I'm a crummy mom? What if I turn out like my mom and hate my kid?" My fingers dug into his shoulders.

In a voice laced with steel he said, "Stop it! Right now January. If I ever hear you compare yourself to that despicable woman again, I will scream. You are *nothing* like her! You are *not* a loser and you will *never* *EVER* be a crummy mother. You have so much love in your heart you could never hate your own child! Do you understand me?"

I nodded.

"This is a joint mission. Parenthood does not fall only on your shoulders. We are a team January. When you become frightened, you come to me and vice versa. We will raise strong, loving and caring children. They will be kindhearted and considerate and they will not fear anything. And we will do it together. I know with every fiber of my being that you will love this child with all of your heart and soul! Understood?"

I nodded again.

"Good. Now, you must promise me something. You must take good care of yourself. I will try not to be overprotective, but it is my nature to be as such so I cannot make you any promises of that nature. And January, nothing says you cannot still become a healer if that is what you wish, love. Motherhood does not exclude you from living you know." He smiled and I melted.

"How did I ever get so lucky?"

"It is I who am the lucky one," he said, as he gently claimed my lips.

"I love you Rykerian."

We decided—well I decided—that we would go back to Vesturon. Rowan went to the Council of Elders and gained approval for my family to go to Vesturon. Times had changed with the war. Earth was no longer safe for anyone so Vesturon was granting amnesty for many individuals.

I knew it would be impossible for us to remain at the Compound on Earth and retain any shred of sanity. My mother was her usual unpleasant and harpy self and my father was as surly as ever. With my pregnancy hormones raging all over the place, we were bound to start our own little war. Rykerian never knew what to expect when he entered the room, so it was for everyone's benefit that we went to Vesturon.

Rykerian found a home for my family and work for my parents. Tommy and Sarah were enrolled in the Academy. They were behind for obvious reasons, but they were smart and with private tutors, they could catch up if they worked hard. Our sanity returned, minus the hormonal issues, since we didn't have to live with my horrid parents anymore.

I also wanted our child to be born on Vesturon. Earth had no functioning medical facilities anymore, and it had continued to deteriorate into a shell of its former self. It saddened me every time I thought of how one incident could snowball into something so fierce and dynamic and change the course of events forever.

Since our return to Vesturon, Athyna and I were able to spend some time together. She had decided, over hours of arguing with Rykerian and the rest of the Yarristers, that she wanted to become a Guardian. She had this pressing need to avenge Therron's death and the only way she could fight the Xanthians was to train as a Guardian. Rowan was livid. Aythyna's nature had never been one of a fighter. In fact, she had been trained as a teacher. She possessed a keen intelligence and I often expressed to Rykerian that she would make a brilliant military strategist. Since I had no known battle skills, Rykerian would roll his eyes whenever I would mention this, but I could see where Athyna's bright mind would be a great asset to the Vesturions.

It didn't take much for me to grow to love her. She was, in a word, fabulous. I was only sorry I hadn't known her my whole life.

Jurek visited often. Rykerian had finally come to terms with our relationship. Jurek's involvement in the war with the Xanthian's and his relationship with Xarrid also cemented that. Rykerian and Jurek would never be the best of friends, but he would always be welcome in our home.

A few times, Rykerian had conceded and given his blessing to me when I wanted to visit Jurek at his space station. Its true name was Lare-Stell Base. His company was known as LS Enterprises. He wouldn't tell me what the Lare-Stell meant and no one knew of its existence, for security purposes. But I intended to get its meaning out of him one day.

I was more than three quarters through my pregnancy when Rykerian allowed me to travel to Lare-Stell. After several days there I was bored to tears. Everyone was treating me like I was an invalid.

"No, January! You cannot fight Tak. I will not allow it. You could get hurt," Jurek explained.

"You never worried about that before."

"You weren't pregnant before," exasperation lacing his tone.

"Oh, so you were never worried about me. You are only worried about the baby!"

He looked at me in that odd way of his and for once, he was speechless.

"Well? No clever retort?"

"Actually, no," he admitted. "For once, you have rendered me speechless. Look, I know you are bored and frustrated, but can you not look at your baby's welfare for one second? If anything happened you would never forgive yourself."

He did make a good point. He saw it too, so he kept pushing.

"You know you would suffer those consequences, and you would carry that guilt and grief with you always. Keep the baby's safety here January," he said as he placed his hand over my heart. "You will be thankful for it when you have a healthy bundle of joy to hold in your arms.

"Why do I get this feeling you know this from personal experience?" I asked softly as I placed my hand over his.

"Perhaps it is because I do. And before you hit me with a barrage of questions, come, I want to show you something."

There was way more to this than he was letting on, but that was all I would get from him right now. I followed him out the door—the one I had wondered about the first time I was here as a prisoner. Yes, there was one. It was hidden in a panel and if one didn't know it was there, it looked like a part of the wall.

We walked down the hall a short distance until we came to another door. Jurek pressed the button and the door slid open to reveal a room that was decorated as a nursery.

It was amazing. There was a perfect little crib with a perfect rocker for me and the room was done in all sorts of pastels. It had a window that overlooked the stars and the ceiling was painted a deep blue and covered in glowing stars and moons. It was the loveliest thing I had ever seen.

"Oh my God! It's beautiful!" I would've jumped in his arms, but my ever-increasing girth wouldn't allow it anymore. Good thing he was strong, because he lifted me up so I could hug and kiss him.

"Do you really like it?" he asked excitedly.

"It's the most perfect thing I've ever seen! So does this mean the baby and I can come whenever?"

"Absolutely!"

"I love you, you know!"

"I know!"

"Well?"

"Well what?"

"This is the part where you're supposed to say, 'I love you too January.'"

"I am?"

I punched him in the arm and stuck my tongue out at him. He laughed at me and hugged me again.

"You do realize you've brought new meaning to my life, don't you?" he asked.

"Is this the part where we go...'No you're the best'...'No, you are!'"

"I suppose so. January, you and I are so much alike. We were like two lost souls weren't we?"

"Are we found now?"

"I think perhaps you are. Me...not so much," he said shaking his head.

"Jurek, you'll always have a place with me you know." I kissed his cheek.

He smiled then, and his lovely lavender eyes were something to behold.

"Hey, will you come to Vesturon when the baby is born?"

"Wouldn't miss it for anything."

"Good cos I'm gonna need the old hand on the forehead thingy. I'm a little freaked out about the whole process you know."

"Um, 'hand on the forehead thingy?'"

"Yeah, you know when you spread the warmth and all."

He threw back his head and roared with laughter. "Only you can do this to me January!"

Chapter Six

Two Months Later

T he pain tore through me in the middle of the night and I woke up
screaming. Rykerian flew out of bed.

"Is it time?" he yelled.

"Yes," I gritted out through clenched teeth.

He started pacing and tearing his hands through his longer than
usual hair. If he wasn't more careful, he was going to yank his braid
right out of his head. He began mumbling something about
transportation. My usually calm and composed husband then charged
out of the room, leaving me standing there, doubled over in pain and
panting.

I projected my thoughts to my in-laws. Thank God we were on
Vesturon! Moments later, they were knocking on my door.

"January dear, where is Rykerian?" Annalise gently asked.

"I don't know. I woke him up and he started jabbering incoherently
and left the room."

"Rowan, go look for him. I will help January downstairs," Annalise
said.

"Can you get Athyna too?"

Seconds later I heard that familiar popping noise.

"Oh thank God!"

"Hand on the forehead thingy?" Jurek asked.

"Yes!"

He obliged and I felt that wonderful warmth spread throughout my body. He and Annalise helped me lumber down the steps. We made it to the front door when a frazzled Rykerian ran inside yelling, "Where have you been?"

"And this is what you married January?" Jurek snorted shaking his head.

"I know, right? Oh my gawd. Annalise, will you go with us?"

"Yes, dear," she said smiling. "Rykerian, everything will be fine," she patted his arm. "Aren't you going to change your clothes?"

He glanced down and noticed he was only wearing his boxers. He had this stupefied look on his face when Rowan appeared.

"Rowan darling, will you go to Rykerian's closet and bring him a change of clothing?" Annalise asked. Thank the holy heavens above for my mother-in-law! "And don't forget his shoes!" she called after him.

He was pale and trembling and if he didn't stop tearing his hands through his hair, he would be bald by day's end.

Another pain hit me then and I clamped down on Rykerian's hand with mine, panting.

"OWWWW!" he screamed. "I think you broke my hand," he whined.

"Deal with it Rykerian!" I grunted in pain.

"Okay, okay! Sooorrrrry!" he said.

"January, squeeze *my* hand if you'd like. I think I can handle it," Jurek said with a smirk.

Rykerian shot him a dirty look.

Athyna came running in at that moment and took in the sight of us. I'm not sure whether she wanted to laugh or cry. Her eyes kept darting between Rykerian and me and she finally bit down on her lip, but a giggle escaped nevertheless.

Rowan reappeared with Rykerian's clothing and shoes and we boarded the transport. Rowan assisted me because Rykerian, who had all but lost his mind by this point, was the first to jump in. Apparently, he had forgotten that his rotund pregnant wife, who could barely walk, much less climb inside one of these wheel-less contraptions, needed a hand.

"Gee, thanks for your help Rykerian," I said sourly after I had climbed aboard.

"What?" He was clueless.

"Oh, my gawd! I can barely wobble, much less walk, and you expect me to hop in this doohickey, not to mention *I AM IN LABOR!*" I screeched.

By this time, the intense desire to slap him had come over me. Annalise reached over and patted my hand, attempting to calm me, and Athyna, who could no longer contain herself, let loose a loud snort.

"I do not understand why you are so upset with me," Rykerian said in complete confusion.

"You have got to be kidding me. Tell me you are kidding me! Because I know you cannot possibly be that stupid!"

"January, I think he is really distressed. You seriously need to give him a break, my friend," Jurek interrupted.

Now I shot Jurek a withering. "Oh my gawd! I can't believe it! How can you side with him? I'm the one in *labor*!!!"

Rykerian gave me another ridiculous look as one more gut tearing contraction hit me. I tried to stop it, but another scream tore from my lips as the pain engulfed me. "Bloody hell, I didn't sign up for this crap!" I yelled. I looked up at Rykerian and the abject worry in his eyes washed away everything else as he grabbed my hand.

"Squeeze it, break it, crush it, tear the bloody damn thing off, I care not! Do what you must to take your pain away. I cannot bear to see you as such." He said those words with such intensity I ground out between clenched teeth, "I love you Rykerian."

He gently brushed the damp hair off of my face and smiled one of those radiant take-your-breath-away smiles that made me forget everything...well, almost everything—except for the fact that I was in the worst pain of my life!

"I love you more than life itself January!" he whispered for my ears only. Then he growled, "Sweet Deity, how soon before we get there? My mate's in serious need of some bloody damn pain relief!"

No sooner had the words left his mouth when Annalise said, "Here we are dears," as we arrived at the medical facility. The robomedics met us with the floating gurney and pain meds. Ah, blessed relief.

I insisted that Athyna accompany Rykerian and me into the delivery room. I'm not sure what I would have done without her because Rykerian was quickly losing his last shred of sanity and mine was going right along with it. He was impossibly anxious over my health and that of the baby's. So thankfully, several hours later our beautiful little boy, Therron Rykerian Yarrister, entered this world with all ten fingers and toes. It was a good thing too, because if it had taken much longer, his father would have driven me and everyone else nuts!

The only time Rykerian let me pry Therron out of his hands was for his feedings. We were like two kids fighting over a new toy. Athyna and Jurek finally left saying they couldn't tolerate us anymore.

We were in the family den one day when Annalise came in and handed us a piece of parchment.

"What is this?" Rykerian asked.

"It is a schedule your father and I have devised for you two. We are truly tired of hearing the two of you argue over whose turn it is to hold Therron," she smiled.

"Well, I never!" he glowered.

"And one other thing...we think it might be time for the two of you to get your own place to live."

We looked at each other, and then back at her, wide-eyed as she walked out of the room.

"She is right you know," I calmly said. "Neither one of us has allowed anyone near him. His poor grandparents haven't had but a minute to hold him. We are arguing all the time like two little brats. Not to mention there isn't room here for everyone when they all get married and have kids. We can't stay here forever."

The look on Rykerian's face was so ridiculous I burst out laughing. It was one of those contagious moments and before long, he had joined in and Annalise was back and she was laughing right along with us. Even little Therron giggled. Annalise picked him up and tickled him, then stole him away. We looked around, then at each other and before I knew it, Rykerian picked me up and carried me up the stairs to our room.

"If we're not careful, we may have a houseful of little Therrons running around before we know it."

Rykerian stopped and stared at me with those incredibly stunning eyes. "Would that be so bad then, love?" he whispered curiously.

I wrapped my hand around the nape of his neck, pulling him toward me. When his lips met mine, I said, "Whatever gave you the idea it was bad?"

I felt his chest rumble as he kissed me back. Then he said, "Maybe then we would stop arguing over who gets to hold the baby!"

The universe was still at war. The Xanthians had made it clear that Earth was their intended target and they would not stop until they had gained control of it. The Guardians had divided their efforts between the two planets, but a full-blown war was now in progress.

Saylan had yet to be found and Xarrid was still searching for her. Rykerian and Jurek were doing everything they could to help, but so far they had found no sign of her.

The task of building our own home had fallen to me and I gladly took that over, with Annalise's help. The work would begin in the next few weeks and our home would be located within walking distance from the palace grounds.

Little Therron was getting bigger every day. He was a perfect blend of his father and me. He had my eyes but Rykerian's unmatchable hair color and his impossibly flawless smile and I think he was going to have his father's build because the kid was huge! He was exactly like his daddy—the sweetest baby boy ever and lucky for us, he loved to sleep!

Jurek visited me frequently, but he was fairly obscure about it. When he had agreed to assist the Guardians, it was understood that the only ones that would be made aware of the Praestani's existence were the Yarristers. Jurek and Xarrid were quite close now, and Rykerian had finally come around, but I wouldn't call them the best of friends. No one but the Yarristers knew of the existence of Lare-Stell and we all planned to keep it that way.

My brother and sister were doing as well as could be expected. Tommy had been giving my parents problems because he wanted to go back to Earth, as did Sarah. They had never gotten very comfortable on Vesturon and missed their old life and friends.

My parents didn't help much either. They complained about everything, especially the fact that they should have been allowed to live in the palace and that as my parents they shouldn't have to work.

One day, Rykerian who was probably the most patient person in the universe, had had more than he could take and had reached his boiling point. My parents incessant whining about every insignificant thing had finally pushed him over the edge. They had shown up this time fussing about my father's supervisor at his job.

Rykerian looked at me, tore his hand through his hair, shook his head and said, "You ungrateful people just will not stop will you? Lives are being lost every day in a war going on and you are oblivious to everything except your petty needs and complaints. What will make you shut up?"

They stared at him, jaws on the floor. Ever since the first time he had met them, he had never spoken to them like that again, but he had finally reached his limit.

"I believe I know what will do the trick and I am going to show you!"

"Rykerian? What are you doing?" I demanded.

"Sweetheart, I should have done this months ago. It would have saved us all from hearing their nasty comments over and over again."

He tapped his shadars and they disappeared. I knew exactly what he was doing. He was giving them a view of how they could be living right now on Earth if it hadn't been for the two of us. I could hear and feel his thoughts. He was laughing his rear end off too!

He took them to their house in Spartanburg...or what was left of it. Then he took my dad to the place he used to work. He gave them a brief tour of downtown Spartanburg. Everything was either burned down or a crumbling mess. Next, he teleported them to downtown Atlanta. What hadn't been destroyed was covered with massive vines of kudzu; it was barely recognizable. The world they had known no longer existed and in its place was sheer hell.

When they finally returned to the palace, my parents were both pale faced and trembling and Rykerian was grinning from ear to ear. I shook my head and smiled back at him.

"You probably should have done this a while ago."

"Yes...perhaps it could have saved me from mountains of headaches!"

"Mom, Dad, now please get out of here and leave us alone. You know, Rykerian's only letting you stay here out of the kindness of his heart. He doesn't have to and he can send you back to Earth whenever he wants. Is that what you want?"

"No... I guess we'll go home now," she said.

After they left, Rykerian said, "At some point, we are going to have to decide what to do about your siblings. Tommy keeps insisting on learning to fight like a Guardian. He wants to back to Earth to defend it January."

"I know, but I worry about him. He's so young."

"Well, he is too young to fight right now, but we could put him in the program that would channel him into the Guardian Academy. I think he would be happy there and he is only twelve right now."

"He'll be thirteen next month."

"He cannot enter the Academy for another five years then. If he knows he is being trained for that, he will be more motivated to work hard. He will also gain the respect of his fellow students."

"So you think it's the right thing to do?"

He put his arm around my waist and pulled me to him, "Have I ever steered you wrongly?"

"No."

"I think it is exactly what he needs. Then he could go back to Earth and be proud of his accomplishments."

"Yeah, you're right...as usual. What about Sarah?"

"I think she should do the same. Of course, she would not enter for what, eight more years?"

"Yeah, she's only nine now."

"That would work well for her, and who knows, she may change her mind by then. We can make her think for now that she can be following her big brother's footsteps. When he's gone, she may go in a completely different direction."

"I am so glad I married you. You are the smartest man." I stood on my toes and kissed him. I should've known better. We weren't very good at just a quick kiss or two. It usually developed into much more, like this one did. In no time, I was being carried upstairs.

"It's a good thing I don't weigh very much."

"Why is that, love?"

"Because you're always carrying me up the stairs!"

"Ah, I see. Well, do you think I am that weak then?"

"No, I would rather you save your strength for other things."

"Hmm...what other things?"

He'd reached our room by this time and kicked the door closed behind us.

"Why don't you put me down and I'll show you?"

He gave me one of those smoldering looks that literally sent currents of heat racing through my veins.

"Have I told you that you are more beautiful with each passing day? When you were pregnant, I thought I'd never seen you look lovelier, yet here you are, stealing my breath away again."

Somehow, even though war raged around us, Earth was under siege, our beloved Therron was gone forever and Xarrid was searching for his missing soul mate, we had managed to persevere. We had quite a long way to go before things were rectified and we knew life would never be as it was, but together, we knew we could carry on. We had been given new hope in the gift of Therron Rykerian and we took that as a message, giving us faith in what the future held. Life was amazing and so were the promises it held.

Epilogue

S aylan had been busy in the small warehouse teleporting all the crates to the Star Freighter. She had devised a system so she could find everything when she got all the crates back on Vesturon. The main thing was to keep it all in some semblance of order.

She had about three hours until she was supposed to meet Xarrid. She still had a ton of stuff to get done between now and then.

She was so excited. She could not wait to tell Maddie her news. Xarrid and she had decided to unite. They had met at the graduation party after she and Maddie completed their Guardian training. What a night that was! They had all been celebrating when Saylan had accidentally mentioned the incident about Maddie's brush with death with that nasty heptamorg (a large, venomous, seven-tentacled beast living in the Unforgiving Forest on Vesturon) and Rayn went ballistic. Maddie hadn't shared that tidbit of news with him, and being the Vesturion that he was, his protective instincts went into high gear and he became so angry with Maddie. Well, in all honesty, she did deserve some of it because, after all, she had hidden just about everything, including the fact that she was even enrolled in the Academy for Guardians from Rayn. She had been sending him on one wild goose chase after another and this one was the final straw.

Saylan still felt remorse for letting that cat out of the bag, but Maddie and Rayn had mended their differences and everything had worked out for them in the end. And now Saylan and Xarrid were going to announce to the Yarrister family that they were going to have their very own unification ceremony. Saylan couldn't wait to see the look on Maddie's face when that happened. Maddie was the one who suggested the two of them get together in the first place.

She chided herself because if she didn't stop daydreaming here, she'd never get her list of chores completed and she'd never make it back to the Star Freighter in time.

Saylan turned back to the next stack of crates and began counting before she would teleport these. Her mind was focused on Xarrid and their upcoming plans so she never heard the footsteps enter the warehouse.

She bent down to snap the lid on the last crate and when she did she noticed three sets of legs behind her.

"Stand up slowly and put your hands in the air," a deeply accented voice commanded.

They were Xanthians. She knew immediately by their odor. It was distinct...overpowering and gamey.

She did as she was told. One approached her from behind and removed her shadars. When he did, her anxiety level just shot up one hundred percent.

"Ahhh...an adrenaline spike on this one. Can you smell it?" one of them rasped.

She heard another of them make a sniffing sound and respond, "Yesth, she isth frightened. That isth good." This one spun her around to face them. She wished he hadn't. He was hideous looking with his huge, deformed teeth bulging out from his thick, slobbery lips. No wonder he lisped, she thought.

Xanthians were disgusting. They were a most unattractive species. Their large stumpy bodies made them appear awkward and uncoordinated, however, they were anything but that. They possessed quick reflexes and had tremendous strength. Their large heads had scale like formations projecting from the top with scraggly hair shooting out behind and around them. Their huge noses were red and bulbous and their yellow teeth were oftentimes large and misshapen.

They always smelled gamey, like wild animals and they had no respect for personal space which was a bad thing because they had the worst breath you could ever imagine. It could seriously make anyone gag.

One of them grabbed her by the chin with his pudgy grey fingers, lifted her head and said, "Hmm, this one could fetch a pretty price on the black market. Beautiful slaves are always in demand. Look at her. That black hair alone would make her worth a lot."

"Haldar, take her clothes off so we can see what she looks like. Maybe we can sell her as a prostitute and make even more."

"Sthop it! You know what our ordersth are. We are to take her to the Rebel Leader. He will insthtruct usth where to go. Now move!"

They bound her wrists and dragged her along with them. Saylan's eyes darted around, trying to seek out a way to escape. If she were going to make it off Xanthus, it would have to be before they arrived at the Rebel Headquarters. If not, she doubted she would survive. The streets were deserted. Everyone had fled the area as the streets here were unsafe and teeming with all sorts of unsavory characters.

Unfortunately, Saylan didn't spy any viable opportunities. She tried to reach out to Xarrid telepathically but for some odd reason, she received no response. Perhaps he was blocking all communications. Too bad she hadn't been gifted with the Powers of Telekinesis or Command. They could have certainly helped her at this point. They rounded a corner and she decided to take a chance and run. She would have to depend on her Power of Speed alone.

Saylan didn't get very far before she was stunned. The beam hit her and she dropped like a rock.

When she regained consciousness, she was strapped to a table. She couldn't move a thing. There was a strap that ran across her forehead, one across her torso and her hips, which also bound her arms and legs. She was essentially locked down. Her mind screamed for Xarrid for she knew she would die if he couldn't reach her.

She struggled in vain against her restraints. Tears poured down her cheeks. How could she have been so careless to let her guard down at that final critical moment?

She heard voices off in the distance. Tuning in to what her captors discussed, she felt herself freeze with terror.

"Remove her tracer and destroy it immediately. We do not need any Guardians breathing down our necks here. If they discover this place, our mission will be ruined."

Footsteps approached her and she felt a hand tightly clench her arm. Something punctured her skin and gouged into her flesh. She screamed for they didn't give her anything to numb the area before retrieving the tracer from beneath the muscle in her arm.

"Shut up or I'll do the same to your other arm," the Xanthian said as he bent into her face.

He was so putrid smelling she nearly threw up on the spot. The only thing stopping her was the pain in her arm. A wave of nausea slammed into her, but she swallowed, forcing down the burning mass of bile. Her eyes darted around the room and she noticed there were other beds like the one she was on with more people strapped to them.

Robots were moving about with drill-like tools. Whatever was going on in here was totally creepy and now she wished they would just kill her. They were performing some kind of twisted experiments on these captives.

Suddenly, she heard the whirring sound of a drill and then one of the people strapped down next to her started screaming. Saylan tried to look at what was happening, but she could only move her eyes. The screaming continued, but eventually turned into a whimper and finally eased off altogether.

"Xarrid, where are you? You have to find me! And now! They are doing horrible stuff to people here! Help me please!"

Saylan squeezed her eyes tightly shut and prayed for help to come. She knew if it didn't, she would rather die than face certain torture at the hands of these cruel evil Xanthians.

Saylan heard footsteps approaching again. She opened her eyes to see a high-ranking Xanthian in uniform.

"Do you know who I am?" he wanted to know.

"No. Should I?"

"Maybe. I am the second in command your Guardians scoffed at whenever we would attempt to negotiate."

"You never attempted to negotiate anything. You always demanded and you were never in a position to do so."

"Is that a fact? I wonder how you will feel in a day or so," he ran his finger down her cheek and she shuddered. "Let me fill you in on something. You are soon going to be wishing with every bone in your attractive little body that your Guardians had negotiated with us." He leaned down cupped her cheek and whispered into her ear, "You, my dear, are going to be a part of an experiment we are conducting here. We are getting ready to implant a nano-chip into your cerebral cortex.

Within days, that chip will begin to transform and mutate. Soon, it will develop and grow, like a cancer, spreading, infiltrating and becoming a part of you so that eventually it will be indistinguishable from the rest of your brain. You will become it and it will become you. You will do exactly as we tell you and you will obey our every command. When we tell you to jump, you will only want to know how high. We will *own* you, to do with exactly as we please. And Guardian, no one but us will know." He took his fat, grey finger and ran it from the base of her throat down to her waist. Then he stood with a satisfied smirk and turning he continued, "Robot, complete the procedure."

Saylan saw the robot approach and heard the whirring of the drill before the most excruciating pain pierced her skull and she began screaming.

The End

ABOUT THE AUTHOR

A.M. Hargrove lives in South Carolina with her husband and two children. After spending years working in management for a large pharmaceutical company, she now enjoys nothing better than spending time at her Mac writing fiction. Her hobbies include hiking, backpacking in the Smoky Mountains, camping, snow skiing, trail running, cooking and snorkeling.

She hopes you've enjoyed *DETERMINANT*, the third installment of the *Guardians of Vesturon*. If so, please consider leaving a review wherever you purchased this ebook. Look for the fourth installment in the series, *reEMERGENT,* in early 2013.

For more information about A. M. Hargrove and her upcoming book releases, please visit her at:

www.amhargrove.com
www.twitter.com/amhargrove1
www.facebook.com/AMHargroveAuthor
www.goodreads.com/amhargrove1

And now…an excerpt of the newly released

ReEMERGENT

Book 4 of The Guardians of Vesturon

Prologue

The Planet Earth

T he female trudged through the streets of Atlanta, *post-pandemic Atlanta*, not focusing on anything but the back of the individual in front of her. Her black hair was filthy and matted, her fingernails ragged and torn with dirt caked beneath them. The sooty streaks covered her skin, but if one took the time to look closely, they would have noticed that at one time she had been quite beautiful. The vacant look in her eyes hid any kind of recognition, any kind of triggered memory that might exist, buried deep within her mind.

"Halt!" the commander yelled.

The line of workers came to a stop as they waited for their next orders.

"This is where we stop for the night."

They were in front of a large empty warehouse in which the

windows had been broken and the doors torn away. The streets had been abandoned months ago, when the hemorrhagic smallpox disease had swept through the city, and then the country and finally the world, leaving millions of people dead in its wake. That's when *they* came...the Xanthians. They came to take over Earth and make it their own. She was part of their scheme, only she didn't remember that. She scarcely knew anything anymore. Her mind was now controlled by them...by the nanochip they had implanted into her cerebral cortex. It had taken over her brain and turned her into a minion. She now belonged to them, doing exactly as they told her, without a thought of her own.

They entered the building and heard the rats scurrying away. Rats and cockroaches...they'd survive anything, it seemed. Many humans had been forced to start eating them to survive, for the food sources had quickly dried up and disappeared. Unless you had a spot of land where you could plant something, you were out of luck.

"Number four, get over here and give us a hand," one of the Xanthian soldiers yelled.

The dark haired girl hurried over to assist him. They were setting up this place as their new headquarters. She was carting crates inside that they had just teleported from Xanthus, their home planet. She had long ago lost her aversion to the Xanthians, when she lost her memory and everything that was herself. She simply existed in her body, a shell, nothing more, nothing less.

The other minions set up pallets on the ground for everyone to sleep on and before long, darkness settled upon them. They were handed their rations which they ate and drank and then were told to sleep. It never occurred to them to do anything else, for they were minions, lacking the ability to think on their own.

CHAPTER ONE

The Planet Vesturon

I *am power. I am strength. I am the wind. I am speed. I am courage. I am faith. I am hope. I am fierce. I am loyal. I am steadfast. I am true. I am protection. I am honor. I am a Guardian of Vesturon.*

Xarrid Yarrister paced within the confines of the Guardian headquarters on Vesturon. Standing at about six feet four inches tall, and nothing but pure muscle, he was an impressive yet intimidating sight. Long wavy dark hair and piercing cobalt blue eyes, he wasn't someone one would merely give a passing glance. In fact, his appearance demanded one's complete and undivided attention. There was a time, and not too long ago, that he simply looked like the young brother of Rayn, Rykerian and Tesslar...softer and youthful. Not so anymore. Scultped and chiseled, he was magnificent to look upon, but Xarrid couldn't have cared less about his appearance.

He had taken some hard knocks over the last year, one of them being the death of his brother Therron. The other one was the disappearance of his soul mate, Saylan. The latter had changed him into the male he was today. Hardened was the word that aptly described him. Most Guardians feared his wrath. Others looked up to him. All of them respected him. He was ruthless and cunning, but that's not to say he wasn't fair, because he was a Guardian after all.

Xarrid was on the hunt...the hunt for Saylan. He would never rest until he had proof that she was either dead or alive. If she was alive, pity the ones that held her. They would have hell to pay if they had made her suffer one tiny bit.

The door to the conference room opened and ten males filed in, including Xarrid's brothers Rayn, Rykerian and Tesslar. His father, Rowan, the Great Leader of Vesturon, was also among them.

Everyone but Xarrid took a seat when he asked, "Well, what have you discovered that prompted you to call this meeting?"

The males looked around uneasily and finally Rayn, the eldest of the siblings, spoke. "The pandemic on Earth is winding down. Our Guardian teams were never able to make a dent in it with any of the vaccine we placed down there. The small pox virus was too virulent and before they could make any progress, it had wiped out sixty-five percent of the population. Our estimates are that it may go to at least seventy percent before it completely runs its course and dies out."

Xarrid flexed his hands and then rubbed his neck. Ever since Saylan disappeared he'd refused to cut his hair which gave him an unkempt, wild look. Since he was a Guardian, he wore a thin braid in the back which was one of their requirements. They weren't allowed to cut it but every ten years, so it added to his long and unruly hair, Xarrid looked the part of a rogue. He was the antithesis of his brothers and the other Guardians that were present as they wore their hair neatly trimmed and were clean shaven. Xarrid didn't take the time to bother with such inconsequential things such as that. He didn't have the time nor did he have the inclination.

"Bloody hell! It would be nice to get some good news for a change, wouldn't it?" he asked no one in particular.

Rayn, the oldest of the brothers, gave him a long, hard look before he spoke. "That's not all."

"Well, what are you waiting for? Go on," he bit out.

"There are reports that the Xanthians have streamed in and taken over. Humans are not only dead from the disease, but the Xanthians are killing anyone that won't agree with their demands."

Xarrid slammed his fist into the palm of his hand. "Those bloody Xanthians. I hate those bastards. My mission is to destroy them all."

Rowan looked at him, his expression grave. The last year had taken its toll on all of them, but Rowan bore the physical signs like a banner.

Tall, dark and handsome, he'd always been robust and full of life. Lately, the purple half moons beneath his eyes had deepened and the lines around his mouth were now more pronounced.

"My son," Rowan began, "I don't want to see you waste your life away by trying to destroy something that may be an impossibility."

Xarrid turned to his father and in a voice laced with steel, said very quietly, "They took from me two of the people I dearly loved. I will live the rest of my life trying to get Saylan back. If and when I do, I will go after them with a vengeance. I will leave and breathe revenge, Father."

Rowan sadly shook his head. "I would rather you focused your efforts on other things."

"I understand what *you* would rather have. Unfortunately, *I* have different goals."

Turning to Rayn, Xarrid asked, "What are our teams doing on Earth regarding the Xanthians now?"

Rayn glanced around at the others before he answered. "We're thinking about pulling out."

"What? How can you think that? What about our Compound? What about the Nunne Hi? Talasi? The others?"

"We would keep the Compound active and the Command Center in Haywood County, North Carolina. All others would be evacuated. The Nunne Hi are safe right now. You know they won't leave their Great Smoky Mountains. They are tied to their ancestors, the Cherokees, spiritually. Their caves are hidden and it would be nearly impossible for the Xanthians to discover their location."

Xarrid started pacing, trying to make sense of what they're telling him.

"We've been through this from all angles. When the virus finishes running its course, Earth will be a different place," Rayn explained further.

Xarrid looked at Rayn like he'd grown an extra head. "That's exactly why we need to keep our presence there. That's when they'll need us the most. Earth will be a hell hole Rayn."

Rayn felt the knots growing again in his gut. He hated this decision. It sickened him whenever he thought of it. "We don't have the troops to spare. We need all the hands we have to get Xanthus back on track."

"We need to blow Xanthus up and forget about it. Then we'll have the extra hands we need so we can rebuild Earth."

Xarrid was losing his patience with Rayn. He let out a loud breath and started shaking his head.

"Xarrid, you know we can't annihilate Xanthus. It's against our covenants. The Council would never allow it nor would the Universal Free Rule. We are protectors of the universe, not destroyers. Besides, are you willing to take that risk where Saylan's concerned, if she's still there?"

Placing his hands on his hips, he stared at Rayn as he began tapping his foot.

"You know she's not. Jurek and his team have turned Xanthus upside down searching for her. With their power, they would have located her by now. The Praestani do not fail in that."

Rayn stared at Xarrid for a moment. He didn't want to start an argument with him because they had been over this time and again. "You have your opinion of Jurek and I have mine. Let's just leave it at that."

"Well then, as far as I'm concerned, this conversation is over. I have things I have to do. Father, give my love to Mother."

Xarrid turned and stormed out of the conference room, leaving them all staring after him.

CHAPTER TWO

"I 'll meet you as soon as I finish," Saylan said.

"Don't be late. I can't wait to share our news with everyone when we're back on Vesturon."

"Neither can I. Do you think your family will be pleased?"

"They love you, not nearly as much as I do, but they will be thrilled, especially Maddie. She will pride herself on her matchmaking skills."

Saylan laughed. He adored her laugh. It did something to him he'd never experienced before. Turned him into jelly and brought him to his knees. If she'd have asked him to move a mountain, and then laughed afterwards, he'd have found a way to do it.

"You know Maddie will be gloating over this, don't you? I can already picture her."

"I can live with that, as long as you're part of the package. Now be safe and finish up. I don't want you to miss that transport. I miss your lovely face already. And Saylan?"

"Yes?"

"You're mine and I love you."

"I love you too Xarrid."

"I have to go, but I'll see you in a few hours." He bent toward her, intending to kiss her, but her face began to fade away, like it always did.

"NO! Don't leave me! Stay this time! Please don't go Saylan!" he screamed.

Xarrid woke with a start, tangled in the sheets, covered in sweat.

He sat up and wiped his face, brushing the tears off his cheeks. He'd had this recurring dream for months, remembering the last time he'd talked with Saylan when he told her he loved her. Then she disappeared, like she always did. He'd driven himself crazy in his search for her. He'd never give up until he found her.

Dragging his hands through his thick waves, he threw off the bed covers, strode to the windows and stared across the dark landscape of Vesturon. His soul knew she still lived. Vesturions were like that. Their souls were attached to those of the ones they loved. They could feel it when they lost a loved one. When his brother Therron was killed, Xarrid felt his soul had been wrenched from his body, and left him battered and bleeding for months. He still hadn't healed from that, and Saylan's disappearance had just poured an extra heaping of vinegar on his raw flesh, burning it like acid. It burned every day. He expected it would forever, unless he found her. He slammed his hand against the window sill and groaned. Why couldn't he get some sign, some small signal where she was being held? Filling his lungs with air, he released it and shuddered as he dropped to his knees and let his anguish flow. The tears gushed like a torrent, as they usually did, and he had long ago quit trying to stop them for he knew it was useless to do so. This had become his nightly ritual, and in the morning, he would awaken, curled up in a tight knot, stiff with swollen eyes from the tears he'd shed.

This is how Maddie, his sister-in-law, found him the next morning. Knocking on his door just after dawn, she entered, calling his name.

"Xarrid? It's Maddie. Are you still asleep?" When she didn't receive an answer, she walked to his bed and noticed the rumpled up sheets. Her eyes landed on a heap by the window and she moved over to find him balled up on his side, asleep. She reached out her arm and gently touched his shoulder.

"Xarrid? Wake up, it's Maddie."

He lifted his lids, and looked at her oddly, trying to put the pieces of the puzzle together. "What's going on?"

"Why are you on the floor?"

His face instantly flamed and he felt the heat of embarrassment that she should find him in this state. The confusion was quickly

335

replaced by a mask of anger, for he was ashamed that she should discover him in such a pitiful state.

Sitting up, he acidly replied, "I don't think that's any of your business. Besides, when did you decide my bedroom had an open door policy for you?"

Maddie looked at him, assessing him. She knew him well, but more importantly she understood his grief. She had dealt with her own issues when she'd lost both of her parents as a teenager. Xarrid was hiding and she was tired of him burying his grief.

She crouched down in front of him and said, "I know what you're doing and it isn't working. Look at yourself. You're a wreck Xarrid. It's obvious you can't sleep. You probably have dreams or even nightmares every night. You have to talk to someone. Please. Come back to us. We're your family and we love you. We only want to help."

Xarrid looked at Maddie and she thought her heart would break from the pain mirrored in his eyes. He looked away and stared at the wall. She saw his lower lip tremble and she took a chance and whispered, "I love her too Xarrid and I miss the hell out of her. Why can't we help each other get through this?"

He turned to her and was in her arms before she could even think of how it happened. She couldn't hear his sobs, but she felt his entire body shuddering from the force of them. The dam had burst and Maddie wasn't sure how long it would take for the lake behind it to empty. It didn't matter though, for she was prepared to stay with him until he stopped needing her to be there.

"I can feel her soul Maddie," he cried. "I know she still lives, but I worry about how and where. Are they torturing her? Is she cold at night? Does she have enough to eat? Is she thirsty? Does she call out for me? Does she think I've abandoned her? I feel so bloody helpless. What the hell could have happened to her?"

"I know Xarrid. I've asked myself the same things. I wish we could find her. But if you still feel her soul, that must mean something. That must mean she's getting food and water. Someone is taking care of her."

"Then why isn't she calling to me? She hasn't even tried. My mind waves to her are unanswered. I'm blocked at every turn, or there's nothing there."

"Same here. The telepathic waves are shut down. I don't know Xarrid, but you need to keep talking to us. We're all worried about you. We can't be worried about Saylan and you at the same time."

He rubbed his face, drying the tears from them. "My mind is so bloody messed up right now, I can barely think straight."

She put her hand on his shoulder and squeezed it. "I know. We all have noticed Xarrid. Look, when Rayn and I were apart, I thought I was losing it. I would work out in the exercise facility until I could hardly walk back to my quarters. But at least I knew where he was and that he was safe. This is crazy with Saylan. Bottling it up inside though will only make you more insane. Talk to us. We can't make it go away, but we can listen and let you vent."

He looked up at her and nodded. "I feel so weak."

"You're not. You lost your soul mate. You're grieving. That's not weakness. That's love Xarrid. Do you remember when we first met?"

He nodded but raised his brows, not really following her.

"You scared the bejesus out of me. I was so intimidated by you. I don't know, you just seemed so in control and powerful. And so smart about everything. But there was something about you that made me turn to Jell-o inside and it was the way you felt about Rayn. You loved him so much that even though you sort of turned your back on us for a while, you did it in good conscience. And it about killed you to do it too. I always loved you after that. So, what I'm trying to say is don't ever think you're weak around me. When I think of strength, a picture of you comes to mind."

He squeezed his eyes shut, trying to stave off another rush of tears. Seeing his efforts, Maddie pulled him back into her arms and said, "Stop trying to fight it Xarrid. Let it go."

She rubbed his back and just held him tight. When at last he felt in control again, he whispered, "I don't know how to go on Maddie."

"I can help you with that. You do it one day at a time."

Rayn, Rykerian and his mate January were sitting in the den when Maddie walked in. Rayn was at her side in an instant.

"Well," he asked. He could tell by her glistening cheeks that she'd been crying.

"His heart is cracked and his soul is splintering. We talked for a long time. He cried and poured his heart out, but I don't know if I helped or not. I hope I did, but he needs more than what I can give him." She looked pointedly at January.

Rykerian started shaking his head.

"It doesn't matter how you feel about this Rykerian," Rayn said. "Xarrid's livelihood goes beyond your petty jealousies."

Rykerian's mouth pressed into a thin line and he said, "Under any other circumstances, I would have something completely different to say to that remark. Given the situation, I will only say this. That was uncalled for. January, please get Jurek here now. My brother is in need of him and contrary to what Rayn may think, Xarrid's needs will always come before my feelings for Jurek."

January hugged Rykerian and smiled. Whenever she smiled like that, he pretty much melted anyway, so what did it matter? Within minutes, they all heard that strange popping sound, and suddenly, Jurek Herdekian appeared in the den.

"You rang?" he asked. He always liked to say that to January because he thought it was funny, even though no one else did.

She flew to him and hugged him because it had been several months since she'd seen him.

"Yes, we did."

"How's little Therron?" Not waiting for an answer, he looked at her and asked, "Are you pregnant again?"

As Rayn and Maddie gaped at the three of them, January replied, "For the love of God, Jurek, can you not be discreet about anything?"

"Oh, sorry," he said. He actually had to good graces to look contrite.

"We didn't call you here for that. We're worried about Xarrid," she said, wanting to get her now exposed pregnancy off the table and buried where it should have stayed except for Jurek's big blabbering mouth.

"What's up?"

Maddie explained about her time she spent with him and how he'd pulled away from them.

"Still no news on Saylan then?" Jurek wanted to know.

"Nothing," Rayn answered.

"We know she wasn't on Xanthus the last time we checked. We scoured that hell hole. We'll check again. I can put one of my teams down there ASAP. I need to check on Xarrid. Where is he?"

"In his room," Maddie told him.

"I'm going to take him away for a while."

"Where?" January wanted to know.

"Some place where his mind can heal. I should have done this a long time ago."

"Are you taking him to Lare-Stell?"

"That would be a big no. He doesn't need to be on an active space station. He needs solitude, away from everything familiar."

"Then where?" January pressed.

"Bloody hell, January. You're a nosy one aren't you?"

Her face flushed in anger. "No, I'm not. I'm concerned about my brother-in-law, darn you! Quit acting like a stubborn fool," she spat, and then she stuck her tongue out at him. She did this a lot, and he just shook his head and laughed.

"The sanctuary."

"Huh?"

"I'm taking him to the sanctuary. My sanctuary. That's all I'll tell you about it because I don't speak of it. It's on my home planet of Praestan and no one, other than myself, is allowed there."

They all stared at him, mouths hanging open, jaws hitting the floor.

"What the hell is wrong with the lot of you?"

"You! You're doing something exceptionally nice for someone other than January. That's what's wrong with us," Rykerian answered.

Jurek narrowed his eyes and growled, "Xarrid is my brother in every way except for blood. Like January, I will do anything for him." Using his Praestani power, he flashed himself out of the room and over to Xarrid's bedroom.

CPSIA information can be obtained at www.ICGtesting.com
Printed in the USA
LVOW01s2322140514

385786LV00039BA/2374/P

9 780615 663456